She walked into my classroom ten minutes early on the first day of the Fall 1990 semester at South Pasadena Adult Education. I sat at my desk with my head down, going over notes and a sheet of mandatory announcements.

It was not hard to hear the entrance, which came with a slight swish to it. I raised my head to greet my first adult education student.

She stood just in from the door: a person—a woman—a person, unlike any person I had ever seen or, indeed, have ever seen since, for she was radiant. Radiant—a not unusual adjective and often a metaphor—but at that moment, as she stood there, and as I possibly held my breath, the word was an utterly accurate adjective that was just barely a metaphor.

Thus begins a very odd love story

BULLY *it* Love

BULLY 4 LOVE

A RATHER ODD LOVE STORY

STEVEN PAUL LEIVA

Magpie

Press

Cover design by Juan Padron https://juanjpadron.com

Interior design by John G. Hartness

Editing by Jean Rabe

ISBN-13: 978-1-7352985-1-1 (PRINT BOOK)

Library of Congress Control Number: 2021902066

"Steven Leiva not only promises but delivers. Bravo!"
Ray Bradbury

PRAISE FOR THE NOVELS OF STEVEN PAUL LEIVA

CREATURE FEATURE: A Horrid Comedy

"Leiva is witty and engaging, stylistically striking an immediate generational middle ground. At face value, the novel would seem nothing more than a boomer's nostalgic wet dream, but Leiva imbues the novel with an accessible comedic edge...Leiva, somewhat of a polyglot of entertainment mediums, employs that mastery as he moves the novel forward in an incredibly charming way. A perfect mix of dynamic action and dry dialogue keep readers turning the pages..."*Creature Feature*" holds enough rich nostalgia for all of us. It's a tender ode to Cold War-era technological anxiety and is a delightful read for a less than delightful time. It's escapism for the gentle masochist, leaving areal-world of trauma for a fictional one of catastrophe." — Areyon Jolivette, *The Daily Californian*

JOURNEY TO WHERE, A Contemporary Scientific Romance

"The author's true strength is in storytelling. The attention to detail is spot on, providing just enough visual imagery to fill the reader's perception without diluting the setting with unnecessary clutter. Throw this in with a strong cast and a nicely paced plot, and *Journey to Where* by Steven Paul Leiva is a fun read sure to entertain fans of the classics." — *Amazing Stories Magazine*

MADE ON THE MOON, A Novella

"Leiva has crafted a satire – perhaps a self-satire – with a very warm heart. If you've ever dreamed of flying in space or walking on the Moon, you'll get the point of this story and you'll love every page." — Russell Blackford, author of *Science Fiction and the Moral Imagination*

IMP: A POLITICAL FANTASIA

"Steven Paul Leiva is a master wordsmith able to take on any genre or blend them as in the case of *IMP, A Political Fantasia*. Once started, I couldn't stop reading. The tale was just long enough, yet had me longing to read more of Leiva's prose." *Zoommmmbizzt!* I highly recommend this novel. — USA Today Bestselling author Jean Rabe

TRAVELING IN SPACE

"*Traveling in Space's* humor and refreshing perspective are thoroughly enjoyable" — Diane Ackerman, New York Times bestselling author of *The Zookeeper's Wife* and *A Natural History of the Senses.*

BY THE SEA, A Comic Novel

"*By the Sea* is a delightfully engaging story about an eccentric community that resides in the foggy environs of Leech Beach...Leiva deftly interweaves characters' past and present to create a vibrant ensemble that is immediately engaging...an appealing comic treatise on small-town politics where sexual liaisons abound, on a collection of individuals who live cheek-by-jowl but find to hysterical effect, that they know each other not at all. *By the Sea* is a light-hearted, clever read."— *Literary Fiction Book Review*

THE FIXXER NOVELS
BLOOD IS PRETTY
HOLLYWOOD IS AN ALL-VOLUNTEER ARMY

"*Blood is Pretty* is a wonderful read, a highly entertaining and impressive debut novel." — Richard D. Zanuck, Academy Award-winning Producer of *Jaws, Cocoon & Driving Miss Daisy*

"A fast-paced thriller with more twists than a box of Rotini pasta. Leiva ratchets up the action to a nuclear level, following his first Fixxer novel, *Blood is Pretty*." — *The Big Thrill Magazine*

For Steven Savile

*Who, like the great Ray Bradbury, has always
shown nothing but encouragement
and kindness to his fellow writers*

And, but for whom...

1

———————

She walked into my classroom ten minutes early on the first day of the Fall 1990 semester at South Pasadena Adult Education. I sat at my desk with my head down, going over notes and a sheet of mandatory announcements. I had prepared the notes over the weekend, as I always did, for I was always prepared. It was not hard to hear the entrance, which came with a slight swish to it. I raised my head to greet my first adult education student.

She stood just in from the door: a person—a woman—a person, unlike any person I had ever seen or, indeed, have ever seen since, for she was radiant. Radiant—a not unusual adjective and often a metaphor—but at that moment, as she stood there, and as I possibly held my breath, the word was an utterly accurate adjective that was just barely a metaphor.

"Is this World History?" she asked with a slightly shy yet determined voice.

"This, um, this would be it, yeah."

"Where would you like me to sit?"

"Oh, anywhere."

"Anywhere?"

"I don't think we need to assign seats in adult education."

She smiled, saying, "Okay." She then surveyed the classroom, looking it over, taking it all in, not in a glance but with penetration and consideration, breaking it down, I guessed, into quadrants, musing on the advantages and disadvantages of various positions. *Should I sit upfront to the teacher's right?* I assumed she was thinking, or *directly in front of him or to the left? Should I sit back a little? What chair looks the most comfortable?* Well, she couldn't have been musing on that last one; the chairs were all exactly alike. They were those smallish blond-wood chairs with collapsible writing surfaces that could be stored to the side or brought up via an ingenious mechanism to flatten and lock in place. There were six rows of six chairs each—little soldiers in the literal support of public education bringing order, if not discipline, to classrooms worldwide, including my classroom here.

I say "my classroom," but that is not accurate. It was Ms. Roberta Boxer's classroom there at South Pasadena High School. During the day, it catered to fifteen and sixteen-year-old sophomores tasked, one fifty-minute session a day, with learning—Ms. Roberta Boxer so passionately hoped, I'm sure—some information and facts about, and possibly some understanding of, American history. On the wall behind my, or rather I should say, Ms. Roberta Boxer's desk, were two large green chalkboards I was not allowed to use. Ms. Roberta Boxer, who, I was made to understand, had only grudgingly given up the evening use of her classroom, demanded that whatever was on the chalkboard remain untouched, and certainly unerased, as it would always be pertinent to her next day's lesson. Due to this hard-as-stone stipulation from Ms. Roberta Boxer (I would have loved to have thought of her as "Bobbie," but somehow I just couldn't), the adult education administration—that is, Adult Education Director, Ms. Deborah Miller—managed to score me a white dry erase board on wheeled legs. Deb had personally wheeled it into my—sorry, *the*—classroom, and I would have to wheel it out at the end of class. Ms. Roberta Boxer had made clear that in no way was it to be evident in the morning when American history would again be ascendant in the world.

2

As might be expected, given the classroom's real subject, a large map of the United States dominated one wall. On another were portraits of all the American presidents (from Washington the First to Bush the Elder) and painted scenes from American history. Most of them were of battles waged in country-sides that otherwise would have been placid. But there were also a few non-violent events, such as the building of the Erie Canal, the hammering of the golden spike, and the first flight at Kitty Hawk. There was the standard large American flag on a pole shooting out on high at a 45-degree angle from a metal flag holder screwed into the wall, which the students in the morning would pledge their allegiance to, never entirely understanding what that meant, except for the rare Boy Scout among them. But more pertinent to this classroom was a neat display poster of the history of American flags—the Don't Tread on Mes, the Liberty or Deaths, the stars in a circle, the stars in a star pattern, even the stars and bars of the Confederacy. All of which seemed a bit more exciting "to die for" than our current flag, which is, let's be honest, a bit dull.

While Ms. Roberta Boxer would be standing in this classroom during the day imparting America's history, I would be a bit northeast in my classroom at Pasadena City College, mostly imparting the history of places that were not America. I had taken this job—a three-hour class one night a week—for the extra income (I had never in my adult life not needed extra income) and as a favor to Deb, a completely cool woman who I really liked.

I met Deborah Miller several years before when I saw her sitting on a huge exposed root of a large Bay Fig Tree on the grounds of the South Pasadena Public Library. I usually would not have bothered anyone sitting alone under a tree. But when I saw this middle-aged Black woman reading one of the Alexander the Great novels by Mary Renault—*Fire from Heaven*, if I remember right—an author I was passionate about, I couldn't help but engage her in conversation. We continued to be engaged in conversation for years after, one conversation being one-sided: her pleading with me to teach World History in the adult education program she had just taken over. So I did it for her as well as for the extra income. And also—I guess I should mention; maybe this won't be terribly embarrassing—as an experiment in enthusiasm.

I wanted to see if I could impart my enthusiasm for history to a bunch of adults going back to school purely for pragmatic reasons—most likely to finally get their high school diplomas so they could get a better job and earn extra income. Everybody needs extra income.

And as I lived in South Pasadena, in a small house that I had managed to purchase during a downturn in the housing market, it was hardly inconvenient to spend one night a week doing a favor for a friend and answering a subtle need of my own.

If we were in a classroom right now, I'm sure one of you would be raising their your arm and flapping your hand at the end of it like a dying fish. Yes, yes, you're right. I should get back to the radiant woman, shouldn't I? But I'm reluctant to do so. For many years I have jealously kept to myself the memory of her, the image of her, all the tones and atmosphere and color and light of her, not to mention my deep feelings about her that all of that informed. I revisit them often. They are almost to me corporeal. But they are now—ironically, I suppose—history. And if I am to tell the story I mean to tell, I cannot hide them anymore.

2

A s she stood in the classroom musing on where to sit, I, not perceivably, I hope but certainly shamelessly, mused upon her. She was about five-foot-five, but this was a guess as she stood in elegant high heels. She wore a dress. A dress! Not blue jeans and a tee-shirt, not fatigues from an Army Surplus store, not anything gangsta-rappers or hip-hopish. Nothing rock n' roll, nothing punk, nothing anti-establishment, nothing that thumbed its nose at convention while, of course, being within her generation entirely conventional. But a dress, a full dress with a billowing skirt, a wide belt that cinched the waist, and a top featuring a v-neck opening and an extended collar upturned in the back. It was white with a pattern of the repeated image of blue flowers—irises, I think. Yet it was restrained, not overdone. She wore a string of blue beads around her neck, set off by the ivory-like skin of her exposed upper chest. She was made-up, but subtly so, with lipstick of a color somewhere between pink and red. She was blonde, and somehow I knew it was natural, although it was not a subject I had ever thought about before in my life: women's hair color and what was natural and what wasn't and why what was natural had become unnatural. Her hair fell down onto her shoulders, not chaotically and yet not seemingly styled. But there was still body to it, and even a bit of a wave. She was pretty. And yet she wasn't. At least not conventionally so. No button nose, no high cheekbones, no well-shaped mouth, all those things that made a face of parts become a whole perfect face. She was striking. Her eyes, which were, I believe, gray, just—I cannot, for the life of me, think of any other word—her eyes just beamed. And she smiled with an irregularly wide mouth, exposing upper teeth that were irregularly long, giving it a somewhat goofy aspect. And yet it was a most pleasant smile to view, a fun smile if that makes sense. Her nose was just a little bit too large, but it did not distract; it was, oddly, attractive. So even though a young blonde of youth and radiance, wearing a dress a gust of wind could blow up, she was no Marilyn Monroe. Especially given the fact that she was thin bordering on skinny with legs that seemed almost like sticks protruding from the billow of her dress. And she certainly didn't have the smoldering sexuality of Marilyn. If there was any blonde goddess filmic allusion in her presence at all, it would have been Grace Kelly. Not because of how that star looked and was presented in, say, *Rear Window* or *To Catch a Thief*—but because she was the most aptly named woman in all of history.

"Anywhere?"

"I don't think we need to assign seats in adult education."

After looking around, she picked a chair three rows back and to my left.

Other students arrived, some dressed as my previous litany indicated they might be, but others in serviceable civilian clothes. It was a good ethnic mix of people—some Blacks, some Hispanics, two Asians, one I guessed was Indian—East Indian, not American Indian. Or, possibly, he could have been Pakistani. And two others who joined the radiant woman as the only ones who would have checked "White" on the 1990 census form without being allowed to indicate their origins: Irish or German; Russian or French or English, and so on, as the "Spanish/Hispanics" were asked to do: Mexican or Mexican-American; Chicano or Puerto Rican or Cuban; or Argentinean, Colombian, Dominican, Nicaraguan, Salvadoran, Spaniard, and so on.

I looked out over this field of adults—not all of them young adults, some were middle-aged, one was an elderly Black woman—who had *chosen* education, as opposed to all the mandated teenage butts that usually sat in these chairs. And I was happy to see that none of them slouched in private pools of uninterest (I had, once, briefly, taught high school). In fact, they were all sitting up tall, seemingly eager to begin. I felt good about that.

"Despite what it says on the blackboard behind me," I addressed them, "I am not Ms. Roberta Boxer."

That got a few laughs and some smiles. I felt even better about that.

"And this is not American history, although there is nothing wrong with American history, mind you, but this is the South Pasadena Adult Education World History course. And I am—" I turned to the dry-erase board on wheels and picked up the one marker I was issued and started to write as I spoke, "Mr. Seruya." Unfortunately, Ms. Deborah Miller had not locked the wheels on the rolling dry-erase board, so it rolled while I started to write. I quickly grabbed it and steadied it as best I could as I finished my signature.

This also got a few laughs, which I did not feel good about. But when I said: "That's okay. My actual signature is about that bad," I got some laughs that I did feel good about.

Teachers have to be performers. But you probably knew that from your own various experiences being inculcated by a lone pedant looming over you. And like all performers, we lust for approval.

"Now, this course is called "World History" because that's what the administrators of South Pasadena Adult Education decided to call it. But we cannot start this course without me being entirely honest with you upfront. This is not really world history. In the short time we will have with each other this semester, I will not teach you anything about the history of, say, Japan or China or Africa, sad to say, or the Middle East or the Pacific Islands or Australia. Although maybe at the end of the semester I'll have a barbeque for the class, and we'll put some shrimp on it."

There's nothing like alluding to a famous TV commercial to win approval.

"No, this course is essentially the history of Western Civilization. I will exclusively cover the history of Europe, England, Scotland, Ireland, America, of course, and unfortunately only a little bit of Canadian history, especially considering what a large landmass Canada is."

That did not register, not even a chuckle. Despite being such a large presence on our northern border, it's incredible how often we don't bother about Canada.

"I make no apologies for this. I would have called the course Western History or History of the West, but, for the bureaucracy to help you all qualify for a high school diploma, it was decided to call it World History. But it is, indeed, the history of the West, which I teach every day at Pasadena City College. I am, admittedly, Eurocentric. Of which I also make no apologies for. That's not to say that I am not eager someday to take some classes myself in African history, Asian history, the history of the Antipodes, the—uh, yes, you have a question?"

It was one of the whites—not the radiant woman, but a young man around twenty-five (which was my guess of the radiant woman's age) wearing an AC/DC tee-shirt. Ironically so, as you shall see.

"What's the antipo, uh, the antipo—"

"The Antipodes?"

"Yeah."

"Well, it refers to lands far south of the equator, the flip side, so to speak, of Europe, often used to indicate Australia and New Zealand."

"Oh. So they don't matter?"

"Well, they don't matter to this course, but I'm sure they matter to Australians and New Zealanders."

"My mother read the *Thorn Birds.*"

"I'm happy for her."

"Twice!"

"I'm doubly happy for her."

"But she didn't like the mini-series. She thinks Richard Chamberlain is queer."

"I have no comment about that. So let's push on, and I'll call the roll, as I have been instructed to do." I moved over to the desk, sat, and pulled out the roll call sheet that was part of the packet of instructions that Deb had given me. "As I call your name, just say, 'Here!' loud and clear, don't just raise your hand, my eyes will be on this list of students, and I will not be raising my head, and I will not see you. So, again, loud and clear, answer with a 'Here!'"

But I did raise my head, once, when I heard her voice, loud and clear, saying, 'Here!' And thereby discovered that her name was Lavinia Carson.

I spent the rest of the class time handing out the textbook the students would use and a sheet I had prepared outlining the main historical points we would cover and the chapters they would be required to read and be tested on. I then, somewhat laboriously, went through the sheet point-by-point, giving a preview. Since it was laborious, I tried to leaven it with some wit and was rewarded with some chuckles and even a few laughs. I was feeling good about this experiment.

It was a three-hour class from seven to ten, and there was a fifteen-minute break at the halfway point. My students dispersed quickly and spread out among the school's hallways, pooling into small clusters in order, I suppose, to get to know each other or to mount an attack on the vending machines. The teachers flowed out of classrooms and headed to the teacher's lounge, which was clearly marked, and especially noted with a red marker arrow on the campus map we were all given by Deb. However, we were deeply disappointed to find the door locked. We didn't know if this was inadvertent on the part of the South Pasadena Adult Education administration or a conspiracy by the teachers of South Pasadena High School. But whatever it was, it was inconsequential as we were still locked out. And as Deb Miller was gone to dinner, we would not likely gain access within fifteen minutes. So those teachers who smoked—mostly cigarettes, one cigar, and two atavistic pipes—huddled together and smoked furtively as if afraid some young, innocent teenage eyes would spy them. Of course, the young, naive adolescent eyes usually attending this high school were either home doing their first night's homework or were out on the town experimenting with intoxicants and carnal lust. Those of us who required something more substantial than smoke to ingest had to suffer the indignity of competing with the students for a place at the vending machines to get our Twinkies. Or, in my case, a small packet of Oreos that I could dunk into my Styrofoam-cupped hot, black, not very good coffee.

The niggardly fifteen-minutes ended, and we all returned to our classes, and I continued outlining the course of our study.

As I wrapped up a little bit early, I let the class go at 9:45, and they happily ejected themselves from their chairs as I dunked my last Oreo into a now cold half-cup of black coffee.

The one student who didn't leave was Lavinia Carson, who was thumbing through her textbook.

"Hi," I called for her attention, "I'm sorry, did you not hear? I let the class go."

Absorbed in the book, there was a beat before she looked up and answered me. "Oh, yes, I know. But my husband isn't picking me up until 10. Do you mind if I wait here in the classroom instead of just standing outside?"

"No, not at all. I'll be here until 10."

"Thanks."

She bowed her head back over the textbook, her blonde waves falling a bit over her face, but charmingly so, and her right hand started tapping out a little tattoo with her long, painted fingernails. Then with her left hand, she gathered up some of her hair that was probably impeding her vision and held it in place against her head. That's when I noticed for the first time two rings on her left hand. Three rows away, and I could still see the details. One was a wide gold band, sculpted and textured with little evenly spaced glints that I assumed were diamonds. Next to it was a companion that had probably served as her engagement ring. It was a plain gold band about half as wide as the diamond-studded one. It supported a large stone, a pink diamond I was sure from its color, that stood out proudly, challenging the wonderfulness of just about anything else in the whole wide world.

Was I disappointed? It's hard to say. At this time, she still wasn't completely real for me, being quite the anomaly inside this high school classroom. She was an intriguing mystery. And I desired deeply, as is the wont of creatures like me, to know her history. So I continued, again without shame, to stare at her, quite prepared to suddenly drop my head and begin to scribble "notes" on a piece of paper, when she would inevitably raise hers. Which she did at 9:59 after looking at her thin, elegant, also diamond-studded wristwatch. I may have been a slight beat behind her head movement because when I looked up after she said, "Well, good night," she was smiling a knowing smile. She stood, gathered up her textbook, and held it against her chest like a schoolgirl of yore, and started to leave. Then she stopped and turned around.

"Mr. Seruya?"

"Yes?"

"I'm really, really going to enjoy this class."

"Well, thank you, I hope so."

"Good night."

"Good night."

She left. After half a moment, I got up and followed her out of the room. And then, being a real fan of mystery novels, I stealthily—rather competently, I thought—followed her to the street where a Rolls Royce sat waiting. A man jumped out of the driver's seat—he was not a chauffeur—and walked around to greet Lavinia, bending down to her as she stretched up to him for a generous kiss generously returned. Then he opened the passenger door and took her hand to help guide her into the car.

There was something odd about the man. No, not odd, but… He was big, well over six-foot, and bulky, with short but styled blond hair. He wore expensive-looking casual slacks and a polo shirt. All perfectly normal, yet it was as if the image of him plucked at some recognition neurons in my brain. But never in my 41-years of life had

I ever met, much less known, someone who drove a Rolls Royce, someone who had a wife like Lavinia, who he obviously showered riches on. I knew this would bother and bug me, taking up precious space in my inquiring historian's mind. Probably for the next week, until the next session of this class, when I would learn if Lavinia Carson was real or just some fantastic manifestation from a brain in decline.

3

"That does seem odd," Peggy Bradford said to me after I had told her about the well-dressed radiant woman wearing thousands-of-dollars of pressurized carbon upon her finger who had enrolled in my adult education World History class. "Not your typical AD-ED student." Peggy was a bureaucrat of sorts and loved abbreviations and acronyms. "And she wore a dress?"

"A dress," I confirmed.

"With blue flowers?"

"Irises, I think."

"What do you know about flowers that you can name the kind of flower it is?"

"I don't know, but somehow I know what an iris looks like."

"And she was picked up by a Rolls Royce?"

"Yep!"

"Are you sure it wasn't a Bentley?"

"No, it was a Rolls Royce. I know the difference between a Rolls Royce and a Bentley."

"Why do you know the difference between a Rolls Royce and a Bentley?"

"Doesn't everyone?"

"I'm not sure I could tell the difference."

"You're kidding me."

"No."

"Well, I guess that's because you're a girl. But me, I'm a boy."

"You're a boy?"

"You hadn't noticed?"

"Well, I saw something hanging down there."

"Boys know about cars. It's—it's genetic, I think."

"You hate cars."

"I don't hate cars. I'm just not obsessed with them."

"And yet you know the difference between a Rolls Royce and a Bentley."

"I told you, I'm a boy. See." I had been laying on my side on the bed, my head resting on my hand, and I turned to lay flat on my back to afford her an unobstructed view of the manhood that proved I was a boy.

"It looks different than when we started."

"Thanks to you."

My tale of the radiant woman was part of a post-coitus conversation we were having. We had not been making love. Peggy and I did not make *love*. We had just had sex. Or, "good mammalian copulation," as Peggy liked to call it. It had featured a lot of laughs, especially when I tickled Peggy under the ribs, as well as uninhibited moans of appreciation and satisfaction. And afterward, as neither Peggy nor I smoked, we filled in the time with good conversation. But then, Peggy and I always had a lot of good conversations, whether sex was involved or not.

Peggy, born Margaret Kathleen Bradford in Columbus, Ohio (a state with a pretty neat flag), was one of my best friends, possibly my best friend. She also worked at Pasadena City College. She was a counselor in the transfer office, helping students choose which four-year college and university they would continue their education. Pasadena City College, or PCC, as almost everyone calls it, is a two-year community college, which used to be known as a junior college. Just like middle school used to be called junior high. I've always resented these name changes. Maybe because I was a proud junior having been named after my father. And I had loved my father.

Like me, Peggy was unmarried; unlike me, Peggy had never been married. But she was quite adept at lying with men—me and, I assume, others, although that never came up in our conversations. I had suspected that she was also quite adept at lying with women, but that is also something we never talked about. Well, I did try to engage her in conversation about it once, teasing her a little bit, for I would have been interested in expanding the extent of our carnal knowledge, but she cut me off quickly with, "I don't go in for three-ways." That was just like her. Peggy had that unique capacity when she was with a person, of giving over her full concentration to that person, of making that person feel that they were the center of all the world's consideration. This is what made her a great counselor and a good friend. To have divided that concentration between two would not have been Peggy at her best. Still, it was fun imagining her trying.

Also, like me, Peggy was a reader of mystery novels.

"What would make a rich woman enroll in adult education?" Peggy put out the question.

"Beats me."

"Well, I will later if you want, but we're talking now. Do you think she has children?"

"How would I know?"

"Well, did she look like she had given birth to a child? You know, carrying some extra weight, big boobs, and such."

"No, I told you she's kind of thin—elegant thin."

"Elegant thin? Not anorexic thin?"

"No, elegant thin like—uh, like Audrey Hepburn."

"And radiant, you say."

"Yeah, that's what I'm saying, radiant."

"Sounds like you fell in love."

"Peggy, I don't fall in love."

Not even with my ex-wife. That was purely a matter of youth, naivety, and the loss of virginity while coming under the spell of the joys of sex.

"Well, A.S.—" A.S. is what Peggy called me, initializing me like an excellent educational concept. "I don't know what to tell you."

"Well, Peg o' My Hard—" That's what I often called her in the right moments. "I don't know if I'm asking you to tell me anything. I'm just relating the incident."

"Still—'tis a mystery."

"Yes, indeed. A mystery"

"You have to get the details."

"It's none of my business."

"What the hell does that mean?"

"Just what I said. I'm her teacher, teaching her something about Western Civilization. That's my business. My business is not to pry into her personal life."

"You're not curious?"

"Of course, I'm curious. Who wouldn't be curious?"

"Then you have to find out more details."

"Why?"

"Because if you don't, I'll never fuck you again."

"Don't make empty threats. You can't keep your hands off of me. Not to mention your mouth."

"Speaking of which, the old A.S. has risen again."

And then she clamped on. Possibly to give me a last—and lasting —memory.

Margaret Kathleen Bradford was two years younger than me, thirty-nine, and was an attractive five-foot-three. Which was precisely the right size for me, especially as she was my favorite person to hug, among other things. Peggy had full, thick, chestnut-colored hair that she always wore down, an energetic attitude, and infectious enthusiasm for many things. She had a cute figure that was all flesh. That is to say, full without being fat, giving without being flaccid. Hers was not really a sexy body, as she was not, in any conventional sense, sexy. But what she was, from her interior to the exterior, was sensual. She loved touch, sight, hearing, and taste. She loved sharing such senses with people, and she loved pushing it forward. I never saw her dressed in anything that did not reveal some cleavage, and her cleavage was very lovely, indeed. It was the kind of cleavage that made you want to come home—so to speak.

Peggy and I connected immediately as friends, started to have those great conversations I've mentioned, and then we began to go out. Not really on dates, but just to accompany each other to events, concerts, movies, plays at the Pasadena Playhouse, musicals at the Music Center in L.A., and lectures on subjects we have mutual interests in. And then, one night after attending a concert of Latin Jazz, which has a tendency to heat the blood, as we were walking to her car (she loved driving, I didn't), she turned to me and said, "I'm horny."

"I rather suspect you're always horny."

"Well, that's true, but I'm especially horny right now."

"Well, what do you want me to do about it?"

"That should be obvious. I want you to fuck me."

"Right here?"

"No, Ass!" Sometimes she expanded my initials into a pet name. "Back at my place."

"Why your place?"

"Because I'm driving, and you have to go where I take you."

"Help!" I whispered-shouted, "I'm being kidnapped."

"So, are you game?"

"Game?"

"Are you up for it?"

"Well, I guess I could rise to the occasion."

"Oh, it's going to be a night of double entendres, isn't it?"

"*Que sera sera*, as that great American philosopher, Doris Day, used to say."

4

As Peggy dressed to go home, I relaxed in that lovely drowsy post-coitus crotch calm. That particular time (hopefully many times throughout one's manly years) when that part of your body is going to feel as marvelous as any part of your body would ever feel without drugs. This is an assumption on my part—the part about drugs—because I've never taken drugs. I mean the radical, elevated-almost-to-godhead-status drugs of my youth in the 1960s. But, given the *ad nauseam* accounts of those who had, I can certainly imagine the feeling. Although friends and colleagues who have taken these drugs tell me—also *ad nauseum*—that I can't even begin to. But I don't believe it, being, I think, an imaginative person by nature, an attribute boosted by being trained to have a historical imagination. So, essentially, I was lying there with most of my body being in South Pasadena, but my crotch being in South Paradise.

"You know," Peggy said as she walked into the bedroom from the bathroom while donning her low cut pull-over sweater, "how about I visit your AD-ED class?"

"Why?" I somewhat groggily said, having been expelled from South Paradise.

"Well, I could talk to them about the advantages of going on to PCC after they get their high school diploma, then transferring to a good four-year."

"I don't think most of them are interested. They're just trying to get their high school diploma to get a better job. It's higher wages, not higher education they're interested in."

"Well, that's why I should come, to open their eyes to another option, greater opportunities, self-improvement."

"You can try to open their eyes, but you'll be defeated by their deaf ears."

"But—"

"Look, these are adults, most in the workforce trying to earn a living, just trying to get one rung up the ladder. Going any higher will take them too long."

"That's a hell of an attitude from an academic."

"Ah, well, that's where you make your mistake. I'm not an academic. I'm just a history teacher sharing a personal passion for selfish reasons, with no illusions of leading a flock into educational nirvana. I'm neither Pollyanna nor Pygmalion. Besides, you don't give a damn about them either—"

"I certainly do. It's my—"

"You just want to meet the mystery woman."

That stopped her. But she began again. "By the way, what is her name?"

"Oh, no, I'm not telling you that."

"Why not?"

"And let you pound the pavements in your two-bit gumshoes investigating the doll," I said with a bit of a Bogart about me.

"You're an asshole!"

"On occasion, I suppose so. Speaking of which—"

"Oh, shut up!"

I felt like wearing gumshoes, a slouched-brim fedora, and a trench coat as I left to teach the second evening of my AD-ED class, for as prepared as I was to teach, all I could think about was a bit of detection. How could I find out what I wanted to find out without her finding out? Was it perverted or absolutely natural to who I was? It was, after all, not her, but her history I was interested in.

All a moot point. When I started to call the roll, Lavinia had not shown up for class. Maybe it was early dementia. Perhaps she was but a lovely figment of the imagination I take so much pride in. And yet, there, on the roll call sheet, was her name: CARSON, LAVINIA. And although I had not seen her enter with the other students and knew she wasn't there, I was obligated to call out her name. "Lavinia Carson?"

"Here!"

I looked up. She was just entering the classroom. She looked at me and mouthed, "Sorry," as she took the only seat left, one far in the back—so far away.

I got up and handed out a short quiz about the chapters they had been assigned. I gave them fifteen minutes of quiet to take it while I sat at the front desk and tried to get a decent view of Lavinia Carson through the forest of seated students. Frustrated in my failure to do so, I did something I had never done in all my years as a teacher—I got up and sauntered around the room as the students took the test. I've always considered this an awful thing to do. Students are nervous enough without a floating pair of eyes looking over their shoulders. But, what the hell, I thought, and I slowly moved in and out and through the students, eventually affording myself a fine view of Lavinia Carson.

She didn't wear a dress this time, but she certainly was not dressed down. She had on a dark blue pair of expensive-looking slacks gathered about her waist by an elastic band. And she wore a dark lavender pull-over top that was full, not tight at all, but well-cut and flowed about her beautifully. She had large hoop earrings and fiddled with one as she wrote her answers on the quiz. But what really took my eye was the sense of pleasure her slightly smiling face evidenced. She was enjoying taking the quiz. Imagine that!

Once the quiz was done, I began my first lecture. Having about two and a half hours, I decided to cover a lot of ground. I started by talking about Greek and Roman mythology and legend and their relationship to those two civilizations' actual History, concentrating on Homer's *Iliad* and Virgil's *Aeneid*. Then, after the break, I moved on to Herodotus, the Father of History. I pull from all of this the historical lesson that ancient war was an unfortunate engine of retribution, saying (using names I thought they would be comfortable with), "Sam kills George because George killed Sam's brother, Frank. The killing of Frank was, of course, a horrible sin. And you can understand Sam's anguish. But John, George's brother, feels this same anguish and sets out to kill Sam. He succeeds, which really pisses-off Sam's cousin Joe, who sets out to kill John, and so on and so forth. Now the anguish and *pissed-off-ness*, if that's a word, is understandable. But is being shocked, appalled, insulted, and dishonored that someone had killed your brother when you had killed their brother understandable? How we answer that question after learning the history determines what lessons we receive. For some, the lesson learned is that honor must be retained, and insults answered, and revenge sought. For others, the lesson is that man falls into these engines of retribution to no good outcome. So it might be smarter to combat the engine more than each other. Now, later in the semester, we will revisit this idea and see how it applies to 20th-century history, specifically World Wars One and Two and the end of this century."

I was hoping I could excuse the students fifteen minutes early again. But it was not to be. We've been on Earth such a short time but seem to have amassed an awful lot of history to lecture about. I actually went past 10 o'clock by three minutes to the consternation and anxiety of some of the students, I supposed (including Lavinia Carson?), for when I finally said good night, they bolted for the door as I shouted out after them, "Remember to read your chapters in the textbook."

The room cleared quickly except for Lavinia Carson. She

remained seated until the crowd dispersed, then calmly gathered up her textbook and notes, stood, and walked toward me.

"That was a fascinating lecture, Mr. Seruya."

"Oh, well, thank you, ah...ah...Lavinia," I said as I gathered my things and stood.

"Yes, Lavinia."

What a lying son-of-a-bitch I was!

"I went out and bought a copy of *The Aeneid*."

"Oh?"

"Well, it was on your list of suggested further reading."

"Yes, yes, you're right. How about *The Iliad*?"

"Oh, I got that too. And *The Odyssey*, although that wasn't on your list. And all by the translator that you like."

"Fitzgerald?"

"Yes, Fitzgerald. But it's actually *The Aeneid* I'm interested in."

"Really? Why?"

"Because I'm in it."

"You're in it?"

"My name."

"Oh, yes—Aeneas's wife."

"I was thrilled to find that out."

"Really?"

"Well, growing up, I always thought it was such a—stupid name."

"Well, it's not, it's—it's beautiful."

"No, no, I mean, well, not stupid but, sort of old-fashioned."

"Well, it is, isn't it? It's from an ancient epic."

"I meant, 'American' old-fashioned. A lot of people where I grew up, they like that sort of stuff."

"Which was where?"

"Pennsylvania, near Hershey."

"Where the chocolate comes from?"

"Yes, where the chocolate comes from."

We both stood there feeling regret—she for having mentioned Hershey, me for having mentioned chocolate. But I wouldn't have mentioned chocolate if she hadn't mentioned Hershey, thus her regret and mine. For it pushed us into mundane chit-chat, an exchange exactly like what hundreds of *hoi polloi* would have had in similar circumstances. But somehow I was feeling, and I was willing to bet that she was feeling it as well, that we both wanted nothing to do with the similar.

"I apologize again for being late."

"Oh, that's okay, you weren't that late."

"Eugene had—"

"Eugene?"

"My husband."

"Oh."

"He had a business meeting that ran long, so he was late coming home to pick me up."

"He always drives you to class?"

"Oh, he insists on it. I drive, of course. I have a car, a very nice one. A Mercedes. But, he always likes to drive me places."

"I hope you're not keeping him waiting right now."

"Oh, the darling won't mind. Anyway, I just wanted to apologize. And I wanted to tell you how much I enjoyed the lecture and how thrilled I am that I'm part of ancient legend. It means more to me than you can imagine."

"Well, good, such connection is good, it's all about connection. Good night, then."

"Good night! See you next week!"

She turned and, despite walking on high heels, I mean not very high heels, but high heels just the same (dark lavender they were, like her top) she seemed to float out of the classroom, out the door, and into the night—like some nymph or possibly a goddess from ancient history.

Lest you think I was only thrilled by the physical being that was Lavinia Carson, let me set you straight now. It was her enthusiastic receptivity for my subject and my poor efforts in trying to convey it (I didn't really believe that—I was a damn good teacher) that was at least half, maybe more, of the thrill. But at *that* moment, I was responding to her delight about her name being part of history—or legend. For I understood it. Understood it? I related to it. Related to it? I knew it intimately.

I was born Adolphus Antonio Seruya, Jr. in Pasadena at the end of the 1940s, a decade that had been divided, almost neatly, into War and Peace. I was born to a father who always had dirt under his fingernails when he came home from work, for he worked among and with plants. My mother had been a Rosie the Riveter during the war, but when I was born, she was "just a housewife." My mother hated me being a junior, she thought Adolphus was a ridiculous name, but my father had insisted. He had always been happy with his name, liked it being unique, and felt it had some weight to it. All of that was no particular reason for being proud of the name, but he was. Even if his three sisters and his many aunts called him "Dolf" throughout his childhood. But he was forced to drop it and be called "Tony" as the 1940s started as it was just too close to the name of that infamous German with the funny mustache and the unfunny murderous intent. After the war, after Hitler was dead and buried, although no one knew exactly where, my father tried to reinstate his name. It didn't work. Tony he had become and Tony he remained until the end of his days when I was in my mid-thirties. But in me, he saw someone who could carry the name, hopefully with pride. And I tried. But memories are long in adults, and children are cruel. Still, I would not give it up. I refused, to my mother's dismay, to be called Antonio or Tony or Tony Jr. or, simply, Junior. I insisted on being called Adolphus.

Why? Because of my father. I was his only son, indeed, his only child. My father was in his early forties when I was born, and my mother was in her late thirties. My birth had not been easy. My mother had said: No more. In compensation to my father, she allowed me to be a junior. If my father had been cold and distant, or hot-headed and brutal, or, even worse, just a man who came home from work, had a beer, ate with no appreciation the dinner laid before him, fell asleep watching TV, and was just tolerant of the other residents in his home, I might have happily adopted a different name. Not Junior, not even Tony, I possibly would have made up a name. Roy perhaps, after Roy Rogers. Or, more likely, Davy after Davy Crockett. But my father, who was a damn handsome man with smiling eyes, who had spent his adulthood nurturing plants, was pretty damn good at nurturing me. And his love for my mother was always on display and evident. His even-tempered relations with relations, not to mention friends and co-workers, led me once to paraphrase Will Rogers and say, "I never meant a man who didn't like my father." He was apolitical, non-confrontational, and had a general and broad-based non-aggression pact with the world. He was both my hero and my best friend. And if he insisted on calling me Adolphus, then, as far as I was concerned, the world would have to call me Adolphus. Not that it did not, as I've indicated, cause me some problems.

But in eighth grade, at Hillcrest Junior High in Ramone, a small, one-time citrus-growing community just a bit east of Pasadena where my parents moved when I was three, my homeroom teacher, Mr. Moore, perceived the troubles I had seen. He asked me to stay after school one day. I was shocked. Was I in trouble, although I had no idea why I would be? I was not "trouble," a bad boy, a difficult student. If anything, I was a goody-two-shoes, a Boy Scout (my father was a Scout leader, of course) who actually believed in being Trustworthy, Loyal, Helpful, Courteous, Obedient, and all the rest. I was a rule follower who felt the breaking of them to be a near mortal sin. It might have been about my grades. They were just okay, me being, at this time, an uninspired scholar. Even before entering my homeroom at 3:05 that afternoon, I had resolved to do better.

"Come in, Adolphus," Mr. Moore said. "Come over here." He was sitting at his desk with a large open book in front of him. I recognized the book as one volume of a set of encyclopedias that was a permanent feature of his classroom. "Take a look at this," he said, pointing to a section of the left-hand page as I arrived at his desk. I was stunned by what I saw. It was an account of the life of Gustavus Adolphus the Great, King of Sweden, from 1611 to 1632. "Do you see what it says here? He led Sweden to military supremacy during the Thirty Years' War. It also says that he helped determine the political balance of power in Europe and that he was one of the greatest military commanders of all time. No wonder they called him 'The Great,' huh?"

"Yeah," I guess I might have said, but I was busy trying to read further. "That's a pretty neat name you've got there, Adolphus, a name from history." I looked up at Mr. Moore, trying to think of what to say. "Do you want to borrow this?" he asked, indicating the book. I nodded my head. "Take good care of it. Bring it back Monday."

A *name from history*. I was hugely impressed by that. Such is the human ego—to make something of significance out of nothing of consequence. I mean, I had the name only because my father had it before me. If it had been my mother's choice, I could just as well have been called Franklin—like many members of her generation, she had worshiped FDR. And my father had his name because…? He never knew. He had never thought to ask his parents. And as his parents had died long before I was born, I had never had the chance to ask my grandparents. They were both native Californians, as their parents may well have been. So I don't think they named my father after the long-dead King of Sweden. If I had any evidence that they had ever lived in or visited Texas, I might have assumed that they had named my father after the famous Adolphus Hotel in Dallas. But as far as I could tell, they never left California, probably had never traveled more than a couple of miles from their birthplaces in the San Gabriel Valley. Now there is the possibility, I suppose, that they had named their son after the man who the Adolphus Hotel was named after, Adolphus Busch (1839-1913), the true King of Beers, the co-founder of the Anheuser-Busch brewing company. Maybe my grandfather was a particular lover of his brews. But if that was the fact, it would be only of minute historical interest and hardly impressive to anyone except those excited by the first pull-tab aluminum cans. It was nothing a thirteen-year-old boy would have been impressed with.

But the generic *name from history* did impress my thirteen-year-old-self as something both momentous and monumental. It elevated me in my own eyes. More important, it elevated history in those eyes. I suddenly knew what I wanted to do in life. I wanted to learn history.

I had not previously been impressed by history. In fact, I didn't care much for it. But then a lot of the history we studied in elementary school and some in junior high was California history, which I truly disliked. I didn't give a rat's ass about Father Junipero Serra (1713-1784) (why anyone would actually be in possession of a rat's rectum that could be relinquished is something to think about). I didn't like his bald pate and his fringe of hair, I didn't like his habit of wearing that heavy, hooded, ugly thick brown dress-thing, and I really didn't like that big image of torture he wore hanging around his neck. I didn't like the missions he founded as they sat out in the middle of nowhere in not very pretty landscapes drawn in black and white in our textbooks, but which I knew were all dusty brown. I hadn't even liked Disney's *Zorro. I* had always been a Davy Crockett man. Mountain tops in Tennessee and rivers keelboats could travel on always seemed to me to be more interesting than scruffy, flat, dry, and dusty landscapes in early California.

But my perception started to change in junior high, even before my meeting with Mr. Moore. I had been assigned a report to write. It may have been in a history class, but somehow I've always remembered it as an English class—composition may have been the thing we were learning, not history. I remember we had been given the freedom to pick our own subject, and I chose the Civil War. I loved the Civil War. Not because I felt that the fight to free the slaves had been a glorious one—I was too young to know what glory was. Not because I worshiped Abraham Lincoln, although I certainly liked him —who didn't like Abraham Lincoln? And not because I believed in Union over Disunion. No, I had always been attracted to the Civil

War because I liked the soldiers' uniforms. It may have been even more than that, for what I liked about the uniforms was the clear contrast they represented, dividing the nation into blue and gray, so simple to understand. Because the uniforms—at least the uniforms I had actually seen, most likely on TV, in my thirteen years—seemed to be designed precisely alike on both sides, the only difference was that the North wore blue and the South wore gray. Something was appealing, I would even say, attractive, in that symmetrical division, that two-sides-of-one-coin dichotomy. And my love for this I can trace, as a good historian should, to a toy.

When I was maybe seven or eight, I was given for my birthday or Christmas a set of Civil War soldiers. They were those little two-inch tall plastic soldiers, and the set contained X amount of officers, X amount of cavalry, and X amount of foot soldiers, all, within their group, in exactly the same pose. And—this is the crucial part—they were evenly divided between those that were blue, including their faces and hands, and those that were gray, including their faces and hands. Over several years, I spent hours pitting the Blues against the Grays in the hallway in our house that our bedrooms were connected to. The hallway's floor was not carpeted, and I played on hard, dark linoleum, not easy on the knees, but then battlefields are not landscapes of the easy, and that's what the hallway became—a battlefield. I didn't know which one; I didn't even know then that the Civil War battlefields had names, so I conducted this plastic-on-linoleum war without the romance of names. No Bull Run, no Shilo, no Antietam, and certainly no Gettysburg. It was just, for me, the battlefield, where on one end I set up the Blues, and on the other end I set up the Grays —foot soldiers on the right and left flanks, the cavalry in the middle, and the officers in the back looking through binoculars. Of course, my army was always the Union Army. To have picked the losing side years after the war's end would have been monumentally stupid. I would get behind the Union troops and take up a small ball. Sometimes it was a golf ball or a small rubber ball, or a tennis ball, all of which would have been brought home to me by my father. He found them lost among the plants he tended. I would roll the ball along the linoleum towards the Rebels, slaughtering a good number of them. Then I would switch sides and repeat the process, sadly felling some of my Yankee boys. My bias led me to be a more competent bowler when I was attacking the Confederates, so The Union troops usually won. But I think I can be forgiven for that.

So when the teacher asked us to pick a subject for our report, I chose the Civil War. I did the research required in the school library. But I also pulled from my own library a Classics Illustrated comic book called *The War Between the States*. Because of that, I committed for the first and only time what, for a scholar, is the equivalent of murder. I committed plagiarism.

The comic had a great cover showing in cameo a battle scene of the blue Union troops mercilessly attacking the gray rebels hunkered down in their position. Dominating the cover in the foreground was a close-up of two Union soldiers on the march, rifles shouldered, one with his head bandaged. When I first saw it in the spinning rack of comic books at the local liquor store, I was immediately taken by it. When I read it, I found its account of the war, the battles of the war, and the conclusion of the war fascinating. But it was the introduction, prominent in a block of type on the first page, that I found moving in a way I didn't quite understand. It summarized the broad historical meat of the war, the brother against brother, father against son, cousin against cousin tragedy of the war. I copied it word-for-word and used it as the introduction to my report, without giving attribution. Of course, I didn't even know the word *attribution* at the time, much less its meaning, nor was I aware that one should give attribution. I just wanted the reader to understand and feel—especially feel— what I had understood and felt when I had read it. But when I got the report back with an A and the teacher's note in red pencil about how much she had enjoyed the introduction and how she was impressed by how truly I had understood my subject—I felt shame. Possibly without really understanding why. Being a coward, for I was one, I never owned up to the truth.

But the important thing was—I truly enjoyed writing the paper. In gathering together the facts, ordering my thoughts about them, wanting to share, if inadvertently take credit for, the comic book introduction, I had been taught something. More importantly, I taught myself something about the past and the pleasure of bringing it forward into the present—my present. This glimmer of interest not just in the history of the Civil War but in the concept of history itself arose. And was there, twinkling, when Mr. Moore said, "A name from history."

5

—————————

"So, did you learn anything more about our mystery woman?" Peggy said to me when she joined me several days later for lunch off-campus at a little Italian restaurant on Colorado Boulevard. She had just gotten back from a conference for community college transfer counselors on all the four-year college and university opportunities available to bright students at the end of the 20th century. She had ordered spaghetti and meatballs on which she put a copious amount of parmesan cheese, and I was munching on a sub.

"Well, she's from Pennsylvania," I said.

"Hmm… Interesting."

"Now, what could possibly be interesting about that?"

"I don't know. It just is. Maybe she's part of the Main Line rich in Philadelphia."

"No, I don't think so."

"Why?"

"Because she said she grew up close to Hershey."

"Where the chocolate comes from?"

"Yeah, where the chocolate comes from."

Peggy suddenly gasped. "Uhhhh! She's part of the Hershey fortune!"

"I don't think so."

"How do you know?"

"Well, outside of the fact that I can't imagine a Hershey heiress from south Pennsylvania attending an adult education class in South Pasadena, she just doesn't come off that way."

"But she showed up to your first class elegant and in a dress."

"And she showed up to the second elegant and in a nice pair of pants. No, I think it's her husband's money."

"Oh…"

"His name is Eugene."

"*Euuugene*," she repeated, extending the name into some sense of significance.

"Do you find something revelatory in his name?"

"No. Just that it's *Euuugene*."

"Peggy, you're an idiot."

"I mean, why isn't he called just Gene?"

"I don't know. Why isn't he called just—"

Something stopped me, some prod, some poke, some prick to my brain. No, no, not my brain, my heart. No, no, not my heart, but that area in the middle of your torso, just above your belly and below your ribs where indigestion rests, where vomit seems to come from.

Peggy could see it. "What?"

"Nothing."

"I mean, who names their kid Eugene anymore?"

"Well, he wasn't named recently. I'm sure he was named forty-years ago or so."

"You think he's that much older than his wife?"

"I think so."

"You could tell? You saw him again this week; you trailed her to the street?"

"No, just the first night. When I saw him, I knew. He's, well, he's not twenty-five years old driving a Rolls Royce."

"So you're just assuming she's a trophy wife, arm candy."

"Not at all—not the way they greeted each other."

"You saw what?"

"Real affection."

"Oh. And that bothers you?"

"No, it doesn't bother me. Why would it bother me?"

"Because you're smitten with her."

"I am not smitten with her."

"Well, she's having some effect on you."

"That I will admit. But I think it has more to do with this..."

"Radiance?"

"Yeah, but... I'm starting to think that radiance is just, uh, an openness to learning, to history. She's really eager."

"Which really makes her an odd duck."

"Why do you say that?"

"A beautiful married-to-a-rich-man-twenty-five-year-old woman eager for education? When she could just sit back and luxuriate."

"Luxuriate in what? In a bunch of glitzy material things? Peggy, don't we do what we do because we believe there is more to life than just glitzy material things?"

"Oh, yeah, sure, sure. I wouldn't mind a few now and then, though."

"Money, Peggy, will not make you happy."

"No, I agree. I absolutely, yeah, sure, agree. But the lack of it can make you seriously unhappy."

"Ah, yes. And therein, I suppose, lies the confusion. But if she is an odd duck, she's a wonderfully odd duck. And I suppose that's what I find interesting about her."

"Not her—her looks."

"Those I can appreciate aesthetically, on a higher plain than the one you might want to think I appreciate her on."

"Like a Greek statue of a goddess, huh?"

"Sure. Maybe she is a goddess. Maybe she's come to Earth, maybe she's the goddess of pure joy in learning."

"Huh!" Peggy said, putting a whole meatball into her mouth and chewing it slowly and methodically while sprinkling more parmesan cheese on the spaghetti. "Speaking of the joy of learning," Peggy finally said after swallowing the masticated meat, "have you decided where to apply to do your doctorate?"

"I haven't decided to apply to do my doctorate."

"Why not? You know, you're getting on in years there, A.S."

"Well, partly because it's not my idea, it's your idea that I should be applying."

"You're being wasted at PCC."

"Thank you. I'll inform all of my students that they are not worth my time."

"No, no, I didn't mean that. You know what I mean."

"No, Peggy, I sometimes often don't know what you mean."

"Well, be that as it may, here…" She pulled out from a large purse she always carried ten brochures from ten universities outlining their ten different doctoral programs in history. "I got them at the conference."

"Jeez, how many trees did they cut down to print those?'

"Take them," she commanded.

"Ah," I sighed and took them and put them in my briefcase.

"I got tickets for a play tonight," she said. "You want to go?"

"I don't know. Where, when, and what's the play?"

"Here in Pasadena. It's a small theater, eight o'clock curtain, we could have dinner beforehand. And it's—get this—Agatha Christie's *Mousetrap.*"

"I saw that in London."

"Well, don't tell me the ending."

"I can't imagine a local little theater production here in Pasadena could be as good as the long-running *Mousetrap* in London."

"You're a snob."

"No, I'm not. It's just a statement of potential fact."

"Hey, it's an evening out."

"I've got papers to grade."

"It's an evening out with *me.*"

"Well, that's a positive. Still…"

"It's an evening out with me that could end with," she whispered quietly, "fellatio."

I perked up, sat straight up, and roared in my best W.C. Fields voice, *"Ah, yes! Fel-la-ti-o! The only time in a relationship—when the boy—really wants to hear the girl say—'I do!'"*

Peggy laughed a piercing, loud laugh and slapped my right hand, which was doing its own Fields impersonation, as her cheeks flushed rosy with embarrassment.

6

S peaking of fellatio. It's sort of the opposite of the weather, isn't
it? It's something everybody does something about, but
nobody talks about it. At least, not in polite company. But as I
write this, I am my own company and have no need to be polite, let
me give it some consideration. For it was the cause of, or inspiration
for, my marriage. *Fellatio and marriage/ fellatio and marriage/ they go
together/ like Horatio and carriage*—assuming the horse is named Horatio. Fellatio is an absurd and silly thing. Especially when looked at
with a cold and analytical mind—as mine has been trained to be. It has
no practical purpose. It is not in the least bit pragmatic, as it does not,
of course, aid in the generation of new little humans. The placing of
one's lips around a penis while simultaneously engulfing that penis,
while then doing whatever needs to be done to make the whole
process, shall we say, fulfilling, is, at face value, bizarre. But is it any
more absurd, silly, and weird than the placing of one's lips onto the
lips of another, then allowing your tongues to do the tango while
exchanging the breath of life? I mean, how would David Attenbor-
ough describe either kissing or fellatio in a BBC life-on-Earth docu-
mentary? But then, in this vast universe, made up of basically matter
and energy and 99.99999999999999999999% lifeless, life itself is

pretty absurd, silly, and weird. If one's cold, analytical mind will give proper consideration to fellatio, it should warm up and admit to the compelling physical facts of stimulus and response. But to mention the inspiration it might engender in at least one poor and naive creature to commit himself to what, at the beginning of such a commitment, is always considered love everlasting.

Her name was Cindy, and I met her in a bar. Now don't stop me and tell me I was an idiot. I know I was an idiot. Worse than that, I was a painfully unknowing idiot.

I've explained how I was a goody-two-shoes in school, and that condition certainly extended into my late teens and to the onset of legal adulthood. For example, drinking alcoholic beverages under the age of twenty-one was illegal in California, and I took that as seriously as I had my Boy Scout oath. But once I turned twenty-one, several things changed. I moved out of my parents' home in Ramone, where I had still been living while attending community college, and moved south to Orange County to attend one of California's many state colleges. And I decided that now that it was legal for me to drink, I certainly would. But not like the communal binge drinking of today's college students. I was not interested in partying with other students, none of whom I really knew anyway. But just decent adult consumption, no big deal, and just a little sophisticated.

The state college I went to was called a "commuter college" because most of its students arrived each day via several converging freeways. According to one of my English teachers, this was a modern and marvelous thing. She waxed enthusiastically for about fifteen minutes one class session about how this fact kept us all out of the dreaded, old-world, old-fashioned, old-fogie academic "ivory tower." Meaning, I suppose, we were all one with the people. The irony of this was that if any instructor I ever had was locked into an ivory tower (possibly one of her own making), she was that instructor. Anyone who made something romantic and appealing out of such a disjointed, disconnected, and non-communal college experience was as absurd, silly, and weird as fellatio.

So, not yet having experimented with booze and not knowing the particular effect it would have on me—Would I have a hollow leg? Would I be a one-drink-wonder?—I wanted to do so in a neutral environment. Besides, I had moved to Orange County to be close to the college; I did not take the freeway to get there each day. I took surface roads. And in taking them, I had spotted several interesting looking bars that seemed to call out, "Psst, hey, buddy, good times inside for a person of minimum legal drinking age."

I picked an attractive-looking bar by the name of Fun & Frolic Lounge and went one early evening.

Cindy, thin and tall, yet sexy, sat at the bar comfortably on a stool, drinking hard liquor and smoking a cigarette. She had short blonde hair, somewhat pixie-like, which was an interesting contrast with her height. And she had as pretty a face as I had ever seen—effortlessly pretty. I was immediately drawn to her and sat on the barstool next to her. Not because I had been drawn to her—I was not just painfully unknowing, but awkwardly shy—but because it was the only empty barstool left.

I ordered a beer. I figured I better start the experiment on the low end of alcoholic content. When the bartender, a man of some bulk, a bald pate, and long sideburns, asked if I wanted a particular brand of beer in a bottle or the house brew on tap, I was dumbstruck.

"Give him a tap beer," came a strong female voice from my left. "In a nice large mug." It was Cindy, rescuing me.

"Thanks," I said, turning to her, seeing her face of fine features, finding her eyes to be green, and longing suddenly for her lips, which were full and smiling as she said:

"You're welcome. It's a good beer. You'll like it."

I nodded another thanks. Then, feeling that it would be rude—not to mention far too transparent—to keep my eyes roaming her face (as much as I wanted to), I took them away and looked around the Fun & Frolic Lounge. The other patrons at the bar were fairly quiet, communing only with their drinks or the bartender. But there were about five tables in the center of the lounge and five booths up against one wall where groups of people sat, talked, and laughed. Loudly. A lot.

"First time in this bar?" Cindy asked.

"First time in any bar," I answered, being stupidly honest.

"Ah, well, you shouldn't overdo it."

"I'll try not to."

"I'll keep an eye on you."

"Thank you, I appreciate that."

"Oh, no problem. I sometimes overdo it, I'll admit."

"Uh, I don't quite know what to say about that."

Cindy stubbed out her cigarette, clearly thinking all the while, then said, "Why don't we trade? You keep an eye on me too."

Then, breaking through my shyness, I shocked myself when I said, "Well, keeping an eye on you will not only be easy, it will be, um, quite a pleasure."

"Ah, that's sweet. What's your name?"

"Adolphus."

"Adolphus?"

"There was an Adolphus who was once the King of Sweden."

"Really?"

"Yes. And, you know, now that I think about it, I should have ordered a beer from Anheuser-Busch because the co-founder of Anheuser-Busch was Adolphus Busch."

"Really?"

"Yeah. They named a big hotel after him in Dallas, the Adolphus Hotel."

"Really?"

"Yeah."

"You're just a font of information, aren't you?"

"Yeah," I said, wondering if I should be embarrassed, if she was kidding me or, worse, subtly putting me down. But she did not turn away. She rested her pretty head on her hand, giving it a cute, not to mention an acute angle, and kept her eyes on me.

"You live around here?" she asked.

"Yeah. I have an apartment close by. I go to the state college."

"Oh, college boy!"

"Do you go to college?"

"No," she said, trilling it with a little laugh. "I'm a working girl. I mean, you know, not in *that way*."

No, I didn't know what she meant by that.

"I work in retail."

"Oh."

"In a dress shop. At the crazy-ass big mall down the street. I'm in line to become the assistant manager."

"Congratulations."

"Yeah, a little bump in pay—never hurts. More responsibility, but I've got the job down pat. Say, did you ever hear that joke about President Nixon?"

"I've heard a number of them."

"Well, this is the one about Walter Cronkite interviewing Nixon, and he asks him, 'Mr. President, what do you think of fellatio?' And Nixon says, 'Well, Walter, let me say this about that, I've got it down Pat.' Ha-ha-ha!"

It was the first time I had ever heard the word—fellatio—so I had no idea what she was talking about. But I followed her lead and laughed uproariously.

I had four or five large mugs of beer that night, and, in an inordinate amount of trips to the men's room, I pissed away my shyness. When I returned from my last trip, I asked Cindy, "You wouldn't want to come back and see my apartment, would you?"

Unfazed by my question, she said, "Why? Is there something special about it?"

"No. It's just an apartment. Furnished. Utilities paid. One-bedroom."

"One bedroom, huh?"

"Have to sleep somewhere?"

"Well, do you at least have some etchings on the walls?"

"No. Don't have anything on the walls yet."

"Is it clean?"

"I haven't been there long enough for it to be too dirty, but I do try to keep it clean, yeah."

"So there's nothing special about your apartment?"

"Well—there will be once you're in it."

"Oh, you sweet-tongued devil, you. George!" She called for the bartender, and we paid our tabs. Then we slipped off our stools, finding ourselves standing close, facing each other if not strictly face-to-face. "Oh, you are a bit short in stature there, aren't you, Adolphus?"

Compared to Cindy, the shrunken condition of myself could well have shrunk so much more, both emotional and physical. But the four or five mugs of beer had given me courage that I heretofore had rarely ever experienced. "Well, actually, I'm six foot two."

"Oh you are, are you?"

"Yes. It's just that tonight I wore my elevator shoes, and I accidentally pushed the DOWN button."

"Ha, haha! You know, you're cute. I mean you are, you are cute." She looked over the landscape of my face. "Actually, you—you're quite handsome."

"Well, thank you."

"Look, you know what? I'm going to lean over and give you a big kiss. If I like what happens, that seals the deal."

And so she did. She leaned down and planted her mouth on my mouth and went spelunking with her tongue, shocking the shit out of mine. But, delightfully so. My heart made itself known by beginning to pound, and I was obviously transported to another dimension, for I hardly heard the generous and appreciative applause most of the other bar patrons gave us.

7

When Cindy and I got to my apartment, we both had to pee madly, which we did—separately and in private, in case you were wondering. She went first, and I followed, and when I came out, she took command, leading me into my own bedroom and telling me to strip, which I did.

Cindy stood before me and made an assessment for several seconds that relativistically warped into minutes for me. Finally, she declared herself not disappointed. Relief must have flashed onto my face, for she smiled.

"Okay, lay down on the bed," she ordered. I did as I was told. Then she proceeded slowly to strip. As she did so, and as she was wearing clothes from the dress shop she was soon to be the assistant manager of, she told me about each piece of clothing, how it was made, the quality it showed, the materials it was made from, and the price before her employee discount. The last piece of clothing was her undies, not available at her dress shop, so she slipped them down and over her buttocks, down her legs, and kicked them away with her right foot without imparting any information about them at all.

And then she stood there in her thin yet fleshy glory—certainly enough flesh to declare her full human femaleness. Her breasts were relatively small and yet nicely proportioned with nipples that definitely made points with me. Her pubic hair had obviously been tended to with care, and it made a triangle that seemed to be pointing to pleasure.

I'm detailing a typical male response and short-list catalog of the essentials, aren't I? Well, I've already mentioned how pretty she was of face and how cute her short, pixie-cut blonde hair was. So let me also add that she had the most beautiful skin—unblemished, healthy color, a silken surface one ached to touch, despite it seeming almost ethereal. There was something incredibly heady in that.

I was as erect as I had ever been in my life, and instinct was calling on me to do something about it fairly quickly. My right hand slowly crept towards it, maybe hoping to catch it by surprise.

"Oh go ahead, honey," Cindy, who was enjoying my enjoying her, said, "give it a wank."

And so I did.

"Nice," she said. "But here, let me do that."

She crawled into bed with me and paid rapt attention to my extension. First with her hand, then with her mouth. I had never been so happy in my life. She stopped for a moment, raised her head, and said quite sincerely, "You see—size doesn't matter. Or, maybe I should say height." She smiled sweetly and returned to her current occupation.

I, of course, fell in love. And couldn't imagine life without Cindy. She was less sure of the idea but found it to be not without amusement. After a period of apprenticeship in which she taught me how to best make love to a woman (subtle stimulus to solicit forthright response), she started taking seriously the idea that we could be married. She liked that I would be a college graduate, for she had taken to heart all the nightly news reports on the more significant earnings potential of college graduates than high school graduates and certainly compared to dropouts. But she never really understood all the time I devoted to the task. She found book reading to be a strange anomaly in human behavior, at least according to her life experience. That should have been a warning to me; that should have bothered me. But, as I said, I was in love. If you could call it that.

My father found our union to be somewhat mismatched. But as he was a man who never had an opinion he wished to express, he kept quiet about it. My mother liked Cindy immediately upon meeting her. As a fellow smoker, I think Mother found Cindy a kindred soul. My father had given up smoking years early when, one evening, he hocked up a huge glob of black phlegm into the toilet bowl. He quit cold turkey that night. And ever since, my mother had missed her smoking buddy. I never learned to smoke, heeding King James the First's counterblast to tobacco, so my mother was delighted to have another smoker in the family. Also, both women had strong, commanding personalities—there was no mismatch there.

The three of them sat together at my college graduation when I was accorded my BA in history. Each displayed proper parental and spousal pride. Pictures were taken of me in my gown and my silly tasseled cap. One was of my parents and me, one was with Cindy and me, one was of me and my parents and Cindy, and one was with me alone holding my diploma. It had been a beautiful day, bright and cheerful.

And then everything went sour.

Although most of my college education had been paid for through scholarships and grants, I did rack up some student debt. Cindy was determined that it should be paid off as soon as possible. I had hoped to go directly from getting my BA to entering a master's program in history, but Cindy said that wasn't workable, that would just amass more student debt, not pay off what was already there. And besides, she said, it was getting to be embarrassing telling people that she was the wife of a "student," a word she effortlessly turned into a pejorative. So employment applications were filled out and sent in, and I was hired at an Antelope Valley high school to teach Freshman Social Studies at a school that sat in the middle of a desert.

We moved, rented a small apartment, Cindy found a position in a local dress shop, and I entered into the most miserable period of my life.

I had not been a happy high school student—not being social, not being cool, not being a bad boy, just being a good student, and not liking most of my peers. This possibly makes it understandable that I would not be happy teaching high school students, seeing ghosts from my own days mingle with the living dead of the current days.

For relief and recreation on the weekend, Cindy dragged me off on quick trips to Las Vegas, which she really loved, taking me from one desert to another.

I hate deserts. I will always hate deserts. Speak to me not of stark beauty, blessed quiet, stunning night skyscapes free from city illumination. None of that will ever convince me that desiccation, dirt, dehydration, searing sun, sweat, and snakes are anything but a ticket to hell. Oh, sure, Las Vegas has large, luxurious, air-conditioned hotels. But if it is an oasis, it is an oasis of mundane, middleclass masses drinking too much, gambling too much, and being tickled to death too much by middle-of-the-road—and thus often roadkill —entertainment.

It was a great revelation to realize that I was a cultural snob: a revelation and a joy.

After my first semester as a high school social studies teacher, and occasional unhappy weekend jaunter to Vegas, I was determined to quit and enter into a master's program.

Cindy was upset. She saw no reason why I wanted to go and "hide in college" again. It was painful trying to explain it to her as I didn't quite have the words, and she wouldn't have listened to them anyway. Cindy stewed for several days and was quite chilly—assuming one can be chilly while stewing. Then she came home one night after working late at the dress shop and announced that she thought we should separate.

The idea roiled me. It seemed impossible, wrong, devastating. I spent much of the night crying profusely. Whereas Cindy took it like a man. In retrospect, I've always felt that Cindy was pleased with my reaction, thinking she had shocked me, thus manipulated me back to good sense.

And she had. For when I awoke the next morning, after my long night of purging tears, I realized that her plan made perfectly good sense, and I gleefully packed a bag and was off.

I returned to Orange County, just made the deadline to get into a master's program in history at the state college I had graduated from and found myself a place to live.

As Cindy and I had no children, no real property to speak of, and hardly anything in our joint bank account, our divorce was easy, quick, and clean. And I came away with a hard and fast philosophy in life: No man should marry a wife substantially taller than himself. Besides putting oneself in a constant physical and psychological sense of diminishment, it has a tendency to diminish one's testicles as well.

8

I've always had a talent for retaining knowledge. Thus my success as a student and, I hope, as a scholar and a teacher. I did quite well in the master's program. And I became quite adept at something else. For Cindy had also been a master's program—of a sort—and I retained the carnal knowledge she had imparted to me in great detail.

I came out of the black and the white, the bad and the good, the dark and the light, and the yin and yang of my twenties a confident person—for the first time in my life. I was now aware of my competence in my chosen field. I was also aware that I was—like my father before me—a damn good-looking guy able to attract women. I had honestly not realized this before; maybe before I wasn't. Although, as I look back at photos taken in my teens and early twenties, I tend to say to myself: Hey, you were a damn good-looking guy. It was a most satisfying epiphany, and I felt quite confident in this knowledge—as well as putting it to use.

Despite the intense time I had to devote to completing a master's program, during this period, I allowed several women—all shorter than me—to fall in love with me and offer themselves to me wholeheartedly. I did not break all their hearts; some I only wounded. Despite this, I would like to think we all always departed as friends.

———

A s positive an attribute as confidence in my competence in several areas was, I lacked a couple of attributes that the world-at-large seems to admire.

Taking after my father, I also had a non-aggression pact with the world. Pushing forward had always seemed to me to be just pushy. In the back of my head was *Pushy pig! Pushy pig!* the elementary school chant used whenever some young snot tried to cut in line. I considered it then one of the gravest of insults, and I had obviously retained that opinion into my adulthood. An aggressive person, I was not.

Nor was I at all ambitious, which is something someone cannot be without first being aggressive. I was not a fan of conflict, controversy, contentiousness, or contrarianism. I had no need to be a rising star on the fast track of careerism and, worse in most people's estimations, I was not enamored with and had absolutely no respect for money. So I was always in need, as I have said, of some extra cash. But only "extra," never a plethora. I didn't believe that all lucre was filthy. I never gave it enough thought to have formed such an opinion.

None of this means that I didn't look out for myself, that I couldn't defend myself, that I didn't, at times, try to manipulate a situation for my greater comfort. I was just able to do it simply, subtly, and, I hope, always with a smile.

For example, I mentioned my success with women. It never came because I pursued them. I had always felt that something was demeaning in that. No, once I figured out that I was reasonably attractive to the opposite sex, I was more than happy to allow them to pursue me—happy, honored, humbled, and often very, very satisfied.

Nor did I pursue a Ph.D., deciding instead to return to Pasadena City College, the community college I had attended, to become a history teacher. I'd had several fine history teachers at PCC who had opened my eyes wider and pushed my mind to be even broader. One of them was the ugliest man I had ever seen. Stan Janis was big, hulking, about six foot five and had a broad and yet long face of massive wrinkles, folds upon folds of them, like one of those dogs that seem all loose skin over a skeleton. And you couldn't take your eyes off of him. Not because of his magnificent ugliness, but because of his transcendent mind. He compelled you to listen to him with a combination of facts, conjecture, questions, stories of great men (and a few great women), tales of anything-but-mundane minutiae, all presented with his gleeful charisma. Besides the *History of the United States 1800 to 1950* course I took from him, I took his *Introduction to Teaching* class. On the first day, he announced, "By the end of this course, you will discover not only if you want to be a teacher, but if you *should* be a teacher. We do not need teachers in it for the huge, vast amount of wealth you can make (chuckles and laughs here). We do not need teachers who do it as a 'fallback' as they write the great American novel or invent a better mousetrap. We need teachers who desire only to teach. Teachers, you must understand, are the first line of defense protecting the future. That's an honorable position. That's a glorious position. That's a position worthy of the medals which you will never receive. And—this is most important—if you really enjoy teaching, there is no more fun to be had on this planet outside of, possibly, conjugal bliss with your spouse—and that's debatable."

He had been absolutely correct. At the end of his course, I had discovered that I wanted to be a teacher. I wanted to be a teacher standing in his shoes.

By the time I got back to PCC, Mr. Janis had died. So there were empty shoes to fill. But I would have preferred to have filled them only after a couple of years of having him as a mentor.

You may now understand my resistance to Peggy when she brought up again the idea of my pursuing a doctorate. I had no plans to. I was comfortable in my skin, a perfectly good skin, and I was pleased to be at PCC, a superior community college. And in all other aspects of life, despite always needing extra cash, I was not in any way uncomfortable.

And then Lavinia Carson came into my life. A radiant and beautiful person carrying the name of a woman of legend who's far-traveling husband was, I assumed, the very essence of aggression and ambition.

9

Lavinia Carson walked into the classroom five minutes early, as radiant as ever. Or possibly even more radiant for she seemed to have about her a glow of excitement. She was wearing another dress, or rather a blouse and skirt combo. It was a high-waisted skirt, burgundy in color, and with an abstract pattern of swirls in slightly darker burgundy, that came to just below her knees. The blouse was long-sleeved yet not quite to the wrists, black and v-necked. On her left wrist rested a solid green bracelet that I was sure was pure jade. It was calmly elegant, if that makes any sense.

"Hello, Mr. Seruya," she said.

"Hello, Lavinia."

"Are you going to hand back the quiz from last week?"

"Yes, I am."

"Did I do okay?"

"Well, if your definition of 'okay' includes getting one hundred percent, then, yes, you did okay."

"Oh, great," she said with a small sense of relief.

"You weren't worried, were you?"

"Well, no, I guess not. But it was the first test I have taken in a long time and, well, you know..."

Besides carrying her textbook and notepad, she had a large, expensive-looking, canvas bag emblazoned with a fashion house logo. I could tell from the way she lugged it that the contents were heavy.

"I have something really neat to show you," she said, lifting the bag a little as if preparing to offer it to me.

"Ah, well, can it wait until after class? We're going to start in a minute." Other students were starting to arrive and take their seats.

"Oh, yes, of course," she said as she took her seat, tucking the large bag carefully under it with her foot.

During this session, I took the students out of ancient myth and legend and into reality, covering what we know—or think we know—about the very early history of the Minoans and the Mycenaeans. How they came into the Greek peninsula, bringing with them the language that would become Greek, and then onto the birth of Democracy and the Golden Age of Greece. After the break, I focused on certain men of action and certain men of thought who shaped this era's history. The men who made the differences. Alcibiades, Cleisthenes, and Pericles, who did things that mattered. And Thales, Democritus, Pythagoras, and, of course, Socrates, Plato, and Aristotle, who thought thoughts that mattered.

As I had so often in my classes, I witnessed that once you start talking about personalities, about individuals, about real people, history comes alive for the students. We are an egocentric bunch, we *Homo sapiens.* Man may or may not be the measure of all things, as Protagoras said, but it is indeed the thing most people take delight in measuring. That's why we are the storytelling species, and we only tell stories about humans. Except, of course, in simple animal fables, but those are just stories about humans dressed up in fur and feathers. We mostly have found our own skins endlessly fascinating in stories tragic, comic, and even salacious. No one ever gossiped about Lassie.

Who we really want to hear about (outside of those in our own, confined little communities, and not always then) are famous people. And in history, famous people were often referred to as "Great Men." And, of course, some Great Women here and there. (That's not a political statement, just the facts). The kings (and a few queens), and emperors (see previous parenthetical note), and warriors (a few of which were women), and great thinkers (you can find a few women here too when they were allowed to think). Later there were popes (no women here, just so-called holy, so-called Roman, and never called emperors in their big, heavy dresses and high hats), and explorers (the women usually stayed home). And, of course, there were the contrarians, the rebels, and the revolutionaries ("Remember the ladies, Mr, Adams.") And, relatively lately, scientists and inventors. There was much professional talk at the end of the 20th century about studying not just great, prominent, spotlight-hogging individuals but ordinary people in their everyday lives and the economy of those lives. And geography, of course, and climate, and the impact of these elements on history; history being so much more than just Great Men (and Women). It was talking I could not argue with; all of that is obviously important. And for some, it's fascinating, especially for professional historians. But for students who are never going to become historians, but who definitely need to know history, give them humans to hang that history on. Give them their glories and triumphs, give them their failures and atrocities. Give them the magnificent ones, and give them the malicious ones. Then, as best as you can, make the connection between then and now; them and us. That has always been my philosophy of the teaching of history.

I dismissed the class right on time. The students were pleased and grateful and abandoned the classroom as if it were sinking post-iceberg—except for Lavinia Carson. She came up to me at Ms. Roberta Boxer's desk, lugging her heavy canvas bag.

"I found these at Vroman's."

"That's a terrific bookstore."

"Yeah, it is, isn't it?"

Lavinia pulled out of the canvas bag a very-much-oversized coffee table book and plopped it with a bit of bang onto Ms. Roberta Boxer's desk. It was *Art in Antiquity,* a book most likely more often displayed than perused. But this one had been heavily perused, as evidenced by the numerous yellow sticky notes that poked out between many pages. She opened it up and started to show me black and white photos and full-page color plates of statues and murals and paintings and mosaics from ancient Egypt, Mesopotamia, Greece, and Rome, but mainly from Greece and Rome. They were pictures of kings, heroes, and gods; of gladiators, slaves, merchants, wives, and children; of land and sea animals, both in the wild and prepared and dressed as meals.

"Aren't these fascinating," she said with her wonderful smile that edged on the goofy but was so wholly excited. "I love these mosaics." She turned to one of Plato debating with students at his Academy, under a tree with grand buildings in the background. "These were real people doing real things."

"Well, yes, but highly romanticized. This was done four, maybe five hundred years after Plato lived."

"Yes, of course, but still, to go from words to this…"

"And Plato, of course, probably didn't look like that."

"Well, then, how about this?" She turned and turned pages until she got to a painted-on-mummy-panel portrait of a young woman from Egypt. Not the Egypt of the Pharaohs, but the Egypt of the first century CE when Egypt was part of the Roman Empire. "That's her, right, I mean the real her, that's a direct portrait of her, right?"

"Yes, so it seems. These paintings on wood panels replaced the plaster masks of the dead in earlier times. They were remarkable, truly capturing the person."

"I feel like I could talk to her," she said happily, amazed at the thought. "You know, get to know her. And yet, she died two thousand years ago. But look at her. She was somebody."

"Well, yes, she certainly would have been from the upper class."

"No, I don't mean that. I mean, she was once alive, living so long ago, but flesh, not dust. She was real and alive and not that much different from me."

"Well, yes, not much, but there were differences. If you were to meet her, you would definitely find her foreign."

"But not in the things that matter."

"What things matter?"

"Oh, cooking and eating, taking care of children—"

"And all the household slaves who did the cooking and probably took care of the children."

"Well, yes, but—"

"And she had absolutely no rights. She was really not much more than a slave to her husband."

"Do you really believe that? Was there no love?"

It was a simple question that slapped away some of my cynicism. For she had asked it, looking straight at me with defiant hope in her eyes.

"Well, yes, of course, you're right. We have evidence from letters to and from married couples that love, affection, existed between them."

"See, she's real. And look at those earrings and that necklace. They're beautiful. She felt a need to be attractive or to carry beauty with her two thousand years ago. That just—just, I don't know, thrills me."

Which was pretty thrilling for me. "It's interesting that you point that out. Because human life is really very simple, isn't it? I mean, basically, we just need to eat, sleep, and reproduce."

"Fuck, you mean. Eat, sleep, and fuck."

I admit to being shocked. I am not prone to being a prude about language and quite enjoy Peggy's sometimes salty mouth. But with Lavinia, it didn't seem right. Was that just me, a professional truth-teller running away from a fact? "Ah, well, if you want to put it that way. But the, uh, genesis, shall we say, is the need for reproduction."

"Okay."

"And, uh, beyond, eating, sleeping, and reproducing, we need shelter, someplace to hunker down. And we need clothes to protect ourselves against the elements, don't we? All elementary, basic needs. They could all be fulfilled very simply with no fuss. Ingest food that won't kill you, but nourish you, sleep safe in a basic shelter that cocoons you against the elements, and, uh, have a quick one with the opposite sex to spread or receive human seed. But we do have a tendency to dress all that up, don't we? That is a mark of our humanity, isn't it? We don't just eat food; we cook it, prepare it, make it presentable. We don't just build buildings to shelter us; we build buildings to please us as we look at them or surround ourselves with them, to be, in a word, beautiful. Or symbolic, meaningful, concrete metaphors—temples, palaces, churches, seats of government, even houses for our dead. If it's a home—" I flipped pages in the book until I found what I wanted, an illustrated view of a Roman villa. "We design it not just as a practical shelter, but as a place to live and to *be* in. So we design it to be pleasing-looking, and we adorn it as this woman adorned herself, allowing for gardens, wall paintings, views. And reproduction? It was often harsh, cruel, and perfunctory in our very early days. But what have we turned it into? Into 'making love' and 'being in love,' which we celebrate in songs, stories, and cheap cardboard cards..."

Okay, I was lecturing. But it was, after all, second nature to me by then. And there was encouragement there. I had leaned back in my chair and placed my hands behind my head, supporting it, as she stood up straight and stood there looking not just at me but at my eyes, connecting with them and never breaking that connection. Her attention was as rapt as her eyes were focused. How could I not keep talking in the hope of freezing her there for all time?

"And clothes. We don't just throw something on to protect us against the cold or accommodate the heat; we style them to express something about ourselves—when we can afford to. And we add to them. Well, look—" I sat forward and pointed to the panel portrait of the young woman. "Earrings and necklaces and what-have-you. And don't think it was just women in history; pay attention to men's adornment as well. Some were really quite the dandy."

"Oh, I have, that's part of what's making them real to me, that makes me wish I could actually go back there and see them, talk to them. But this—" Lavinia indicated the portrait. "This is the next best thing, and I'm just really, really fascinated by them. And I really do love her earrings and that necklace."

"Well, they help you to relate to her. Especially you—" I wondered if I should pursue where this was taking me, was there dangerous ground ahead? But the path was so well marked out. "Because, well, because you have a wonderful sense of style, I mean, you know, you're always so well dressed."

"Yes, my husband, Eugene, he insists on it."

"He insists on it?"

"Well, it doesn't take much convincing. I've never had such wonderful clothes. And it pleases him so much to see me in them."

"Speaking of which, isn't he out there waiting for you? Are you keeping him waiting?"

"Oh, no, I drove myself tonight. In my Mercedes. Eugene's at a big convention back East."

"Oh, I see. What's the convention for?"

"It's all about construction aggregates production."

"I have no idea what that is."

"It's basically for people who run rock and sand quarries and provide rock, sand, and gravel to the construction industry. That's his business. He owns quarries all over America, and some in Canada and Mexico. He started real close to here at Ramone Rock and Sand in—"

"Ramone? Yes, I know the quarry there. I grew up in Ramone."

"Really?"

"Yeah."

"Neat."

"Well, I don't know how—"

"Eh-um!" It was Ms. Deborah Miller, who stood in the classroom doorway. "Hey, you guys, the cleaning crew needs to get in here. This is the last one, and I can't go home until they are done."

"Oh, sorry, Deb, we'll be out in a second." I then turned to Lavinia. "Well, thanks for bringing this in," I said, referring to the book, which I started to put back in the canvas bag for her.

"Oh, can't we talk some more? I don't have to go home right away."

"Well—"

"Do you live far? We could go to a coffee shop or something where you live."

"Actually, I live here, pretty close, just four or five blocks away. I walk."

"Oh, neat. Well, I know then, how about we go to this old drug store I've seen on Fair Oaks. They have an old-fashioned soda fountain, they say. I've always wanted to drop in. We could go for coffee. Or better yet, malted milk!"

"That's the Fair Oaks Pharmacy. A bit kitschy, but yes, they do make good malts."

"I think it will kind of remind me of home."

As we left, Deb, who was still standing in the doorway, gave me a distinct and meaningful look and, out of Lavinia's sight but not mine, pointed to her own wedding band on the ring finger of her left hand.

When we got to the student parking lot, it was empty except for her silver Mercedes SL60, a two-seater, slick looking machine, sitting directly under a lamppost, beautifully illuminated, as if it was in a print ad in *Vanity Fair*. Especially considering it sat at an angle to the lamp post, taking up two parking spaces.

"Eugene says at night to always park the car under a street lamp," Lavinia said. "That way, no thief can steal away your car in the dark."

"Yes, but they also won't find it hard to see while they're trying to break into your car," I pointed out with some little glee.

"Well, that's true. I guess that's something Eugene never thought of."

"And why did you park this way?"

"Eugene insists. Says that way, my beautiful 75,000-dollar car won't get dinged by a crappy 10,000-dollar Corolla."

We got into the Mercedes, and the first thing I noticed was that the passenger seat did not just support me but welcomed me. It was a leather seat, and somehow it communicated its luxury to me directly (hide-to-hide?). I found myself surreptitiously stroking it. "Nice car," I complimented, feeling required to do so.

"Eugene picked it out," she said, brushing off the compliment.

Then she turned to me and said in a near confessional tone, "Do you know what I really wanted?"

"No. What?"

"A VW Bug. I always wanted a VW Bug. But Eugene, you know, did his 'no wife of mine' bit, and, well, I find it very hard to deny the sweetie-pie."

"Oh, he's a sweetie-pie, huh?"

"Yes. Nicest guy in the world—now."

On that last somewhat cryptic word, she started the engine, took off the parking brake, set it into the gear she wanted, and hit the gas. Hit it? Slammed it! I felt like John Glenn being hurled into space. I guess she was taking advantage of the empty lot to show me what this car could do. It was knowledge I would have been happy to forego. At the exit, she came to an abrupt and possibly rupturing stop to take a quick look right and left, then we were off again as she turned left, dashed up to Monterey Road, made a sharp—very sharp—turn right to lightspeed it two blocks to Fair Oaks Avenue. There was a green light facing her at Fair Oaks and no oncoming traffic, and she made the left turn sacrificing not even a minuscule of momentum. Then the next three blocks strobed by, and when she saw a convenient parking spot across from the Fair Oaks Pharmacy (under a streetlamp). She pulled over in a blink and secured it. Not once in this quick trip had she used her turn signals.

"Ah," I said, then needed to take in a good breath of life, "Lavinia, you really should have used your turn signal several times back there."

"Really?"

"Uh, yeah, it would have been a good idea."

"Eugene says you only need to use your turn signal when someone is close behind you or in front of you."

"Eugene says that huh?"

"Yeah."

"No, I don't think that's right. I think the law is you should always use your turn signals. Besides, on Fair Oaks, there were cars behind you when you, um, suddenly pulled over."

"Really?"

"Yeah."

"Shit!"

The dawn-to-midnight Fair Oaks Pharmacy and Soda Fountain was becoming an institution in South Pasadena. It had been around since 1915, giving it a historical patina that few going concerns in the Los Angeles area could boast of, and that in itself may have been enough to institutionalize it. But recently, after years of trying to keep up with the times, the store metamorphosed backward and recovered, as best as possible, the look and feel it is purported to have had in an earlier part of our 20th century. The owners looked for and found in Joplin, Missouri, a bunch of antique pharmacy fixtures and an original soda fountain to add to the store's vintage interior décor. It was a time warp for good, stable business reasons—the nostalgia trade in coming in as the 20th century was going out. As a historian, I find such recreations lacking. As a person, though, I can happily gather the nostalgia around me for comfort. I just would never have admitted it to my colleagues.

1940s big band music came out of hidden speakers as we entered —Glenn Miller or Artie Shaw or some band like that—and Lavinia stopped immediately and looked around, taking everything in.

Although there were several soda shop tables, all curving metal and red padded seats on the accompanying chairs, she said, "Let's sit at the soda fountain." And so we did, planting our butts on the round stools resting on shiny chrome columns—she, delicately and with grace; me, a bit less so. A young Latina was behind the counter in an apron and a little paper hat, and she greeted us with a smile and asked if we wanted to see menus. Lavinia answered quickly, "I don't. I just want a vanilla malt." And I nodded, extending the order to two vanilla malts.

"Whip cream?" the waitress (I don't feel comfortable calling her a soda jerk, and certainly not a jerkette) asked.

"Of course!" Lavinia answered.

"And a cherry on top?" We were further asked.

"Goes without saying," I, nevertheless, said.

Lavinia continued to look around as we waited for our malts. "This is nice," she finally said. "Not quite as, I don't know, 'real' I guess, like the one we have back home."

"So, Pennsylvania, you said, right?"

"Yes. I grew up in a tiny town called Andersberg. One of those, you know, one-industry towns. It was built up around the Anders Quarry. That's where I was working when I met Eugene."

"Oh." The shape of things to come was taking shape. And I did nothing to discourage her from taking it there.

"He was there buying the quarry."

"Buying it?"

"Yes. I told you Eugene owns quarries all over America. I was the secretary slash office manager to Young Bob Anders, who owned the quarry. He was selling it because he couldn't keep it going anymore."

"Was he really called *Young* Bob Anders?"

"Yeah, he was. He was actually Robert Anders, Jr. His dad had gotten to be known as Old Man Anders, so it was natural, I guess, that we all started calling his son Young Bob. It stuck on pretty good, even after his dad died, and he inherited the quarry."

"So, being a one-industry town, that was the only job you could get?"

"Well, actually, no, I mean, it's more complex than that. I mean, I'd been working there since I was sixteen."

"Sixteen? You got a part-time job there?"

"No, I started full time. Had to quit high school."

"Oh, that—" I checked myself. I don't know why. It wasn't quite like I was going to say, *That explains why you have that hump on your back*, but it felt the same. And Lavinia could see that.

"Yeah, you've been wondering what I'm doing in adult education, right?"

"From moment one," I admitted.

"Well, my family has worked at the quarry forever. My dad was working there, from the time he was a teenager, and there was an accident. An accident that shouldn't have happened." Her gray eyes became steel-like with indignation. "And he was killed."

"Oh, gee, I'm sorry."

"Yeah—thanks. Anyway—"

The malts arrived, and Lavinia gave the waitress the sweetest' thank you' I had ever heard. Then she took the standing-up-straight straw and plunged it up and down in the malt a few times before taking her first sip. "Ah, good, this is good."

I was getting tired of keeping my neck turned to look at her, so I suggested, "Why don't we take these and go sit at one of the tables." We did, settling in, then, after she took a few more sips, she continued.

"Anyway, that just left my mom, me, and my two brothers, twins, who were only seven at the time."

"Was there any insurance or worker's comp?"

"No insurance. And the quarry had no union. As for worker's comp, well—well, it's all complex. And a long story."

And yet, I knew she wanted to tell it. "Well, you said you didn't have to go right home, and I don't have any classes tomorrow until the afternoon."

"Okay. If you think it might be interesting."

"I don't see how it could not be."

She took a really long sip of her malt. "This is good, really good. But how about some coffee?"

I got the waitress's attention and ordered two cups of coffee.

"Young Bob was running the quarry at the time. Running it into the ground. His dad had been great, loved the business, took it over from his father. But Young Bob would have preferred doing anything else. Still, it had been his big payday, so... Well, when my father was killed, Young Bob came to my mom and begged her not to sue, which she had threatened to do. You see, the accident came from a safety violation that my dad had kept warning Young Bob about, and he had told my mother all about it. Young Bob told her that the quarry was on the verge of bankruptcy, even closure, and he needed every dime he had to try to save it. So even defending a lawsuit would kill the only real employer in the town, and so would kill the town, and put all our neighbors out of work, and she didn't want that, did she? As for worker's comp—my mom is not a very, well, informed person. She didn't really know anything about worker's comp, and Young Bob certainly didn't tell her anything. So he put this pressure on her, even got neighbors to pressure her, to save the town. Mom grew up there— what else could she do? But Young Bob said he had a plan to compensate us—he would offer me a job in the office and pay me exactly what he had been paying Dad, which was quite a bit more than he usually paid office workers. So we would still have an income, and Young Bob wouldn't have any extra expense. He thought it was a brilliant solution. But it meant I would have to quit high school, and that devastated me. I was a good student, a really good student. I loved high school, and my friends there, and even my teachers, and I was just starting to look into colleges."

"Towards what goal?"

"Just that. College. I would have been the first one in my family to finish high school, so just going onto college was goal enough. But, Young Bob kept putting on the pressure and finally convinced my mom, who put the pressure on me."

"Didn't any of your teachers object?"

"Sure, but they had no influence. Wouldn't have had any even if it was just me saving my family, but saving the whole town—who could argue with that?"

"So you quit high school and went to work at the quarry."

"Yeah. in the middle of a school year. On a Tuesday. I couldn't even finish off the week. Showed up at the quarry on Wednesday morning. I found the office mess. So I was cleaning lady first, then an office manager—I insisted on that title. And I was good. I had gotten an A in typing at school. I hate messes, so I'm really good at organizing files and such. I'm even good at math, so I made sense of his accounts. I had that end of the business running smoothly pretty quickly. Young Bob was thrilled, said I was a natural, that I had found my calling. Every time he said that, I wanted to throw-up. It was all typing and paperwork and rock dust from the quarry all over everything. But, if

I'm given a job to do, I like to do it right. That's what I learned about myself, being thrown in that. I suppose I was proud of that."

"No reason not to be."

"Yeah, that's what I thought. I became indispensable to Young Bob. There's a certain satisfaction in that. And Young Bob was certainly free with expressions of gratitude. Sometimes too free."

"Oh?"

"I don't need to go into that. Doesn't matter anyway, because one day last year, Eugene came walking into the office. Then everything changed."

"You guys fell in love."

"Sure."

"And got married."

"Yep. Honeymooned in the Bahamas. It was beautiful."

"And now you're here, in South Pasadena."

"Well, we live in San Marino."

"Oh, of course." Of course, because more affluent people live in that little enclave than live in Beverly Hills, often in houses bigger than the ones they have in Beverly Hills, and yet—in a far more subtle manner.

"San Marino High doesn't have adult education," she said, answering a question I hadn't asked out loud.

"Yes, I guess they don't need it, do they? Which begs the question, why do you need it?"

She smiled, knowing I had probably already guessed. It wasn't a question of need, something so mundane; it was a question of want, something, in this case, so sublime. But I wanted to hear her say it. "When Eugene and I sort of suddenly decided we were going to get married, I had a condition. That I could finish high school and get my diploma."

"And go on to college?"

"We haven't really discussed that yet. I don't know. Eugene's uncomfortable with the idea, but—but he also wants to make me happy."

"So, if you go on to college, what do you want to study?"

"Everything, absolutely everything. Is that weird?"

"Well, daunting, if not weird."

"I just want to learn things. I don't have to worry about a future profession. Eugene is as rich as Croesus. I read about Croesus in our textbook, and now understand that saying."

"Well, there you go—learning things."

"It's neat."

"So, college seems—"

"Eugene wants to start a family."

"Oh."

"Eugene's older than me. He's in his forties, so he feels we need to start soon. So I said, look, let me get my high school diploma, then we'll have children."

I drained the last of my malt with a chaser of lukewarm coffee before saying, "Yours is a unique love story."

"Well, there's complexities. But that's an even longer story than the one I've been boring you with." She laughed.

"Really? Well, now, you've intrigued me. And you haven't been boring at all."

"I think they want us to leave," she said, referring to the waitress and another worker, obviously beginning to close.

Thinking that Peggy would kill me if I didn't learn the whole story, I said, "There's a 24-hour coffee shop just down the block on Mission."

We sat in that coffee shop for an hour or so. Lavinia talked about how her life had so completely changed. Such alterations in destiny are always fascinating. It was history being told to a historian. And now I want to convey it to you. But no historian relies on only one source. I have subsequently done further research, have gotten several points-of-view, learned things maybe even Lavinia did not know. And will present it in the next chapter as objectively as I can.

10

L avinia Ritter did not like her job of nearly ten years as the office manager at Anders Rock and Sand. And lately, she had been resenting it. Despite this, whenever Lavinia came into the office on workday mornings, even Mondays, she felt like she was coming home.

She was always the first to arrive. She would open up the office, enter into the darkened suite of three rooms—Young Bob Anders's office, her office, and the reception area—and turn on the lights. Brightness was bestowed upon the landscape of the dull—the basic desks and utilitarian chairs and tables centering the room. The dirty walls were covered with maps, charts, state employment information, and a cheaply framed photo of Pit Number One. An out-of-date first-aid kit was mounted on a wall by a row of heavy metal filing cabinets, gray by their nature and even grayer by the film of rock dust covering their tops and adhering to their sides. In fact, rock dust covered much of the office. Between Lavinia and the begrudged efforts of Ellen, the nineteen-year-old receptionist, they did their best to keep the office clean. But the dust never really went away, maintaining its presence in a thin layer over everything. She had often asked Young Bob to approve the expense of a nightly cleaning crew. It was an idea he was not fond of, so he buried it away behind the rock wall of, "I'll take it under advisement."

And yet it felt like coming home? Yes. Repetition of place, repetition of the actions one takes in that place, repetition of fellows who occupy and visit that place, and the deep familiarity this builds, can do that to you. Prisoners with long sentences probably come to feel this way even about bars; heavy metal doors that shut them off from and rarely open up to; walls both thick and high, and lock after lock after lock clicking into place behind them.

So it is not inconceivable that Lavinia Ritter would feel this way about this location of her daily grind. Especially given that the small house on Ash Street she shared with her withering mother and lugubrious twin sixteen-year-old brothers, whom she referred to as Dullard One and Dullard Two, was an oppressive, tepid hell of unenthused half-hearts.

She had been working in that office, in the same position she was in now, doing the same things day-after-day, from the age of sixteen. In essence, she grew up there, forced, prematurely, into being a "grown-up," with the delight of youth taken from her, but the joy of responsibility given to her. Not everyone, of course, would have found joy in responsibility. It was just one of Lavinia Ritter's unique qualities, qualities unrecognized by all and so appreciated by no one.

In this office that she managed—and controlled to a certain extent —she every day became freshly self-aware of her qualities. She found the surroundings a comfortable if not a loved home for herself, her ego, and her essence. It offered no sustenance for who she was but did offer a measure of protection from the malnutrition of self-loathing.

Lavinia had taken the job—or had it thrust upon her—to save her family. And—it had been made clear to her—the small town of Andersberg. Her birthplace could, no, *would* die without her sacrifice. Being young, she was, of course, a romantic. Being young, she was, of course, a romantic clothed in melodrama. After fighting off the disappointment of leaving high school, she found honor in her sacrifice and decided to make the best of it.

That meant not just quitting high school, but quitting books.

Lavinia was an "odd duck," as her mother called her, always with her nose in a book from a very early age. Andersberg had neither a bookstore nor a library, but once every two weeks, a bookmobile arrived from Hershey, Pennsylvania, funded by the worldwide ingestion of sweetened cocoa. Waiting for the bookmobile every other week was the sweetest anticipation she had known. But now she entered into her savior-hood with her head held high, which did not allow it to be bent in reading books. Her grandmother, a wise old woman who had died three years before, might have said that she was cutting off her nose to spite her face, but that was not true. It was more like the newly pious avoiding temptations at all costs.

She did read magazines. Magazines were okay. Magazines got thrown away. She subscribed to *Time*, the *National Geographic*, *Travel & Leisure*, and *Playboy*. They were magazines read by adults, and since she was being forced to be an adult...

When Lavinia arrived at Anders Rock and Sand on the first day of her employment, she found the office so totally disorganized, so fundamentally a mess, that she almost broke into tears. But tears do not become a savior—at least until one is nailed upon a cross—and she bucked herself up, rolled up sleeves that didn't actually roll up, and got to work. Work that took time, attention, deep concentration, and a rational and logical mind that she found herself enjoying being able to apply to the tasks at hand.

The real mess, though, within the Anders Rock and Sand's walls was its owner. Young Bob Anders' mind was so totally disorganized, so fundamentally chaotic, that Lavinia quickly saw the real problem. Organizing and managing the office would be difficult but doable. Organizing and managing Young Bob Anders—which she was not being asked to do but knew she had to do it anyway—would be far more difficult.

Young Bob Anders grew up the richest boy in town. Which wasn't saying much. Andersberg was a one-company town, and that company within its industry was small potatoes. Still, relatively speaking, he was the prince of the town, the leading employer's son, the grandson of the town's founder. No one would be surprised to hear that he was spoiled. Or that he grew up privileged. Or that he did not go to the local high school, but to a private school in Hershey, where "Hershey's Kisses" had taken on a secondary meaning. Nor should anyone be surprised to learn that all he had ever wanted was to continue being spoiled, even if he had to do the spoiling himself, to remain privileged, and to be private. He loathed Anders Rock and Sand. He hated Andersberg. He could barely tolerate the townspeople. Had his father not died suddenly when Young Bob was twenty-six, he might have remained a prince for a good number of years. But his father did die, and a mantle had fallen on Young Bob. It was a mantle made not of gold but of lead.

Young Bob Anders's lack of passion, and even respect, for his only source of income soon diminished that source. But he kept a tight grasp on whatever was available, and a tight grip, by its nature, squeezes.

Lavinia did her best as the years passed to help Young Bob maintain that grasp, but to loosen it a bit. Not for his sake, nor even hers, but for the quarry workers. No worker ever dared complain to Young Bob. Or, if they did, they knew it would be useless as he simply would not listen. So they came with their complaints and grievances to Lavinia, who they adopted as a kind of den mother. She did what she could for them, often by cajoling Young Bob Anders and berating him, even shaming him now and then. She developed quite a "mouth" on her but used it almost exclusively on Young Bob (it also had its uses at home and with people she found incredibly stupid). How could she get away with that? He held her livelihood, her family's solvency, and, indeed, the solvency of the town, in his hands. But when she realized what a minimally humane person he was, combined with an overabundance of selfishness and a profound deficit of intelligence, she found him relatively easy to manipulate by not taking him seriously and letting him know that he was a walking joke. Plus, there was the fact that while she was still underage, yet fully a woman, in the office covered with rock dust, he had made sexual advances toward her. They were advances Lavinia repelled by taking advantage of the tenderness of testicles and the threat to tell the world if he did not behave himself.

So the office of Anders Rock and Sand was the closest thing to home that Lavinia had. Or maybe it would be more accurate to say that it was her territory, within the borders of which she reigned, if not wholly supreme, nearly so.

Still, despite the appearance of a strong young woman who took no guff off anyone, not even her boss, and who always knew what-was-what, Lavinia was miserable. Miserable because of the past near-decade, miserable in the moment, miserable in contemplating an unchanging future. Miserable with no solace. Not even in books, which she still refused to read. No solace whatsoever.

And then Eugene Carson walked into the office.

Ellen, the receptionist, had called in sick, a not unusual occurrence. Lavinia was at Ellen's desk in the reception area, searching for a file when Eugene Carson walked in. He had opened the door quickly and with force as if he had intended to tear it off its hinges. He surveyed the perfunctory office like a conqueror looking over a territory to decide if it was worth his time. He was wearing a charcoal gray suit, an obviously expensive suit, something this office had not seen for a very long time, if ever at all. He was a bulk of a man, an oversized package, Lavinia thought, with blond hair slickly combed straight back and held in place with some hand-applied, patented, possibly exclusive combination of chemicals in a cream. He had a slightly florid face that set off blue eyes that were not charming, as blue eyes often are or disarming, as blue eyes could be, but instead were stone-like—hard if, on the surface, pretty.

Eugene's survey stopped when it came to Lavinia, and something stopped within him. It was a most unusual feeling, not unpleasant, but unknown to him and deeply disturbing. He quickly shook it off.

"Hey, sweetcakes," Eugene said to Lavinia, "let your boss know I'm here, will ya."

Lavinia stood up from the receptionist's desk and decided to look this fellow over. She started with his feet (at least one of them being the wrong one). She then moved up, visually caressed the fine material of his suit, surreptitiously measured his waist and his barrel chest, until she came up to his well-shaven face, and finally to those blue eyes. "Do you have an appointment?"

"Of course, I have an appointment. Tell him Eugene Carson is here."

"Well, I'm sorry, Mr. Carson, but I make all his appointments, and I don't remember you having one."

"Really?"

"Yes."

"Good! I told him to keep our appointment secret. I'm glad to see he can take orders."

"Take orders?"

"Yeah. Like a puppet on a string, sweetcakes. Now, tell your boss I'm here."

"Well, as at the moment I have no idea where he is, I find that hard to do."

"What do you mean, you don't know where he is?"

"Young Bob—"

"Young Bob?"

"That's his name."

"He lets his receptionist call him Young Bob?"

"I'm not the receptionist; she's out sick today. I'm the office manager. And yes, everyone calls him Young Bob. As he always says, rather boringly, 'Mr. Anders was my father.'" She said the last in a mocking, deep voice.

"Well, where is *Young Bob*, then?"

"As I said, I have no idea, although I assume he's somewhere between wherever he was last night and the office. He's the boss. He sets his own hours."

Frustration confused while anger welled. "But, he knew we had an appointment!"

"Yes, yes I did, Mr. Carson," Young Bob said as he rushed through the still open door wearing a disheveled brown suit as cheap as Eugene's neat suit was expensive. "I'm sorry for being late, but I saw an accident on the way in, and I had to stop and help the people. Horrible, horrible! But luckily I had the car phone, so I called 911 and got an ambulance there. Everybody's going to be okay, thank God."

Lavinia knew this to be a lie. It was one of three standard ones that he often told.

"So you're a good Samaritan," Eugene stated.

"Well..." Young Bob said, preparing to take the praise with humility.

"Or possibly just a sucker."

"Ah..."

"We are already ten minutes into our meeting. Can we go into your office and discuss some business?"

"Yes, yes, of course, Mr. Carson, please come in."

As they started for Young Bob's office, Eugene turned to Lavinia and said, "Can I get a cup of coffee there, sweetcakes?"

"Sure," Lavinia answered with cheerful alacrity. "You'll find a freshly made pot of coffee and some clean mugs right over there." She pointed to the unit provided by a coffee service with a countertop, storage drawers, and a mini-fridge. "Oh, just don't use the one that says WORLD'S GREATEST BOSS—that one belongs to Young Bob."

What's the term? Thunderstruck? Gobsmacked? Whatever it was, it was intense, making Eugene incensed over the insult, over the injury. Nevertheless, outside of staring at Lavinia—who stared right back—for two seconds, he turned, not quite meekly, but certainly mildly, and went to the coffee, grabbed a mug that said, QUARRYMEN DO IT DEEP, scoffed at it, then poured himself a cup. Almost reluctantly, he asked Lavinia, "Milk?"

"Sure. In the little refrigerator there under the counter."

He opened it. Found it. Poured it into the cup. Returned it to the refrigerator. Then, he escaped into Young Bob's office without looking at Lavinia, closing the door behind him.

What the hell was that all about? Lavinia thought as she moved into her office, having found the file she was looking for. It was a most unusual occurrence; well-heeled men just did not usually drop by this office. And yet, it did seem to go along with what had been occurring for the past couple of weeks. Strangers had been coming to the quarry, looking around, sometimes even guided by Young Bob. She had assumed that they had been some sort of state inspectors, but when she asked Young Bob, he was noncommittal and seemed embarrassed to be so. The quarry workers were buzzing about it whenever they came into the office. They mentioned that whoever the strangers were, they were knowledgeable and asked pointed questions, which the workers had been told by Young Bob to answer honestly.

Then the big man's name came back to her.

Eugene Carson.

Eugene Carson.

Had she heard it before? Or seen it? Just recently, maybe, or relatively recently? And there was something about that florid face.

Ah. Wait-a-minute.

Lavinia got up and went back into the reception room, to a set of two chairs where people waited, and the table between them laden with slick industry periodicals. A good number of them were the *Quarrymen's Quarterly,* and she went through them quick, finding what she had expected. Him, Eugene Carson, that florid face on the cover of an issue from three quarters ago. She grabbed it, went back into her office, opened it up to the cover story, and soon realized what was going on. For Eugene Carson was the president and C.E.O of Ramone International Aggregates, Inc., the second-largest conglomerate in their industry.

He's selling out, she thought, *the son-of-a-bitch is selling out.* What was this going to mean? For her, for her family, for the town? This nice little company town subsumed within the tentacles of a corporate octopus?

The meeting went on for half an hour, and the voices got loud, although she couldn't make out anything that was being said. Then she heard Young Bob's door open, and she got up and stood in her office doorway.

Eugene Carson came out, followed by Young Bob. Eugene turned to him and said, "The contracts will be with you by Thursday. They will detail exactly what we agreed to here. So there is no need for your lawyers to spend a lot of time on them."

"Lawyer."

"What?"

"I only have one lawyer. I don't have lawyers."

"Well, tell him to have a good look, by all means, tell him to protect your interests, but also tell him that if he asks for any substantial changes, the deal is off right then and there."

"Okay, Mr. Carson," Young Bob said, then turned and walked back into his office, closing the door behind him.

Lavinia stood there, on her ground, making herself as tall as she could.

Eugene turned and looked at her. "You know, little lady—"

"Don't call me little lady."

A slight smile popped onto Eugene's face, a papercut of a smile, barely noticeable, yet capable of sharp irritation. "You know, *diminutive dame*, you're the kind of woman whose ass I want to kick—or marry."

He obviously had not planned to say those last two words, and it appeared to surprise him as much as it surprised Lavinia. Eugene handed her his QUARRYMEN DO IT DEEP mug and walked out of the office, pointedly slamming the door behind him.

———

Three weeks later, Lavinia Ritter and Eugene Carson were married. That this was absurd, ridiculous, silly, astonishing, unusual, surreal, and just plain stupid cannot be denied. But Eugene could not get the "little lady" out of his head; he could not exorcise the "diminutive dame" out of his mind. A romantic would say his heart, but Eugene Carson was not a romantic. The heart was an organ for pumping, period. And women, whether little and diminutive or tall and statuesque, were mainly good for sex. An atavistic concept, yes, but one not yet an anachronism. And as he preferred quality in everything, Eugene had never been reluctant when he wanted sex to pay top dollar for it in a simple financial transaction. It was nice and clean that way. (Well, it was also nasty and dirty. In fact, it had better be nasty and dirty, or he wouldn't have thought he had gotten his money's worth. But it needed to be clean in what really mattered.)

This "little lady," this "diminutive dame," whose name he did not even know, had inserted herself into him in a way he could not understand. As he flew back to Los Angeles, Eugene kept seeing her in his mind, whether his eyes were open or closed, but mostly when they were closed. He saw her in other short-statured blonde women that he caught glimpses of in the airport, in the airplane. He realized that he was aware of things about her that he had never paid attention to in any woman before. He knew her eyes were gray! Gray! He had never known the color of any woman's eyes, not even his mother's. He knew she had a really sweet figure. That's how it presented itself to his mind—as sweet. Sweet? The only time he ever used the word sweet was when he ordered sweet & sour shrimp. But that was all he could think of her figure: as sweet. For it was so attractively curved and somehow just the right size and potently solid, even if he knew it wouldn't take much for him to crush it.

Her wide mouth, he kept seeing her wide mouth. And although he had absolutely hated every word that had come out of it, he found it— alluring. Alluring! It was not a word he had ever used before—even when ordering Chinese food. Why did he think of it now? *How* could he have thought of it?

He scoffed at himself. He wanted to push his own face into a stucco wall and rub it there. He wanted to get drunk. Upon landing in Los Angeles, he excused the limo driver who had been sent to pick him up and booked a flight back to Pennsylvania.

E ugene walked into the Anders Rock and Sand office the next day in a friendly and slow, almost supplicant manner. Ellen was sitting at the receptionist's desk.

"Hello, yes, may I help you?" Ellen asked.

"Where's your boss?" Eugene asked politely.

"He's not in yet. Uh, in fact, I don't think he's coming in today."

"No, no, no, I mean the woman, the other boss."

"You mean, Lavinia?"

"Lavinia," Eugene stated quietly, embracing this knowledge.

"She's in her office."

"Can I go in?"

"Sure, why not?"

Eugene walked over to Lavinia's office door and knocked gently.

"Come in, Ellen," came Lavinia's voice from beyond the door.

He walked in and found her, head bowed, reading a piece of paper. "It's not Ellen," he said.

Lavinia looked up from what she was reading. For such a young person, she was rarely shocked by anything. But seeing this bulk of a man looming in her doorway did take her aback.

"So, your name's Lavinia."

"Yes. Lavinia Ritter."

"I'm Eugene. Eugene Carson."

"Yeah, well, I think you established that yesterday. Young Bob's not here. He's not coming in today. In fact, he's going to work from home until..."

"You know I'm buying the place."

"Yeah. Young Bob and I had a pertinent conversation about it after you left."

"You're not happy about it?"

"Should I be? Young Bob is completely incompetent, he's been running this company into the ground, and I've been doing my best to try to save it, but, at least, he's an incompetent that I know."

"*I* am not incompetent."

"No, there are probably other words for you."

"I've bought dozens of these companies."

"Yeah, I've read up on you. You come in. You fire many of the old workers. You bring in some of your own. You bring in new technologies. And they all become little cogs in your big, fat wheel."

"Is that the way you see it?"

"I wouldn't have stated it that way otherwise."

"It's consolidation and competence to do so."

"I think that's arguable."

"Well—"

"What are you doing here? I mean, I know, I've read that you *personally* handle every purchase, that you don't send lawyers, that you don't send sycophantic minions to do your dirty work, you somehow delight in doing it yourself—"

"That's been my method."

"But afterward, your sycophantic minions descend from the sky onto the companies and gut them like fishes."

"Maybe I'll do it differently this time."

"Well, how blessed can we be! Why would you do that?"

"Instinct. I have the best instincts in the business."

"Instinct for pounding the crap out of rock and stone—that's something to write home to your mother about."

"I want your help."

"My help?"

"You've admitted it quite clearly, and I could see it myself, your Young Bob is a doofus. I'm purchasing this company, I need to know about it. I'm going to bet—it's my instinct—that you know more about this company and what's gone on with it than he'll ever know."

"Well, you got that right."

"So I want you to work with me, hand-in-hand, as I start to—"

"—absorb this company like some space alien blob?"

It was an accusation not to be answered. But Eugene's paper cut smile quivered just slightly. "Dinner tonight. Drinks beforehand. I guess the best restaurants around here are in Hershey, right? I'll send a car for you. Give me your home address. You'll have to change into something nice."

"Must I?"

"Lavinia Ritter, I'm about to give you consideration I don't think I've ever given to anybody else in the whole of my life. Don't pass up this opportunity."

Lavinia thought for a brief moment, then shouted out into the reception area, "Ellen, write down my home address and give it to Mr. Carson as he leaves."

Eugene smiled something quite a bit more than a paper cut smile. "I'll have the car pick you up at...?"

"Seven."

"Seven," he acknowledged, then turned, moved, picked up the slip of paper from Ellen, and left the office.

L avinia was happy to have drinks before dinner. She started drinking at seventeen, saying, "If I'm going to do an adult job, I'm allowed to drink an adult drink." And although she had never allowed herself to overindulge, she had found alcohol to be a tonic for her life.

The car dropped her off at the fanciest restaurant in Hershey, and she was instructed to meet Eugene in the bar. He was sitting there, in another expensive suit, drinking a beer.

They greeted each other somewhat awkwardly, then she sat upon the barstool, and he asked her what she would have.

"Jim Beam Black on the rocks."

"Well, that's a pretty powerful drink for a—"

"Don't say, little lady."

"Oh, no, I wasn't going to say that."

"Really? What were you going to say?"

"Uh, for a woman of, um, low—body—mass. You know, not a lot there to absorb the alcohol."

Lavinia enjoyed and appreciated the effort. "I do okay."

When their drinks came, Eugene said, "I think our table's ready. Would you like to go sit down?"

"Why not?"

She followed him into the dining area and to a window table with a RESERVED sign on it. The *maître d*, having spotted them, rushed over and pulled a chair out for Lavinia. She placed her whisky on the table and sat with effortless grace. Then Eugene sat, not gracefully, but rather somewhat lumpish-ly—as he always did, as a man should. And yet, this time, after the heavy load that was him hit the seat, he felt chagrined.

He took a sip of his beer, she took a sip of her whisky, just as menus were being presented before them. They took their time looking them over. Then Eugene ordered a New York Steak, and Lavinia did the same, adding a dinner salad as a starter. The waiter wanted to know if Eugene wanted a salad, and he said, No, not for him.

"Oh, go ahead, have a salad," Lavinia urged. "It's good for you."

It was an argument Eugene had never found convincing, but he looked at her, he looked at her gray eyes and found them not to be unkind. "Okay, fine."

"And what kind of dressing, sir?"

"Uh, whatever she's having."

"French?" the waiter asked to confirm.

"Is that a creamy one?"

"Ah, no, sir."

"Oh..."

"Have the blue cheese," Lavinia said.

"Why?"

"I don't know. You just look to me like you would enjoy blue cheese."

After the waiter left, Eugene took another sip, or more like a gulp, of his beer, and Lavinia took a swallow of whisky. Eugene then decided to look right at her and tried to make his stone-hard blue eyes penetrate her soft gray eyes. "All right, just tell me everything I need to know about Anders Rock and Sand."

L avinia told him all about Anders Rock and Sand, eventually getting to the business and financial details he was mostly interested in. But she started with history. She told him of Richard

Tilden Anders, who had come into this county in 1885 and founded the quarry, thus founded the small town that had grown up around it. Eugene wanted to say that he didn't give a crap about that stuff, but he didn't. For Lavinia, across from him, so much less than him in flesh and bone, yet not fragile, not frail, talked with animation that was direct and potent. She displayed an energy that sparked and an articulation of words that seemed to dance around his head, showing themselves off before entering his brain, splintering, and lodging in several centers of cognition, memory, and, oddly, pleasure. Instead of pleading, "cut to the chase," as he had commanded others in the past, he remained mute while giving her rapt attention. It may have been in the way she was telling the history, with a strange, proprietary passion. Since Anders Rock and Sand had become her surrogate home, it had become vital to her to know about it. And she had gone about researching the history she was now conveying. Lavinia talked to many people in town, especially the older ones. She went to the county seat and looked up records. She went to newspaper offices and bothered them to pull out their archived past issues. She was now the only person who knew the full history of Anders Rock and Sand and Andersberg. She was undoubtedly the only person who wanted to know it. But now Eugene was coming to realize it. It had a profound effect on him, although he never, ever, would have admitted that to anyone, much less himself.

Young Bob Anders' lawyer had only minor requests for changes in the contract of sale, and Eugene accepted them without passing them by his own lawyers. Usually, Eugene would exit the scene at this point in the process, and his "people" would come in. But he didn't. He surprised many back at Ramone's home office, telling them to just "hold their horses" while he further assessed the situation. "Further Assessing the situation" meant spending a lot of time with Lavinia. Young Bob, not being nostalgic at all about Anders Rock and Sand, nor his time there, moved very little out of his office when he vacated not only the company, but Andersberg, and, indeed, Pennsylvania. He took what money he personally realized from the sale (not nearly as much as he had hoped for, but more than he deserved), and took himself down to Florida, to the Keys, and bought himself a boat.

When Eugene came in and occupied Young Bob Anders' office, he called Lavinia in, asking her to close the door and have a seat before his desk. He then started to dictate precisely how the changes to Anders Rock and Sand would occur and in what order. Lavinia sat there quietly, listening but not taking the notes he had expected her to. The changes included assessing all the employees' salaries and seeing if the highest-paid employees could be let go to be replaced by lower-wage workers, or not at all if they could get away with it. He told her of updated technology his people had recommended, which would allow them to let go more workers. The Ramone International Aggregates, Inc. computer system would be installed and tied, of course, to the main computer in the home office. Signage would have to change; this was now to be Ramone International Aggregates Quarry Number—well, he couldn't remember the number, but he would get that. And he saw no reason why they should have a receptionist, as this was going to be a working quarry office from now on, not a company office, and he would install a manager to run the quarry. Lavinia herself could double as the receptionist if needed. He dictated all this from notes that the head office had faxed to his hotel in Hershey, as this little speech was usually given by the newly installed manager. Eugene had never done it before, and he read everything from the notes rather stiffly and, quite frankly, unconvincingly.

"Uh-huh," Lavinia said as she got up from her chair, walked around the desk to Eugene, and reached out to brush some rock dust off the left shoulder of his expensive suit. "If you're going to be around here for a while, you're going to get a lot of rock dust on this suit."

It was a tender gesture that Eugene had a hard time computing. Possibly when the new Ramone International Aggregates, Inc.

computer system came in, it would be easier. "I would like to stay for a little while more," Eugene said, surprising himself with the unintended tone of request in his voice.

"Then I suggest you come to work in a nice pair of blue jeans and a white shirt."

"Oh, okay, that's probably a good idea. Um, I noticed you didn't take any notes. Are you going to remember everything I said?"

"Well, you're reading off notes. Why should I take notes? Why don't you just hand that to me?"

"It's an internal Ramone International Aggregates document."

"Well, aren't we now a part of Ramone International Aggregates?"

"Uh, yes, I guess that's true." Eugene handed the document to her. Lavinia took it and sat back down in front of the desk and looked it over.

After a minute of consideration, Lavinia said, "Well, we have one man, Frank Spencer, who's going to be retiring. In fact, I'm starting to plan his retirement party right now. Possibly you won't need to replace him. That'll save you some lunch money. The other highest-paid workers—and believe me, it's not that high—are all invaluable. They know the quarry intimately and understand it. You will not let them go."

"Oh, I will not, will I?"

"No, you will not because you are not a fool. You are not a fool, right? As to the other employees you intend to replace with technology, well, that's just plain stupid."

"What?"

"You've got to have someone run this technology, I think."

"Well, yes, but—"

"And you're thinking of bringing in people to do that. Why? Train these people."

"But, what if they don't have the capacity to learn?"

"We can cross that bridge when we come to it. I mean, hell, what are you? A puppy dog taken by shiny new toys? Try to exploit the assets you've already got. As I told you, for Christ's sake, it's a one-industry town. You let a bunch of people go, and you're going to have a good percentage of Andersberg living in poverty."

"Lavinia, that's hardly my problem."

"Bullshit! Of course, it's your problem. You buy Anders Rock and Sand, you buy Andersberg."

"Well, no, I don't think—"

"Oh, come on. We're not talking about your Harvard MBA business school thinking here. We're talking about people. Do another assessment to see if we really need that new technology."

"It will make the quarry's output much greater, which will justify what I've spent buying it."

"Okay, I can understand that. We'll just have to make it work for everybody."

"Business doesn't run that way."

"This one does. New computers? I love that idea, as long as you provide excellent training so we can use them competently. And Ellen? You want to get rid of Ellen? So I don't get any support staff? I've got to sit at the front desk and be mistaken for a receptionist when I'm the office manager?"

"Actually I was thinking of giving you a title boost and making you the assistant quarry manager."

"Why not the manager?"

"Would you want to be the manager?"

"No, of course not. I don't even want to be here, to be honest with you. I was going to quit."

"But—but you know everything, I'm going to need you for the transition."

"Yeah, you do. And the workers need me to speak up for their interests."

"That's not your job?"

"As what, the office manager?"

"That's right. Your loyalty has to be to the company."

. . .

"Maybe you're right. But my job as a citizen of this town, as a neighbor to everyone who works here, as a woman who has worked here for ten years and, quite frankly, gave up a lot to do so, it's my *job* to protect their interests, and, by God, Mr. Carson—"

"Call me Eugene."

"And, by God, *Mr. Carson*, I will do that. Now, here's what we're going to do."

What?"

"This is your first day here. Take off your damn coat, one, then, two, I'm going to start bringing in the employees, one-by-one. You're going to meet them, talk to them, you're going to hear about them, you're going to hear about their families, spouses and children and fathers who worked here, and mothers who have cared for them, sometimes working shit jobs to boost the family income. You're going to ask them if they have any dreams beyond working at this quarry, and, if so, is there any way you could help them, so they might quit on their own. *Then* you can bring in other people. But most of these people, quite frankly, don't have dreams. They just want to work and draw a salary that allows them to take care of their families. Quarry work is the only work they know. But they're not stupid people. I think several of them who would be happy to learn how to use new, fancy machines, as long as they still get to work."

To Eugene, it was a typhoon of words and his instinct was to put up the shutters. "Why would I do this?"

"Because it's the right thing to do."

"The only right thing to do in business is to earn a profit."

"No, the only right thing to do in business is to provide a service or product that you have some affinity for, that you think serves some purpose that you can be proud of and happy to provide. And then to earn enough revenues to keep that business running, to pay your employees a decent wage for their hard labor or good thinking, and to upgrade when need be. *And* to make sure working conditions are safe. Whatever is left, that is your profit, and you're welcome to it."

Eugene shook his head a little, amazed by the naivety on display.

"This is the rock and sand business, Lavinia. It's the only thing I've ever done, and I guess I enjoy it. But it's just rock and sand. It isn't rocket science."

"Or brain surgery. Yeah, yeah, I know, it is neither of those things. But it provides the raw materials that help build our buildings, structures, bridges, roads, and what have you, the hallmarks of civilization. Haven't you ever thought of it that way?"

"No, of course not."

"Of course not, you say. Well, that's your problem, Mr. Carson—"

"Eugene."

"*Mr. Carson!* You don't enjoy the business. You just enjoy making it grow, like some many-tentacled monster."

"There's a certain satisfaction in conquering—"

"*Conquering*—that's an interesting choice of words."

"In—acquiring and growing, then."

"So the whole business is just your hobby, then, and everybody else be damned."

"Well—no."

"Are you going to meet with your employees? Or am I going to walk out of here right now?"

What the hell, Eugene thought, *where the hell, how the hell...?* "I told you I wanted to kick your ass."

"Yeah, yeah, or marry it! You're not likely to do either. You can be the big boss-man, but you're going to do it without me."

Lavinia's turn toward the door to exit was nearly mythological and completely epic.

"Okay, stop, wait a minute," Eugene shouted, rising from his chair, reaching out as if he could grab her.

Lavinia turned back to the large bulk of a man.

Eugene gestured to the chair in front of his desk, silently requesting her to sit again. Lavinia did not move. So Eugene sat instead and was only slightly uncomfortable looking up at her. "Okay, listen, upon reflection—"

"Reflection? You reflect?"

There was no answer he could give that would not lead to an even more full-frontal attack. Acquiescence was the only strategy left for Eugene. "It's a good idea. Let's, uh, let's go ahead and meet the employees."

Throughout the morning, one-by-one, Lavinia brought in Anders Rock and Sand's employees to meet Eugene. They were of various ages, but all basically healthy and strong men, if apprehensive at this moment. Lavinia talked to them and assured them that Eugene was nothing but a bully, and if you face down bullies, you can usually come to some kind of accommodation with them.

The lunch hour came, and Eugene said he needed a break, but Lavinia wouldn't let him have it as he had not yet seen everyone. She picked up the phone and ordered a bunch of pizzas. Not just for Eugene and the men to be interviewed during their lunch hour. But for all the employees. It was a pretty hefty bill, and Eugene paid for it out of his own pocket.

When he finished talking to the last employee at about one forty-five, Eugene turned to Lavinia and said, "I need a drink. Did Young Bob ever keep a bottle in here?"

"He tried. I would constantly pour it out."

"You're kidding me."

"You would have nothing here to buy if I hadn't."

"Well, I still need a drink."

"Fine. There's a nice little bar in town. Let's go there."

The "nice" little bar Lavinia took Eugene to was called, appropriately, The Rock and Sand. It was both a working man's bar and a community center and, on election days, the town's one polling place: "No Vote - No Booze." It was owned and operated by Hubert Bacon, known as Hube and, on occasion, due to his surname, as *Sizzlin'*. He was a veteran of World War II, a paratrooper who had a metal plate in his head that was put there after a not wholly successful jump into Belgium. His wife had died ten years before. His two children had moved out of Andersberg for careers in the military and the ministry. So he considered his patrons his family, and he treated them that way, greeting them with open arms, taking the time to listen to their troubles and share in their joys, and imposing upon them strict family rules. Discussions, yes, arguments, no, whether it be about politics, sports, or social issues. No descending into sloppy, maudlin, or aggressive intoxication. No driving home if Hube did not think you could do so safely. He had a contract with Andersberg's one taxi, operated by his third cousin, Joe, and he would send over-inebriated patrons home in Joe's cab, adding the fare to their bar tab.

Hube was surprised but delighted to see Lavinia walk into his bar midday, and just surprised to see this tall bulk of a man in a well-cut suit follow in behind her.

"Hube, this is Eugene Carson. He just bought the quarry."

"Oh." Hube put his hand out, and Eugene took it. "Nice to meet you, Mr. Carson, welcome."

"Thank you," Eugene said.

"Hube, what's your most expensive beer?" Lavinia demanded to know.

Hube named the one he always had on reserve for the three epicures in the town.

"Fine. Pour one for Mr. Carson."

"Uh," Eugene stepped in, "I'd rather have a Budweiser."

"I'd rather you let Hube show off how worldly we can be here in Andersberg. It is an imported beer, right, Hube?"

"Absolutely!"

"See," she said, smiling at Eugene.

"And, Lavinia," Hube said as he opened the cold bottle of beer, "Your usual?"

"What, this time of day? I'm going to have to get back to work."

"Ah, no," Eugene said. "Let's, uh, let's take the rest of the day off."

"Really?"

"Yeah."

"Well, in that case—yeah, Sizzlin', give me my usual."

Lavinia was showing off, putting on display that sense of ownership that natives of close-knit communities liked to flaunt to outsiders, especially outsiders from a world so much larger than their own.

They sat at the table that Lavinia considered her own, but only unofficially as Hube never played favorites. It was midday, though, and patrons in the bar were sparse, and the table was free.

Hube brought over Eugene's beer and Lavinia's whisky. Eugene took several welcomed swallows.

"Good?" Lavinia asked. "Yes, it's fine," Eugene answered. "Good," Lavinia said again.

They sat there silent for a moment, Eugene towering over Lavinia even in their sitting positions, just enjoying their drinks. Finally, Eugene said, "Well, you've given me a lot to think about."

"Do you do that often?"

"What?"

"Think about things."

Eugene subtly nodded his head two, three, four times, not at what Lavinia had implied, but at what he was thinking. "You've got me pegged as a bull in a china shop," he stated in a slight accusation. "Or a bull-headed bastard."

"Well…"

"Which I am. The bull is my favorite animal."

"Not surprising."

"I went to Ramone High School, mostly."

"Okay."

"We were the Ramone Bulls."

"Ah."

"I like their strength, their locomotive push-ahead power."

"Do you like their snorting?"

"Of the hot breath of determination, not of cocaine."

Lavinia laughed. It wasn't derisive, it wasn't dismissive, it was hearty. And it took her by surprise. The surprise started her laughing at the fact that she laughed, and then she couldn't stop laughing. She couldn't stop. She slammed her right hand on the tabletop repeatedly and tried to mute her mouth by covering it with her left hand to regain control, and Eugene had to pick up his beer to make sure it didn't fall over and spill. Lavinia offered no such protection to her whiskey glass, and some of the aged intoxicant sloshed onto the table. Eugene sat motionless and unmoved and stared at Lavinia for some moments. But laughter, as everyone worldwide knows, is contagious, and so the bull finally laughed and continued to do so, his bulk taking on a humorous vibration, which made Lavinia laugh all the more. Then the sparse patrons started to laugh, even though they didn't know what they were laughing about. And even Hube, even Sizzlin' Bacon, began to laugh.

The rest of the afternoon was joyful. Much was discussed. Personal histories were shared, even Hube's parachute-assisted ascent into Belgium. And at some point, Eugene and Lavinia found themselves smiling at each other—smiling—while stone-hard blue eyes met soft gray ones. Then both suddenly stopped, and both pairs of eyes looked away. But only for a few seconds. They looked back at each other in a movement that seemed coordinated. Then their smiles slowly uplifted again.

Over the next week, Lavinia and Eugene worked closely together, designing the future of the new Ramone International Aggregates Quarry number whatever. There were compromises: his usual corporate plans melded with her sense of taking care of family and community. Lavinia even convinced Eugene to seriously consider signing a union contract. She told him that he would save money in the end because this particular union had a generous retirement plan and excellent health insurance that was better than what he was probably planning to provide his employees.

He was planning to offer one, wasn't he? Because God knows, Young Bob never did. Young Bob became her talisman of evil, her whipping boy of everything awful in the world, and she so propagandized this to Eugene that any hint that he might be in the same sad company as Young Bob caused him extreme embarrassment.

Eugene knew he was out of control, out of control for the first time in his life, and it scared him. And yet, when he went back every night to his luxury hotel in Hershey and went to bed, he would feel a deep comfort and satisfaction that had nothing to do with the high thread count Egyptian cotton sheets that the hotel provided.

Two weeks to the day from when Eugene had barreled into the offices of Anders Rock and Sand like the bull he so admired, Lavinia said to him, "Take me to dinner tonight."

"It seems to me we've had dinner together every night."

"No, I mean in Hershey. Let's not just have dinner together—*take* me to dinner."

"To that restaurant we went to before?"

"No. I think your hotel probably has a restaurant."

"Oh, sure, yeah. It seems okay."

"That will be fine then."

"But that other restaurant is, like, five stars."

"Hey, I'm a small-town girl, it'll be okay."

"Okay. When we leave, you can follow me in your car and—"

"No, no, let's go the whole hog—escort me in your car. Pick me up at home at seven."

"But how will you get back?"

Lavinia just looked at Eugene with articulating soft gray eyes. Eugene—and I must report this for historical accuracy—gulped.

The menus were presented to them, and Eugene's eyes went directly to the list of various red meat and near red meat offerings: New York Steak, Rack of Lamb, Prime Rib, Pork Chops, and such.

"No," Lavinia said behind her menu.

"No?" Eugene asked. "No, what?"

"No steak or lamb or any other heavy meal."

"Oh. So what are you going to have?"

"A salad. And you are too."

"Me? You mean, just a salad? I don't want just a salad."

"They look good."

"Lettuce never looks good, just—leafy. A juicy steak looks good. Succulent lamb looks good."

"It would be best if you have a salad."

"Why?"

"For later."

"Later?" The word ran through Eugene's mind squeezing the most out of specific neurons.

"You don't want to feel heavy and lethargic, do you?"

"Well…"

"Heavy and lethargic and ready for bed—no, let me amend that—ready for sleep."

"Lavinia…" Her intent could not be denied. "You're, um—I've got to be honest with you—you're kind of shocking me."

"What? You didn't think I did it?"

"I haven't thought about it at all."

"That's absurd! Of course, you have."

"Well…"

"I'm having a Greek salad. I've always wanted to go to Greece. That's nice and light."

"Uh, okay. So I should have…?"

"Well, you're going to want some meat, aren't you?"

"I suppose, but—"

"A Cobb Salad then, or, I know what, a Chinese Chicken Salad."

"Chinese?"

"Surely, you're not prejudiced."

"Of course not. I just have never had one before."

"An adventure, then."

"Well, okay. And what do you drink with a salad? Should we look at the drinks menu?"

"No."

"No drinks, either, huh? Why not?"

"Sleepytime down south," was all that Lavinia needed to say.

The dinner was eaten, and conversing took place. Lavinia chose the subjects, most having to do with travel and locations traveled to. Lavinia was, of course, an armchair-in-front-of-the-TV traveler, but Eugene had actually been to places, and she wanted to hear about them firsthand. Eugene strived to make his accounts interesting, but he had traveled exclusively on business and never as a tourist. It took a deep dive into his memory to recall things seen and impressions received that were not about corporate offices and convention centers and airport lounges. In doing so, he surprised himself that there were such things in his memory, and he enjoyed recalling them as much as Lavinia truly enjoyed hearing about them. Which was good because it masked, if not diminished, a certain nervousness and particular anxiety he was at that moment afflicted with, stemming from anticipation and a vain—as opposed to vain—attempt at predicting the near future.

Lavinia allowed for, even encouraged, dessert and coffee. She had no objections to sugar and caffeine.

When they were both finished and had declared themselves happy with the meal ("I liked the crunchy things on my salad," Eugene had said.), Lavinia said, "Let's stop by the lobby store. I want to buy a toothbrush and some other stuff. Then—let's go to your room."

"Ah—you sure about this?"

"Do I seem hesitant?"

"No."

"Are you?"

"I don't want to be."

"Well, then?"

"Okay. Okay. Uh—"

"Okay?"

"Okay."

W hen they got to Eugene's room, Lavinia looked around and explored it and declared it, "Very nice." Eugene stood by the door, which he had closed and locked. He moved no further into the room as he was losing his battle against his nervousness and anxiety. Lavinia finished with her survey, turned to him, and could see plainly that he was in a state of mild crises.

"What's wrong?"

"This has all been...."

"Awww. Has the heifer scared the bull?"

Eugene said nothing.

A sudden possibility occurred to Lavinia. "Surely, you're not a virgin."

"No! No, no, not for a long time, I mean..."

"And you're not gay?"

"Are you kidding? Me?"

"Then you just don't like me? That way?"

"Oh, no, yes, I mean, I do, I certainly do, like I've never liked any girl, uh woman, before."

"Well, then?

"I've—Well, you see, um—I've never fucked a woman that I hadn't paid for."

"Oh." Lavinia considered this information for a moment. "Well, that's okay then. I wasn't planning to fuck you."

"Oh, um. I'm sorry, did I—"

"I intend to make love to you—a completely different thing. Come here," she commanded sweetly and gestured gracefully. "Come sit on the bed." Eugene moved to do so. "Take off your coat first." He did so, placing his coat on the back of a chair, then went to the end of the bed and sat. Lavinia came up to him and put herself between his legs, and started to loosen his tie. "Now tell me, why have you never fucked a woman you hadn't paid for?"

"Too busy—easier—you get what you pay for. If you pay a lot, you get quality, excellent, um—quality."

Lavinia took the tie from around his big neck and threw it onto the chair to join the coat. She then started to unbutton his dress shirt. "My dad—well, step-dad, really, took me to my first whore—"

"Don't call them whores."

"What?"

"You seem to have too much respect for their professionalism for that. Call them, um, erotic engineers."

"Erotic engineers?"

"Why not?"

"Okay. Dad took me to my first erotic engineer."

"Was she good?"

"She was wonderful. Older. I mean, I was seventeen. She must have been thirty, thirty-five. She had wonderful skin."

His shirt being fully unbuttoned, Lavinia pulled it off Eugene to reveal the white cotton tee-shirt beneath. She pulled the tee-shirt out from his pants, tugging mightily, bringing herself close to his face. He could smell her clean, flower-scented self and feel her breath warm and caressing. The tee-shirt off, she ran her hands over his shoulders, arms, and chest as he talked.

"I worked for my step-dad, at Ramone Rock and Sand. He worked me hard but paid me well, so I just continued seeing…"

"Erotic engineers."

"Yeah, erotic engineers. It—was—less complicated. You know, a simple transaction. I didn't have to try to, um, impress a girl, make, uh, you know, nice to her. I could be myself."

"A bull?"

"Well, uh, yeah, I guess, but not—"

"Besides, you didn't think women were attracted to you."

"Well, I don't know about that. It's more, um, I wasn't sure I would like the women who were attracted to me."

"Or to your money."

"Yeah, sure, that was part of it."

"I'm attracted to you."

Eugene was struck by the statement. He grabbed her face gently and held it still. Lavinia thought he would kiss her, but he didn't. He just questioned with his eyes, which covered the fullness of her face but landed on her eyes, then he asked, "Why?"

"Because you've only allowed women to fuck you, and you've never been made love to. I want to say that you're like an unloved little boy, but you are anything but a little boy. But you are unloved."

"Maybe I'm unlovable."

"Maybe." She took his hands away from her face and put her hands on his. "Let's see." Lavinia leaned in and kissed Eugene, a kiss returned by a man no longer nervous and anxious, but grateful and appreciative, and something else besides. Something Eugene had never felt, could not define, wanted not to end, and was moved by in a way so unique to his life up to that moment that I think he can be excused in thinking it was divine.

A week later, they were married. This despite Eugene having never made a formal proposal. Nor, for that matter, had Lavinia. There was just a natural progression into a shared assumption that they were now bonded, together, a couple. It was shocking to them both, and yet not at all unpleasant. The world, indeed, the universe, seemed to split into two. There was now *Us*, and then there was everybody and everything else in the universe. It was obviously not two equal parts. But neither Eugene nor Lavinia felt diminished because of that.

They got married in Andersberg so that Lavinia's withering mother and lugubrious twin sixteen-year-old brothers could attend, as well as Hube "Sizzlin' Bacon, Ellen, and the other Quarry workers, who got the day off *with* pay, and most of the rest of the town.

Eugene arranged for a new manager to take over Ramone International Aggregates Quarry number whatever. He was a man of vast experience in the business, usually surprised by nothing, who was "floored" by Eugene's very detailed directions for this quarry's operation.

Eugene also arranged for a retroactive death benefit and pension for Lavinia's father, which her mother was the beneficiary.

Eugene suggested a honeymoon and asked where Lavinia would want to go for a week or two. "The Bahamas," she answered without hesitation. She had never been farther from Andersberg than Hershey, and so had never seen the ocean, and she wanted to be surrounded by it. The fact that the National Geographic's current issue, which had arrived in the mail the day before, had a cover story on the Bahamas might have inspired her desire. Eugene made the arrangements quickly, booking a suite in a luxury resort and two first-class tickets flying out of Philadelphia. Lavinia had a sudden concern that she had no clothes for such a trip and extended stay. "Don't worry about that," Eugene said. "They have plenty of shops at the resort." And she was concerned about the resort. She did not want to be "stuck" in the resort. She wanted to actually see the islands, she wanted to learn to scuba dive, she wanted to know the life of everyday people there. She showed Eugene points of interest on the beautiful pull-out map that came with the issue of National Geographic. He told her that what-ever she wanted would be hers.

He drove them to Philadelphia for an overnight stay and some clothes shopping for Lavinia. She was delighted by the shops Eugene took her to, by the quality of the dresses and outfits on offer, and Eugene's natural instinct for what would look good on her. With his help, she made choices quickly, and there was time to see Independence Hall. She had demanded to see Independence Hall.

The world shrunk when they were in the Bahamas. There was just them and a cast of characters to serve, entertain, and amuse them, instruct them directly or through exposure. The light was unique, the air invigorating, the ocean surrounding, vast, and blue, and yet—so strange that this was true—intimate.

After several nights, in the casual comfort of ocean breezes and the warmth of each other's bodies, they began to talk of the future beyond this shrunken jewel of a world.

"We've never talked about this," Eugene said.

"What?"

"We've just done all this without really talking about it."

"So?"

"You know you'll have to move to California with me."

"Well, of course. To Ramone?"

"Oh, good God, no! I have a house in Pasadena. But I'm thinking of buying a new house in San Marino."

"Where's that?"

"Right next to Pasadena."

"Why move then?"

"Very big houses in San Marino."

"Do we need a very big house?"

"*I* need a very big house."

"Then *we* need a very big house."

"Good."

"I want to go back to high school."

"What?"

"I never finished."

"I know that, but—"

"I will not have you married to a woman who doesn't even have a high school diploma."

"I want children."

"I will not let your children have a mother without even a high school diploma."

"Thank you."

"You're welcome."

W hen they left the Bahamas, they flew to New York. Eugene wanted Lavinia to have the opportunity for some more clothes shopping. Lavinia wanted to see the city, visit places she knew about from movies, TV, magazines, and the Macy's Thanksgiving Day Parade. There is the possibility that no one has ever enjoyed shopping and sightseeing in New York as much as Lavinia did. At least not with the particular pure joy she felt and passed onto Eugene, which gave him an odd satisfaction he had to get used to, not having had it before.

One day, after she and Eugene had walked through Union Square and explored the East Village, they found themselves in front of the Strand Bookstore. It is not a place Eugene would have thought to enter. But Lavinia, who had boycotted books a decade before out of love painful to pursue, entered through the front door without hesitation in a trance-like walk and spent the next three hours there. A crate had to be ordered to ship all the books to California she had Eugene buy for her.

The next day they flew to Los Angeles, then took a limo to Pasadena, to Eugene's house, which was immediately put on the market as Eugene looked for a bigger home in San Marino. It did not take him long to find one he considered to be perfect. Lavinia had no objections to it, and it was soon furnished. They moved in—husband and wife, lover and lover, bull and heifer, President & CEO of Ramone International Aggregates, Inc., and high school student at South Pasadena Adult Education.

———

T hat is the history of the meeting, romance, and marriage of Eugene Carson and Lavinia Ritter. History? Possibly a fairy tale. *Beauty and the Beast* comes to my mind.

11

Lavinia and I left the 24-hour coffee shop at three in the morning. I could have easily walked home—really wanted to walk home—but she insisted on driving me. I screwed up my courage and shut my eyes for most of the ride, opening them only to give her directions. As it was such a short trip, just a little of my life passed before me—none of it terribly interesting.

Lavinia had really wanted to talk about the extraordinary alteration in her life, circumstances, environment, and wardrobe. And I was a more than a willing listener. How could I not have been? It was but a small and very personal history, but a history nevertheless, and histories fascinate me. Thank goodness. My life would be rather a waste if they didn't. But more than this, of course, was my fascination with the teller of this particular history. Lavinia had lost none of the radiance she had projected when I first saw her, the eager first arrival in my World History class. In telling her story, she gestured with her hands in a smooth, improvisational choreography (which I'm aware may be a contradiction in terms) that danced with her kinetic face; her wide mouth articulating in variations of her smile, her eyes widening and narrowing as needed for different moments in her story, even her nostrils flaring in punctuations, all charmingly so. I was an observer as well as a listener, obviously an admirer. But was I also someone falling in love? I cannot answer that. It would have been not only a stupid thing to do but highly unlike me. The mere hint crossing my mind unsettled me and led me to suddenly ask her if she had a photo of her husband. I needed the intrusion of hard reality, the image of the mythological creature that was so much a part of her story, to wipe the hint away.

"Oh, sure," she said as she reached for, grabbed, and opened her purse, pulling out of it a soft leather wallet. "Eugene had this picture that's his company photo showing him all hard and serious, so I made him get a new photo where he smiles, looks a little more like my Eugene."

Her wallet had one of those flipping photo holders, and she held it up to display the first photo in the flips.

I could have lost my breath and chased around the coffee shop, trying to catch it. I could have had a heart attack and died clutching my chest, falling out of the coffee shop booth onto the floor with the dull thump of an inanimate object. I could have screamed in shock, surprise, and existential dread. I did none of that. I somehow had the strength to take in the image of Lavinia's husband and deal with the sudden surge of sharp, stinging emotions without displaying anything but the casual looking of an interested party.

It was a nice picture of Eugene Carson. Not quite as Lavinia had described him when he first showed up in Anders Rock and Sand's office, for he did not have the combed back "Gordon Gekko," severely-held-in-place hair. She had obviously gotten him to change his style. His hair was now a little longer, softer, looser, and dryer. And he was not wearing in the photo an expensive suit, but a nice, comfortable-looking sweater. Even though I noticed these details, they were meaningless for me. For all I really saw in this picture, coming out from behind the mask of age, was unmistakably the youthful bane of my high school existence. Here was the terror of my teen years, my pubescent tormentor, the author of the scars on my face's right cheek, which is why I wear a beard (have I not mentioned before that I wear a beard?). This, to me, was not Eugene Carson, businessman, newlywed, sometimes snorting bull. But Gene Pytka, the young bull in the china shop of self-repressed memories in my head.

As I've mentioned, I grew up in Ramone, a small, suburban city east of Pasadena. Suburban yet not lacking a manufacturing base. Besides Ramone Rock and Sand, there was an aerospace engineering and manufacturing plant. And the brewer of a beer popular with the working class—especially the working class that worked at the brewery. Ramone had an agricultural history of vast citrus groves and a Native-American tribal history before that. But when my working-class family moved there, it had become a haven for the working class. It was a compact community of nice little stucco-covered houses of no particular distinction, where families could be raised because families raised were really the main product manufactured in Ramone.

The only time the outside world had any inkling that Ramone existed was when it became the butt of a running radio gag in the 1940s, a joke that never made it onto television in the 1950s. Despite this, during the Cuban Missile Crisis, at least half of Ramone's residents were convinced that the first Russian nukes would land directly on Ramone because of our aerospace plant. Even though I was only a young teenager at the time, I was amused by this. It was the first of many anecdotes I've gathered over the years that have convinced me that no matter how small and insignificant one's world really is—and Ramone was pretty small and insignificant—one still considers it the center of the universe.

My family moved to Ramone in the early 1950s and bought a new small stucco-covered house in the southern half of the city, just a few blocks from our high school. I was very much a 1950s kid, running around in my Davy Crockett coonskin cap. It was a really good one, entirely covered with fur. Most kids had "coonskins" with fur only on the sides and a plastic skull cap emblazoned with the face of Fess

Parker. I watched a lot of television, of course. TV first entered our house the year I was born. It was not my babysitter; it was my only sibling. And I played in the neighborhood unsupervised and unwatched by any adults. They seemed to have had other concerns to occupy them.

It was in the 50s that Eugene/Gene Carson/Pytka came into my life. I was small for my age; he was large for his. With my one-half possibly Sephardic Jew/Gibraltar Island/Spanish ancestry, I was of a dark hue, especially in the summer sun. He was so white he seemed bleached. Even his naturally blond hair, cut into a flattop, seemed more white than yellow. He lived one block over on a street parallel to my street. In fact, we shared a numerical address—I lived at 545 E. Orange Street, and he lived at 545 E. Lemon Street.

We met in the Cub Scouts and were pushed into each other's company more often than just that fact—and our geographical close-ness—would typically dictate, as our mothers were the co-den mothers of our Cub Scout den. So we had to be friends, according to our mothers, whether such closeness would have come naturally to us or not. But we were young, and we tolerated it, despite not having much in common. Gene was strong and athletic and a daredevil. I wasn't and wasn't and certainly wasn't. He liked to build plastic models of various engines of destruction—warplanes, tanks, battle-ships, even "Little Boy," the first atomic bomb. I read comic books when I wasn't watching television. He was most comfortable with a gang of kids around him, especially if they acknowledged as the head of the gang. I was most comfortable playing by myself. He was an alpha male.

I'm not sure I even qualified to be an omega.

And yet, I guess it is not inaccurate to say that we were childhood friends. I made it work by remaining the quiet one, listening to him rattle on about things he liked, watching him do handstands (which I, of course, could never do), and other displays of impressive prowess. And he made it work by deciding that he was my protector. It was natural, of course, for he was bigger and stronger and saw me as a runt, in the purely biologically descriptive use of the word, not as a derogatory slur. Not that there was much for him to protect me against. After all, this was a sleepy 1950s' calm and placid community under the temperate climate of Southern California in Eisenhower's America. Still, it gave him a reason not to push me down on the ground.

Then things changed—which, of course, is what creates history.

Gene's father, who Gene was a smaller copy of, died. It was cancer. Which came on suddenly, rapidly shrunk the big man down to near non-existence, then finished the task. It was horrifying for Gene, and he seemed to fold into himself, becoming quiet and quite intolerant of others. He was sent away for a summer to his uncle's little ranch in Oregon. It was devastating for Gene's mother, but she had the strength to rise above it—she was, after all, a den mother. Or had been, as she stopped doing that and other volunteer activities and went to work to earn a living. She found a secretarial job at Ramone Rock and Sand. Gene returned from the ranch bigger than ever, tough and solid in his bulk, and just plain mean when he wanted to be.

We were no longer friends of any sort. We went to the same elementary school, fortunately never sharing a teacher, so never being in a class together. I hardly saw him, except at recess, and managed to avoid him well enough most times for him not to see me. This was not a conscious move on my part, just some survival instinct guiding my actions. We went to the same junior high. There I came under his gaze on occasion, followed by a snort and sneer, but no words, no actions. He had few of either for anyone. He had become a loner, looking for trouble more than companionship. He was often in detention, often sent home for a day or two, often absent from group activities. He was caught smoking, defacing property, and peeing on our baseball diamond's home plate. He was called a "juvie," a juvenile delinquent. But he really wasn't because "juvies" usually ran with a gang. He was just angry at everything and everyone at every moment of the day.

Then we were in high school. Something happened to him over the summer between junior and senior high school. Maybe he had been sent to his uncle's farm again. Perhaps time had begun the process of healing. Possibly hormones deserved the credit—or the blame. He was social again; alpha again; athletic again. But without giving up a certain meanness, which he had decided to direct almost exclusively toward me.

"Hey, *Adoofus!*" was his call of the wild, which he started when we were freshman, and for which he received the "Clever Boy of the Year" award from his surrounding gang, handed to him with chuckles and laughs and other derisive sounds. They were delighted to add insult to what they perceived to have been the injury of my name, Adolphus, not knowing I wore it with pride. But that made the insult all the more injurious. This, in the first months of that school year, was all Gene threw at me, yelling it out whenever he saw me—in class, across the campus, at P.E. on the athletic field ("Come on *Adoofus*, run faster" "Jeez you're lame, *Adoofus*" "Don't throw it to *Adoofus*, the only thing he can catch is a cold"). It wasn't easy to ignore, but I managed it by seeming to be oblivious to its intended hurt. That, of course, was a mistake, as it provided Gene with no satisfaction. So, just before Christmas vacation, as I was walking across campus to the cafeteria for lunch, weaving around pockets of congregated students, Gene took the advantage. He snuck up behind me and followed me until he surreptitiously tripped me into a group of cheerleaders in full uniform. Feeling myself falling, I reached out to find something, anything, to hang onto. Which, determined by some obscure universal law, turned out to be one reasonably fresh breast of the head cheerleader. I then tugged and stretched her uniform's sweater as I twisted and fell down hard on my back, bringing her down onto me. She screamed and cursed me as she quickly leaped up with a fine cheerleader's agility. I tried to apologize but had no words for it as I struggled to get up with what little physical skill I had.

"Jeez, you really are a doofus, *Adoofus*," Gene said as he grabbed me under an armpit and jerked me up. "If I ever see you attack girls again," he said with his face pushed up close into mine, "I'll beat the crap out of you." I can still remember the smell of his breath. It was unpleasant.

There were laughter and other vocal expressions mixed with the sight of many students swirling around me like a chilling fog. A hollowed-out pit formed within me and filled with a kind of nausea. Then a striking push against the back of my head delivered by Gene commanded me to get the hell away. Which I did, walking rapidly, forgetting about lunch, to a distant place at the other end of the campus, to a Boys Restroom, to a stall, to tears.

Usually, Christmas vacation was a wonderful time. It was not only a break from school, which was always welcomed but was suffused with the season's excitement. Even to a young teenager not wanting to be a child anymore, yet full of fresh childhood memories of past Christmas times, it meant presents under the tree and the sweet suffering of wondering what unwrapping them would reveal. But, no longer a child, you tried to keep that to yourself and strike a more giving, family loving, peace-on-Earth-wishing attitude. While still selfishly soaking yourself in finding and trimming the tree; the smell of goodies baking; the joys of television filled with Christmas specials—Andy Williams and Bing Crosby and Perry Como and Alvin and the Chipmunks leading the sing-alongs—and at least two versions of *A Christmas Carol* on TV. And *It's a Wonderful Life*, of course, thinking only you had discovered that it's a wonderful film. You looked forward to visiting relatives come to exchange gifts and sampling their homemade goodies; and counting down the days to the 25th, both in agony that it wouldn't come fast enough and in dread that it would all be over too soon. All this was no less true for my freshman year Christmas vacation than previous ones. But despite the red and green, the silver and gold, and the pure white visions of snow, the whole damn thing that year was bordered in black.

I had never felt hate before. Or the utter disdain Gene had breathed into my face with his foul breath. I was both too young and too insecure to have ever thought of myself as significant in any way, but now I had to fend off the stomach-sick bile of my complete insignificance. And as the multi-colored lights of Christmas delighted me, as I warmed to humanity when Scrooge found redemption, as sugar cookies melted in my mouth and pralines made me slightly sick, as pervasive Christmas music from the sacred to the secular to the silly lodged into my head and spun around there, I often and suddenly felt an absolute fear. I wanted to run scared and hold my breath as the expected blows of having the crap beat out of me fell upon me from somewhere in the new year.

I lived all this completely alone. Who could I tell? Escape was desired, but escape was impossible, for fate was giving the orders.

It was the first year I managed to stay awake to see the old year's passing. But was the neighborhood horn-honking and other noise-making, the drunken shouting out of *Happy New Years!*, even the rapid, sharp pops of firecrackers, ushering in the New Year, or tolling the last year of my life?

I returned to school to finish my freshman year. My Christmas fears proved not unreasonable. Gene Pytka "had it in for me" (horrible, horrible words), and his presence was often near and always felt. We had only one class together—Physical Education or P.E. as it was called with tribal familiarity. Can you think of a worse class to share with your nemesis? There was nothing to hide behind. If you were not in your P.E. outfit of shorts and tee-shirt, you were naked in the communal shower. My not-likely-to-ever-really-be-educated physical self came under constant review by Gene. His comments in the gym or on the athletic field, within earshot, sometimes shared in a gleeful whisper to one or two of his appreciative gang, always hurt. But the second was more hurtful, for being left to my imagination made it so. In the showers, it was, of course, my "manhood" that came under scrutiny, declared in several unclever ways to hardly be even a boyhood. And my buttocks provided Gene with a handy target to hone his skills at wet towel snapping. It was such a standard, crude, cliché oppression, but it stung none the less for that. Once, the welt on my left buttocks rose so high, I could not sit on it the rest of the day and, in my next three classes, sat angled at about thirty degrees. There were titters from those in the know and feigned obliviousness from teachers who just didn't want to know.

I knew of no way to avoid this pain until another pain came to my rescue. Due to a young child's stupidity, I had spent some time, at the age of seven, trying to fly, which meant falling—as I never did fly— from a not safe height onto the ground. Damage was done, and by high school, it meant various days of back pain. I took advantage of this to get out of unwelcome tasks at home and to extend blessed weekends without the danger of running into Gene. After several absences, the school called my mother for an explanation. She offered the truth. They suggested that I should be put into Limited P.E., but would need a doctor's note. She got it from a chiropractor with the unlikely (well, maybe it was likely) name of Dinkel. I was free! Even if Gene loudly laughed at me for now being in the "Gimp P.E. class."

Outside of P.E., I had always done my best to avoid Gene, but he had developed an uncanny sixth sense of where I might be and often was suddenly there to mock, sneer, and put down with verbal cuts. After my P.E. "end run" (not that I knew what an "end run" was) around him, he stepped up his efforts and expanded them to the whole wide world of our campus. He now would come up silently behind me when I was at my locker and slam it shut when I had just opened it, once catching one of my fingers in the slam. It swelled and turned black and blue, and I lied to everyone, including, of course, my parents, as to how I received the injury. He loved bumping into me, tripping me, pushing me into walls, and knocking books out of my hand. I became afraid to go to the restroom for fear he would be there or come in as I was in mid-urination. But I often had to, of course, for nature can be denied but not often delayed. So I would go quickly and pray—the only time I have ever prayed—at the porcelain altar to some porcelain god to keep Gene of the White Porcelain Skin far, far away. My prayers were not always answered.

Since we walked home from school in the same direction, I often had to suffer Gene walking behind me, taunting me all the way until I turned, taking a longer route to my house, but one that did not pass Gene's house. The taunts were always prognostications of a violent future at his hands. And his feet when kicking was predicted— "kick the shit" instead of or in addition to "beat the crap." This sinister following-saunter of his only ended when he turned sixteen, and he got a driver's license and a used car.

The harassment did not end with our freshman year. Gene continued it for the next two grades—it became his hobby. Something he could pursue as a diversion from the rest of his high school days. Days of growing bigger and bigger each year, excelling at sports, having slight brushes with the law, disrespecting teachers, spitting a lot on the school grounds, and spreading stories about his drunken escapades.

And yet he never did beat the crap nor kick the shit out of me. However, I never stopped fearing it and would have been relieved to have gotten the beating over with. But what he did to me in the last week of our junior year, if not as violent as multiple body-blows with big, pounding fists, and gut-kicks with swiftly moving feet, causing broken bones, damaged organs, eyes gouged out, was violent in its unique way. Indeed, in a worse way. The former would have been but the outcome of rage, whereas the latter demonstrated pure hate.

It was the last week of school, a warm late spring day. It had been relaxed, as finals were over, and it was just a time of summing up and saying good-bye and getting yearbooks signed. I had gotten back two of my finals with As on both, and I was feeling good about that and looking forward to telling my parents as I walked home from school. I did not have a car, had not even bothered to get a driver's license as my parents couldn't afford the insurance to allow me to drive our one car. I didn't mind it. The idea of driving intimidated me. The worst grade I ever got was in Driver's Ed. Unlike my peers, I did not see driving a car as freedom, but as the oppressive slavery to a multi-horse powered metal entity which could capriciously crush you within its being. Yes, melodramatic. But not at all unrealistic.

I recently found the walk home enjoyable, knowing that automobile-enhanced Gene would not be walking and taunting behind me. It was a good time for thinking and musing and daydreaming. Occasionally, if I had a test coming up the next day, I would try to remember the pertinent facts of the subject, the dates, and peoples of history, for example, or the parts of a worm or a frog or a bird or a man for Biology, without having to look in the textbooks tucked in my hand. So the walks passed quickly, and I hardly ever noticed my surroundings.

I don't remember what on this day I was concentrating on. Not an upcoming test, of course, possibly I was just musing on how to spend my time over the summer. I had recently discovered the historical novels of Mary Renault and could have been planning out which ones to read. But whatever it was, it must have been something deeply engaging, for I failed to make a turn down the street I usually turned down to avoid the block Gene lived on. I was just walking past a vacated house for sale when suddenly a car pulled into its driveway a little too fast and braked a little too hard.

Gene Pytka emerged from the car quickly and with a strong determination, and I saw on his face darkness I had not seen before, and I had seen various shades of dark there in the past. "I think it's about time I beat the crap out of you," he announced.

He grabbed me by the back of the neck, clamping on in a tight vice, and pushed me, then dragged me, to the backyard and slammed me up against the rough stucco of the back of the house, right by the back door, and told me to stand there and not move as he took off his jacket. I thought of running but knew he would catch me, and I was afraid it would be by the throat, and he would squeeze the life out of me. So I froze everything but my mind, which reeled in thought and weighed options of pain and painful consequences preparing for slamming fists and swift kicks. But it also somehow found a corner from where it wanted to talk.

"Why?" I found myself asking in panic, that panic somehow giving me a voice.

"What do you mean, why?"

"Gene, it's not a hard question."

"Shut the fuck up!"

"Why do you want to beat the crap out of me?"

"Because you're so full of crap."

"I don't get it. Why have you hated me all these years? We used to be, you know, friends."

"Because you're a wuss, because you're a weak little turd, and because you're not fit! Haven't you ever heard of survival of the fittest? Well, you're not fit, so you don't deserve to survive."

"That's idiotic."

Gene's jacket was off now and on the ground. He pushed me once more up against the back of the house. "You're a short little shit. You're an ugly little bug. Bugs are to be stomped on, to be gotten rid, they're disgusting, you little cockroach."

"Actually, cockroaches will probably survive a nuclear war."

"And you're a smartass."

Then Gene slapped my face. Which was really strange. It hurt like hell, and it made me dizzy, but all I could think of was that it wasn't a slug, and it wasn't a kick, and it wasn't a knee to the groin. I think the slap took Gene by surprise also. I'm not sure he knew why he did it, instead of a slug or a kick or a knee to the groin.

I started to cry, having no free will not to.

"Oh, now the baby tears come," he taunted.

"We used to be friends," I pleaded to him.

"We were never friends. I hated every fucking minute I had to spend with you. It was my mother's idea. You were so boring and so dull, and you couldn't do anything I could do."

"You could show-off. That's what you could do. You kept showing off to me."

"Yeah. And you were too stupid to be impressed."

"But that makes no sense. None of this makes any sense. If you didn't like me, why didn't you just stay away from me?"

"Because you offend me."

"Offend you? What have I done to offend you?"

"Shut up! I'm going to beat the crap out of you now. For once, take it like a man."

"But I'm not a man. I'm just a kid."

"I said, shut up!"

"You hate me."

"I hate you!"

"I don't know why you hate me."

"Shut-up. Close your eyes if you want, but be prepared. I'm hoping to break your jaw."

"But why? Why? Why? Why? Why? Why?"

"Shut-up, I said, I said, shut up!"

But I just kept going, "Why? Why? Why? Why? Why? Why?" I wouldn't shut-up. I wouldn't stop. "Why? Why? Why? Why?" Somehow it seemed perfectly logical that as long as I asked the question, he wouldn't hit me. "Why? Why? Why? Why?" It was having some kind of effect on him. I could see that in his eyes. I could see it in confusion and rage. I could see it in the spit coming out of his mouth. I could see it in the flare of his nostrils and hear it in what I perceived to be uncontrollable snorts. And then I saw it in the unclenching of his right fist as he took that hand and grabbed me by the shirt collar and pulled me up to him as I kept saying, "Why? Why? Why? Why?"

"Because you have a father, you shit!" He yelled it into my face, spittle sprinkling forward. "Because you have a father. The great father of the neighborhood. Everybody knows what a wonderful guy he is. And you love him. I've heard you talk about him even at school. You don't talk about your parents at school, you're supposed to hate your parents. But you love that stupid shit who named you *Adoofus*." He was breathing rather heavily—expending hate takes a copious amount of energy. "And I hate you because you have that kind of face I just want to rub up against a stucco wall."

And that's what he did. He grabbed my head, and he turned it to the side, positioning my right cheek against the stucco on the house. He grabbed a fistful of my hair in one hand and my neck and jaw in the other, pushed my head into the wall, and started to run my face back and forth, back and forth, back and forth over the stucco as if trying to scrub it clean. It hurt like hell, the pain welling up from the surprise and the shock. And then the pain found its voice, and I screamed and screamed and screamed. I felt wet. My peripheral vision saw red. Then I heard another scream—his, as he kept filing my face back and forth, back and forth, back and forth against the wall; his, as he pushed my head harder and harder into the wall; his, as it increased in volume and harshness of tone manifesting his own particular pain.

Then Gene stopped. He let go of me. I fell down against the wall, exhausted. I looked up at him. I had no idea what I looked like, but he looked at me, horrified. Then he grabbed his coat and ran, disappearing as in a magic act. I heard his car door slam, its engine start, and the roar of its quick escape. I collapsed onto the ground, feeling faint. Then I heard another scream, a woman's cry, the next-door-neighbor, a lady who knew my mother. She ran to me, picked me up, took me into her kitchen, quickly grabbed a dishtowel. I heard the faucet run, and soon the wet dishtowel was being applied to my cheek. It stung. She told me to hold it there as she sat me down on a kitchen chair. I heard her call my mother on the phone. Soon my mother was there, and then the neighbor drove us to the hospital.

One part of my cheek was split all the way through. I could have stuck my tongue through it. They figured it was a raised bump in the stucco that had acted like a knife. There were stitches to take care of that. Other areas of my cheek were missing deep layers of flesh, which they assumed had been rubbed off onto the wall, and no stitches could close up those gouges.

My father had been called at work, and he rushed to the hospital to join my mother. I don't remember much of what happened there as they put me under anesthetic, not just because of the delicate stitching that needed to be done in an awkward place, but because I had become hysterical. When I came out of the anesthetic, I found myself laid out in a hospital bed feeling light-headed, or, actually, light-bodied, floating on the wind of painkillers. Mom and Dad were there talking to a doctor not far from my bed, and yet they seemed to be miles away in another dimension, the Phantom Zone, perhaps, or perhaps I was in the Phantom Zone. I lifted my hand to my face and felt a sizeable thick bandage covering most of its right side. In mid-sentence, the doctor separated from my parents and gently took my hand away from my face and placed it under the covers. "No touching the bandage, champ," he said, smiling. "You might loosen it."

Champ? Champ at what? Getting picked on? Getting rubbed out?

The doctor returned to my parents and spoke some more. I heard it quiet and muted, but I got enough from it to realize that I would be spending the night in the hospital for observation. That did not worry me because it had an exciting drama about it. After all, the three of us, Mom and Dad, and I had weekly watched both *Dr. Kildare* and *Ben Casey, M.D.* Then I was out again. I remember waking in the middle of the night, hearing hushed conversations and quiet activity outside of my room, for hospitals do not close at night. I remember a nurse coming in and tending to my bandages. I think she may have changed them. I remember asking for water, then feeling a straw placed between my lips. "Slip slowly," she told me. I told her it hurt. She told me they would be giving me more pain medication soon and try not to talk much. The water relieved my thirst; the medication relieved me of consciousness.

I woke up in the morning upset because my parents weren't there, but the nurse told me they were on their way in. When they arrived, they told me the doctor wanted to keep me in the hospital one more night. They brought me a stack of brand-new comic books to "While the time away with." I was thrilled with the super-hero ones—Superman in *Action Comics*, Superboy in *Adventure Comics*, *The Fantastic Four*, and *Iron Man*—but disappointed that they had also brought me one *Archie*, one *Jughead*, and one *Betty and Veronica*. Strangely enough, I enjoyed those three the most that day. I guess I needed an escape from Ramone to Riverdale.

As I had been told not to talk much, I said little, but then I had little to say. Later a policeman came in, and I heard him say to my parents that they had no idea who might have done this. It was such a strange attack that didn't fit with the ways of the local gang members.

I'm not sure my parents had ever known that there were gangs in Ramone. The neighbor who had found me had not seen the attacker. She had only heard my cries and a car leaving before she made it out of her house. So he asked their permission to ask me if I knew who it was. They told him I wasn't supposed to speak much, but I could nod, and if I had a name, I could write it down. The policeman came over. I remembered him from a visit he had made to my junior high to talk about bicycle safety. Ramone did not have that many policemen. He told me he was sorry for what happened to me, and it would help them a lot if I could tell him who did this to me. "So," he said, "do you know who did it?" Without hesitation, I shook my head, "No."

***

T he next day my parents took me home with instructions about changing my bandages, when to give me pain medications and a medication to prevent infections, and when to bring me back in for a follow-up. They had made up the couch in the living room as a bed and told me I'd be resting and sleeping there for a while. We were a one-television family, and they wanted to make sure I could watch my favorite shows. But I didn't want to watch anything at the moment. All I wanted to do was to sleep, to be—for the moment, at least —unconscious.

I woke up to the sound of an unfamiliar voice. It was evening. I could tell, as the living room lamps were on, and I could smell that dinner had been prepared and possibly eaten. It was a deep, solemn voice, somewhat gravelly. I looked up and saw a big man, huge in presence, especially in relation to my parents and the small, low-ceilinged house we lived in. He dominated the room as he entered from the front door and planted himself in front of my parents, who stood between him and me as if he possibly posed a threat to their cub.

"I'm Stan Carson," the big man said. "I own Ramone Rock and Sand. I think you know Mrs. Pytka. She works for me. Actually, in fact, we're going to be married."

"Oh. Well, congratulations," my mother said.

"Yes, congratulations," my father said. "She's a nice lady."

I could hear the confusion in their congratulations, wondering why they were being called upon to offer them.

Stan Carson made no acknowledgment of the congratulations, showing that they had not been called for. His announcement had only been a preamble to establish his credentials for the mission he had in mind.

"She asked me to come and see how the boy was."

"Thank you," my father said. "He's doing okay."

"No, he's not doing okay," my mother countered, irritated a little. "He was almost killed."

"No, he wasn't," my father said quickly, wanting to defuse my mother's outrage, which he may have been feeling himself, but saw no practical use for it. "But, as you can see, he's been hurt pretty bad, and he's still in sort of a shock, the doctors say."

"Yes, I imagine," Stan Carson said while giving over his eyes to me. I closed mine. I didn't like the scrutiny. "Has he told you who did it?"

"No. He says he doesn't know who did it," my father answered.

"Doesn't know or just doesn't want to say?" the man asked.

"What? Why—"

Stan Carson cut my mother off as he moved between her and my father, parting them easily. He walked over to me, lying on the couch, and looked down at me from on high. I thought he might smile at me—but he didn't. "Adolphus, isn't it? Your name is Adolphus?"

I nodded my head.

"You know who did it, son. And I'm here to tell you that you don't have to be afraid of him anymore."

"How do you know that?" my father asked.

The big man turned to my parents. "Gene did it."

"Gene?" Gene's once co-den mother, who remembered him as always wanting more than his share of refreshments at the den meetings, who possibly still thought of him in his blue and gold Cub Scout uniform, asked, "Why would Gene do such a thing?"

"He's told me over the past couple of days that he's been tormenting your son for years."

"Tormenting? Why?" Father asked. The mystery disconcerted him greatly.

"I don't really know. Gene, well, I guess... Look, he came home right after he did it in, also, I guess, a form of shock, telling his mother that he had done something really, really bad. Then he just sort of— collapsed, his mother said. She called me, and I came over. I like the boy, but I've always known there was something needed—to be corrected. So I had no problem believing something bad had happened. That *he* had done something bad. He couldn't tell his mother. He seemed ashamed, which was not something I'd ever seen him show before. I sat him down. I told him I wouldn't let anything bad happen to him. But if he didn't tell me, I couldn't do anything for him. That opened him up. He told me what he had done."

My mother came over to me. "Honey, is this true?"

I nodded my head.

"Why haven't you told us this?" My father wanted to know. "He's been tormenting you for years? You should have told us, we could have talked to his mother, or—or the school."

"It's admirable that he didn't," Stan Carson said. "Boys know that only rats snitch. They've got a natural sense of honor."

It wasn't honor, of course. It was nothing like honor. It was the pure embarrassment that I was a victim, a small, weak, nondescript, hastily-drawn-with-little-detail victim of a supervillain when I should have been the superhero putting the bastard away. But I was happy to take the compliment.

"Look, I love Gene's mother. And, like I've said, I've known for a while that Gene has some problems. But he's basically a—well, he has potential. I'm going to marry his mother and adopt the boy. I'm not letting him go back to Ramone High. We're taking him out of school. I'm going to get him a private tutor to finish up high school, get his diploma. Then I'm going to take him into my business. He needs, uh, guidance is what he needs. A strong hand, you know."

"He needs to go to jail." My mother had been listening to this with a slightly opened mouth.

"Mrs. Seruya, that would be a mistake. For one thing, he's underage. And you've got to see that if he did go to jail, then he would be lost. It would set him on a path leading to, believe me, no good. Despite what we might like to think, we don't "correct" people by sending them to jail. We set them in stone, making them worse than when they went in. Especially when they are young. But, if we keep all this to ourselves, you can trust me to take Gene in hand, to shape him right, to make him a man."

"So he'll suffer no consequences?" my father asked.

"Oh, there'll be consequences, Mr. Seruya. I'll not be easy on him. I'll make him tough in the right way. In a sense, he'll have less freedom than if he goes to jail. He has some ideas about going into professional football. I'm not going to let that happen. He's good, but he's not that good. Playing sports would just feed his aggression rather than focus it. Business will shape him into something useful. That's my plan, in any case."

"But, Adolphus…" I think my mother was about to go crazy. All the talk had been about Gene, what was best for Gene, what would make Gene a man. And her little boy—seventeen-years-old though I was, I was still, of course, her little boy—seemed to have been pushed into the shadows. Possibly that's where I should have been.

"Listen, I know what Gene did is inexcusable and untenable, and amends must be made. I've contacted the hospital. All the hospital bills will be sent to me, and I'll pay them. And I can give you, right now, a check for twenty five thousand dollars. It doesn't go far enough. I know that. I don't know what can. But I know where you work, Mr. Seruya, I know that's about four times your yearly income, so I figured it would at least help ease things."

Neither mom nor dad spoke. It was for them a lot to take in. Years later, Mother told me that she didn't know what to say, that she thought she should mention doing something legal, suing or something, but she wasn't sophisticated enough to understand how to speak about it. Plus, the big man before her—big in stature, big in influence, big in power—was so commanding that it seemed natural to fall in with him controlling the situation.

Stan Carson pulled out of his pocket the check he had mentioned and handed it to my mom. Then, from another pocket, he brought out a little leather case, and from that, he withdrew a business card. He pulled a pen out of his breast pocket and wrote on the card, "This is my personal phone number. If there are any complications, any problems in the future and you think I can help, I will listen and do what I can. Nothing frivolous, mind you. But if you or your son ever need some urgent help, let me know. This is what I can do for you right now. You could still go to the police if you want, but I think you know it's best to keep this to ourselves."

Stan Carson left, saying nothing more.

"Well," my mother said, not really knowing what to say, "it'll be nice to get some new carpets."

Nothing urgent ever came up, and my parents never called him as far as I know. Well, possibly they did once for something that Mr. Carson would probably have seen as frivolous, so I can't be sure, but I've always suspected. After my mom died, three years after my dad, I found the card in her jewelry box showing its age, a little brown around the edges. By that time, Stan Carson was dead as well.

<hr />

When I returned to school in the fall, everybody had questions. Rumors had been flying, and some had been perceptive enough to wonder if Gene Pytka, who had suddenly left town with his mother, had anything to do with it. But I adamantly said no. And I had made up the story that I had been attacked by an escapee of an insane asylum. It was just the sort of thing kids would believe. I had several ugly scars on my cheek. I romanticized what I might tell people in my future adult life. Dueling scars? Atavistic and unbelievable. Got them during some heroic act saving some damsel in distress? Melodramatic and unbelievable. Maybe I could just remain mysterious about them and let others make up outrageous but intriguing explanations.

Finally, my father, a man always clean-shaven, but a man with an obviously thick beard, told me to grow one. It was my senior year in high school, and he got permission from the principal for me to breach their dress and grooming code. At that age, my beard was not as thick as my father's beard would have been, but it was thicker than most of my peers could have managed. It was the first thing of distinction in my life—it wasn't the beard of a wuss. As I matured, my beard thickened, and it became quite formidable. I was fortunate that it was the late 60s and early 70s, a new era of masculine facial hair, significantly not neatly trimmed facial hair. This was important as hair would not grow from two of my scars, and the longer the beard, the more I could cover them up. Although I now prefer it less wild, I keep my beard full and dominant. I have not seen the scars for years.

1 2

I have related this little history of my adolescent bedevilment in a strict linear timeline. The memories that make up that history, though, came to me in a chaotic flood. These damn memories stayed dammed up while Lavinia drove me home—fear for one's life takes full concentration. But once I entered my house, turned on the lights, and crashed onto my couch, they engulfed me, each discrete recollection pushing for prominence (*Pushy pig! Pushy pig!*).

It was nauseating. Deeply so. I ran to my bathroom and threw up what was left of malted milk, coffee, and the late-night cheese fries we had ordered at the coffee shop. I hate throwing up. I always have. Your body takes over, leaving behind the most godawful taste and burning nostrils. It was the worst moments of my childhood merging: Regurgitation and Gene Pytka. I climbed into bed and tucked myself into my blankets as if somehow they were a strong defense.

I woke up in the late morning in a normal state of mind. There's nothing like a stretch of unconsciousness to make consciousness bearable. I was left, though, with a serious concern. Lavinia, radiant

Lavinia, a special woman of grace and a budding intelligence married to Gene Pytka, who was now Eugene Carson, adoptive son, and heir of Stan Carson. Why hadn't I made the connection before? A choice of suppression over oppression or, worse, obsession? If memories of Gene, and what he had done to me, and what little I knew of what had become of him had not faded—I might have. The ego does its best to self-preserve. But now, faced with Gene again...

But I wasn't faced with him, was I? I didn't need to see him. I was just teaching his wife. A singular human creature being wasted on the bastard!

You see my dilemma? How was I to see her every week without offering to save her from the Beast? Would she take it as sexual attraction, or possibly true love (on my part), or perhaps something creepy?

I saw a restraining order in my future.

There was nothing to do but be the excellent teacher I was and expand her knowledge of Western Civilization. The course wouldn't last forever. She would eventually exit this stage we were on, and all would be well.

I had almost convinced myself of this by the time of the next class.

I was sitting at Ms. Roberta Boxer's desk in Ms. Roberta Boxer's classroom and going over announcements that Mrs. Deborah Miller wanted me to make when I heard the door open. It was precisely thirteen minutes (by my watch) before the start of the class, and I assumed that the early arrival was Lavinia, maybe with something exciting to show and tell me. I kept my head bowed over Deb's list of announcements. It was as if my neck had locked into place. I found myself in a state of dread. Then I heard a voice that may well have been a death knell.

"Adolphus?"

I looked up. It was him. It was Lavinia's husband. It was my youthful tormentor.

"Gene," I said, looking up at the towering man. "Or do you prefer Eugene these days?"

"Friends call me Gene."

"Then, I will call you Eugene."

He smiled the very slightest of smiles, which quickly faded. "I just came to tell you that Lavinia won't make class tonight. Or, actually, ever...um...ever again."

This pissed me off. Not much pisses me off, but this pissed me off. I stood from the desk. I couldn't rise to Gene's heights, but I could at least close the gap. "This is your doing, isn't it? Did Lavinia finally mention my name, and you said, 'No wife of mine is going to be taught by a wuss, a short little shit.' Well, fuck you, Eugene, she's bright and smart and you cannot—"

"Lavinia's dead."

Horrible confusion struck me. "What?"

"Car accident."

A grab for making sense followed. "Oh. She was such a lousy driver."

"Yes, she was. She was such a lousy driver. I tried to keep her out of her car as much as possible. But, you see, I had to go to a convention. I offered her a driver, but—she only liked being driven by me."

The reality of it all moved me from behind the desk. I walked up to the big man. I surprised myself by putting my hand on his big, beefy forearm. Needing to connect, I suppose. I said, "Oh, shit, Gene. I'm so very, very sorry."

"Thank—thank you."

It was too much. Gene, up in his tower, holding the fort down, allowed something human to penetrate his defenses and started to cry. Tears ran in succeeding gushes from his eyes, as his cry became a bawl. His sinuses let loose a vast amount of mucus as the bawl became a wail. And yet he continued to stand tall and straight, ramrod and stiff. His only movement was an up and down shudder that moved most prominently his big, broad shoulders. What could I do? What could I do but offer succor, more human touch as I tighten my hold on his forearm and move in to—to what? Hug him? I would be hugging his midriff—hardly manly condolences. So I just took hold of his other forearm and squeezed there also.

Gene grabbed and pulled me in as if trying to absorb me, transferring his shudder to me as we now both did a little dance of vibration, which hit a pitch matching his wail, and I became light-headed with lack of oxygen from my face being crushed into his chest.

Gene collapsed. Just crashed. And took me with him. We fell upon several classroom chairs, my head banging on hardwood, before we settled on the floor, tangled among the chairs, Gene's weight crushing me, squeezing out what air was left in my lungs. Darkness enveloped me.

The fall dislocated my right shoulder and fractured my left arm in two places; two of my ribs snapped, and my spleen was ruptured. I soiled my pants.

Gene Pytka had finally beaten the crap out of me.

13

My next conscious moment was a short one. And so dream-like that I thought it was a dream, and it will always seem like a dream in my memory. But the reality of it has been confirmed by Ms. Deborah Miller, for it was Deborah, my good friend Deb, whose brilliant, smooth, ebony face of extreme concern filled my conscious vision as her voice filled that other prominent sense.

"Hey! Hi! Welcome back to the land of the living."

The land of the living? Where the hell had I been? I tried to articulate something of some intelligence and pith, but Deb has confirmed that I just uttered, "Uhhhh," then exited the land of the living once more.

My next conscious moment was filled with the face of Peggy, looking at me in a way I had never seen her look at me before. It was somewhat akin to Deb's look of concern but had a sharper, teary edge to it.

"Wha— what happened?" I said with a weak voice I hardly recognized.

Peggy was caught by surprise that I had returned from the dark nothingness, and she sat up straight on the chair that was pushed close to the institutional bed that held me captive. She palmed moisture and a fragile emotion from her face, replacing it with a cheery and seemingly unaffected *Ain't the vicissitudes of life a kick-in-the-head* attitude. "You fell down and went—boom! With a ton of bricks named Eugene Carson landing on you."

"Oh." Memory started to seep back—it was unpleasant. "Hurt," I managed to say.

"Yes, I don't doubt that, Ass. But if you will pick unsuitable dance partners, you have only yourself to blame."

"*Really hurt*," I emphasized. And I did. Everywhere. Everywhere, it seemed, on my body and possibly in a few places outside of it.

"Oh." Peggy realized she had to take me seriously. "I better go get the nurse," she said, getting up and moving out.

"Good—good idea," I said with some effort after she left. I wanted to close my eyes then, but I was curious as to where I was. A quick scan confirmed that I was in a hospital bed, in part of a hospital room bordered by a flowing, curving curtain. "*Ohhh-ahhh-owww!*" came a cry from beyond the curtain but within the room. "You said it, brother," I whispered back.

The nurse came in, followed by Peggy. She was a middle-aged, efficient woman in an outfit that had little blue flowers on it. Not irises—but they reminded me of irises. "Hello, Mr. Seruya, are you feeling some pain?"

"Some?" I said. "I think it's all the pain in the world distilled and concentrated into little old me."

"Oh, I'm sure it's hardly that bad. But let me check a few things." She read my chart, took my temperature, checked my blood pressure, then said, "Okay, I'll be back in a moment with something for the pain."

"With alacrity, please,"

"I'm sorry, I don't know what that is."

"He means quickly," Peggy interpreted.

"Yes, yes, as soon as possible," the nurse said as she left.

"Just tough it out until then, A.S.," Peggy said.

"I've never been tough in my life. I don't see why I have to start now."

"Well…"

"As that great American philosopher, Daffy Duck, once said, 'I'm not like other people—pain hurts me.'"

Peggy snorted—but with a smile. "You're such an ass sometimes, Ass."

A snort, a smile, and something in her eyes—it was the "something in her eyes" that concerned me.

I was a bit more conscious the next day and was told the extent of my injuries and that they had cut me open and removed my ruptured spleen. I was now spleenless, less of a man than I had been before. I grieved for my spleen. Not that I knew what the hell a spleen was, and, indeed, remain ignorant about that to this day. But, still, it had been mine, and I had been attached to it.

In the late morning, I was visited by Deb, who brought the uniformed Officer Cameron from the South Pasadena Police Department with her. He was relatively short, although taller than me, and stocky. I guessed the tall and well-built ones worked for the Los Angeles Police Department. They probably all had the same size guns, though.

"Mr. Seruya," Officer Cameron said, "if I could ask you a few questions about what happened? We are trying to see if assault and battery charges should be made against Mr. Eugene Carson."

"What?"

"Did Mr. Carson attack you? Ms. Miller here thinks there may have been some confrontation between you and Mr. Carson over his wife."

"What? Deb!"

"Well," Deb said, "you were, I mean, it seemed—"

"We went out for malts and coffee and chit-chat. That's all. A student and a teacher communicating as people, that's all."

"She was a student?" The law wanted to know.

"Yes, and—and Gene, or Eugene, or whatever, came to tell me she wouldn't be back in class because she, uh—oh, God, I just remembered—"

"It was a pretty bad accident," Officer Cameron confirmed. "He, um, he didn't blame you for it?"

"No! As I said, he just came in to tell me and then, well, I was trying to offer some simple human condolence when he, uh, he had been trying to hold it together, you know, be a tough guy, but then he just—just started to cry. A lot. And then he grabbed me."

"Grabbed you?"

"I mean to hug, or, or, hold onto. He just needed another, you know, human to hold onto."

"But, your injuries didn't come from a hug."

"No, because he collapsed, he just suddenly collapsed."

"Collapsed?"

"Collapsed from grief. Have you never heard of anybody collapsing from grief?"

"Yes, sir. Heard of it. Seen it," he said, making short work of what was possibly an interesting history. "I'm just trying to get the details."

"Well, thems the facts. If the son-of-a-bitch wasn't so huge, and I wasn't so—not huge, then—"

"Okay. I see. Thank you for your time, Mr. Seruya. I wish you a speedy recovery."

Then Officer Cameron left the stage of this stupid little drama, and I focused my eyes on Ms. Deborah Miller. "Deb, how could you think I was—"

"Well—"

"Well?"

"She was attractive, and you're, well. Um, you know—"

"I'm what?"

"Well, you like women."

"Along with billions of other men."

"But, I know you, and—and—"

"Deb," I suddenly realized something I had been oblivious to, "have I got a reputation?"

"Yes," Deb said with no hesitation.

"Really?"

"Yes."

"Well—that's pretty cool."

———

Later that day, Peggy came to visit bearing gifts. It wasn't flowers. Many of those had been sent from PCC. From the college president, the history department, and from several of my students. And a big bunch from a cousin in Arizona and roses from cousins in Central California, and even some from Ms. Roberta Boxer, who I still had not actually met. It wasn't a cute stuffed animal, with a cute broken arm in a cute cast, which I might have expected as the perfect ironic gift from Peggy. Nor was it something more personal, sexual, and downright dirty, which would also have been no surprise coming from Peggy. It was a generous stack of comic books fresh from Pasadena's premiere comic book store, Secret Identities. Mainly superheroes and the kids from Riverdale. And a *Little Lulu* and a *Casper the Friendly Ghost* because Peggy thought that would be funny. It was.

"Comic books?" I said with some astonishment. "I haven't read comic books in years."

"Yeah, but I know the story."

"What story?"

"About the only other time you've been in the hospital."

"I told you that story?"

"You were drunk. And sexually satisfied."

"So, I must not have been too drunk."

"You were drunk enough."

"What exactly did I tell you?"

"That you were in the hospital—I don't think you said what for—and that your parents brought you a bunch of comic books and how much that meant to you, and what a good memory it was."

"Oh."

"Plus, they are quite practical."

"They are?"

"Well, they're so much lighter than regular books, and you should not be hefting any heavy historical tomes right now." Peggy smiled. Or someone who looked like Peggy smiled.

"You could have brought me some mysteries."

"You only like hardback books."

"True."

"And they're still too heavy for you to handle."

"Agatha Christie, heavy?"

"You know what I mean. Comic books aren't going to hurt you."

"That's not what they said in the 1950s."

"You're no longer innocent, and you've already been seduced."

A doctor walked in. I think I remembered him from my pain-killer fog. He explained how I was doing, that I would be in the hospital a few more days, and what to expect once I was released. Then he left.

Then Peggy kissed me. It was sweet. And then she left.

And then I fell asleep. But not before reading a *Superman comic*, a *Fantastic Four*, and a *Casper the Friendly Ghost*.

Two days later, in the middle of the afternoon, I woke up from a nap after having dreamed a series of surreal dreams (but then, what dreams aren't?) to find Eugene Carson looming over my bed.

"Jesus Christ!" I said in a purely secular exclamation, and not in a call for divine intervention—although such intervention would not have gone unwelcomed. Gene or Eugene or Pytka or Carson, for I didn't know how the hell to think of him, stood there in a black suit and tie and with a profoundly introspective and somewhat tortured face staring at me.

"I am so—so—very—very sorry," he said.

"You scared the shit out of me!"

"I'm sorry about that too. But I mean, I'm sorry about—having—fallen on you and…" Gene gestured toward my broken body.

"Oh. Well, don't, um, don't mention it, as my dear old dad used to say."

"Well—but I already have."

"That's true, you already have. Thank you. But I think I'll go back to sleep now. I just had a particularly nice wet dream, and as I'm somewhat physically limited right now—"

"We had Lavinia's funeral today."

Damn! There he was being human again, and fragile, more sand than rock. "Oh."

"Her family wanted me to take her back there."

"To Pennsylvania?"

"Yeah. To Andersberg. But I couldn't let go—of her. I had to have her here."

"Okay."

"So, I flew them out."

"Private jet?"

"Sure."

"They must have enjoyed that. If that's not an inappropriate thing to say."

"Tomorrow, I'm sending them to Disneyland."

"Well, that's—that's appropriate, I guess. It's what you do with relatives from back East."

"I'm sorry you couldn't be there."

"At the funeral?"

"Yes. Lavinia would have wanted you there."

He still stood there at the foot of my bed, large and looming, moved but unmoving. I wanted to suggest that he sit down, but I didn't think he would, so I just said, "Well, I think I actually would have liked to have gone."

"She liked you." He did not say it with jealousy or bitterness, but just as a fact that he was slightly astonished over.

"I liked her. She was very, um, very bright. Unique. Different."

"She was excited about what you were teaching her," he said. Again, with a tinge of not understanding, but not being upset about it.

"Well, that's the best words a teacher can hear."

"I guess I ought to go."

"Uh, yeah, well, thanks for dropping by."

"I didn't bring you anything."

"You didn't have to bring me anything."

"Look, don't worry about the bill. I told the hospital to send the bill to me."

"Eu—Gene—Eugene, you don't have to do that. I have health insurance, you know, I have an excellent job, and I have health insurance."

"It's done."

"Well—I guess that's appropriate too. Sort of your family tradition, paying for my hospital stays."

"I—uh—okay." He looked at me strangely. I realized that he didn't know what his adoptive father had done all those years ago. "So, all your bills will be paid. Any complications, what-have-you, you know, later, I'll cover that too."

"Well, if you look a gift horse in the mouth, you might get bit, so…"

"Can we keep in touch?"

"Um—why?"

"I don't know. I didn't even know I was going to ask that."

"Well, you know where I am. I teach at Pasadena City College, I—"

"Do you want anything of hers?"

"Why would I want anything of hers? I don't think her clothes would fit me."

"She bought a bunch of books that she said she was showing you."

"Yeah, um, they're good books."

"Do you want them?"

Then I got an idea, a sudden flash of an idea, a rather dumb and silly idea. "No, uh, Gene, um, what I want, um, uh—do you know what I want?"

"What?"

"I want you to keep those books—and read them."

"Read them?"

"Yeah. And I want you to write me a report on them."

"Really?"

"No, not really. But, if you want to keep in touch after you've read the books, I'd be happy to sit down and talk to you about them."

"Oh—okay." He looked down as if figuring out how he would deal with the books, maybe worrying that he wouldn't know how to open them. "Well, I've got to go, I've got—"

"Business to attend to? Rock and sand, I understand, providing the materials for the building of America."

"No. I'm taking Lavinia's family out to dinner."

"Well, I'm sure they'll appreciate that."

"She didn't like them much."

"Yeah, she told me."

"But they're—" Something caught in his throat; something moistened his eyes. "They're all that's left of Lavinia."

"Gene—"

"I've got to go," he said, then did.

I thought long and hard until I came up with the opinion that this had just been another surreal dream. Then Peggy breezed in, all smiles and cleavage, and made a case for conscious, physical reality.

14

I didn't believe that Gene would actually pay my hospital bill. I thought it was just something he said in the emotion of the moment, a grandiloquent conversation filler. After all, he wasn't legally liable, nor was he trying to protect anyone as his stepfather had so effectively protected him. And he was a bottom-line businessman, a rock-solid Rock and Sand man groomed, I assumed, by Stan Carson to be tough and uncompromising and to keep that bottom line always as fat as possible—the bully-made-good, San Marino-living, Rolls Royce-driving, eight-tentacled, plutocratic son-of-a-bitch (although, his mother had always been nice to me).

But when the hospital bill finally came about a month later, it was fat and scary with strange names and unbelievable numbers, the most incredible being the big zero after CURRENT AMOUNT DUE. I called my insurance company to see if possibly they had covered one hundred percent of the bill, but they said they had no record that it had been submitted. Damn, I thought, do I have to send the bastard a thank you card?

So Gene had been a man-of-his-word. Or possibly he was just showing off.

When I left the hospital, I was escorted home by Deb and Peggy. They had thoroughly cleaned the house and filled it with flowers. I like flowers. I never thought to bring any into the house, but I like them, so the riot of soft textures and colors was welcomed. I did note, though, that there were no blue irises. Possibly they were out of season. They had also stocked the refrigerator with easy-to-microwave meals, store-bought, and home-cooked. They said they would take turns visiting and driving me around, especially to follow-up doctor visits. Deb's husband had made a bunch of small repairs around the house that I had been putting off for months. It was all lovely.

I was anxious to get back to work and relieved when I could. Deb had found a permanent substitute to take over my adult high school class, so I didn't have to return there. But getting back to PCC, back with my students, made my life purposeful again and, I'm sure, helped me heal faster. Peggy and I started to go out again to events we both enjoyed, and she was very creative in gently satisfying my sexual urges, which we both enjoyed a lot.

I found that I kind of liked being pampered. But I figured I better not get used to it.

Soon my life was pretty much back to normal. I was teaching, getting a lot of reading done, having intelligent conversations here and there, and trivial discussions now and then. I joined a book club that Deb started. Well, drafted more than joined. The club members were all women, and Deb felt a need to have at least one male perspective. I told her I didn't know how "male" my perspective was, but she figured that was okay, as they wouldn't have wanted anything "too male" anyway. I didn't quite know how to take that. And I started seeing Peggy even more than I previously had. At the time, I didn't really make note of that. Although my memory now tells me that I stopped seeing several other women of diverse attractions that had previously extended, rounded out, and deepened my intimate physical experiences. My injuries, of course, took me out of that loop for a while, and I guess I just hadn't gotten back into it. Some of my casual female friends visited the broken me. But only once each and not all of them that was on the list.

But Peggy was always there. I put it down to our unique relationship due to our proximate careers and shared place of employment. I don't remember being either bothered by this or lodging any complaint with myself or the universe.

Life was good. That's all that I knew.

One day I got a call from Dr. George Eggers, the president of Pasadena City College, asking me to drop by his office after my last class. George was a comfortably professional administrator who spent an inordinate amount of time talking about sports. He had been a star player in some sport in some East Coast university and, I believe, was once on a U.S. Olympic team. I always liked to imagine that his sport was Greek nude wrestling, but I don't suppose that was it. In any case, he was a big man who nicely filled out a suit and had one of those broad, open faces that seemed to exist mainly to serve as the foundation for a smile. His academic field, before moving into administration, had been Economics. And although economics and history cannot be divided, I've never been empathetic toward the area. I admired George and respected him but could never really get close to him.

"Adolphus, come in, sit down," George said as I entered the office. He was smiling a non-economical smile. It was big and broad and full of giddy delight.

I sat. George looked at me, still smiling, and seemed to be scanning the totality of Adolphus Seruya. It was scrutiny both creepy and, oddly, sweet—which made it even more bizarre.

"I wanted to let you know that the college has received a rather sizable donation," he paused for what drama he could milk, "in your name."

A featherweight boxer could have knocked me down. Hell, the

infant son of a featherweight boxer could have knocked me down. "In my name?" I questioned with deeply sincere incredulity.

"Yes! It's wonderful. And it's multi-faceted."

"I don't understand what that means."

"Well, there's money there to support, even expand, the Department of History, if we want."

"Well, we do want, don't we?"

"Yes, yes, sure, but there's also an endowment for scholarships for our brightest students to go on and get degrees in history, and the donor has stipulated that you are to be in charge of picking the recipients. They're to be called the, uh," he checked some notes on his desk, "the Lavinia Carson Scholarships for Advanced Historical Studies."

"Oh, Christ!"

"What?"

"Is the donor Eugene Carson?"

"Yes, that's right, Eugene Carson, the president and C.E.O of Ramone International Aggregates, Inc. Why? Is there a problem with it? It's a very reputable company. Do you know something? Is his money not good?"

"Oh it's good alright, about as good as it gets. Eugene Carson is the man who fell on me."

"Oh. You mean your accident?"

"It's nothing but a guilt payment."

"Well, good for guilt then!"

"We can't really take it, can we?"

"What the hell are you talking about?"

"Eugene Carson doesn't give a rat's ass about history."

"Excuse me, Adolphus, but it doesn't really matter if he gives a rat's ass about history or not. *You* give a rat's ass about history. The students getting the scholarships give a rat's ass about history. And this college, as represented by its president, gives a huge rat's ass about big fat donations that help it fulfill its mission."

"I hate that."

"Hate what?"

"Having a mission."

"What?"

"Love of knowledge should be—natural, innate, not some damn mission. Every time we discuss the 'college's mission,' I see students in camouflage fatigues and blackened faces hacking through a jungle."

George Eggers stared at me for a moment, then said, "You're a strange little guy, you know that, Adolphus?"

"I suppose."

"I'm sure we can budget an increase in your compensation with this money."

"Well, I can always use a little extra cash."

"So you should be incredibly pleased."

"Well, yes, I am. Of course, I am."

"There's only one condition."

"A condition? Of course, there's always a condition, isn't there?"

"It's not onerous. You just have to go and thank Mr. Carson."

"*Go* thank him?"

"He wants you to have lunch with him this Sunday at his house."

"A really nice Hallmark card wouldn't suffice?"

"Adolphus?"

"Or a really nice, heartfelt letter on that fancy new college stationery you ordered. He's a businessman; they like stationary."

"Look, are you mad at him still? I mean, really holding a grudge just because he fell on you?"

"No, uh, jeez, of course not, George. It's more than that. We actually grew up together."

"Really?"

"Long story. Boring."

"But, obviously, with a happy ending."

"One can only hope."

"You know, this could mean a lot for your career. I mean, with this happening, with you having generated such a large donation—"

"Well, I didn't really generate it."

"But it will be seen that way. Which means we should seriously consider, when the position becomes available, making you the history department chair."

"I don't want to be the chair of the history Department."

"Why wouldn't you want to be the chair of the history department?"

"Because, I'm not an administrator. I just want to teach, that's all I want to do."

George looked at me—a strange little guy. "Well, you'll change your mind."

"I will?"

"They always do."

"They?"

"When the call comes from above, it's hard not to answer."

"You see it as a holy quest?"

"No, Adolphus, I see it as a human one."

15

There were many things in my life that I didn't want. I didn't want Richard Nixon to be elected—twice. I didn't want to have my first colonoscopy. I didn't want to be as short as I was. I didn't want to ever feel intimidated again. I didn't want to do anything in life but teach history to bright students, enjoy the literary and lively arts, and have "good mammalian copulation" with women of various attractive attributes. I didn't want to ever lose my teeth and have to wear dentures. I didn't want to have any more of my bones broken. I didn't want to ever get married again, and I didn't want to ever eat eggplant parmesan. I also didn't want to be bullied again, have my face rubbed against a stucco wall again, and be hated again. But none of those did I not want as deeply and intensely as I did not want to go have a "thank you" lunch with Eugene Carson.

But there I was that Sunday in my ten-year-old brown Celica of no distinctive design, driving up a long driveway that ended in a curve before Gene's house in San Marino. House? An utterly inadequate word. It was a mansion. It wasn't a modern one or even a post-war one. Instead, it was pre-World Wars. I guessed it was built at the end of the nineteenth century or soon after the start of the twentieth. It was three stories and castle-like with turrets. But it wasn't built of stone or brick. It was constructed of wood, possibly California redwood. (I quickly checked my pockets for matches, but as I don't smoke…) This being California, there were several very tall palm trees here and there dotting a massive front yard—if you could call it that and not a park. There was a metal sculpture of a stag standing atop a substantial sort-of-square boulder. There were no other cars parked in front of this mansion and no indication of where I should park. So I choose to park as far to one side as possible so my little Celica would not be an embarrassment to the structure. Although I was silently embarrassed that I did this.

I walked up to the front door. There was a doorbell button in the belly of a brass relief of a pheasant (yes, I made the silent joke that maybe it should have been a peasant), and, after taking a deep breath, I pushed it and heard musical chimes beyond the door. I expected a butler in full livery to answer the door while he answered to Jamison or Jeeves or possibly Lurch. But it was Gene.

"Oh, hello, hi. Come on in, Adolphus."

Gene's big frame was covered in a pair of gray slacks and a light blue polo shirt. On his feet were brown loafers and no socks. I wore a suit. I don't know why I wore a suit. I've always looked more rumpled in a suit than I do in blue jeans and a tee-shirt.

I walked into a grand foyer with two sweeping stairways at the end of it—one to the right, one to the left—each leading up to the second floor. Why two? What could two possibly do that one couldn't? Was it some form of discrimination? Boys to the right, girls to the left? Beautiful to the right, ugly to the left? Was one a UP stairway and the other a DOWN? If that was the case, they were inconveniently unmarked. But then, if that was the case, I supposed the rich would have learned which were which at their nanny's knees.

"Well," I said, "it's a bit bigger than our little *stucco* houses in Ramone."

Yes, I did. I did emphasized "stucco." I got only a slightly quizzical look from Gene.

"Well, yes, a bit too large, actually. But, you see, I was hoping to raise a family here."

It was a graceful and sad note. I tried not to let it get to me.

"I thought we would have lunch on the patio out in the back if that's okay with you."

"Well, you're the king of the castle, Gene."

"I just thought it was a nice day, Adolphus. And it would be, you know, pleasant."

He started to lead me out of the grand foyer when he suddenly stopped, making me stop short. He turned around and looked at me. Some thought was wrinkling his brow. Or rather a memory. "I used to call you, *Adoofus*, didn't I?"

"Uh, yes. For some years."

"God, what an asshole I was," Gene said, reflectively.

"I always thought so."

"Ha!" Gene laughed a laugh that one might have taken as dismissive, but I don't think it was. "Well, I don't blame you for that. Late apologies, but I do apologize."

"Long time ago. No apologies necessary," I said, not at all believing it.

He led me through a couple of rooms, all well-appointed, as a magazine might say, and it all reminded me of glossy rich-people primetime TV soap operas. Not that I ever watched any, but I would get a glimpse of them now and then when Peggy would stay over and watch them, especially after coitus. We finally entered a room where large glass doors opened up onto a huge patio. Beyond the patio was a stunningly green lawn, somewhat rolling—into infinity, it seemed. Off to one side was a sparkling pool that looked like you would break it if you dove in.

There was a large round table on the patio with ten chairs around it. At two of the chairs were complete place settings with what looked like fine china plates—quite a difference from the Melmac plates I, and I would guess Gene, ate off in our childhoods. Gene gestured to one chair for me, and he took his place at another.

Then two maids, fully uniformed and visibly invisible, came out from somewhere carrying our meal. I was somewhat startled because I actually had begun to think that we were alone. It was a lunch of prime rib, little potatoes nicely browned, asparagus with the required hollandaise sauce, and a side-salad, well tossed and already dressed.

"I hope you like blue cheese dressing. I love blue cheese dressing," Gene said.

"Who doesn't like blue cheese dressing? Especially when the only restaurant your family ever went to when you were a kid was Bob's Big Boy Hamburgers."

"You guys went there too?" Gene seemed delighted with the revelation.

"Sure. After visiting relatives in Pasadena, who never seemed to feed us."

"I loved the free Big Boy comic books they gave you."

"You did? Somehow I didn't think you ever read comics."

"Oh, I didn't. Stupid stuff, mostly. I didn't even like Superman on TV, all that fake flying. But this was... Well, what else was a kid going to do while you waited for your double cheeseburger?"

The maids, both Hispanic and possibly undocumented, soon disappeared into the bowels of the redwood behemoth, and we were alone again. I looked at the spread and said, "Well, this all looks good."

"Forget looks—dig in!"

Not unexpectedly, the food was delicious. I think the hollandaise sauce was laced with cocaine or something equally addictive. The wine, which I'm sure had been brought up from some extensive cellar, was intoxicating for more reasons than its alcohol content. Even the blue cheese dressing was far superior to any I had ever had at Bob's Big Boy. There were many pleasing smells, tastes, and textures to consume and be consumed by. What there was not, as we were both consuming with single-purpose dedication, was sparkling conversation.

But I knew I had to say something. I had to eventually speak. I was, after all, there on a diplomatic mission. So finally, as one of the maids returned with dessert, individual fruit tarts with vanilla mascarpone cream (or so the maid announced), and a silver carafe of coffee, I spoke my prepared speech.

"Gene, I want you to know how deeply the college, and, of course, myself, appreciate the generosity of your gift to the history department."

He looked up from his tart to look at me directly and intensely for a moment. It scared the shit out of me. "Do you think Lavinia would have been pleased?"

The mention of her name seemed to darken the sky. It was sobering. I had forgotten that this was all about her. But I was having a problem seeing Gene as a great lover, as possibly a passionate, sensitive man. I could see only the big bulk of the beast, for it was only the beast I saw. The beast of my childhood, the beast who had fallen on and crushed me, the beast covered not in fur but in hate. I had forgotten about the beauty.

"Um, uh, Lavinia? Oh, uh, yes, sure, I do think she would have been pleased."

"She's still with me, you know."

"Really?"

"Oh, I don't mean like a ghost or anything, I'm not an idiot. But, what she brought to me, which was—herself, I guess. That which she brought to me is still here." He put his hand on his chest.

"In your heart?" I asked, thinking it a silly, non-scientific analogy.

"No, more! My whole person, my whole being. She resides in me."

"Well, that's um, well, that's pretty wonderful, I guess. Lavinia was —she was a special woman."

"You saw that, too? You saw that."

"From the moment she walked into my classroom," I said, hearing myself be wistful, then wondering why.

"Did you fall in love with her?"

Such a loaded question. Was a weapon being cocked?

"Uh, well, no, Gene, of course not. I mean, not that she wasn't worthy of love, but I was more, uh, taken by her, I think you would say. She had one of those personalities that definitely radiated out, that seemed to be its own source of energy. Special, that's all I can say. I think she was exceptional. You were fortunate to have had her, even if it was for a short time."

Gene said nothing at first. He just sat there in deep thought, a process as visibly invisible as the maids. Finally, addressing something quite a bit larger than me, he said, "I know that. I think about it every day. She was the only person I've ever loved. Except for my father, of course. Not my step-father, who made me the man I am today, but my real father—who just made me. Do you remember my father?"

"I have a vague memory. We were pretty young when—"

"Yes. True. But, of course, you don't love a father like you love a woman or a wife."

"Hopefully not."

"It was the most unusual feeling for me. It altered me."

"Really?"

"Can love do that?"

I guess he was asking me. At least, there was no one else around. Being put on the spot to answer such a monumental yet mundane question made me giddy with nerves. "I'm, uh, ha-ha," the nervous laughter expelled as I tried to answer, "probably the wrong person to ask, Gene. If I ever saw cupid hovering around me, I'd probably smack him down like a fly."

"You're cynical about it?"

It was such a damning and perplexed accusation! I became something I had no real quick understanding of, but it was some combination of being embarrassed and defensive. "I wouldn't say, you know, cynical. Just, um, just sort of not interested in it."

"You've never loved anyone?"

"Well, you know, as a kid, I loved my mom and dad and all that normal stuff you do. I was married once, and I thought that was a love story, at first, but it twisted into something somewhat the opposite of love. And, um, you know, I love my work. I'm pretty passionate about that. Which is why, again, I really want to thank you." I very much wanted to get the fuck out of there. "I mean, deeply, sincerely thank you for what you've done for the college and—and for me. I mean, hell, you know, I'm completely honored."

"Well, I broke your arm and stuff."

"Uh, yes, yes you did, but, um, I'd hate to think that your benevolence toward academics here was just because you did that. I mean, I hope this gift, especially in my name, doesn't come from guilt."

Gene thought about that for a moment, giving the idea courteous consideration, but coming to a quick conclusion. "No. No, that's not likely. I don't feel guilt. Ever. My step-father taught me that that's a mug's game."

"Oh."

"I only meant that, well, um, that in breaking your arm, and the other, you know, the spleen stuff, it sort of formed a relationship between us."

"It did?" It was such a curious idea.

"Sure. When Lavinia told me her history teacher's name, I knew right away that it was you. I mean, how many people are called Adolphus?"

"True."

"But I had no interest in seeing you again or anything like that. I mean, childhood—so long ago. I didn't particularly like it, and I'm glad to be away from it."

"I see."

"But, for some reason, I felt the need to inform you of Lavinia's death. In-person. I told you, she's inside me. I know what her wishes would have been. By going to see you, I was allowing her to say good-bye. You too, I guess. But that was going to be it, that was going to be all. But, when, hell, I practically crushed you to death, it, sort of, I think, threw us together."

I smiled. I smiled because I didn't believe Gene at all. I smiled because I had another theory. "Might it not have been, also, possibly, that I witnessed you in extreme and very fragile, distress. Not so flat-tering for a big man." It was uncalled for, unfair, and mean in several senses of the word. And for it, I got that look again, focused and unwavering, and displaying clearly his stone-like cold blue eyes. When he spoke again, I felt incredible relief, as it was evident that there would be no dire consequences.

"Possibly," Gene stated. "In either case, I decided I needed to know more about you. I mean, more than I knew from when we were kids.

So I had a long talk with the president of your college, and I hired a private investigator to look into you."

"What?" I said, somewhat alarmed. What I was alarmed about, I have no idea.

"Oh, not to find anything bad or anything like that. Just to gauge your standing as a teacher, and for, you know, a personality profile. I kind of wanted to know why Lavinia liked you. But mainly your standing among your colleagues and students, past and present. Turns out you're well-respected and liked and have even been, for some, an inspiration."

And then I, not having learned anything, stupidly and cynically said, "Were you disappointed?"

"No. Pleased, actually. Very pleased that my faith in Lavinia was justified. So, my gift, you might say, is to honor her—as well as you."

His sincerity was unquestionable—as much as I wanted to question it. "Well, I—I don't quite know what to say."

"You've already said it. A sincere thank you is enough."

"Okay. Sincere it is and grateful I am."

"And I'm going to keep in touch with the college. So if needs come up in the future, I'll know. I'm going to be moving soon. I'll send the college my contact information."

"Where are you moving to?"

"Andersberg. I'm going to headquarter there."

"Really?"

"You know—I don't have any family left. As you know, my dad is long gone, and mom died five years ago, my step-father before that. I have no brothers or sisters. So Lavinia's family is really the only family I have. And I want—I want to have some family around me. So I'm going to Andersberg. I'm going to take care of her mother and her brothers and set up a house there, probably build something for all of us. And, you'll like this, I think; I've decided to build a library there and give it to the city and fund it. It will be the Lavinia Carson Public Library."

"Gene, that's great." Damn! I was beginning to feel entirely moved by all this. "I'm sure she would have been pleased."

"I want to love somebody," Gene said, almost as if it came from another conversation.

"You—you want to get married again? You're hoping to meet somebody there?"

"No, no, no—I'll never get married again. I can't imagine anyone replacing Lavinia. But she started something in me. I found something in there. Like a new muscle. A love muscle. And I don't want it to atrophy. So I'm going to exercise it on Lavinia's family. Does that make sense?"

It was laughable, but I couldn't laugh. Maybe the beast was falling away, even for me. "Um, sure. It's quite a change from, you know, the kid that scraped my face across a stucco wall, ha-ha."

"I'm sorry?" It was a question, not an apology.

"Well, I mean, you know, you were young and, as you said, back then, you were, you know, well, an asshole. So I'm—I'm very pleased that Lavinia had this effect on—"

"What are you saying?"

"Well, I'm—I'm just, you know, talking about the time you—you grabbed me, took me in the backyard of that empty house and, you know what you did—" I reached up to my face, separating part of my beard, exposing some of the scars. "You know, the thing you did that caused these scars that I hide."

Gene sat way up in his chair and straightened his back and seemed to grow a foot or two as he leaned in toward me. "What are you saying? That I scraped your face against a stucco wall?"

"Of course you did."

"No, no, that can't be right. I know that certain people rub me the wrong way, and I always have it in my head that I'd like to rub them the wrong way against a stucco wall, you know, like little snot-nose kids and know-it-alls and government regulators, like that, but I don't think I ever would have done it."

"What are you talking about? You did it. To me. At the end of our junior year in high school. It was horrible. You ripped my face, for Christ's sake!"

"Adolphus, I'm sorry, I truly don't remember doing that."

"Why—why do you think your step-father took you out of school? Why do you think—"

"Oh, I had problems, I'll admit that. My step-father helped me a lot. But, you know, I don't—"

"Holy shit, somehow you've suppressed the memory."

"A-A-Adolphus, I don't—"

"Is it hard for you to actually say Adolphus instead of Adoofus? It seems not to be coming out of your mouth very naturally."

"I'm sorry, but I—"

"You know—thank you for everything," I said as I stood up. "The money, the gifts for the college. And thank you for this, um, this wonderful lunch. But I really—I really do have to be going now."

"Well—"

"I would like to say, 'I'll see myself out,' but I'm going to get lost in there. Can one of your maids see me out?"

"Yes, of course," Gene stood and called out for a Maria, then said, "Really, truly, I don't—"

"Look, let's not talk about it. It's all just history, I guess. Which is pretty ironic, isn't it, me being a history teacher and all."

I left with the strangest damn feeling inside me—churning, rising and lowering, sloshing. A mixture of anger and disbelief and something I could not name—nor wanted to.

16

I don't know why I was so upset and angry. Or, actually, deeply sickened over Gene's lapse of memory. I had done my best to forget the face-scraping incident; why shouldn't he? In fact, most of my youth, especially my teenage years, rarely fired up neurons in my now fully adult brain. And that's the way I thought of myself then—fully adult and mature, being in my early forties and all. Because, what are your twenties but an extension of your teenage years, but now with legal status? And what are your thirties but a decade of pinning over the loss of your twenties? But the forties, ah, the forties! Now I am genuinely an adult; now, I am fully a Man. Or a Woman, depending on your genitals or sense of self-identity. Of course, there are those with arrested development. You know, the little Peter and Petra Pans out there, who don't want to grow up, who don't want to take on adult responsibilities, who don't want to feel like a Man or a Woman. But I think, or I certainly hope, that they are a minority. For those of us who are happy to frame and put on our walls our certificate of competent, mature, and responsible adulthood, the forties become who we are. Everything before that becomes, if not an embarrassment, at least something we tend to forget in a discounting sort of way.

Of course, while celebrating having reached this height after a slow trek upward, we also forget that we will soon be facing a somewhat quicker roll downwards. But, as that is a depressing thought, I'll leave it there and return to the rubbing out of history.

Why was I sickened? Maybe because while I had done my best to leave my past and that particular incident behind me to not spend any mental and emotional time on it, Gene seemed to have genuinely eradicated the experience from his memory. And thus, of course, from any emotions he might have had about it. How did that come about? A form of battle fatigue, shell shock, or what we call today PTSD? But it was just a trivial and brief awful incident in the whole history of humanity. Whereas battles in wars that reverberate for years are horrific, horrendous, horrible, and traumatic. But maybe trauma, like the trivial, is an individualistic thing. Stan Carson, who became Gene's step-father, had indicated to my parents that day that Gene was much upset over what he had done to me. They didn't believe it. I had never believed it. But, thinking back now, I have to ask, why did he go right home to confess to his mother—to his shame? Unless it wasn't a confession but a boast. It would have been just like Gene to have boasted over what he had done. But a boy to his mother? And why did Stan Carson even come to us? I was too afraid to "rat out" Gene.

And surely a man with Stan Carson's community influence would have been able to find out that the police did not have a clue as to who had done it. If he had just left well enough alone—well enough for Gene, but not for me—Gene would have been able to skip, tra-la-la, happily into the rest of his life. But Stan Carson was compelled to set things right. Not just the incident, but—more important—the author of the incident. For what could he really do to right the traumatic experience? He couldn't change it. He couldn't turn it from awful to terrific. He could only put some sort of monetary cost to it—and pay up. The author of the incident, though, the author could be changed, could be turned, it was hoped, from awful to, if not a terrific person, at least no longer a horrible human being. Once he was Gene's legal guardian through adoption, did he put Gene into therapy? Did some shrink hypnotize the memory of the incident out of Gene so he could have mental health? Like you take a burst appendix out to recover physical health? Did Stan Carson pay who knows how many thousands of dollars to have in Gene—at least regarding the incident, and maybe what underlined the incident—a *tabula rasa* that he could write upon? To script Gene into a tough-as-nails, take-no-prisoners, smart and canny businessman? A man who was as hard and ungiving as rock while also as slippery and wily as sand. A bully, yes. But a bully not for momentary visceral sick pleasure, but for long-term financial gain. And Gene would have stayed that way, one hundred percent, "apology" not being in his lexicon or his suite of actions.

Except he met her.

He met Lavinia.

And Lavinia obviously saw something in him, something to love. But it wasn't unconditional love. She may not have been as hard as a rock, but she certainly wasn't soft. And if I say she may have been as slippery and wily as sand, I certainly don't mean it as an insult. I think what she saw in Gene, what she loved in Gene, was not what he was, but what he could become. Or maybe it was something he was hiding, even if not consciously. Love sometimes, so I've been told, brings out the best in a person—assuming there is some best in there. So Lavinia may have gotten Gene's bully percentage down to ninety or ninety-five percent, but then she died. She didn't have time to complete the job. A pity. Such a horrible, sad shame.

The upside was that PCC now had a lot of money for the history Department! And some outstanding students, some from disadvantaged circumstances, would get the opportunity to get a full and fine education and maybe, just maybe, have a positive influence on the world. So I decided, to hell with all this post-traumatic analysis! I just concentrated on the money, the moola, the dinero, the filthy lucre, and what could be done with it in my competent, mature, and wise hands.

And here's what I did with the money.

First of all, I put in for and received a substantial increase in my compensation. Then I went out and bought myself a new car. No, I did not get a Mercedes or some fancy sports car. I didn't want to recapture a youth I wasn't that fond of in the first place. I bought a nice, ugly, dull, and safe Vovo. I'm one of those rare Californians who don't like cars. Personal freedom for me has never meant sitting alone in a metal pre-coffin barreling down the freeway at eighty miles an hour, lulled into thinking you were not really going *that* fast and, besides, your control over its momentum was eternal, wasn't it? But, this being California, I have always needed a car. And if I now had my choice, my choice was for the one that would protect me the best, one that gave me the best chance of not becoming a traffic accident statistic. So a nice, heavy, boxy, tank of a Volvo to get me from South Pasadena to Pasadena five days a week and, on nights and weekends, to the occasional venue of fine dining or swell amusement, was just fine with me. Otherwise, I was happy to stand and ambulate on my own two feet.

Those two personal items out of the way, I worked with Dr. Eggers and Grace Van Egon, the head of our history department, in redesigning our history curriculum. We added a course in African History and imported a brilliant, young, Kenyan-born professor. He had been teaching at the University of Birmingham in England and loved Raymond Chandler and, therefore, the "idea" of Southern California. For our new Asian History course we found Trinh Dinh, a newly minted Ph.D. She had escaped to America with her family after Saigon's fall in 1975. She had a Valley Girl accent that contrasted weirdly with her exotic look. Not exotic solely because she was Asian, but because she always wore traditional Vietnamese clothes. We all assumed it was a statement, but none of us felt comfortable questioning her about it. Besides, the clothes were as beautiful as she was. Both courses proved very popular, many of our African-American students going to the one, and many of our Asian students going to the other. Getting the Africans to Asia and the Asians to Africa, not to mention our white European-American students to either, did prove to be a bit of a task. But I found myself up to it. I simply suggested to Eggars and Van Egon that we make both courses mandatory for graduation. I sold them on the idea that the twentieth-first century would be a global century, so we better prepare our students.

I continued to teach the History of Western Civilization and loved it. It was suggested, though, that I take on the extra duty of teaching a course in Latin American history.

"Why?" I asked Grace Van Egon, who had put forward the idea.

"Well, because, one, you are a superior teacher, and, two ... I mean, your background, you know, your family ... I mean, you're Spanish, aren't you?"

"Spanish? Well, my paternal—and *only* my paternal—ancestors seem to have come from Spain, from Gibraltar, a British territory, actually, but that was a long time ago. The 1700s, best I can figure."

"Oh."

"I've never even been anywhere in Central or South America."

"Oh."

"Except, as a kid once. I went with a friend's family for a day trip to Mexicali. But it was really stupid. My friend's father went past the border, drove quickly around the city, never stopping, never letting us out, even to pee, then drove back into the good old U.S.A. I never have figured out what the hell that was all about."

"Oh."

"To be perfectly honest with you, and maybe we should keep this to ourselves, but I don't even like much to do with Latin America. I mean, Aztecs, and Mayans, and the Incas, and conquistadors, revolutionaries, and cattle ranching, you know, that sort of stuff."

"Oh. I scc."

"I mean, I like bossa nova music. If it was all quiet nights and girls from Ipanema, I might be interested."

"I see."

"And I *really* dislike Mariachi music. I won't go to a Mexican restaurant if they have a Mariachi band."

"Now you are just being silly, Adolphus."

"Grace, I'm just trying to deflect you away from this idea."

"Consider me fully deflected."

"Ah, thank you."

"So you only want to teach old dead white men's history?"

"Hey! I'm going to be an old dead white man someday."

———

I n all of this, I found a real joy in using Gene's money. Every time we decided to expand the history department, a cartoon cash register appeared above my head (in my head), clicking off the thousands and thousands of Gene's dollars that we were spending righteously and well. My greatest joy, of course, was picking the students to give the scholarships to. There's nothing quite like the brightest of the bright. In this, I am not an egalitarian. I am egalitarian in the idea —or rather, the fact—that the brightest of the bright can come from anywhere. That's why PCC was an excellent place to be; it had a pretty full complement of students from "anywhere." Discovering the brightest of the bright in such a place was an exciting adventure compared to tripping over them in some posh private paradise of academic achievement. Most PCC students were ordinary and average. But then most people are ordinary and average in general. Although protected by their own home-grown egos, few ever feel less for it. The ordinary and average in this world are not a persecuted minority. But the brightest of the bright can be if they are not found, encouraged, and embraced. It was a joy to discover such students, ascertain their dreams, figure out what the fulfillment of those dreams was going to cost, and earmark for them Gene's money to pay for it. I made every one of them write a long and sincere thank you note to Gene.

In reports I sent to Gene detailing the Lavinia Carson Scholarship recipients, I included my view of each one. I wrote about their past accomplishments and their hopes for their futures. I had no idea if Gene ever read these reports, for we never heard back from him. The endowment he had given the college was a self-sustaining entity. On occasion, more monies were funneled into it by Gene, but never with a specific reason why. Possibly it was in response to my reports; perhaps it was for his tax purposes; maybe it was continuing guilt. I didn't really care. I came to see the endowment as an ever-flowing spring, and I found much refreshment in it.

───────

About two years into the endowment, I came up with what I thought was a delightful and brilliant idea. PCC faculty-led summer tours for select students to the geographical area of their main historical interest. In other words, our Kenyan Brit would take four of his brightest of the bright on a tour of Africa. Dr. Trinh Dinh would take four of her students on a tour of Asia. And I elected myself to take four of my brightest students on a tour of the United Kingdom and Europe in the early summer. And a tour of the Mediterranean locales of ancient civilizations—Greece, Italy, Asia Minor, with a brief stop in Alexandria—in the late summer. The question did come up if such a use of the endowment was kosher since they were not inexpensive and benefited only a relatively few individuals. But this new program was duly reported to Gene and hearing no objections from him, flights were booked, and shots were received.

The tours were successful, eye-opening for everyone, spirit-enhancing, and mind-expanding. And on mine, I managed to take Peggy along.

(There is something almost magical about carnal bliss on a Greek island—just in case you were wondering.)

As school started the next fall, I was feeling pretty happy, pretty self-satisfied. We had received some laudatory press for our program, and I was becoming a rising star in California education. I did not seriously know how life could be sweeter or how I could be happier. I hadn't thought about Gene as anything but Mr. Generous Moneybags for maybe a year and a half. The stucco scrape, the extreme pain that Gene had caused me, twice, I tucked back deep into my past and away from my daily considerations.

And then...

And then, one day in early October, I was coming out of the rather blunt main entrance of PCC after my last class, ready to walk to

Peggy's house for a little late-afternoon tickle and squeeze, and feeling the warmth of anticipation. Then that warm anticipation was over-awed by cold consternation. Standing at the bottom of the broad steps that descended from the entrance was Eugene Carson. He was in a business suit that wore its price tag not only on its sleeves but throughout and stood in the shiniest shoes I had ever seen. Although I was at the top of the steps, and Eugene was at the bottom, he still seemed to tower over me. And he looked strange. He *looked* strange. It was his face. It appeared to be a new face, and one I couldn't read. I was fearful. Did he come to admonish me? Did he come to put the brakes on? Did he come to stop the bleeding?

As Eugene did not ascend the steps to greet me, I had no choice but to descend them to greet him. With every step down, he grew in my vision. *My God, what the hell is going to happen*, I thought. Gene was not smiling, not even a papercut of a smile. But he also was not frowning. He didn't look happy or unhappy; he didn't look benevo-lent or malevolent. He just looked at me with his stone-cold blue eyes. No! *That* was the strange thing. Not so stone. Not so cold. I stopped just before him, staying on the last step to have some height in this confrontation.

"Hello, Gene," I said, still having to look up at him.

"Hello, Adolphus," he said.

"It's good to see you. Are you here for a personal report on the endowment? Are you here to see Dr. Eggers?"

"No."

"Oh."

"I've come here for one reason and one reason only."

What reason would it be? What frightful, burning hell would it be?

"I've come here to tell you that I love you."

17

"What?"

Gene's face went through a rapid and damn frightening metamorphoses. Suddenly he had a broad smile, which forced his cheeks up into a cheery elevation. And his eyes, his previously stone-like and cold blue eyes (do believe this, I am not exaggerating), his eyes began to twinkle.

"I said, I love you. Love, Adolphus," Gene threw his arms wide. "Love, the most powerful force in the universe." It was surreal, Eugene Carson, who used to be Gene Pytka, a bully and a bull, had become a hippie, a damn hippie.

"So, you're loving everybody now, are you?"

"No, not everybody. Who the hell has enough love for everybody? No, you, only you, I love only you. Lavinia opened up love in me, and I can't waste it. It would be like throwing shit on her memory."

"Yeah, okay, right, I remember. You moved back to—what was that place?"

"Andersberg."

"Yeah, Andersberg. You moved back there to love her family, her mom, her brothers. It was going to give you a family."

"Yeah. It was initially a good plan. But there was a problem with it."

"What?"

"Her family is so damn unlovable. I mean, her mother is as dumb as a damp mop. And her brothers are—her brothers are, like, I don't know, they're like two single-cell organisms. They kind of just move by reflex, and their reflexes aren't very sharp. But—I built a nice house for them all."

"You were going to live with them."

"Yeah, well, I found a warmer hearth and home in a hotel in Hershey."

"Did you build the library?"

"Yes! The Lavinia Carson Public Library is up and running with a million dollars' worth of books on its shelves. I brought in some other businesses to Andersberg, rather than just the quarry, so it's growing, it's thriving, so I did my job there. And in memory of Lavinia, I let all my Ramone quarries worldwide become unionized."

"You're kidding?"

"No. It's working out." Gene seemed almost reluctant to admit it. "But I couldn't think of any more ways to love her, to keep her memory alive."

"Just do it in your head, Gene, like everyone else has to."

"Head, heart, yeah, I got all that. But what I need, Adolphus, like an addict needs dope, is someone alive to love. I've decided it has to be you."

There must have been a lot I could have said, but I couldn't think of anything except, "You know, I'm not gay. Did you think I was gay when we were kids?"

"No, I'm not talking about that, I'm not gay either. I'm not even talking about sex. *Love*, Adolphus. It's not physical, it's—it's a binding force in the universe, that—that if you don't have it for someone, it sets you adrift. Do you understand?"

"Well, then, get yourself a dog, for Christ's sake, Gene! Leave me out of it."

"No, it's you, Adolphus, it has to be you. I *have* to love *you*."

"Why? I mean, I'm pretty damn unlovable too, you know."

"No. You can't be. Lavinia would not have liked you if you were. And Lavinia tells me to love you."

"Are you—are you talking to her now?" I was suspicious, of course, suspicious that Gene had had a total mental breakdown.

"No, come on! Metaphorically, I mean."

"That's a good word for you."

"I'm not as stupid as you think, Adolphus."

"But, Gene, I think you need to calm down here. You're talking sort of silly, okay? Look, uh, you want to be friends, you know, like we were when we were very young? Well, yeah, sure, maybe that's okay. You want to go out for pizza and beer one night, fine, but—"

"Don't trivialize this, Adolphus. I'm going to love you. It has to be you, only you, because..."

"Because, why?"

"Because I remembered."

"What?" I wasn't asking what he had remembered; I was pretty sure about what he had recalled. I was asking what the hell was going to be thrown at me now.

"About a year ago. I was taking a walk, late at night, in Hershey, eating a chocolate bar."

"Well, yeah, they're probably easy to come by there."

"It wasn't a Hershey's Bar. It was Nestlés."

"You're a damn anarchist, Gene."

"Shut-up, Adolphus, this is serious. I suddenly remembered, you know—scraping your face against that stucco wall."

It was like I had suddenly swallowed shit: awful taste, gag reflex, and the premonition of a dire illness.

"What you had told me plagued me. I couldn't get it out of my head. I knew you were wrong. I thought you had told me that just to be mean to me."

"Mean to you? You had just gifted the college thousands of dollars in my name. Why would I be mean to you?"

"Yeah, that's why it plagued me. But how could I check up on it? My mom's dead, my step-father's dead. I went to a psychiatrist to, um, to talk it out. He did some hypnosis, what they call memory recovery

—nothing. He told me there was no such memory, or I have a solid block against it. But there I was that night, walking the streets of Hershey, eating a $100,000 Bar—"

"*That* seems appropriate."

"It's my favorite candy bar."

"I would repeat myself, but why bother?"

"Take me seriously, Adolphus."

He *was* serious. And unsmiling. The twinkle was gone from his eyes.

"I was chewing a big bite of the bar. Slowly, very slowly, and I just kept chewing and chewing—and chewing. It was as if I couldn't swallow. I started to panic and was ready to spit it all out when, and I mean this literally, in a flash—really, of light—I was there again. I was rubbing your face against that stucco wall. I could see the blood smearing it. And I was feeling—I was feeling the most godawful—godawful hate. And it… Well, it scared me—twisted me with fear. I mean, there's a whole hell of a lot of things about life and people and, hell, inanimate objects even that I don't like, that I would like to just—steamroll over. But hate like this?"

"Okay, so, what—"

"Then, suddenly, I could swallow. And once I swallowed, I knew that if I couldn't turn that hate into love—I would be lost. I would not be a man that Lavinia could love. But I didn't know what to do about it. I was too frightened to come back here. So I just—I just sent the endowment more money. I knew that if I had sent money directly to you, you would have rejected it."

"Yes, I probably would have. Silly me. Maybe it's not such a bad thing to profit from another's guilt."

"I never felt guilt."

"Oh, thanks."

"I felt loathing. For my action then. And for my inaction now. I needed courage. For the first time in my life, I lacked it. Then, Lavinia came to me in my sleep and—"

"Oh, for Christ's sake, don't tell—"

"It was just a dream, Adolphus; stop thinking I'm an idiot. It was actually a, well, you know, a wet dream, like we used to have as teenagers. She didn't say a word. It was all just—sexy. And I woke up, you know, wet. But—but so satisfied and—and happy and—jolly."

His smile got even broader. I was afraid it was going to knock something over. "Jolly?"

"That's the only word I can put to it. It was just this—this jolly understanding that I could now come here and tell you I love you."

What was I going to do with this? What could I do with this? "Well, Gene, look, you know, I've got an appointment and—"

"You don't have to do anything but accept my love."

"That's not as easy as you might think."

"I know you hate me for what I did to you."

"No, I don't hate—well, you were not anyone I would have put on my Christmas card list, Gene, but... Look, I did my best to forget also. Why don't we just go back to that tactic? How about a mutual pact of memory loss? Much easier, much cleaner."

"No, I have to love you. I have to take you in my arms and embrace you."

And, indeed, he did open his arms. And then he stepped up onto my step. And then I backed up to the step above. And then he followed me up to that step. And then I dashed to the side and leaped down from that third step to the ground and stumbled slightly but recovered my footing and ran. I ran to the edge of the long mirror pool that graces PCC's front grounds and stretches from close to the main entrance to just before the sidewalk on Colorado Boulevard. Gene calmly turned around and smiled and, with his arms still wide open, walked toward me. I was desperate to escape but to where? Where couldn't he follow me? He was a big man but probably fast. I'm a small man and pretty damn slow.

I looked behind. The long mirror pool stretched before me, with six inches of water reflecting, I assumed, the college's educational mission. A manifest metaphor made of concrete, concrete possibly made of Ramone rock and sand. But the water! Gene had had nothing to do with the water! I jumped up onto the edge of the pool, then jumped in, the water coming up to my ankles.

Gene started to laugh. "What the hell did you do that for?"

"Get away from me, Gene! Go away!"

"No," he said in a statement of undeniable fact.

"And that's why I did this. You see these?" I raised my right foot. "These scuffed brown loafers—Twenty-nine ninety-five at Florsheim. Your highly polished black dress shoes, I'll betcha—what?—five hundred dollars?"

"Fifteen hundred, actually."

"For a pair of shoes!"

"They're custom made, Adolphus. They're the most comfortable shoes you could ever wear."

"Well, I'll never know that, will I?"

"I could buy you a pair."

"Shut-up! I'm going to stand in this pool until you go away, knowing full well that you would never sacrifice a pair of fifteen hundred dollar shoes."

Gene stepped up on the edge of the pool. I backed-up two or three paces. "Gene, get down! I'm all for soaking the rich, but not their shoes."

"I'll come in," Gene said with a smile and his arms still wide open.

"No, you won't."

"I have lots of shoes."

"Fifteen hundred dollars, Gene!"

"Sure. But to me, that's pretty much equivalent to your twenty-nine ninety-five."

"You bastard!" I said, backing up a step.

Gene, smiling the smile I had become sick of, stepped into the pool. I screamed. I hate to admit it, but I screamed. Not only like a girl, but *exactly* like a girl. And then I turned around and started to run down the length of the mirror pool. It's a long run and not fun in six inches of water. Assuming I would ever have had any recorded speed records for running, I would have broken them. Splash, splash, splash went my feet followed by the splash, splash, splash of Gene's. He was chasing me, he was actually chasing me! The panic I felt was unreasonable but not unreal. I just kept running and running, "seeing" what was behind me—this massive man, this monster from some 1930s horror film chasing after me and growling. Although he wasn't really growling, he was shouting out, "Adolphus, Adolphus, wait!" That's what I saw in my mind, seeing nothing before me in reality. I was aware of nothing but momentum. I didn't even realize I had leaped out of the pool, onto the sidewalk, straight into Colorado Boulevard— and right into the path of an oncoming SUV.

The blare of a horn. The screech of brakes. Suddenly, I was embraced by two beefy arms, lifted up, swung around, and carried with leaps and bounds back to the sidewalk. Then there was stasis. But the embrace did not end. It became tighter and tighter and tighter.

"Oh God, oh my God, God, I thought I was going to lose you too!"

"Gene," I squeaked out, "Gene, you're crushing me."

But the gigantic python inside Eugene Carson just kept squeezing me, tighter and tighter and tighter as his "Oh God, oh God, oh God!" keep looping into my ear.

Gene re-broke the two ribs he had broken before. And I squeak-screamed precisely like a girl.

1 8

It must have been a funny sight—or sights—for the few students left on campus, especially the front of the campus. First, there were two men at the bottom of the steps. A big and tall man and a slightly-below-average-in-height man, having a somewhat agitated conversation at the bottom of the steps. Most of the students would have recognized me. None, I assume, would have recognized Gene. The few who passed us, coming up and down the steps, went by quickly and probably did not catch a word of our conversation. They certainly would not have been curious if they had. It was none of their business, and to Youth, there is no business but their business. When Gene, though, with wide-arms-enthusiasm, declared that he loved me, that might have caught some attention and generated some amusement. But otherwise—just another agitated conversation on a college campus—no big deal. The mirror pool sprint, though, the Coyote chasing the Roadrunner, *that* would have gotten everybody's attention and certainly given them much amusement.

Then they may have been horrified by the potential tragedy of my death by a faster-than-the-speed-limit SUV and, hopefully, were relieved when I was snatched back into life by what seemed to be a larger-than-life "super" hero. Then amused again when that big hero picked me up like a baby, cradled me in his arms, and walked me back slowly, because he knew I was in pain, to the main entrance, yelling, "Where's the school nurse?" upon entering.

There was just one person in the entranceway, a student sitting on the floor, his back up against the wall, studying a biology textbook.

"What? Uh, you're going to need the Medical Center."

"Fine. Where's that?"

"Uh, well..."

I recognized the student, but I couldn't think of his name, so I just yelled out, "Just lead him the hell to it, man!"

Soon I was laid out on a medical bed being examined by a nurse, Claire, a nice lady, been with the college for thirty years. We'd had a party for her just two weeks before and gave her a gift card to Nordstroms.

"Well, Adolphus, your ribs are broken again." An ice pack was applied as she called for an ambulance to take me to Emergency. "You need x-rays and some strong painkillers, and you're going to be pretty damn uncomfortable for a month to six weeks."

All this time Gene stood there asking if there was anything he could do, and Claire said, "Outside of staying the hell out of my way, I can't think of a thing."

Finally, the paramedics came in with their wheeled gurney and gently—somewhat—lifted me up and put me on it. As they started to wheel me away, I asked Claire to please call Peggy and ask her to meet me at Emergency. Before we got out the door, Gene stopped the paramedics with an authoritative voice.

Eugene came up to the gurney and looked down at me. Son-of-a-bitch, he was big! He was distraught and in a kind of pain himself. Then he obviously decided to put on the best face and offered me a smile somewhere between the paper cut and the horrible gash of his I-love-you smile. "Pizza and beer?" he queried.

"What?"

"You said we might go out for pizza and beer. Why don't we do that? Once you're feeling better."

"What! Why?" I asked with disbelief. I could have attached a whole essay to that, "Why?" But what was the use?

"Because you said we could."

"Gene—really—I think you need help."

"I love you."

"Shut-up!" I said as I noticed the paramedics noticing what Gene said. And not the grimace of pain it had caused me to shout.

"Excuse me, sir," one of the paramedics said to Gene as they rolled me away.

But Gene followed us to Emergency, went directly to the financial office, told them not to bill my medical insurance; that he would pay for everything. And then he went and sat in the Emergency waiting room, where Peggy, who reported this to me later, found him when she arrived.

"You must be, *Euuuugene"*

"Huh? Uh, Yes. Eugene Carson."

"I'm Peggy, friend, and occasional paramour to Adolphus."

"Oh, hello."

Then they had a conversation. I did not know this at the time because I was being tended to by a doctor. Had I known it, I would have been willing to break two more ribs to get out into the waiting room to physically separate the two. Why? That's a good question. The subsequent telling of this chronicle may provide an answer.

The x-ray confirmed that the two ribs had been broken exactly where they had been broken before. And that, thankfully, no organs were damaged. The doctor considered wrapping my chest, but that was a technique being frowned upon now, as it restricted the breathing, and restricted breathing can sometimes cause pneumonia. But he said if I thought I would feel better…

"No, no, please, pneumonia on top of this I don't need. This pain is an old friend, and I'll just take it home and put it up for a few weeks."

I was released into Peggy's care. Gene was nowhere to be seen. She drove me home, put me to bed, and went into the kitchen to make some soup. Why do people always make people soup when they are sick or injured? What made her think that just because my ribs were broken that I wanted soup? I was actually craving hot pastrami on rye with a lot of mustard. But she told me that lifting the sandwich, biting, and chewing would hurt my ribs. She was probably right. Still, I would have liked to have tested her hypothesis and tasted some pastrami.

On the bed tray that Peggy had bought me the last time I was invalid, she brought me the soup—tomato, of course—with three saltine crackers on the side.

"Well, if I can chew the crackers, why can't I chew a hot pastrami on rye?" I asked her, still mourning the pastrami's loss.

Peggy just stared at me. She has a particular stare, which I think she has reserved just for me. It is an unequivocal, undeniable, and unarguable declaration that I was a fool. Then she gathered up the three saltines in her right hand, palmed them, swiftly and powerfully closed her hand into a tight fist in a technique of compression that one could imagine Amazon warriors had used on the testicles of their male opponents. She positioned this fist over the bowl of tomato soup, turned it around, and opened it, releasing the pulverized saltines into the soup. "Eat," she commanded.

"You don't eat tomato soup. You drink it with a spoon," I said, leaving the soup untouched.

Then she spooned some soup and presented it to my mouth. "I could force-feed you, you know."

"Have you ever thought of becoming a warden at a women's prison?"

"No, of course not, don't be silly. I would only consider being a warden at a men's prison."

I quickly took the spoonful of tomato soup into my mouth and ingested it. "Umm—umm, good!" I said, quoting a TV commercial from our childhood.

Peggy pulled up my wingback reading chair and sat, and we settled into her spooning the soup into me. "Well—I met Eugene Carson," she said between my ingestions.

"You did?"

"He was in the waiting room."

"He wasn't?"

"He was. He had already arranged to pay the bill."

"Great! It's like he's bullying me with obligations."

"Well, he did break your ribs again."

"Yeah, after saving my life. Oh, crap! Does that mean I belong to him now?"

"I found him interesting."

"You found him interesting?"

"Yeah. I did."

"A twenty-car pile-up on the freeway is interesting, but it's still a bloody mess. The man is nuts!"

"He didn't seem that way to me. He was just—well, half distraught and half..."

"Half what?"

"I don't know how to explain it?"

"Try, crazy as a loon."

She ignored me, of course. "I know! Beatific!"

"What!"

"As if he had found Nirvana or the key to human happiness or maybe just a solid purpose in life."

"You got that from a brief encounter in the waiting room of the emergency ward?"

"We had a good conversation. I, of course, thanked him for his support of the college. Something both of us have benefited from. And that got him started talking about Lavinia."

"Oh."

"He really loved her."

"True."

"I mean, *really* loved her. Capital L, boldface, deep, abiding—"

"Pathological?"

"Shut-up, cynic. I'm just saying that—"

"Okay, you're right. He obviously had a deep love for Lavinia. And her death has, I think, pushed him over the edge because—"

"Because now he wants to love you."

"Oh, shit! He told you that?"

"He told me everything."

"Do you agree, then? Pathological—weird, cuckoo, nuts! Over-the-bend. An accordion with missing keys. An exile from the Bizarro World."

"I think it's sweet."

"What?" I tried to sit up a bit more. It hurt like bloody hell.

After the reverberations of my scream ended, Peggy asked, "You finished with your soup?" She stood and took the tray off my lap. "Now, why don't you try to get some sleep?"

"Sweet?"

"Yes. Unusual, I'll admit, but—"

"You only like him because he's tall."

There was that stare. My testicles tightened.

"Listen, Ass—this is a rich, powerful man who has greatly bene-fited the institution we both work for and love who wants nothing more than to just simply—love you."

"With a capital L? Boldface? Abiding?"

"I don't know. It's interesting."

"There's that twenty-car pile-up again."

She started to leave, then turned around. "Oh, by the way—"

"Is that a new blouse?" I had just really noticed it. It was white, with ruffles, and very low cut. Her cleavage outlined a path—a path to —well, a way to Nirvana.

"Yes. Remember, you were coming over. I bought it for tonight."

"I like it."

"Thank you."

"It inspires me."

"What? To get a blouse of your own?"

"No. To take it off."

"And then do what?"

"Well…"

"Whatever you could do would hurt."

"Yeah, but—"

"I prefer you screaming out in joy, not pain."

"For some people, pain is joy."

"Ah, yes, but not for you, my little man."

"Ouch! Now that hurt."

"That's why you need your sleep so you can grow big and strong."

"Okay, okay, I'll sleep."

"Fine. I'm staying the night, of course. In case you need anything. I'll sleep on the couch."

"Talk about sweet."

"Yep. I'm just an angel of mercy." She started to walk out again.

"Hey!"

"What ?"

"What were you going to say?"

"What?"

"You had a 'By-the-way'."

"Oh, yeah. I committed to Eugene that I would make sure you go out with him for pizza and beer. He offered to send me to a spa for the weekend."

"What?"

"Yeah."

"He bribed you?"

"Yep. But he didn't have to. I think it's a good idea. I would have done it for nothing. But this is a very nice spa. I'm going to come home with very smooth skin."

"I'm aghast."

"You can't be aghast."

"Why not?"

"Because it's the late twentieth century and 'aghast' went out with the nineteenth."

"Well, just how do you plan to make me go out for pizza and beer with him?"

She smiled, leaned forward just a little, becoming just a little Marilyn Monroe. "Oh, I have my ways. Now go to sleep, sweet prince, go to sleep."

L et me tell you about Margaret Kathleen Bradford as she was at this time. She was a feminine feminist. She was very *Flower Drum Song* as she enjoyed being a girl. And she didn't mind being called a girl. She preferred mammalian/*Homo sapiens*/female, but as that was a mouthful, she accepted *"girl"* as a competent signifier. She hated the word, woman. "It sounds like it means that we are just 'Wo(e) to man' or just a man with a wo(mb)," she would always say. "No, give me 'girl' anytime. And just like the restrooms in elementary school, we have our own door to go through."

She was feminine, but not frilly. Although she did wear frills on occasion. Maybe it would be better said that she was feminine, but she wasn't a "doll," a "babe," a "hot number," created by the application of paint, and powder, and unnatural colors around the eyes. She always wore nothing but clear nail polish.

"That's how James Bond likes his girls, by the way," she often said. "I mean, in the books; don't even talk to me about the movies. He likes women who wear clear nail polish. He doesn't like women who wear red nail polish. *I* don't like red nail polish." She wore make-up only on special occasions, and a minimal amount at that. And she wore clothes that did not call attention to themselves, but she had no objections to clothes that called attention to her body.

She liked her little sexy body. She liked that it curved where it should curve and protruded where it should protrude. She absolutely adored her breasts. And her cleavage was never unexposed except at those times when she wore a coat to fend off the cold. When puberty hit her, so did a theory: much exposure to open-air would help her breasts grow. An idea I always suspected she had ripped off from Santa Claus regarding his beard as stated in the 1947 film classic, *Miracle on 34th Street.* In any case, they were fully grown now, and she loved them as much as she had when they were young and developing. There have been a few occasions in venues where the main business was the consumption of alcoholic beverages, when some asshole, whose brain was currently being pickled by said consumption, would look at her and declare, "You, lady, have very lovely breasts." Far from being insulted, offended, or even miffed, Peggy would just sit up tall, thrust them out, smile broadly, and say, "Thank you, I grew them myself!" Then the asshole usually climbed into himself.

I have often seen Peggy in the shower running her hands over her body in deep appreciation, following curves and cupping and squeezing protrusions. She did not erotically do this (although it always inspired erotic thoughts in me). Instead, she was reveling in the totality of her fleshy body and making a connection with her animal self.

But as intense as her morphological self-love was, it could not hold a match, candle, torch, or klieg light to her love of that other half—in importance if not in volume—of her body: her brain.

Although Peggy was an administrator, a counselor charged with helping students moving from our two-year college onto even higher education, she had gotten her B.S. and Masters in Biology. She had taught the subject for several years. In all the diversity of life, her preferred group was the mammals. Her main interest, concern, and, it must be said, love was for them. No houseplant could ever survive under her care. She became quite a connoisseur of artificial flora. And in the diversity of parts that made up the living entity of a mammal, her deep fascination was reserved for the brain, especially the one residing in *Homo sapiens*. She loved getting lost in the brain's complexity. She was always in awe over its malleability and frequently debated with herself and others the question of whether we owned the brain or the brain owned us. She spent a lot of time reading the current literature on the brain, partly to conclude that debate and to develop her own. This led her into contemplating consciousness and the mind. She came to her own conclusion—although she was always open to other thoughts—that consciousness and the mind were but attributes of the material brain, and as the brain was a part of the body, then consciousness and mind could not exist outside of the body. She was never shy about saying that "Descartes was just an old fart," which did not please certain faculty members in the Philosophy Department. But she insisted, in several staff gatherings, both official and casual, that the body couldn't function without the brain—obviously—and that the brain, thus the mind, couldn't function without the body. Peggy absolutely hated the idea of artificial intelligence. She thought the precious prediction that someday soon we would be able to upload our minds into computers was nothing but wishful thinking at best and a grave intellectual fallacy at worse. In her mind, we were biological units with the brain and the rest of the body feeding each other on a constant information loop to the great benefit of both.

So why wasn't she teaching this? Why did it remain, basically, a private matter with her? Well, this is where her feminism came in. She was ever angry that the mammalian/*Homo sapiens*/female had of late ("of late" being the past five hundred years or so) been faced continuously with mammalian/*Homo sapiens*/male constructed roadblocks to realizing the full potential of their brains. She was willing to admit that in earlier days of hunting and gathering, and cave-dwelling and such, the natural division of labor ("labor" being the operative word here) kept the two sexes on different paths. Or rather, in the same direction, just with one leading the other (and we know who that was) instead of moving forward side-by-side. But as life for mammalians/*Homo sapiens* became easier and easier, with advances in technology, science, and medicine providing rosy-cheeked leisure, there should no longer have been any roadblocks for any female to reach the full potential of her brain. So she took it as a calling, her mission at PCC, not just to help the female students who came to her but to search out and find ones that she could encourage, cajole, and sometimes even bully into considering further education. She was also there for the male students, of course, but the male ego rarely needed extra encouragement.

Peggy couldn't nurture a houseplant if her life (not to mention the life of the houseplant) depended on it. But she could and did, quite tenderly and with a form of love, nurture student brains. Of course, her actual job was just to find seedlings of potential to send off to be nurtured by others. But she kept a database of all the students she had helped move on to four-year colleges and universities. And she kept in touch with them, following their progress, sending them notes of encouragement if she thought they needed it, and letters of congratulations when they deserved it.

In nurturing others, she did not ignore the nurturing of her own self, which she saw sitting quite comfortably within the folds of her brain. She felt it was absolutely necessary to continue to feed it with information and knowledge and art and music and drama and comedy and good conversation.

And mystery novels, of course, her beloved mysteries. A relaxing pastime we shared. Although we liked mysteries for different reasons. She loved mysteries for the puzzles, the complex laying out of clue after clue as to who had done the dirty deed. And I liked mysteries for the characters. She was always miffed if she couldn't figure out "whodunit" before the denouement. I could not have cared less. Sherlock Holmes that I liked, not the game that was afoot; it was Nero Wolfe and Archie I cared about, not the murder victim; it was Philip Marlowe's cynical view of the plot, not the plot itself that I found fascinating. But all that was fine—between the two of us, we made one excellent mystery fan.

Besides Peggy's self-caressing of her body in the shower, you just knew that in quiet moments of contemplation, she was self-caressing her brain, gleefully traveling among the folds of the cerebral cortex, skipping happily from neuron to neuron along dendrites and axons. This was the way she enjoyed being a total, living mammalian/*Homo sapiens*/female. She actually thought about her breathing, not allowing it to just be a reflex. She never let a taste pass her lips without savoring it. And she, daily, I believe, thanked nature for adding pleasure to copulation, saving it from just being bluntly utilitarian.

This was Margaret Kathleen Bedford at this time. How could one not have wanted to have her as a pal?

2 0

Ost likely because this was the second time these ribs had been broken, healing took longer than expected. My doctor had some small concern about this and suggested —by way of a rather commanding order—that I not go back to work right away. He told me, in fact, to stay housebound, to limit my activities to within the house, and to pamper myself. I didn't have to bother with pampering myself, for Deb and Peggy happily shared the job, which was nice of them and no less than I deserved. But they couldn't be with me all the time, so I was often left alone.

One might have thought I would have taken this opportunity to work out my whole Gene-Me problem. But I didn't. I did my best to avoid thinking about it, filling my time with other, more appealing activities. There were the visits and pampering from Deb and Peggy, sometimes individually, sometimes together. Deb bought me a VCR and hooked it up to my TV. She and Peggy would go to the video store and rent old movies. We would have movie nights, for which they would make thematically compatible meals and intoxicating drinks— cold fried chicken and mint juleps for the night we saw *The Long, Hot Summer*, for example. They also left behind nutritious home-cooked meals that I could warm up when I was tragically alone. I have some female cousins who phoned a few times to see how I was doing. We would chit-chat for a few minutes, ending each call with mutual *love yous*, although that probably was hardly the case. And some of my favorite students would drop by in small groups, and we had improvisational symposiums on some subject in history. Those were wonderful.

But, as I said, I was alone much of the time. As I was sanctioned against practicing any athletic skills (of which I have none) in the backyard, I had to fill the time with more mental activities. That meant, of course, the reading of books. I read the mysteries Peggy and I were reading together. I read historical novels (I reread all of Mary Renault). I read the occasional sci-fi time travel novel—I'm a historian, how could I not like time travel stories? But what I really found myself getting into were non-academic, popular books on history and the personalities who populate it. I had previously been a bit snobbish about such books. But I found them, the good ones anyway, to be great storytelling. I read mainly books covering historical periods, both focused and broad, and biographies, which tied personalities to their periods. I found myself making a list of subjects and people I thought I might want to write such books about someday—although I assumed that I never actually would.

So my convalescence—despite the pain, despite feeling a bit like a prisoner, despite missing being in class (sort of)—turned out to be a good time. I almost hated getting back into the world. But not, of course, back into Peggy's bed.

"Pizza and beer," Peggy said, her head on my chest, her left arm around my torso, a few calm minutes after some most welcome bit of renewed sex. I was, of course, wholly healed now, or I could not have enjoyed the welcome of renewed sex, and Peggy certainly could not have laid her head on my chest. Peggy liked putting her head on my chest as part of the post-coitus cuddling she had instituted and which had become, by now, a cherished tradition. For her. It's something *girls* like to do. Men don't seem to cherish it quite as much. I mean, it can be nice on occasion, but every single time? Some men, I suppose, might like to rest their head on a woman's chest, but rarely after sex, more often, I suspect, when both are clothed, maybe lounging on the couch. And then, again, maybe men never like doing this—there's something little-boy-with-mother creepy about it. If they do it, perhaps they only do it during the early stages of a courtship (assuming courtships even still existed) to convince the female that they are not dangerous despite being, in most cases, larger and more robust. (My marriage to Cindy was not one of those cases.) When women place their head on a man's chest—clothed or unclothed—it is never like a little girl hugging her father. At least, I don't think it is. No, I think for women, it is just a disconcertingly endearing thing to do with their mates. Or maybe it's something more profound than that; perhaps it actually comes from our hunter-gatherer past. For, let's be honest, sex for men is a concentrated period of mounting loss of control, combined with intensifying sensitivity. It's a focused time of just letting go as the rest of the world seems to drop away, melting into non-existence. Finally, when the uncontrollable big burst is over, or shortly thereafter, the world comes back in a rush, reconstituting itself into something tangible and demanding. Sensitivity leaves. Poof! It's gone. Now the most demanding urge in your whole body comes from your legs wanting to get up to put you back on your feet so you can go out and hunt for meat. Women, on the other hand, love to keep men immobile after sex by putting their surprisingly heavy heads on the manly chests and—this is important —bringing one arm around the men's torsos, literally holding them down, non-verbally saying, "Stay awhile. Maybe later we'll go do some nice gathering." Even Peggy, as independent a woman as I have ever met, had the instinct to do this. But what the hell? I wasn't reporting back to work until the next Monday. I had nowhere to go anyway.

"What?"

"Pizza and beer."

"You're hungry? Should we order some and have it delivered?"

"No. We should get up and shower and get dressed."

"You want to go out for pizza and beer?"

"Well, we have a date to do so, yes."

"We do?"

"Yeah. With Eugene."

"Huh?"

"I made a date for us to go have some pizza and beer with him tonight to fulfill your commitment to do so."

"Oh. Without consulting with me?"

"Didn't have to consult you. You made a commitment."

"Oh. Interesting logic, there. What if I already had something to do tonight?"

"Like what?"

"Like, um, washing my hair."

"I'll wash it for you in the shower."

"It'll be wet afterward."

"Ever hear of a blow dryer?"

"I don't have one."

"I brought one."

"Well, maybe I have to clean the lint out of my belly button."

"Your bellybutton is devoid of lint."

"How do you know?"

"I've been intimate with your belly button."

"Okay. So we're going out to have pizza and beer with Gene, an appointment you made."

"That's right."

"Which means you've been in contact with him."

"Oh sure, we've seen a lot of each other."

"Really?"

"He was too shy and, I guess you would call it, chagrined to come and see you. I told him it probably wasn't the right time, anyway, you know, let you heal, get over the incident."

"I'm over the incident, but I think I'll pass."

"No, it was probably traumatic, and you're probably not over the incident, but it's time anyway."

"I know whether I'm over an incident or not."

Peggy laughed—derisively. "If people knew things like that, there would be no need for psychiatrists."

"Yeah? Well—I think there really is no need for psychiatrists."

"Now you're just being stupid."

"Sure, maybe. I've been stupid before."

"Come on. It'll be fun."

"Do I have to? Not one encounter I've ever had with Gene Pytka Carson, from my early childhood to now, has ever been fun."

"Did you agree to it?"

"Well, yeah, you know, for sometime in the vague future."

"Well, here we are, Buck Rogers, in the vague future."

"Okay, fine, defeated. Where are we going? Don't tell me he wants to go to a Shakey's."

"No, it's some family run place in Madison."

Madison was a city between Pasadena and Ramone that had retained a real charming, almost 1940s small town feel. It had a busy main street of mainly independently owned shops and restaurants, having avoided national chain establishments taking over. That would happen later, of course, but that is another, and not very interesting, story.

"I don't want to drive to Madison."

"You don't have to drive."

"Oh, okay, so you're going to drive."

"No."

"We're walking, maybe?"

"No. Eugene is sending a car."

"Of course. *Euuuugene* is sending a car?"

"Dress nice."

"Why do I have to dress nice? It's just pizza and beer."

"Don't be such an asshole, Ass."

Peggy slapped my stomach, jumped out of bed, grabbed my arm and pulled me after her.

Peggy said that Gene's car would be there at six-thirty and she kept hurrying me on as I tried to dress. Of course, most of my delay in dressing was caused by her rejecting what I had picked out to wear. Finally she approved a nice pair of charcoal gray slacks and a black, long-sleeved shirt. Casual classic, she called it. I called it charcoal gray slacks and a black, long-sleeved shirt.

The collar on my shirt being askew, she faced me directly and put her hands up to un-askew it while looking at me, deeply, which was just a bit unnerving. "You know, you are a very handsome man."

"Well, sure, relatively speaking."

"What do you mean, relatively speaking?"

"I mean, it's usually a relative speaking when you are told such things. You know an aunt or grandmother or something."

"Well, I'm not a relative and you know damn well that other women have found you handsome."

"Yes, and I've always found it best not to argue with them."

"Well..." Finished with my collar, she stood back and stuck a pose. "And how do you think I look?"

"You look fine."

"Not pretty maybe, maybe beautiful, possibly enchanting?"

"Uh, well..." Peggy was wearing a gray knit dress that hugged her as tightly as I liked to do, and that gave ample exposure of her cleavage, as I also liked to do. She also wore these dangling earrings that I believe were her favorites. I always noticed these earrings when she wore them—because they dangled. "Um, you seem clean, well-pressed, and, um, totally put together."

"You a—"

"And your eyes are bright and lively, your smile lifts my spirit, and your complexion is healthy and vital, smooth and, dare I say, creamy. And your hair, which I see you had cut today, although just brown, as opposed to, say, raven black or platinum blonde, has always been, I think, rather lustrous, and has never failed to inspire me to stroke it."

"Holy, shit! What brought all that on?"

"Hey, you were the one fishing for a compliment. I'm just the mackerel you landed."

She laughed. "Well, I would like to think there was some sincerity in what you said."

"Sure—you can *think* it."

Peggy smiled a lopsided smile, then turned away from me.

"And you wouldn't be wrong."

She turned back to me, her smile now a perfect one. "You've just earned yourself a gold star, Adolphus."

We went outside to stand on my front porch to wait for this "car" that Gene was sending. I fully expected it to be an ostentatious stretch limo. More than that, I expected it to be a cartoon ostentatious stretch limo. You know, it would pull up to the front of the house and keep pulling up and keep pulling up and keep pulling up until its mile and a half stretch ended. But when the car came it was not a cartoon ostentatious stretch limo, or even a real world ostentatious stretch limo, it was just a simple, black town car. A driver popped out and opened the back door for us. We got in and thanked him in our best *noblesse oblige* voices. We drove out of South Pasadena into Pasadena and up to the 210 freeway, which we got on and traveled along smoothly and safely at the posted speed limit until we reached the Downtown Madison off-ramp. We went north to the charming Madison downtown nestled under the San Gabriel Mountains.

Peggy truly enjoyed the ride. She kept stroking the leather seats and pushing herself into them, testing the extent of their luxury. I found that somewhat unbecoming of an academic, but then I was feeling testy about this obligatory evening and even more testy that I was putting on a good face for Peggy, who was being sensual with a leather seat instead of me.

The town car pulled up to the front of Schwarzkopf's Pizzeria and stopped.

"*Schwarzkopf's* Pizzeria?" I said incredulously because, well, how else could you say it? Peggy just looked at me bereft of any comeback.

As we entered the front door, we noticed a sign saying CLOSED FOR PRIVATE PARTY. That immediately worried me. I don't know why, but it was a signal that Gene was in charge, calling the shots, the Grand Poobah. Maybe now the Grand Poobah over my life, and that was worrying.

It was a larger restaurant than I had expected with five long communal tables with bench seating. I hate communal tables in restaurants, absolutely hate them. Forced camaraderie is not true camaraderie, and I hate eating with a crowd. In a normal restaurant, even one with many tables and copious seating, as long as you are at your own table you can exist comfortably in your own bubble, and that's exactly how I like it. Not that I don't peek out of that bubble and spy on other diners and even, on occasion, have possibly caustic, but certainly at least witty, comments to make about them. This you cannot do at a communal table sitting around like Robin Hood's merry band of men (and women). But one quick look around and I was no longer worried about the private party sign, but relieved by it. For there were no other diners to be seen in Schwarzkopf's Pizzeria, only Gene, who came up to greet us.

"Hey, Peggy, Adolphus! Great! Good! You made it!"

"I never ignore a summons," I said, looking up at the big man wearing light brown slacks, a cream-colored pullover v-neck sweater with chest hairs poking out to say hello, and, I'm sure, shoes hand-crafted by some little old man in some little old village in little old Italy.

"Summons? Hey, this was your idea."

Peggy lost her elbow in my ribs. But I found it quick enough. "Uh, yeah, well, I guess it was."

"Pizza and beer, that's what you said, pizza and beer, and they got the best of both here."

"Are we the 'private party'?" Peggy asked.

"Yeah, I figured that would be best."

"Kind of unfair, isn't it? A party of three, denying them all those other customers and all that other business." What a thrust I gave him, I thought, poking him in his rich, capitalist belly.

"It's no problem. I co-own the place. I own forty-nine percent. Come," Gene gestured us further into the establishment, "let's sit down."

At the end of one of the long communal tables, there were three place settings. One at one end of the table and two immediately to either side. Gene pulled out the chair at the end and said, "Peggy, take the seat of honor."

"Thank you, Eugene," Peggy accepted with grace. Why did she always call him Eugene? Eugene was a stupid name.

"And us boys will take the other two seats."

Us "boys" sat, and then there we were facing each other. Although one of us had to direct his vision on an incline and the other on a decline. Still, we were face-to-face. But would there be a face-off? If there was, I supposed that's why Peggy was between us—sort of like the Speaker of the House in the British Parliament. *ORDER! ORDER!* Once settled—napkins on laps and all that—Gene said, "What I've asked George to do—"

"George?" I asked.

"George Schwarzkopf, my partner here. Well, him and his wife."

"Yeah, you've got to explain that."

"Explain what?"

"*Schwarzkopf's* Pizzeria?"

"Oh, well, that's easy. George came over from Germany in the fifties, settled here in the San Gabriel Valley, and became an importer of German beers. Became quite an expert in them. He met Bettina, a third-generation Italian who had all these family pizza recipes. He liked her pizzas, she liked his beer, it was a natural. They fell in love, got married, and opened this place, Schwarzkopf's Pizzeria—it's been here forever. Serves only the best of German beers and pizzas made with Italian family secrets. And new pizzas, international pizzas. Bettina's very innovative. She even went to Tokyo once and found out they make pizza with cuttlefish. So she's adapted that. Makes it with pesto instead of tomato sauce. It's surprisingly good; you should try it."

"I think I'll pass," I said. But did I say it because I was revolted by the idea of cuttlefish on a pizza—weird, alien-looking, creepy little creatures that they were? Possibly. Or possibly I was not passing on this innovative pizza delicacy, but rather on Gene's enthusiasm for it. Or maybe just Gene's enthusiasm for anything. The Gene I had known was not really a creature of enthusiasms. Enthusiasms are a positive thing. The Gene I had known had been a creature of dislikes and their negation, by definition a negative thing. Why was I uncomfortable with positive Gene? Maybe I just didn't like change. Perhaps I didn't believe in change.

"Lavinia discovered this place," Gene said, almost as a justification. "She used to like—" He stopped for a second and cleared his throat or his memory or his heart (a romantic might say) of some little impediment. "Uh, she used to like, as you know, driving around in her Mercedes. She —" He took a quick, deep breath. "She never knew where she was going. She was just exploring the area, to get the—the lay of the land, as she said. One day she wound up here in Madison around lunchtime and stopped here to eat. She loved it. But, at that time, the place wasn't really doing so good. George had been sick. Some weird disease. They finally figured it out, but the medical costs were a lot, and they were going to lose the place, and Lavinia thought that would be a damn shame, as she said, and so I came in and, you know, gave them a lot of money."

"And took half interest in the place," I said, meaning to be just factual, but even I could hear the underlying accusation.

"Forty-nine percent," Gene corrected my fact. "They wanted to give me fifty, but I said, no, forty-nine percent. What do I know about German beer and pizza?"

"It couldn't have been, like, say, a low-interest loan, and they could have kept it a strictly family business?"

"Adolphus..." Gene looked at me and leaned in toward me, and looked even more at me. At his size, leaning in was an intense thing, making the looking damn scary. "Lavinia changed me. Made me more, uh, whatever. But she didn't make me *not* a businessman. It was a fair deal, and George and Bettina have had no complaints. Speaking of which, here they come."

Out of the kitchen, each carrying a large platter, came a couple, maybe in their sixties. For a lover of German beer, George looked as if he never touched the stuff. He was a thin, medium height man with a sharp face and a long nose under which there was the most precise mustache I had ever seen. He had slicked-back black hair with gray extending up just a little bit from the temples. Bettina had a perfectly voluptuous figure, even if it carried a few more pounds than it should have. Her hair may have been going gray, but she wasn't about to let the world know that. She had a sensual mother's face, which was less disturbing than it sounds. They laid down their platters, and our eyes feasted on individual slices of many types of pizza. It was like a convention of pizza species.

"So, what I asked George and Bettina to do was to bring us a bunch of their different pizzas we could sample. Fun, huh?"

"Wow!" Peggy said. She was ready to dig in.

"Oh, yeah, fine," I said, in a fit of sudden offended anger. "But we can't eat all this food." I was thinking of the whole pizzas back in the kitchen from whence these representatives to the convention came from. "How much food is going to go to waste? In a world of hunger? Christ, can you be anymore the typical oblivious millionaire, Gene?"

Peggy looked at me as if I had just insulted a king or a queen or a god or a screen legend. Gene, the smug bastard, just smiled and said, "Troop 414."

"What?"

"Boy Scout Troop 414," Bettina said.

"They have more Eagle Scouts than any other troop in the San Gabriel Valley," Gene stated the simple fact.

"All of Madison is very proud of them," George said and pointed to several pictures on the walls of the pizzeria featuring eager young scouts doing eager young scouting things.

"Tonight's their Merit Badge Awards Dinner," Gene said. "It's a huge troop. Usually, it's a potluck. You know, each family brings something."

(All this gave me a slight horror movie chill, but I can't explain why now).

"But tonight," Gene continued, "all the pizzas these slices came from are over at the high school gym where the dinner is being held, and George and Bettina's waiters are there serving the scouts and their families. All donated, of course. No beer, though. We obviously didn't send over any beer. But *we* can have some beer, though, can't we, George?"

"Of course," George said, and, with alacrity, fetched some laminated drinks menus that listed all the German beers on offer, each with a short explanation of their particular virtues. George handed one menu to each of us. I thanked him for mine and immediately hid my chagrined face behind it, studying it with an academic's passion for particulars. Peggy seemed genuinely fascinated by the list. But that didn't stop her from chuckling breathily and quietly, although not so quietly that I couldn't hear her.

When we got to the sampling of pizza slices, I stuck mainly to the most traditional ones, although Peggy, using very subtle shame, made me take a bite of the cuttlefish pizza. The smile on my face as I chewed belied the abomination of taste happening behind the smile. I wasn't sure I was actually going to be able to swallow it. But I managed—with an image of little cuttlefishes swimming down my gullet and into the pool of my poor stomach. I took a swallow of the beer I had chosen, the lightest one on the menu, assuming the alcohol would kill the little creatures. Peggy seemed to enjoy her slice. But then she, throughout the evening, also swallowed three mugs of different very dark samples of liquid German pride. She was a happy *Frau*. Gene seemed to be in his element, consuming many slices of pizza, feeding the man-monster that he was, and lubricating the feed with mug after mug of beer.

And yet, when we came to that moment when we all knew we were done, I was the first one to burp—several times. Peggy competitively tried to match me burp for burp. And Gene, who one would have expected to have been the champion of burps, burped not once.

But he did give me a long look, bringing a silence upon the near-empty pizzeria. Finally, he said, "So, how are you feeling?"

"Feeling?"

"I mean, your ribs? Are you fully healed?"

"Uh, yes, that's what they tell me. For the *second* time."

"And I'll always be sorry for that. But, you do understand, neither time was from, you know, meanness, or anything?"

"Yes, Gene. Oddball accidents, that's all they were," I conceded for some reason.

"I'm glad you're fully healed again."

"Yeah, me too."

"That means you can get back to having some good sex with Peggy, right?"

I would not have believed it, but Peggy blushed. I forcibly stopped my jaw from dropping. And Gene remained obliviously unchanged. "Uh, well—I've never had bad sex with her," I was happy to admit.

Peggy stood suddenly, swaying just a little, and asked, "Does this pizzeria have a piss-eria?"

"Over there," Gene said, pointing to *over there*.

"Thanks!" Peggy headed to *over there*, shouting back, "Don't talk about me when I'm gone."

Now it was my turn to look at Gene. I mean closely—something I had mostly avoided doing during our adult encounters. I didn't really want to look deeply into the face of evil, the smug, twisted, mocking one I remembered from our high school campus, the gym showers and locker room, the student store where he once surreptitiously punched me in my kidneys. And certainly not from that moment of immediacy and concentration his visage had displayed during the backyard flailing of my face. But that face of his was no longer there, except in the basic configuration of parts, parts now grown older, bulkier, wider. But what was there? This is what I didn't know. And a lack of knowledge often generates assumptions, fears, and prejudices. Not that those assumptions, fears, and prejudices are always wrong.

"So you guys," I said to Gene once Peggy had fully exited, "uh, have been seeing a lot of each other during my, uh—convalescence."

"We've become, I would like to think, friends, yes," Gene said. "It was a way to get to know you better."

"To get to know *me* better?"

"Well, I have to know you, don't I? I mean, to love you."

"Gene, let's stick with the pizza and beer."

"Well, Adolphus, it's just the facts. You're a historian. You should like the facts."

"So you've been pumping Peggy for information about me?"

"I wouldn't quite put it that way."

"Okay. Well, have you been pumping Peggy herself at all?"

"I don't know what you mean by that."

"Oh, come on, Peggy's a highly sexual person. I've been out of commission. Have you been filling in for me? Out of love for me, of course, which would be damn nice of you."

"What? No, of course not—unthinkable."

"Unthinkable? So you don't like my taste in women."

"No, it's not—you don't—I mean—" Then Gene said the most surprising thing I think I had ever heard. "Look, I will never, ever have sex again for the rest of my life."

"What?"

"You know, I only had sex with whores before Lavinia."

"Really?"

"Mainly for convenience sake."

"Well, yeah, I can see the advantages there."

"They were professionals," he said with a measure of admiration.

"Well, yeah, sure. Did the whores have an association? I mean, like the AMA or the Bar Association?"

"No. But we did often associate in bars."

I laughed. I laughed at the son-of-a-bitch. No! I laughed *with* the son-of-a-bitch. It was funny, damn it! I hated laughing with the son-of-a-bitch!

"Many of them were pretty good businesswomen too. Knew what they were doing. I mean, how to market and provide a service."

"I'm happy to hear the American prostitute is a credit to commerce."

"Oh, they weren't always American."

"Okay."

"But—with Lavinia—it wasn't professionalism."

"No, I don't suspect—"

"She took me to sexual heights I never knew could be reached. I was, you know, really taken aback by that. I tried to figure out the difference. I mean, Lavinia was a woman, like the prostitutes were women. Had the same, you know, equipment and stuff, but—I mean the whores were good, very good, I mean I could afford the best. But still, with Lavinia..." He stopped. He knew the answer, but I think he was afraid that the answer was too simple, too facile. It was the only one he had, though, so he finally just said it. "Look, the difference was, you know, that I didn't love any of those prostitutes."

"Which makes me nervous when you say you want to love me."

"No, no, you know there is nothing sexual in our relationship."

"No. Physical on occasion, but certainly not sexual."

"Get serious here, will you, Adolphus."

"I'm sorry."

"I'll never know love like Lavinia's again. The idea of even thinking I could makes me—and I'm not kidding, now—physically ill. As for sex again, with prostitutes or whoever, what would it be? Just a mechanical process. No, that part of my life is over. But love, Adolphus, love that is the counterweight to hate, which I have known—sadly. That's all I have left. But not some, you know, dorky, spiritual love for everybody and everything and the whole world, which is the field upon which I conduct business—that's not going to happen. Things irritate me too much. I may no longer be a bully—and, yes, I admit I was—and Lavinia snatched that from me, which I don't regret, but I still think of myself as a bull. I used to be mean and unfair and tough. Now I try to be dispassionate and fair, but still tough—just a good businessman. But I have to have love, Adolphus; I have to have some focus of love—to counteract hate. That's what Lavinia gave me. That's all that I have left from Lavinia—a capacity for love. And you, you damn, sorry, short son-of-a-bitch, whether you like it or not, you are going to be the focus of that love. As you once were the focus of my hate."

My jaw now slowly dropped as my whole mouth widened. I struggled to find something to say. I made two or three attempts, but nothing coherent came out of my mouth. Then I was rescued by Peggy's return.

"Well, boys, miss me?"

"Peggy, you drunk?" Gene asked her.

"Not anymore."

"Good, then come home with me, you and Adolphus. I want to show you guys something."

21

W e thanked and said goodbye to George and Bettina, and then Gene marched us out of Schwarzkopf's Pizzeria and down the street to his Rolls Royce. Peggy called shotgun and slipped into the front passenger seat as if she had done it often. I got into the back, which was cavernous, and sat there alone, feeling abandoned and foolish and childlike. Peggy and Gene chit-chatted as we drove to San Marino, and I sat there doing my best to ignore whatever they were talking about while hearing every word.

When we got to Gene's home, the same mansion I had been to that strange and disturbing afternoon a few years before, he pulled up to the front door and hit the car horn, letting it blare for a couple of seconds. As we were getting out of the car, Maria, one of the two maids who had served us that afternoon, opened the front door, and a golden illumination spilled out. "Good evening, Mr. Eugene," she said.

"Hi, listen, Maria, how about making a pot of coffee for us? We'll have it in the great room."

"Of course, Mr. Eugene," Maria said as she left on her mission.

"Come with me, come with me," Gene said to us, a little anxious excitement in his voice as he led us through the grand foyer, between and under the two sweeping staircases, through a door, and into what

I would call a living room and Gene had just called the great room. Well, it was awfully large, and if people think that's a "great" thing, then so be it. I had briefly been in it once before, and it was as richly appointed as I remember it and unchanged, except for an addition that I knew must be the reason Gene had brought us here. He walked over to it and stood before it, looking up at it while gesturing toward it to direct our attention. "What do you think?"

Over a massive fireplace was a large oil painting of Lavinia.

It was stunning. I was almost overpowered by it, feeling suddenly unbalanced, although I didn't lose my balance. I have no idea why not, but somehow I managed to stand my ground. And yet, it didn't quite feel like I was standing on it. "My, God... That's—it's—her."

"Good, isn't it," Gene said without taking his eyes off the portrait.

Good? It was an entirely accurate representation of a woman I had known for only a short time. And yet, staring up at it now, it was as if I had never known anyone as intimately. It would be facile to say that it "looked just like her" for it was far more than that. It *felt* just like her. It radiated her in precisely the same way she had radiated herself. It wasn't a full-length portrait. It was from the mid-torso, and Lavinia was placed in front of a nondescript dark, almost black background. She existed there not in a place—how ordinary—but a space —how celestial—that she occupied fully. Her hair was exactly as I remembered. Her mouth had that slightly goofy look as it formed a smile. And her eyes—well, they were really the focus of the whole piece. Unlike some portraits, she was not looking off to the side or somewhere beyond in the distance; she was looking right at you, compelling you to look right back. The portrait was embracing, enchanting, and delightful. I knew as a hard and solid fact that the painting was nothing but an inanimate object, just a canvas in a frame covered with oil-based paints. And yet, I was convinced that I could see Lavinia's chest rise and fall with breath. I expected this oil-based Lavinia to say something. But the next voice in the room was Peggy's.

"She was quite beautiful. It's lovely, Eugene, just lovely."

"Thank you."

"How…?" I asked, wanting to know where the hell the magic of this thing came from. Gene knew exactly what I was asking.

"The interesting thing is, Adolphus, I commissioned it and had it painted after her death. I did a lot of research into artists, I mean world-class artists, who paint real portraits. I mean, you know, I didn't want something that looked like Picasso or any of that crap, couldn't have that. Anyway, I found this artist in Canada, in Montreal. I really liked her work. She's actually the granddaughter of a famous photographer of portraits. I can't think of his name; she doesn't have the same name. She spent her childhood practically in his studio and, oddly, didn't become a photographer. But she got this passion for capturing people in the old fashioned way, I guess, you know, with paint. But the way she works is from photographs, usually from ones she's taken, posing the subject out and everything. Of course, we couldn't do that for Lavinia, but, fortunately, I had taken a lot of pictures of her. And video—a lot of videos. She hated that. I snuck up on her a lot. And yet—I think she loved it too. It was attention like she had never had before. Anyway, Sarah—that's the artist—Sarah took them all to study. And I told her what I wanted. I told her I didn't want her to memorialize Lavinia with some—dead picture of a dead woman. I told her I wanted this Lavinia, as alive as possible. She took everything and went back to Montreal and worked on it for a year. She told me it drove her nuts, that it was the most difficult commission she had ever had, but she was determined to get it right. She kept apologizing for taking a long time. But I never pressured her. "You're not God," I told her, "I don't expect it in seven days." It was a strange year. I felt—empty. But I filled it with anticipation. Then Sarah called me up and said, 'I've got her!' I rushed up to Montreal. And, as you can see—she had. I paid her twice what she had asked."

"Can I sit?" I asked.

"Of course you can sit; why would you think you couldn't sit?"

"I don't know. It's a room that almost looks like you shouldn't sit in it. You just stand and look at it."

"Don't be stupid. Of course, you can sit here, anywhere. Sit on a damn table if you want to."

I did not sit on a damn table. I sat on a chair that somehow was luxurious in its utilitarian function. I picked it because it was positioned to allow me to continue to look up at the portrait of Lavinia.

Peggy could not then, or possibly ever, have felt what Gene and I felt. A feeling Gene had by now long reveled in, but one intensely new to me. It must have given me an unusual aspect, something alien to the Ass she knew so well. "Are you okay?" she asked with genuine and anxious concern.

"Sure he's okay," Gene said rather cheerfully. "Except that he loved Lavinia too."

"No, I didn't, I…" I was trying to figure out how to defend myself.

"Sure you did. Not like I loved Lavinia. Not romantically, I know that. But, well—that was Lavinia. Do you think there has ever been anyone ever like her?"

"Gene, I can't answer that. But I know I've never seen anything like this before in my life. Of course, I don't think I've ever seen a painting of anyone I actually knew, but I've certainly seen a lot of portraits. But this is… It's quite a tribute you've made here."

"I didn't do it as a tribute. I did it totally for selfish reasons. I couldn't live without Lavinia. I couldn't go on. But what do we love when we love a person? Not the hair and the eyes; an attractive figure or the face. Not even their personality or smile or laughter or voice. But a combination of all those boiled down to some essence. I told Sarah, don't paint the person, paint the essence."

"When did you become a poet?" I asked Gene quite seriously.

"I'm not. I just broke it down, analyzed it, like I would a business I'm considering investing in."

"You mean, you wanted to find Lavinia's bottom line?" I said, meaning any and all of the insult Gene may have perceived from the question. But it did not faze him.

"The bottom line is not the essence of a company. Lavinia taught me that."

That was all he said, obviously feeling he needed to say no more.

"Well," Peggy said, still on the outside, "it's beautiful, absolutely gorgeous."

"It's not gorgeous," Gene said.

"I agree," I said. "It's just—"

"Lavinia," Gene made the statement for both of us.

We were both still staring at the portrait. And I suspect Peggy was staring at us, most likely desperate to crack wise. But she didn't.

"But, there's more," Gene, in a burst of bright cheer, said.

Maria walked in with coffee.

"And once we've had our coffee, I'll show it to you."

T he coffee was a good idea. Maria laid the coffee tray down on a large and long, heavy, dark wood table surrounded by an arrangement of big, well-cushioned furniture. Facing the table on each of its long sides were couches big enough to bring refugees over from Cuba, and at one end sat two very ornate matching chairs. Gene led us to sit on this furniture that still looked to me as if it was for display only. He sat on one of the couches, and Peggy joined him on that same couch. I sat on one of the chairs. I was afraid I would get lost on one of the couches. Also, sitting on the chair conveniently positioned me with my back to Lavinia's portrait. Otherwise, I would not have been able to take my eyes off of it.

Maria poured us each a cup of coffee and indicated the plate of small pastries on the tray. I decided to concentrate wholly on whatever Gene and Peggy had decided to chit-chat about, and chit-chat they did, talking mainly about the extent of Gene's rock and sand empire.

"It's a stupid business in some ways," Gene admitted. "I mean, just digging up crap from the ground; selling it to people. And yet..."

Peggy looked at him and angled her head in a sympathetic and encouraging gesture that may also have been a bit flirty. You know, that feigned interest in what interests your interlocutor, usually a member of the opposite sex, or even same-sex if sex was the real subject at hand. "And yet?"

"Well, it does provide building material, doesn't it? Man the builder, and all that. Essential stuff, I suppose."

"Sure," Peggy said. "Not a bad legacy."

"Yes," I was compelled to contribute. "You could have a great big gravestone that reads: HERE LIES EUGENE PYTKA CARSON UNDER A STONE THAT CAME FROM ONE OF HIS OWN QUARRIES."

After giving all her attention to Gene, Peggy gave it to me with a look of disappointment that tried its best to shame me. But I was not in a mood to be shamed.

Gene, oddly, looked up to the ceiling, which was far above us. At first, I thought that he was looking for something or seeing something up there he thought was wrong. But I was wrong. He stayed in this position for just a second or two, then lowered his head and said, "How about: HERE LIES EUGENE CARSON UNDER THE GROUND HE SO OFTEN DUG UP.

Peggy laughed a reflex laugh. Gene looked satisfied. I silently damned the man for not being susceptible to my passive-aggressive bullying. There would be no scars on him, no-siree!

"In any case, I've decided to diversify."

"Into what, soil?" Abject failure didn't seem to deter me from failing again.

"No," Gene pretended to take my question seriously. "I'm moving outside of the solid material of aggregates to something a bit more ethereal, although hopefully not ephemeral. I'm talking about capital investments."

"So, you're just playing the market."

"No, not at all. I'm talking about venture capital. I have a lot of it."

"Venture or capital?"

"A bit of both, I guess. What I'm getting into is these dot com ventures,"

My head being much in history, I was often not cognizant of the present. I had no idea what he was talking about.

"It's the internet and all that, the World Wide Web. I'm finding all these companies, bright young guys—"

"No women?" Peggy wanted to know.

"Not so far. But if you hear of one... Anyway, companies that use the internet, or build services for the internet, or are provided through the internet. I mean, there's so much potential there. When some proposal instinctually hits me as useful, that's when I go in and invest. It's, uh, it's kind of exciting."

"I can see," I said without realizing I was going to say it, "Lavinia getting excited about that."

"Yeah." Gene's eyes darted up toward the portrait. "She would have, wouldn't she? Maybe..."

Silence suddenly came upon us. I'm not sure it was awkward, but it certainly wasn't comfortable. Finally, Peggy spoke up. "Hey, Eugene, did you, uh, ever read that, uh, that thing I gave you?"

"What?"

"You know, that thing I gave you." Peggy not-so-subtly gestured with her head toward me.

"Oh, yeah, I did. It was excellent, Adolphus."

"What are we talking about?" The scent of a conspiracy was in the air.

"You're, um... What do you call it, Peggy?"

"His Master's thesis."

"Yeah, you're Master's thesis."

"You read my Master's thesis?"

"Yeah, I gave it to him to read," Peggy said with some defensive pride.

"You gave it to him to read?"

"Yes, A.S., I just said that."

"I found it fascinating, Gene said. I didn't realize that our Founding Fathers had been so inspired by Greek and Roman history, you know, early democracy, and the Roman Republic and all that."

"And *all* that," I said defensively, although I had no idea what I was defending.

"It wasn't hard to understand."

"Oh. Well, good. I'm happy to hear it." So it was rudimentary, was it? Simple, was it? If the likes of Gene Pytka could understand it.

"You know, I think of writing coming from colleges and such as being kind of, you know, elitist and obscure for the likes of me to understand."

Now the son-of-a-bitch was a mind reader!

"But yours was good. Even funny now and then."

"Yeah, which almost prevented me from getting my Master's. A couple on the thesis committee—"

"But you did get it," Peggy cut me off. She had heard the story before.

"I squeaked by."

"Does it matter? Now?" Peggy asked.

"No, I guess not. What really matters is why you gave it to Gene to read."

"Why not?"

"Don't do that, Peggy. Answer me directly."

"Was it private?" she asked, smiling.

"No, of course not, but—"

"Adolphus, I asked her for it. Or, rather, she suggested it when I asked for a way to get to know you better while you were healing and, let's face it, you would not have welcomed a visit from me. She said you put a lot of yourself into this thesis, so it was a good start. And I was very impressed."

To impress a beast—this was the goal of my life? No, but... "Well, okay. Thank you."

"Now, are you all done?" Gene meant done with our coffee and not with my protestations. "Let me show you that something else."

Gene marched us—again—through the house, toward the back, through a utility area, to a door. He opened the door while hitting a light switch next to it, and illumination was brought to a long stair-case heading down. He led us down it to a small room. At the far end was a vault-like door, which Gene opened through a combination. As he swung that door open, the room beyond it was dark, but by the time the door was completely open, the room was brightly lit. It was a long, high-ceilinged, rectangular room bare of any furniture and nothing on the walls except a small climate control panel and—

To our left, side by side with ample space in between, hung three portraits of Lavinia. They were all the same size as the one in the great room. In each, Lavinia was in a similar pose as in the portrait upstairs. But there were differences in the clothing and the background. At first, I thought these were rejected attempts until the painter had gotten it right. But in looking them over, the reality of what they were became strangely, oddly, surrealistically clear. They were portraits of Lavinia progressively aging.

"The first one," Gene said, pointing to the one on the far left, "is of Lavinia in ten years' time. The next is Lavinia in twenty years. And the third is, obviously, Lavinia as she would have looked in thirty years. In ten years, the first one will replace the one that's in the great room now. In twenty years, the second one will replace that one. And in thirty years, the last one will replace the second one."

"Gene, I…" I found no more words to complete a statement.

"I brought in a couple of experts on aging, even a forensic anthropologist to consult with Sarah. She found it, as she said, a most fascinating experience and experiment."

"Eugene… Why?" Peggy asked, finally, *finally*, flummoxed by this man.

"I wanted to grow old with her," Gene said. "I didn't want to become an old man daily staring at a portrait of my young, dead wife, like someone out of some old black and white movie. I want to grow with Lavinia. I want our love to mature along with us."

"There's only three," I noted.

"Well, I figured in thirty years I'll probably be—what?—within ten years of death. Plus, she'd be younger; she might have chosen to have a facelift. Well, anyway, this is where I stopped."

It was the type of evening that in a movie would have given the protagonist weird dreams and possibly nightmares. And I fully expected to have some and may have had some if I had slept that night. But it was one of those nights—you've had them—where the mind refuses to shut off, it kept replaying the evening—not just our time with Gene, but some unpleasantness with Peggy after that.

Gene had the town car take us back to South Pasadena. We rode in silence. Of course, we were tired, but it was more, at least in my case. Anything I wanted to say, I didn't want the driver to hear. When we got to my house and entered, and turned the lights on, we stood in the middle of my living room—so much smaller than Gene's great room —and stared at each other for a few seconds.

"Well," I finally said, "he's either the most romantic grieving lover in the history of mankind—excuse me—humankind. Or he's a total nutjob."

"Well," Peggy said as she laid her purse on the couch, "I vote for romance, grief, and love."

"Yeah, you would, but you're a girl."

"Oh, don't do that, little man."

"You guys have more natural empathy than men."

"That should be a good thing, shouldn't it? Shouldn't men maybe learn something from that?"

"Look—he's a bully, he's nothing but a big bully. He's a big beast of a hulk of a bully. You may think he's been doing some altruistic things that we've benefited from, but, basically, he's been forcing himself on us, buying us, owning us, manipulating us."

"He's a man in pain, Adolphus."

"He's a man in pain? It seems to me that in my relationship with Gene Pytka that I'm the one who's been in pain."

"Not like this. This is a true psychic suffering. Eugene's in pain and suffering from grief and looking for redemption, all at the same time."

"Redemption? I don't believe in redemption. Gene's the same ugly bastard he was when we were kids, except he talks better now."

"You're truly an ass, Ass! I'm going home."

I'm going home—such a horrible thing to say, such a slice-of-the-heart and impalement-of-the gut thing to say. Like, *I'm taking my ball and going home.* Or, *I'm going home to my mother.* Or, *I don't ever want to see you again.* Or, *I don't ever want to speak to you again.* Or, *Get away from me, you stink!* "No, please, stay, it's late."

"I'm going home."

"Why go out again? Stay. Come on, let's go to bed, let's go to sleep."

"I'm not sure I can sleep."

"Okay, so, I'll tell you what, I'll make us both warm cups of milk, and we'll put on one of those Bill Moyers' *Power of Myth* videos you got me. You know they always put us to sleep."

"No. Thanks, Adolphus, but I want to go home to *my* house, to *my* bed, and not sleep all alone in my extreme and deep disappointment in you."

She grabbed her purse on her way to the door, which she opened, passed through, and slammed shut behind her, leaving me angry—at myself.

I *had* been an ass. The truth was that I had seen something in Gene I had never seen before. The human. The frail, juggling emotions while trying not to show them, trying not to get beyond grief but to manage it human. Not to mention the desperate, trying to control reality human. Not to come to terms with it, but to dictate the terms of it. He was such a businessman. But then, I had to admit, business is such a human occupation.

Where was the Bully? The bully hadn't gone away. I had not been wrong in what I said to Peggy. I just hadn't been thorough. I was admitting this to myself now. But did I have to admit it to anybody else? Wouldn't that diminish me? Wouldn't that be giving in to the bully?

So I laid awake—all night. I did not make myself a warm cup of milk. I did not watch Bill Moyers. Because—honestly—I did not want to go to sleep.

And in the morning, a Saturday morning, I called Peggy.

"Oh. Hello," Peggy answered unenthusiastically when she heard my voice.

"Did you sleep?"

"Actually, yes, I did, like a baby."

"I've always thought that an odd phrase."

"What?"

"'Sleep like a baby.' Don't they keep their parents up all night crying?"

She sighed, her warm breath exciting her telephone mouthpiece. "You know nothing about babies, do you?"

"Well, I was one once."

"I have my doubts. Babies sleep most of the damn day. You know, twenty hours or something."

"How would you know that?"

"I know that because most reasonable, non-oblivious people know that."

"I'm sorry."

Peggy did not respond.

"I think," I added.

"Sorry about what? And why do you have to think about it?"

"Sorry I made you mad last night—I don't have to think about that. I truly am. And sorry that I seem to have been unfair about Gene. That's the one I'm still thinking about."

"Well—at least you're thinking."

"Yeah. It's painful. Sometimes I think non-thinkers have it easier."

"Ignorance being bliss and all that?"

"Sort of. But more, that it's not that non-thinkers don't think, but that they think only once. You know—stick with first impressions and defend them to the death. Gene was a monster in my mind, hard, unbending, you know, rock-solid."

"No pun intended?"

"No, actually, I intended the pun. He dwelt there—in my mind— heavy and hard and bruising. I had managed, though, to push him into some dark corner, tuck him away, out of sight of Mnemosyne."

"What?"

"That Greek goddess of memory."

"Stop showing off."

"What? Everybody knows—"

"No, everybody doesn't know."

"Yeah, okay, you're right. Crap, I'm really feeling horrible."

"Why?"

"I don't know. Peggy, you don't really know Gene, the Gene I knew, and what—"

"I know he bullied you without mercy."

"How did you—"

"He told me. He told me all about it. He told me some of the things he did to you. Some of them were actually kind of funny. Like how you got your first boob feel."

"What?"

"Look, kids get bullied, Adolphus, happens all the time. Most live through it, and most forget about it."

"Well that's what I did, but—"

"No, you just suppressed it. But, geez—"

"Are you going to tell me to 'Man up'?"

"Well, no, what I'm saying—"

"I mean, you are trying to trivialize something that is not trivial."

"But it is, don't you—"

"Did he tell you how I got the scars on my face?"

"What scars?"

"Oh, come on, Peggy, we've been as intimate as a couple can be; I'm sure you've noticed the scars under my beard. Haven't you combed it for me on occasion?"

"Well, you comb my—"

"Let's stick to my face?"

"Okay. Yeah, I've noticed them."

"You never asked about them."

"You were covering them with a beard. I figured it was none of my business. Probably fell off your bike or something, I assumed. It didn't matter anyway, it didn't matter to me, I still loved your—"

"Gene caused them."

"Oh."

And then I told her the story. The event I have already described here, so I will not repeat it. But besides the, shall I say, raw details, I tried—ironically, given our previous evening—to paint her a portrait of Gene's stunning visage of hate that had been pushed through my eyes and into my brain. And of how it felt to have been the object, the recipient of that hate. The voice coming out of me telling this story, painting this portrait, was certainly different than any voice she had ever heard coming out of me before. A voice indicative of something grave, profound, disturbing within an exposed emotion, the kind women sometimes like to see in their men because women are, after all, maybe, sort of, or at least it seems, more empathetic than men. Or, if not more compassionate and understanding, more willing to enjoy the catharsis of being empathetic.

"The funny thing is," I continued, "when you feel so much hate coming your way, you want to jump on the bandwagon."

"What?"

"You want to hate you too. There must be some reason to because there it was—in your face."

"But, Adolphus, I've never known anyone less prone to self-loathing than you."

"You called me 'little man.'"

"Um…"

"Last night."

"I was mad, you were—"

"Not 'Ass,' which I'm happy to acknowledge on occasion. But 'little man.' Compared to what, Peggy? Your Eugene? Or worse, my Gene?"

"I wasn't comparing you to anything—anybody."

"The son-of-a-bitch, the man-monster, suddenly shows back up in my life announcing death and then crushing me. But not just physically. With his success, his wealth, his—his striding across the open land while I—I scamper from bush to bush."

"Adolphus, are you drinking?"

"Only coffee."

"Why don't we—"

"Hate. Hate in many guises. Hate hidden and hate out in the open. I'm sick of it."

"As is, I think, Eugene. Did you ever consider that?"

"Maybe. So I will let Gene love me. Not that I know what that really means. But I'll stop fighting it. Not for his sake. For mine, I guess."

"How?"

"I don't know. More pizza and beer?"

"But no cuttlefish."

"No cuttlefish."

"I think that's wise."

"I think it's unavoidable."

"Do you want me to come over?"

"I want to sleep. *I'm* the one who didn't sleep last night. But later, maybe, tonight."

"Do you want to go to a movie?"

"No. I want you to fuck me."

"You don't really have to be crude."

"It's just a man's excuse to get the woman to hold him."

I'm willing to bet Peggy smiled at that. "Okay," she said, "I'll see you tonight."

22

Letting Gene love me was the worst mistake I ever made. It was also, outside of one other, the best decision I ever made. But knowing that would take a while. I didn't announce to Gene, as I had to Peggy, that I was going to allow him to love me. I figured I would just let things flow naturally. After all, I had gone out and had pizza and beer with him; he probably assumed everything was okay after that and that everything was as he would wish. Besides, how does one make such an announcement in a situation like this? You couldn't tell me. No one could have told me. For there had never been a situation like this. Also, I was afraid if I made some grand announcement, he would be so happy he would give me a great big hug, and there I would be again with two broken ribs.

So I returned to PCC, happy to be teaching my classes again, getting back into the life of a community college teacher bathed in the sunshine of Southern California. And the smog that backed up against the San Gabriel Mountains and settled down upon Pasadena. Things pretty much returned to normal. I liked some of my students; I didn't like others. I avoided most administrative duties and tried to avoid being put on committees. Peggy and I attended concerts, plays, and comedy shows together. I managed to deflect a big-eyed little girl from the neighborhood who tried to get me to adopt a kitten from her cat's recent litter. The thing I most loved returning to was planning our summer study trip with select students. Preparing it in detail while gleefully adding up how much of my new "lover's" money we would spend. That year, though, even if it meant spending less of Gene's capital, I decided we would not go to Europe and the Mediterranean terrain of ancient Greece. I decided to pay attention to those students most interested in American history. I put together a six-week tour of Revolutionary and Civil War sites, during which I would conduct a running seminar not only on those two book-end wars but on the development of America in between them.

Peggy came along but often went off on her own to explore and visit with neurobiologists she had started corresponding with. One day she came to my hotel room (we always took separate rooms for propriety and privacy). She told me there was something she wanted to show me, so I and everyone else were going to get the afternoon off, no matter what I had scheduled. The students were not unhappy with this change in the schedule. Unbeknownst to me at the time, and I still find it a bit surprising, too much of me can be, I guess, too much.

We were in Pennsylvania at the time. But in a rented car, she drove me to Delaware, to Wilmington, to Brandywine Park, where we parked. She took me by the hand and guided me through the lovely grounds until we got to—

"The Brandywine River!" Peggy swept her right arm out toward the river as if she was Mother Nature bringing it into existence.

"Some people call it a creek."

"'Some people' can go to hell. I think it's the most beautiful thing I've ever seen."

"You know, it was on my itinerary. The Battle of Brandywine Creek and all that."

"That's in Pennsylvania."

"Oh. Same water, though."

"I didn't want you to see it first with anyone but me."

I had to admit, there was something nice about that. But I didn't quite know how to address it. So I looked out over the river, which wasn't that wide, which is probably why it is also called a creek. There were masses of green foliage on each bank: tall trees and squat bushy trees (pardon my lack of a botanical vocabulary). The water flowed rapidly, sparkling in the sun, but looking deep, cold, clear, and vital when it passed through shaded areas. Reflections of the trees that caused the shade danced on the kinetic surface. The facile thing to say was that it looked like a painting of an early American landscape (or a late *Native-American* landscape, some might think), so I won't say that. But that doesn't mean I didn't feel it.

"Growing up in L.A.," Peggy said, "living in L.A., my God, we don't live with something like this. I mean, the Los Angeles River, give me a break."

"I know." There was regret in my voice, which surprised me.

"Can you imagine living by a river like this? To be able to see it daily."

"Oh, come on, don't make yourself dissatisfied with your life."

"I'm serious, Adolphus. I would kill for this."

"Peggy?"

"I just feel so *real* here. That's why I wanted you to see it with me. To see if you feel it."

"I don't quite know what that means: feeling real here."

"Then you don't feel it."

"Well, I don't know. It's beautiful, of course. It's good, I like it. But you know what I like more?"

"No, what?"

"Seeing you loving it."

She looked at me. Askance at first, then sweetly, then askance again. "I can't judge your sincerity in that."

"I'm always sincere."

"Sure, sure, now and then, on occasion, when you can spare a little."

I'm sorry to report that she was entirely sincere in that assessment.

One of the best things about this study trip was that Gene was nowhere in sight. I was able to forget about him for a while. But such wasn't the case about a week after the pizza and beer and aging portraits night. It was a Saturday afternoon, and I was alone in my house reading a mystery that Peggy had challenged me to figure out who the murderer was before I got to the end. I don't know why she insisted on doing this, knowing that I almost always fail. But I suspected it was a display of her superiority in this that she thought I needed reminding of to keep me in line. No—that's mean. Maybe it really was just her enthusiasm for the book. Which I also liked, I just didn't really care to expend the mental energy to—

There was a knock at the front door. Unless it was a delivery of food, of which I had ordered none, or Peggy, who I knew had booked herself into a neurobiological weekend seminar in Phoenix, or possibly a couple of my students, or Jehovah Witnesses or Mormons, who I have cursed at the door so often I was pretty sure that by this time I was on their blacklist, or Deb—no one ever knocked at my door. So I fully expected when I opened the door to find Deb.

It was not Deb. It was Gene, that tower of strength, standing on my porch, his huge Rolls Royce parked in the street in front of my house, which slightly embarrassed me.

"I thought I would come by and see where you live," Gene said, dispensing with any greeting.

"Why?"

"Because as the object and focus of my love, I need to be able to visualize your natural environment when I'm not with you. I can see you in a classroom standing before students, that's no problem, but I couldn't get a picture of you at home."

"You could have sent your painter."

Without hearing or possibly not acknowledging my subtle witticism, Gene walked into my home, not waiting for me to invite him or even move out of the way. But my reflexes being pretty good for one who had no athletic ability, I managed to make a backward hop, skip, and jump and got the hell out of the way.

Gene stood in the middle of my living room. Dominating it, of course. "Not really what I expected."

"Sorry," I apologized insincerely.

"I mean, it's minuscule."

"Minuscule?"

"Yeah, small, you know, tiny."

"Well, it only has to fit me."

"But what about when Peggy's over?"

"She doesn't take up much space."

"It's really crap, *Adoofus*"

No, he said, "Adolphus," I just heard Adoofus. "Hey!"

"I expected something more, you know, something *proffsoral.*"

"You mean, professorial."

"Yeah, whatever the fuck."

"Well, I'm not a professor, just a lowly—"

"You know, something with nice, uh, dark heavy furniture here in the living room, and a big den where you do your thinking work. You do have a den, don't you? Or do you call it a study?"

"You're standing in it. Unless you mean my shower. I do a lot of thinking in my shower."

"This," he indicated the room with a broad gesture as if to sweep everything aside, "is both your living room and your den?"

"Gene, it's just a room, a space. Call it my all-purpose generic room."

"And those are brick and board bookcases."

"They are, yes, certainly. That's rather apparent by the fact that you can see the bricks and the boards. I haven't tried to hide them."

"I expected big heavy, tall bookcases for all your weighty tomes. But this is just pathetic.""Gene, what the hell?"

"Brick and board bookcases," Gene repeated as he shook his head. "Isn't that what young people do, I mean, you know, in their first apartment, college students in their dorm rooms or something?"

"Well, I teach college…" Was I groping for an explanation or an apology?

"Christ. Pathetic. Are the bedrooms through there?" He gestured with a nod toward a hallway.

"Bedroom, yes."

"Let's see."

"Hey!"

He moved with a lumbering grace—if you can imagine such a thing—to the hallway, through it, and into my bedroom. "Hell, there's hardly room for your bed in here."

"Well, as long as there is room for the bed, it being a bedroom, and all."

"Is this where you fuck Peggy?"

"I don't fuck Peggy; I make love to her."

Gene snapped his head around and looked at me with a piercing eye. "Bullshit!"

He was right, of course. "Well..."

He then moved out of my bedroom and took a self-guided tour of the rest of the house, which didn't take long as it consisted only of a small bathroom and a no-where-near-gourmet kitchen. "Well," he concluded, "at least it's neat."

"Neat?"

"Neat and clean. Tidy. But then I would expect you to be a good housekeeper."

He was calling me a girl! I knew that's what he was doing. Or, possibly, a girly-man, a hell of a thing to say to someone you supposedly loved. "Well, you're wrong. I happen to be a lousy housekeeper. If it was up to me, this place would be a pigsty."

"Yeah?"

"Yeah!"

"So who keeps it clean? Some illegal alien?"

"No, of course not. Peggy and Deb."

"Who's Deb?"

"She's a friend of mine. She runs the South Pasadena adult education program, you know, where I met..."

"Lavinia."

"Yeah." Sad. Suddenly I was sad.

"Would I like this, Deb?"

"I don't know. Deb's likable. I've liked her for years."

"You 'make love' to her too?"

"No, no, we're just, you know, simpatico, good friends."

"So you make this good friend, Deb, and Peggy, who you 'make love' to, clean your house?"

"I don't *make them*; they just, you know, started doing it."

"And they are both highly professional educators?"

"Well, yeah, sure."

"Pathetic. I'll tell you what, let me buy you a house."

"No!"

"Why not?"

"Why would I let you buy me a house?"

"So you don't have to live in a dump like this."

"Or so you don't have to think about me living in a dump like this."

"Okay, I'll buy that. I'll send over my real estate man with several options for you to choose from."

"No, Gene, no, you are not buying me a house."

"Huh." He was quiet for a moment. I think he was trying to see around, or through, or past the absurd notion that *I* would not let *him* do something. Then he said, "Let's see your backyard."

"No, Gene, you are not seeing my backyard."

"Why not?"

"Well, because it's basically a shit dumping ground for certain neighborhood dogs."

"Huh."

But there was no stopping him, and soon we were surveying the extent of the grounds of my estate.

"Broken fence," I said as some little explanation for the canine traffic and dumping.

"You could go out there and shovel that shit up, you know."

"I could."

"Or poison the damn dogs."

"Oh, sure, that's an option I've put on the table."

"All that brown overgrowth is dangerous, you know. Could cause a fire."

"Yeah, you're right. I should do something about it."

"I'll send over my gardeners. They'll take care of it."

"Gene—"

"Unless I can get you into a new house quickly, then we don't have to worry about it."

"You are not buying me a new house!"

Gene gave me that piercing look again, which I suddenly recognized—it was John Wayne! He stole it from John Wayne! "You like John Wayne movies, don't you?"

"Love them, why?"

"Nothing."

"You open to negotiation?"

"Negotiation for what?"

"I won't buy you a house—"

"Thank you."

"If you let me send my gardeners to take care of your yard and you let me pay for a cleaning service—legal and bonded—so that poor Peggy and this Deb don't have to pick up after you anymore. That's not fair, you know, they are two professional women, for Christ's sake."

He was right; it wasn't fair. I knew that. I had always known that. But what's knowledge when convenience is at stake? So I was thinking about it.

"Come on, make a decision."

"Okay. Agreed."

"Good." He held out his big hammy hand, and I shook it. "One other thing."

"Hey, we just—"

"I'm still going to send over my real estate man to show you some houses—just in case."

I never did let him buy me a house. His real estate agent did have me drooling a couple of times, though. But his gardeners—well, really, there was a landscape artist, then there were gardeners—turned my backyard into a paradise. Putting smack dab in the middle of it what they called a reading gazebo where I could sit in a comfortable chair and read to my delight, even at night, because they installed lighting. And I must admit I was a bit shocked by how happy Peggy and Deb were with my new cleaning service. I was not unhappy myself. I did refuse delivery on new bookcases. Which did not make Gene happy —"I mean, Christ, Adolphus, they were only from Ikea." But as I told him, I had a particular emotional investment in my bricks and boards and wanted to keep it that way.

All this was the beginning of this strange, one-sided, non-sexual "love" affair that I found myself in. A very easy affair, for I really had nothing to do to reciprocate except be the willing recipient of the benefits of Gene's love. And yet, I couldn't just let it be easy. I kept wanting to complicate it. Like when Gene called me and said:

"I'm going to take you to a ball game."

Upon hearing those words, I sunk to the lower depths of a particular hell. It's not a very crowded hell. You can stand in the middle of it and look out on a landscape of brimstone and spouting flames, and you'll be lucky to see only one or two other "souls" in torment. For it is a hell reserved for those who *hate* sports.

(Is "hate" too harsh of a word here? Especially given the unadulterated hate that I have reported on? Okay, how about abhor, dislike intensely, loathe, or have a low tolerance for?)

What? You question this? How can anyone hate sports? This is the primary reason I dislike sports—everybody else expects you to like them. But let me assure you, there are those of us who dislike sports. I have disliked them since childhood. I was probably the only person living in Southern California who hated the sound of Vin Scully's voice. It often permeated my childhood living room on a Saturday or Sunday afternoon as my dad sat in his easy-chair, a can of Lucky Lager beer in hand, watching a Dodger's baseball game on television. Watching squeezed little men running around a tiny diamond or scattering about like insects in the outfield, as Scully announced the play-by-play. Or, worse, the players standing around for long periods doing jack shit as Scully riffed on this, that, and the other. My dad always tried to get me to watch the games with him. But I refused, claiming homework or other important things to do, like rereading comic books. Dad would look at me with disappointment and pity. You see, this hell I speak about is not for those who just dislike sports. It's hell for those who have to put up with other people thinking they are weird for not liking sports and try to initiate you, rope you in, inculcate in you, or brainwash you to enjoy sports. In other words, sports evangelicals. Just as annoying as religious evangelicals. Or the bubonic plague. Why they aren't sent to some hell instead of we poor bastards, I don't know, except to say that life ain't fair.

Now let me stop you before you get started. Because I know you want to tell me that sports builds character, engenders camaraderie, and offer the joy of being part of a team. Well, so does serving in a war, and that can get you killed. I mean, let's break that down. *Builds character.* The only thing sports builds is massive, expensive stadiums, usually with taxpayers' money. *Engenders camaraderie.* Yeah —for one team only. Other teams can go to hell as you crush them into the dirt. *The joy of being a part of a team*—tell that to those usually stuck on the bench or in the dugout earning a pittance compared to what the "star" players make and who will never have an athletic shoe named after them—not even a jock-strap. And shouldn't we finally dispense with the old canard, "It's not whether you win or lose, it's how you play the game"? It *is* about whether you win or lose, usually because a monetary value is attached to the outcome. How you play the game only comes up when a decision has to be made: Steroids or no steroids. All this is true even in the amateur athletics—as it is still laughingly called—of the Olympics. You don't think money is involved in whether you win or lose in the Olympics? Have you never heard of commercial endorsements? And didn't you grow suspicious about the whole concept when suddenly the American Olympic basketball team was fielding a bunch of off-season pro-ball players? But I'm not just bitching about the money and chemical cheating. I don't even like the Special Olympics! And I know when I'm sent down to *that* particular hell, I will be very much alone. I mean, the modern Olympics started in

1896, at the end of the nineteenth Century, to bring nations together. And soon after that, we had two world wars in the Twentieth Century. Now that's really bringing nations together on the field of competition.

I will admit, though, that sports do bring people together—in clumps, in little clusters of humanity. And those clumps hate all the other clumps. It never fails to amuse me—am I the only one?—that when a team, professional or collegiate, wins some important championship, its home city breaks out into massive street celebrations. Featuring the excessive imbibing of intoxicating liquids, riots, and destruction of property. And, on occasion, harm to random members of this little clump of humanity. There's Character Building for you! There's Sportsmanship! It has also never failed to amuse me how a team's win is celebrated by the fans as if they—each and every individual one of them—are responsible for the success as if it was a personal win for them. But what the hell did they do? Ah, yes, they supported the team. That takes me back to high school and school spirit and the pep rallies. You know, those little incubators of unthinking, knee-jerk patriotism, which really has no relation to a genuine love of nation, but only to *Be True To Your School* morphing into *My Country Right or Wrong*. I mean, sports fans are so—tribal. And tribes are so—atavistic.

But here's maybe the real thing. As I have mentioned, I have absolutely no athletic ability at all, which I'm sure is true of many of you. And I see absolutely no reason why I should worship at the feet—or feats—of those who do. What would I be trying to do? Absorb their abilities into my own body, whose natural position is "at rest," in the hopes of experiencing what it might feel like to have those abilities? Isn't there something psychologically off about that?

Disliking sports is akin to being a socialist in a Republican household—it can deduct a bit of cheer from the holidays. But I have always stood my ground. Maybe *that's* my only athletic ability.

So when Gene called up and said, "I'm going to take you to a ball game," I thought, *Oh, God, here we go again.*

"What kind of ball game?"

"Any kind of ball game. There are a number of them, you know. Base, basket, foot."

"No, thank you, I'll pass."

"No, you won't."

"Gene, I don't like ball games."

"I know, I remember from high school. But that's why I want to take you to one."

"Why would you want to put me through such torment?'

"Because I love you. And I don't want you to miss out on something essential about the beauty of it."

"Well, if you love me, you wouldn't ask me to do something I don't like."

"You probably wouldn't like having open-heart surgery, but as someone who loves you, I would press you to do it if you needed it."

"That's a stupid analogy—no one needs ball games."

"We can bring Peggy along."

"Oh, Peggy doesn't like sports any more than I do."

"I think you'll find that she does."

"How would you know?"

"Been spending a lot of time with Peggy."

"I thought it was me you loved."

"Jealous?"

"No, but—"

"She doesn't tell you everything, you know."

"And she tells you?"

"Sure. I don't judge Peggy."

"Why not? You judge me."

"Which should prove to you that I love you and not her. You know, sometimes she's afraid of you."

"What?"

"You're a man of strong opinions."

"What's wrong with strong opinions?"

"I don't know, let me think." And he did. I guess. In any case, there was a moment of silence. Then: "Maybe strong opinions are like a strong smell. Not everyone likes them coming into their space."

"And not everyone likes ball games, so just leave me alone in this."

"No, I really don't think I can."

"Okay, I'll make a deal with you."

"A deal?" If human ears could actually prick up, I'm sure Gene's would have.

"I'll let you take me to a ball game if you come to the theater with me."

"The theater?"

"Shakespeare."

"Shakespeare?" His ears now would have drooped.

"The Royal Shakespeare Company is coming to the Ahmanson at the Music Center. Come with Peggy and me."

"Shakespeare, huh?" He was trying to find an angle out of this; I could feel that, even through the phone. "Which one?"

"*A Midsummer Night's Dream.*"

"Is that the queer one?"

"What?"

"You know, full of fairies."

"Well, yeah, fairies, but real fairies, you know, fluttering around, little wings on their backs. Not the 'I'm casting aspersions on your character' definition of the word."

"Well, look, I'm with you in concept. But instead of Shakespeare, how about a Neil Simon? I liked *The Odd Couple*. I liked it when Jack Lemmon snorted, trying to clear his ears. And that sloppy guy was really funny."

"Nope. It's either the Bard or no balls."

"Christ—you're better at negotiations than I thought you were. I'm proud of you, Adolphus!"

It was like he had patted me on the head. *Patted me on the head!* Well, I guess that's better than if he had smacked me upside it.

Unfortunately, Gene was able to arrange getting us to a basketball game before the Royal Shakespeare Company got to downtown L.A. (Damn Brits!). I was hoping that Shakespeare would scare the shit out of Gene, and he would give up this particular enterprise. But it was not to be, and one early evening he came in his Rolls Royce to collect Peggy and me and drove us to the Inglewood Forum where the NBA's Los Angeles Lakers played. The seats he got us were at the very bottom of the stadium, right there butt up against the court where you could almost smell the players' sweat. *Oh, swell!* I thought. *He did this on purpose, giving me the lowest vantage point so I would have to look up at all these abnormally tall men running frenetically back and forth for no apparent reason in their loose shorts.* Being a millionaire several times over, I thought he would put us up in some enclosed box way up high. With comfortable easy chairs to sit on, some fancy layout of delicious food to munch on, and high-powered binoculars I could use if I deigned to feign interest in the game. But no, there we were sitting on these not-comfortable seats at ground level. If this was the theater, we would have been the poor, unwashed, groundlings. Later, I found out that these were actually expensive prime seats where you can be close to the action. My question at the time, of course, was, "Who the hell wants to be close to the action?"

And then the game started.

It was the most exciting time I had ever had in my life.

The players, distinguished by their different colored jerseys if not by their heights, moved in almost vibrating, certainly kinetic patterns, seemingly random but yet not at all. Back-and-forth, time and time again they went, trying to get that damn ball through those damn hoop-secured baskets. There was speed, there were feints, the strategic passing of the ball, and unbelievable human-powered launches of that ball from long distances in gorgeous arches right to and into and through the baskets. These were moments that, to me, the most naive of neophytes, seemed to be purely supernatural and bore no relationship to the physics of the material world. But, of course, they absolutely did. It was just that my mind has never had a relationship with the physics of the material world. I got so caught up in the excitement, being right there, courtside, that if I had not had superior control over my reflexes, I swear I would have joined the game.

I became a basketball fanatic and remain so to this day. But only if I can see the game live—I never watch it on TV—and only if I can get courtside seats. Which, for years now, thanks to Gene, I've been able to afford.

Nevertheless, I still proudly maintain my extreme dislike of all other sports and stand by all my previous comments on the subject in this account.

Gene—not to mention *Eugene*—did *not* become a Shakespeare fanatic. He deeply hated *A Midsummer Night's Dream.* I got Peggy and Gene and me the best seats I could afford (I insisted on buying Gene's ticket), which were not the best seats in the house, but they were not horrible either. And Gene sat in his not-the-best but his not-horrible seat, not liking, first, the production design, which he called, "A bit airy-fairy for my taste," a comment he thought to be amusing, but it was not. And second, the production itself, which was slightly radical. And third, Shakespeare's magnificent language. "I can't understand a fucking word they're saying. Why don't they put subtitles up, like they do at operas?" I was shocked that he even knew that about operas and embarrassed by his comments because he made them as the actors were on stage in nowhere near a hushed voice. He did like Puck giving Bottom the head of a jackass. Does that surprise you?

Afterward, Peggy got me to admit that what I had forced Gene to go through was unfair. Four hundred years on, Shakespeare's words are, practically, a foreign language. Before genuinely being able to enjoy a production of any of his plays, you should study it. I have a method of doing this. First, I read a play's chapter in *Asimov's Guide to Shakespeare.* Yes, yes, I know, not quite academically accepted, but the robot master gives a clear outline of the plot while putting the play and its subject matter into historical context and decoding some of the more obscure language. Then I'll sit down and read the play while listening to an excellent audio version of a production (stage or radio), hopefully a British one. Seeing the words, reading the poetry, while a good actor is coloring them with the proper emotions and attitudes makes them far less obscure. Then, if one's available, I'll find a video of a film or television version of the play. Thus armed, I can sit relaxed and comfortable during a live production and experience it with almost Zen-like acceptance.

But I did not arm Gene with this method. I just threw him in, as one might throw a young child into a pool to teach the little snot to swim. Which is the action, I have to admit, of a bully. Peggy said I should have been ashamed of myself. And—I was. To make it up to Gene, we found a production of Neil Simon's *Brighton Beach Memoirs* and took him to it. *That,* he enjoyed. I enjoyed it also. We laughed both simultaneously and together. Believe it or not, there is a difference between those two words. And that difference was the beginning of not this cockeyed "love" affair of Gene's, but of a relationship between the two of us, which became much to my shock, but no longer dismay, an actual relationship.

A barrier came down. What had seemed an unnatural co-mingling of two disparate personalities became—friends hanging out together? Well, Eugene—yes, I started to think of him more as Eugene than Gene—thought of it as more than that. To him, our relationship was his very own love project, almost, I supposed, an emotional business arrangement. But he was nuts. I just think I got used to him. That Eugene, rather forcefully, imprinted himself on me, got into my head like a song can do, even one you don't particularly like, and the next thing you know, you're humming that damn thing or, worse, singing it in the shower. But whatever the reason, we found ourselves sharing each other's lives.

I got Eugene more closely involved in what we were doing at PCC. I wanted to show him how his money was being put to good use. I introduced him to students past and present whose lives he had changed, trying to get him to understand that they were not really just "collateral benefit" to his campaign to love me, but the central good he was doing. I think he got it and became proud of what he had done. He started teaching me some basic principles of business. Not to make me a businessman, but to explain himself, as if it was vital for me to be proud of him. I'm not sure I got it. I wasn't, quite frankly, as good of a student. To this day, I still have a natural (to me) bias against business-people. But I did manage to take the person out of the businessperson and find some common ground with him.

Which was, more often than not, Schwarzkopf's Pizzeria, where we spent many nights, sometimes with Peggy, frequently without. We actually found things to talk about; some subjects were more inter-esting to him than me, some more interesting to me than to him. And a surprising number of topics that we found equally interesting. It's a big world, after all, no matter what the late Mr. Disney had to say about it. And we had laughs, lots of laughs, often at the expense of others. Well, most laughs do come at the expense of others, don't they? Nothing brings two people closer than finding the frailty in others. Our mutual laughs usually came after several beers. So if we were ever mean, and I'm not saying we were, but if we ever were, in our little confederation of two, mean (if hilarious) in our verbalized thoughts about others, I blame demon Deutschland brew.

One of our best evenings was when Peggy and I took him to one of the last revival cinemas in L.A. to see John Wayne in *The Searchers* and *Red River*. I don't think he had ever seen John Wayne on the big screen, and he was profoundly moved. "Tell me it was Adolphus' idea and not yours," he privately asked Peggy. "Oh, it was his idea," she lied—Peggy's nice that way.

Eugene traveled a lot on business and often asked Peggy and me to go with him. Most of the time we couldn't leave because of school, but we would take him up on it when possible. We would have been fools not to. Especially if it was a trip to New York ("Give your regards to Broadway," he would say as an inducement). Or New Orleans ("Come on, you like that jazz shit, right?"). Or Amsterdam ("Stay away from those girls in the window, Adolphus"). Or London ("The place is like a damn history theme park, you gotta love it, right?"). And once Peggy and I actually took a three-week leave of absence to go with him on a business trip to Tokyo ("Home of cuttlefish pizza!"), Hong Kong ("See it before the damn Commies get it back!"), and Seoul (he tried to make a statement about "Seoul food," but it fell flat). As Gene was often concentrating with a deep focus on the business at hand, putting in a lot of time on it, Peggy and I were often off on our own in these places. We didn't think of these trips as vacations, or ourselves as tourists, but as continuing education and ourselves as students of the world. Not that we didn't have fun, enjoyed good food, marveled in the gorgeous scenery, and kept a chart of all the countries, cities, and hotels that we had sex in. But that was just "collateral benefits."

Most of Eugene's trips at this time had little to do with Ramone International Aggregates, Inc., which he had installed a new CEO to run. But with his new diverse interests as a venture capitalist, especially those dot-com companies he was always talking about, which all seemed pretty dumb to me at the time. But, of course, when quite a few of them had spectacularly successful IPOs, Eugene was transformed from a multi-millionaire to a bloody billionaire. He never crowed about this, only reported it to us as a simple matter of fact. The more successful Eugene was becoming, the more humble he became. This meant that when the dot-com bubble burst, I felt it like a blow to the gut—for him. I could have gotten some satisfaction in being right—it was all dumb after all—but my first thoughts and deep concern were for Eugene: How many millions, maybe a billion, had he lost? I called him immediately to console him if he needed it. Yes, this surprised me too.

"Don't worry about it," he said. "I got out of all those companies months ago. I didn't lose a dime."

"You son-of-a-bitch," I said, in wondrous admiration. "Was it smarts or luck?"

"Every business success is a combination of both, but probably more luck than smarts."

See—humble. I had to ask him why.

"Lavinia."

"Really?"

"With every success, I go home to share it with her. I look up at her portrait and tell her all about it. Then I hear her tell me, 'Keep it humble, Eugene, keep it humble.' So I do. Not that I'm not proud of what I've accomplished, but...."

"I understand."

When Peggy and I did not accompany Eugene on his trips, he would give us the run of his mansion in San Marino. Once he became a billionaire, you might have thought he would have left the old San Marino neighborhood behind and got himself a really nice place. You know, on Mt. Olympus, or something like that. But he didn't. It was quite apparent why; it was Lavinia's home after all. It had become quite clear that Eugene's motivation for everything in business and daily life was Lavinia. Not the memory of Lavinia, but Lavinia. Was he obsessed? I guess so. This not being a highly fanciful and romantic account, I can offer no other conclusion. Was this something I should have counseled him to seek help with? Would you have?

But it was not Lavinia's home to Peggy and me. On those times we stayed there, it was a vast funhouse of luxury, relaxation, and comfort. Just what all hard-working educators should be able to enjoy. Eugene had this incredible home theater built, and we spent many nights watching movies we loved on a big screen he had lately installed that descended from the ceiling. We slept in a guest bedroom as his (and Lavinia's) bedroom was the only room off-limits to us. But we certainly did not feel deprived. The guest bedroom was about the size of my whole house. "Of course," I could hear Eugene say, "that's not saying much." We enjoyed his big, gorgeous pool quite a lot, swimming in it and sunbathing around it in the nude. Which amused the hell out of Maria, who was always there, taking care of us, seeing to our needs, waiting on us, and, surprisingly, did not seem to resent us. If I were her, I would have wanted to kill me, who deserved this luxury no more than she did.

We were becoming spoiled, and we knew it. We searched for some guilt within us but found none. We suspected that Eugene had "bought us," that we were just living accouterments to a rich man, the latest in loyal friends—or pets. Then we scoffed at the idea. Then tried to analyze the scoffing. Then decided that we just didn't care, as the sun bathed our backs and we dreamed of the lovely meal Maria was going to prepare for us, and I looked at Peggy's perfect ass.

"Things are a lot different than they used to be," Peggy said one afternoon when we were lounging out by the pool.

"Yeah," I agreed.

"You and Eugene have become real pals."

"It's the oddest thing that's ever happened to me. I like the son-of-a-bitch. I mean, I don't like everything about him, but I do like him."

"Well, he could probably say the same."

"No, he *loves* me, remember?"

"Yeah, you've sort of become his child."

"His child? We're the same damn age."

"What does that have to do with it?"

"You're weird, Peggy."

"Yeah. But sexy, right?"

I looked over at her, lounging there, sunbathing in the nude, her skin, her lovely skin, glistening in the sun. "You're a vision; that's what you are, Margaret Kathleen Bradford."

"You're not bad yourself for an old man."

"*Older*, Peggy, but not old."

We smiled at each other, and both laid back and were soon snoozing in the sun. Later Maria came out and covered us in large beach towels to keep that sun from burning us.

I have to admit it—life was good. And Eugene was the author of much of it.

And then he blew it.

Some fluttering fairy with gossamer wings put the jackass head on him, and he became once again the bully pressing his ugly face into my handsome one.

23

I t all started with a simple, dumb question.

Eugene and I were in Schwarzkopf's Pizzeria, which, as I've mentioned, had become our hang-out. It had surprised me how relaxing those evenings were, how I could let the rest of the world fade. Which was another surprise—that I enjoyed letting the rest of the world fade. We didn't have many of them, both of us being busy, but when I knew one was coming, I began to look forward to it with warm anticipation. We had just finished consuming a super-extra-large sized sausage, mushroom, olive pizza, and not a few German beers when Eugene turned to me, leaned back a little bit, looked down on me (physically, not psychologically), and asked, "How come you're not a doctor?"

I looked back at him, wondering where the hell this came from. "Uh—because I can't stand the sight of blood."

"You know what I mean, Ass."

"Hey, Peggy is the only one who can call me Ass."

"Not when you're being an ass."

"Okay, so, you don't mean a Doctor of Medicine?"

"Of course not."

"Doctor of Chiropractic, maybe?"

He looked at me with a combination of disdain and disappointment.

"Okay, okay, so you mean Doctor of Philosophy."

"No, stupid, of course not."

"No, really, that's what you mean."

"That's not what I mean. I know what I mean; I'm not stupid."

"Then you become a doctor."

"Come on! What would a doctor of philosophy be? You have to be a philosopher? They don't even have those anymore, do they?"

"Oh, more than you would imagine."

"I thought they were all Greek or something. You know, old Greek, you know, toga Greek."

"Toga Greek?"

"Yeah."

"No, they have them today."

"Really?"

"Yeah, I'm not sure what use they are, but they have them. And everywhere. Not just in Greece. Of course, what they have to say is 'Greek' to most people, but that's an entirely different matter."

"Well, let's get back to the real matter."

"Let's get back to some more beer."

"Why aren't you a doctor?"

"A Doctor of Philosophy?"

"Are we going to start that again?"

"Look, Eugene—you're talking about a doctorate, right? A Ph.D.?"

"Yeah, that's it!"

"What do you think Ph.D. stands for?"

"I don't know, I never thought about it."

"M.D. What does M.D. stand for?"

"A doctor, I mean, you know—"

"A medical doctor, right? M.D. Which, of course, really means, Doctor of Medicine."

"Okay."

"So—Ph.D. The Ph stands for philosophy. So a Ph.D. is a philosophy doctor or a Doctor of Philosophy. Get it?"

"Oh."

"But then, you see, all philosophy really means is 'love of wisdom,' so what it means is, you are a lover of the wisdom of some particular thing. See? So you could have a Ph.D. in engineering or literature or cognitive science or—"

"History."

"Yes, or history."

"Which is what you would be."

"One assumes. If one were to also assume that I was going to go for my doctorate, which I'm not."

"Why not?"

"Because I don't want to."

"So you're okay with just being a teacher, a student herder, you might say, there at a *junior* college"

Of course, he made the word "junior" sound like—sound like what?—well, sound like *Adoofus*. "We don't call them junior colleges anymore. They're community colleges, locally based, serving the community, giving the students the exact same education they get in the first two years of a four-year college but at a much lower cost, and much greater care and attention paid by their instructors."

"You sound like a brochure."

"It's been a good career."

"Huh."

I *Huh-ed* him right back. Then we became quiet, both of us starting into our beer mugs, each of which was about half full. Or maybe one was half full, and one was half empty.

"So, what do you have right now?" Eugene asked, breaking the silence.

Still staring into my mug, I said, "Some light beer from the Rhineland."

"No, no, I mean, you know, I mean your school thing, your academic thing."

"You mean my degree?"

"Yes!"

"I have an M.A. in history. M.A. means Master of Arts. It's sometimes just known as a Master's."

"Oh, you mean, like an M.B.?"

"You mean an MBA."

"No, M.B. Master Bator?"

I snorted a contained laugh. Which is not the best thing to do after the number of beers I'd had. "No, that would be a high, but not the highest, degree in self-eroticism."

"Have you ever heard of the word, 'ambition'?"

"No. What is that? Yugoslavian?"

"Obviously a Ph.D. is higher than a Masters."

"Yes, if you want to look at it that way."

"What other way is there to look at it? It's on a scale, am I right?"

"Yes, you are right. But for what I want to do, which is to teach at PCC, a Master's is just fine."

"Peggy says you are so much better than that."

"Peggy says? I get it; you've been talking to Peggy."

"I always talk to Peggy, you know that. You don't own her, you know."

"No, that would be slavery."

"I mean, look, Adolphus, don't get me wrong in all this—I'm really proud of you."

I wanted to say, "What fucking right have you got to be proud of me about anything?" But I didn't. Even Germany's finest brew couldn't prod my brain into that. "Can we just drop this," I found myself pleading, then found myself disgusted that I found myself pleading. But I continued nevertheless. "I mean, if you want, we can talk about sports. It doesn't even have to be about basketball. Talk to me about baseball."

"Why do you want to drop it?"

"Ah—really—because I have to pee real bad. And then I think it's time to go home."

"I'm not going to let you drive home in your condition."

"You had your driver bring both of us in your Rolls, remember? That's the way we come whenever we come here, remember?"

"Yeah. Pretty smart of me, huh?"

"Actually it was Peggy's idea."

"Ah. Peggy's pretty smart."

"I have to go to the *piss-eria.*"

"Which Peggy named."

"Yes, yes, she did. Clever woman, that Peggy."

I was furious at Peggy. I wanted to have it out with her the next time I saw her. But I didn't. I hated arguing with Peggy. I mean, I enjoyed spirited discussions with her, usually about something to do with academics, or a play we just saw, or a movie. Rarely about politics; we pretty much agreed on politics. But arguments about us, if there was an us, or emotional arguments, things about our persons or personalities or personableness, those are the kind of "discussions" I hated. Because somehow, after the fact, I always felt as if I had lost the argument, even if during the fight, I thought I had racked up the most points. The next day I would feel like shit, and I would call her and apologize. Harsh words, I hated harsh words between us, so I said nothing. I chalked it up to heavy consumption of German beers and let it lie.

But Eugene did not.

He went to see Dr. Eggers, president of PCC, and asked him if it would be advantageous for me to have a doctorate. Even if I only was teaching at PCC. And he said to Eugene, and I quote because Eugene told me:

"Well, Adolphus is a very talented teacher, and he is also very, very, smart, very astute. He's got a good eye regarding history. But there's not an academic in this world that doesn't need continuing education. Honing, we might call it. Yeah, and going for his Ph.D. would offer that to Adolphus. Despite history being, obviously... Well, our understanding of it is always evolving as we move into the future. Adolphus surely wouldn't want to be stuck with old ideas. It wouldn't be good for the college, either. So, yes, it would be quite to his advantage to get his doctorate."

"And *he's* a doctor!" Eugene declared, metaphorically waving George's credentials during halftime at a Lakers game.

"Well, next time I have a bellyache I'll go to him."

"Damn it, you know what I mean, don't be dumb."

"So he's a doctor, so he's smarter than me?"

"No, but he's higher up on the scale."

"Well, that's a matter of perspective."

"Hey, no, it's not. A Ph.D. is better than an MA; that's just a matter of physics."

"Physics?"

"I mean, if you look at it physically, like a ladder, you know, there's the higher rungs, and the lower rungs and the lower rungs are always lower than the higher rungs, you can't argue with that."

"How about when the ladder is flat on the ground?"

"What do you mean? Ladders aren't supposed to be flat on the ground. What use is a ladder when it's flat on the ground?"

"Well, sometimes—"

"I just think—"

"Eugene!" I stopped looking at the Laker Girls leading cheers and turned to the hulking cheerleader of doctorates next to me. "That's not your forte!"

"What isn't?"

"Thinking. You're a—you're a—you're a doer. The best doer I know. Look what you've done, building up your adopted father's business, diversifying, becoming a billionaire. You're a—you're a man of action, a big man of action, why don't you leave the thinking to the squirts like me."

"I've never been so insulted while being complimented."

"And you wouldn't have even gotten that if you hadn't been thinking so much lately. I'm telling you it's not good for you. Okay, look, the game's starting again. I'll bet you a hundred dollars that the Lakers are going to win."

"I'm not going to bet against my team."

"Okay, can we bet on the point spread? Not that I know what a point spread is."

"You don't gamble."

"Yeah, you're right, I don't normally, but—"

"That's why you don't want to go for your doctorate!"

"What?"

"Because you don't want to gamble."

I hated that. I absolutely hated that. I hated that during the rest of the game, which I gave only seventy percent concentration to. I hated that on the way home. I hated that as I tried to fall asleep that night. I hated that when I woke up in the morning. I hated that! I absolutely hated that!

I have mentioned previously that I had been a Cub Scout and that it was in the Cub Scouts that I first became "friends" with Eugene. Or Gene, which I think I'll go back to calling him. And I've mentioned that our mothers were co-den mothers of the pack we were in, which helped form the false friendship Gene and I had, thus the quote marks above.

Well, here's a scouting story that has nothing to do with Gene. And yet, it does. From Cub Scouts, I naturally graduated into being a Boy Scout. Whereas my mother was heavily involved in my Cub Scout life, my father became heavily involved in the Boy Scouts. He loved it, became a scout leader, and wore a scout uniform, just like I did. He was beloved by the other scouts and the other fathers, and the other scout leaders. He remained a scout leader even after I had left the scouts in my late high school years because I felt I had outgrown them. Feeling that I had "outgrown" anything was so unique for me that I embraced this decision wholeheartedly, and nothing my father could say would dissuade me. But he stayed a scout leader. He loved it.

When I had joined the Boy Scouts, though, I was a perfect and utterly enthusiastic recruit. I loved the Boy Scout uniform and the uniformity it imposed, which offered this odd comfort, a cozy sense of camaraderie, and a bucolic (Boy Scouts spend a lot of time camp-ing) brotherhood. All opposed, I supposed, to the gangrene of gangs, of which Ramone had a few. The irony is that it was the uniformity that I outgrew when I left the Scouts. But in the beginning, it was neat. I also loved reading *Boy's Life,* the official Boy Scout magazine. It had a great series of short stories about a pack of Boy Scouts who traveled through time having adventures with historical figures. I was crazy about those stories. I took being a Boy Scout very seriously, almost as if it was a calling, as if I was part of a unique and special cohort set apart from the rest of humanity. And being serious about being a Boy Scout, I was deeply serious about the Boy Scout law. You know, being Brave, Clean, and Reverent, that sort of stuff.

Of course, any bravery I may have had was never tested during this time, and had it been, I'm afraid I may very well have come up short. As for clean, I suppose I was as clean in my body as any boy of my age. But I interpreted it as meaning pure in spirit and thoughts and action, which meant following the rules. I liked following the rules. And reverent? Not coming from a family that attended church much, I interpreted it as maintaining an earnest demeanor. There's a good chance I may not have been a lot of fun to be around.

My father's involvement meant more time spent with him, which was great as I liked my father. And because he was so well-liked, it didn't matter that I was not.

The most memorable moment of my Boy Scout years, though, was one that led to the only real conflict my father and I ever had. Boy Scouts, you see, spend a lot of their time advancing up the ranks. Like the military. Like life, some might say. You start out as a Tenderfoot. Then you work hard to achieve Second Class. Then harder still to make First Class. After that, you focus on earning merit badges. The more badges you earn, the higher up the ranks you go from Star to Life to the coveted Eagle, soaring high with achievement. For my dad, being a Boy Scout leader who looked quite snazzy in his uniform, it was important for his son to eventually wear a sash full of sewn-on little round merit badges and look quite snazzy in his own. Especially as his father handed him his Eagle Scout badge in front of their congregated cohorts. The badges were symbols sporting symbols denoting what specific scouting or general civic knowledge you had acquired on your Boy Scouts of America march to manhood. Expertise in things like camping and citizenship and canoeing and first aid and archery and fishing and even—the only merit badge I actually earned—library science. Going after each merit badge meant not only learning specific skills but studying each badge's own little textbook. So it was essentially a school outside of school, and I already was in school, and the school I was already in was the school, I concluded, that really mattered. So, I'm afraid I disappointed my father. After his pride in my reaching First Class, he was disappointed when I stalled in the onward and upward achievement of the honors that could be accorded a Boy Scout. He never really harshly pressured me about going on. Or approached me about it in a passive-aggressive manner. He just simply wanted to know why.

"Hey, Dad," I said to him in the flippant manner I was beginning to hone, "I made First Class; you can't get any better than that!"

I was too young, stupid, and insensitive to see the bit of hurt that may have been perceivable in my father's eyes. I've had some recurring regret about this, but it passes. And I've wondered now and then if I should chastise myself for having settled. But what's wrong with having settled? Because when you settle, you're settled. And isn't that what most people look for—to settle down and be safe somewhere within the chaos we call life? Or maybe it's just finding who you are and sticking with it. Even if it's not going to bring you any great honors. I've read enough history—obviously—to know that sometimes chasing after accolades can be *un*settling and can stir up that chaos of life.

So you see how this story sort of relates to Gene. Now, let me tell you another quick one that may or may not relate.

I once went through a period of crisis in my life. I mean, besides having my face grated against a stucco wall by Gene Pytka. After I had gotten my master's degree, I was trying to figure out what precisely to do with them—my master's degree and life. The original plan, of course, was to go back to PCC to teach history. But it had been a challenging program. I had never worked so hard. And I had been taken aback when several of my professors told me that I was the perfect candidate for a Ph.D. Was going "backward" really a good idea? Pasadena, after all, was in a valley, weren't there mountains out there to climb? But I was tired. No, more than tired, tired is just yawning and nighty-night. I was exhausted, deeply, with that limp feeling as if you had been jellified, flesh and bones and all. Which meant to roll out of bed and get the day started, I would have needed someone to push me. But I had no one. Besides, I hated being pushed. And yet, I was still in some kind of state over my marriage (when I had someone) and subsequent separation and divorce (when I gave up someone). I don't really know what that state was, but then that was part of the problem. I kept dreaming about getting away, ideally to Europe, where I could tramp around, visit historical sights, try to see and hear and even feel what had just been accounts, descriptions, assessments, and conclusions formed into print pressed into books. But I knew it was only a dream because it was something I just couldn't afford. Yes, I know, young people travel to Europe on the cheap all the time. But when I say "tramp," I mean it metaphorically. Hoofing it and hostels were not for me. Comfortable transportation and cozy hotels were what I wanted.

I mentioned all this to my parents to explain my mood, and a week later, somehow, they came up with the money to fund the trip. I thanked them profusely. My dad, as he always did, just said, "Don't mention it." I should have wondered at the time where the hell they got the money, but I wasn't about to, having an aversion to obligation —not to mention guilt. I now suspect they went to Gene's adopted father, Mr. Carson. I imagine him musing on it for a moment, then writing out a check. And why not? It's not like it wasn't in his self-interest to foot the bill.

So off I went to Europe. Alone. And I remained alone as if I was traveling those lands in an impenetrable bubble. Not that I didn't enjoy the trip, I enjoyed much of it immensely. It fulfilled a deep desire to touch history, it presented a kaleidoscope of grand images, both tangible and almost ethereal, and it gave me many moments of quiet contemplation.

But I was lonely, not knowing how not to be or too shy to remedy the situation, and unsure of my future. It all may have just been my mid-twenties brain trying to finish its development—perfectly understandable. But that didn't make it any less intense and disconcerting.

One evening I was in Milan. Milan is not a gorgeous Italian city like Venice or Florence, being somewhat industrial and commercial, so not a great place to feel adrift in. But I was there, not planning to leave before I could get up to see nearby Lake Como. I walked the streets rather aimlessly until hunger gave me a mundane, if necessary, aim. I found a small North African cafe. It was getting darker outside, and that made the light within the restaurant warm and inviting. I had never had North African food, and although I wasn't ordinarily adventurous, I decided to go in. I was greeted by a friendly man and taken to a table and given a menu. In reading it, I was lost. It was in Italian and Arabic and French, none of which I could read. So I asked in English, gesturing toward the menu, what he recommended. The friendly man, who spoke English well, told me I should try couscous with lamb and mint and feta cheese, his own creation. I said, okay, that would be fine. To drink? He asked. I asked for coffee and water.

The friendly man left, and I was left adrift again. I looked around the cafe. I took in the decor and the atmosphere. I looked at the few other customers, including two middle-aged men having a spirited discussion that I found amusing, despite not understanding what they were saying. Then the door opened. A tall, lanky man came in and answered the call of the two spirited men, joining them at their table. He was their age, but with a full head of prematurely gray hair. It was combed back and wavy, slightly long, and beautiful. He had a long, well-shaved face that somehow should have been craggy but wasn't. And when he smiled, it was not insubstantial. He wore blue jeans, a blue denim shirt, and black boots. Right after he sat, he pulled out a pipe and pipe paraphernalia. He went about preparing for a smoke as he listened to his companions, who continued with their spirited conversation. Once prepared, he placed the pipe in his mouth as he crossed his right leg over his left, then lit the pipe with a long match and vigorous inhaling, causing the tobacco to glow in the bowl of the pipe. Once satisfied with the pipe's draw, he shook the match dead, took the pipe out of his mouth, and exhaled a long billow of white smoke. He did not join the spirited conversation unless invited and then added only a few, I assumed, pertinent words. Otherwise, he sat silent and seemed as amused by the conversation as I had been—he smiled throughout except when he puffed on his pipe—although more rightly so as he understood what it was about.

My food came, and I turned my attention to it, approaching it shyly. But once I got to know it, I embraced it wholly. Although I had a book with me, as I always did, I found myself, once comfortable with my meal, eating it while staring—unobtrusively, I hope—at the seated, tall man. Something was compelling about him—something magnificent, yet something simple. I was trying to define it, to find a way to think of it, when a familiar phrase popped into my head: *Comfortable in his own skin*. That was it! This was a man who seemed—no, obviously was—comfortable in his own skin. Had I been religious, I might have seen him as an angel or a saint or a divine messenger from some god or other, modern or pagan, giving glad tidings, or something. But he was not. He was just a man who had no idea that he was becoming for me an ideal. *To be comfortable in your own skin.* That's what I wanted, that's all that I had ever wanted, without knowing it. I made a pact with myself that evening as I finished my couscous and lamb and feta. I would strive to become comfortable in my own skin. Not a particularly monumental goal, not a world bending or changing one. Not an objective bringing relief or sustenance or liberty or happiness to millions. Not an end purpose that would benefit anyone at all, except me. But it was a goal I became determined to reach. Twenty years later, teaching at PCC, fucking Peggy, living in my little house, I had felt that I had reached that goal. I was comfortable in my own skin.

So, do you understand how I might get angry at anyone who would suggest, subtly or strongly, that I change that skin, slough it off like some damn snake?

Gene was aware that I was angry, for we didn't see each other for several months after that last Lakers game. He was traveling, deal-making, acquiring even greater wealth. I was busy teaching, grading papers, enjoying good books, and Peggy's body. Peggy herself was confused. She knew something had happened, but she couldn't get either of us to talk about it. It was a lousy position for Peggy to be in. But—she knew the job was dangerous when she took it.

24

After several non-Gene months, he communicated with me using Peggy as his surrogate, or, as he might have said, his go-between, or, as I might have said, his advocate. Why she agreed to function as any one of those, I just didn't get. I mean, how many times can you go to a luxury spa?

Peggy and I had gone out for an evening at the Pasadena Ice House for some stand-up yucks. The Ice House had become a local institution, now prominent on the stand-up comedy circuit, but it was known as a folk music venue when I was in high school. That was during that short period nestled between the early 60s, when Rock n' Roll, which was considered thoroughly American music, was declared a dying musical anomaly ("Thank God" some elder squares proclaimed), and when the British Invasion landed on our shores via airwaves and airplanes ("The British are singing! The British are singing!"). It seems that folk music had just been there to fill the gap until John Henry-like, it had to lay down its acoustic guitars and twangy banjos and die, unable to beat electric guitars and percussive drums.

Okay, put your hands down. I know, get on with the story.

Well, sitting in the Ice House bar at the end of the evening, Peggy said to me, assuming, because I had been laughing, that I was now in good humor, "Oh! I forgot to tell you. Eugene's back in town."

"What town is that?"

"What do you mean, what town is that?"

"Well, I mean, he lives in San Marino, you live in Pasadena, I live in South Pasadena. But he's an international traveler, so maybe you mean something bigger, the Los Angeles area, which we all live in."

"Shut up, Ass."

"Okay." I shut up, happy to drink my drink, the better use of my mouth for the moment.

"No, I mean shut up being stupid. Gene's *home*—how's that?—he's home, and we were talking, and he said, 'Hey, let's go to Schwarzkopf's Saturday night!' and I said, 'Great! Love too!' 'And Adolphus too, of course,' he said, and I said, 'Well, of course, we couldn't do Schwarzkopf's without Adolphus.'"

"Why not?" I asked, giving her my open face of genuine curiosity. "You guys can go to Schwarzkopf's alone. I don't have to be there."

"But, you know, come on, we're the Three Musketeers."

"The Three Musketeers?"

"Yeah! Aren't we?"

"Do you see a D'Artagnan hanging about?"

"Oh, come on, I know there was a riff, or something, between you two, but he wants to get together, so let's get together."

I started singing, slightly under my breath, a song that Haley Mills sang with herself in this Disney movie, *The Parent Trap*—"*Let's get together, yeah, yeah, yeah...*" The weird things you remember when you are trying to avoid the weird.

"Adolphus!" Peggy said with snapping, schoolmarm admonition.

"Okay, okay, Saturday night."

"Fine, we'll pick you up at about seven."

W hen the giant Rolls Royce pulled up in front of my tiny house at seven, Gene was alone if you don't include his driver.

"Where's Peggy?" I asked.

"She said she couldn't make it. Some crisis."

"Crisis?"

"I mean at school."

"Oh, yeah, sure." I was incredulous. I smelled a trap.

"Seriously. A student freaking out over what college to transfer to. That's her job, helping them, isn't it?"

"It's Saturday."

"Yeah, the kid just showed up on her doorstep."

Now I didn't know what to think. It is what Peggy did. Even if it was Saturday, she wouldn't have said to the lost lamb at her door, "Make an appointment during office hours." That just wasn't her. Thank goodness. "Well, okay," I said as I climbed into the capacious back of the Rolls, joining Gene.

"But she sent me with a message. I quote, 'Hey, Ass, grow a pair and have the cuttlefish pizza.'"

I laughed. It was involuntary, it was knee-jerk, therefore, it was real and genuine. And I had to admit, it was a good start to the evening.

On the drive to Madison and Schwarzkopf's, he told me about his latest trip back to Lavinia's hometown, Andersberg, to check on things. Not just stuff to do with Ramone International Aggregates Quarry Number whatever, but also the Lavinia Carson Public Library and the Lavinia Carson private family. He didn't like his in-laws, but he always made sure everything was all right with them. And he was checking up on the general economy of the town and found it booming because of the other businesses he had attracted to it. He was, of course, accorded a hero's welcome.

"That really bothered me."

"Really? Why?"

"Well, you know, I was used to, even possibly kind of liked, people bowing and scraping to me when they essentially were afraid of me. But, um, this genuflucking—"

"Genuflecting," I corrected, the good pedant that I was.

"Oh. But it means bowing and scraping, right?"

"Right."

"Oh. I kind of prefer genu*flucking*."

"Nevertheless…"

"Yeah, okay. Well, anyway, they were genuflecting just because I was, uh, I mean, I did these, um…"

"Absolutely humane and wonderful things?"

"Yeah—okay. I find that, um—embarrassing."

"That's probably healthy. If you didn't, it would mean you were a megalomaniac."

"Oh. And that's bad, right?"

"Well, from my perspective, it's horrible, yes."

"Is it good from any perspective?"

"Only from that of a megalomaniac. But then his problem is he's suffering from megalomania and can hardly be considered a credible source."

"Okay, so, I should embrace my embarrassment."

"Yeah, I would if I was you. So everything is fine back in Andersberg?"

"Sure."

Later that evening, after a large pizza sampler (which included no cuttlefish) and much beer, some conversation about the Lakers, and his inquiry as to my at-that-moment brightest student (who he seemed genuinely interested in), Gene suddenly said, "I know I need to apologize to you."

"Apology accepted," I said without hesitation.

"You don't even know what I'm apologizing for."

"Sure, I do."

"What?"

"For being a dickhead and bugging me about things I don't want to be bugged about."

"You mean getting your doctorate?"

"Yeah, that."

"Noooo." He stretched out the word as if he wanted it to cover many things.

"No?"

"No, that's not what I'm apologizing for."

"Well, you should."

"Why?"

"Because—it—bugged me!"

"Well, that's your problem. I only want what's best for you."

It was a stupid thing for him to say. And, for me, it was a shocking thing to have heard. "You only want what's best for me?"

"Of course."

"What right do you have to only want what's best for me?"

"The right of one who loves you, you idiot."

Not wanting to have to hear that again, I'm not sure I heard it. "I mean, that's the kind of thing your parents say to you. You know, a hardass father, which, by the way, my father wasn't, or a doting mother, which mine wasn't. So which one are you? I mean, by gender, I suppose we could call you a father, but, to be honest with you, Gene, you're coming off to me as a mother—you know a girly-girly smothering mother."

"You're an ass."

"I told you only Peggy can call me that."

"I didn't call you Ass. I called you *an* ass."

"Short for an asshole?"

"That'll do."

We sat there, silent for a few moments. Finally, because I am by nature a curious person, I had to know. "So what are you apologizing for?"

"For being insensitive."

"Oh. Is this for a particular thing or a blanket apology for just being yourself?"

"No, for not realizing that maybe you're turning down the idea of going for your doctorate because, well, you just can't afford it."

"Oh, for Christ's sake!"

244

"I didn't know you were religious."

"You know, sometimes your humor is as ham-fisted as your—as your—ham fists."

"Well, it's true, isn't it?"

"If I wanted to go after my doctorate, I'm sure I could raise the money."

"No, you're not."

"I could take out a second mortgage on my house."

"On that piece of shit!"

"Hey!"

"Look, I'll fund it for you. I could give it to you directly, but I just started a higher education foundation that will pay for a student's full higher education, for as far as they want to go. From the first four years right through to a Ph.D., if they commit to that. That's why I was asking you about your brightest student. I want to give a grant to your brightest student. And I can give you a grant to pursue your doctorate."

I looked at him—the big massive man, the manly man, a man with his head in the clouds, or maybe just a man with a cloudy head. I grabbed my mug of beer that had lately been refilled and chugged down the full contents. Then said to him, without a quiver or quake in my voice, totally in command of myself, "There is no hope on Earth or a chance in heaven or hell that I would allow you to do that."

"Why not?"

"The fact that you have to ask that question is why not."

"I don't get it."

"And that is also a fact!"

"I only want what's best for you," he said on the edge of plaintivity.

"You said that. And I've already issued my commentary on it."

"You could go to any college or university you want. You love England, how about Oxford?"

I've got to admit, I started to get a cultural boner on that one. But I persevered and gave Gene the exact same stare my mother used to give me when she was mad. "I'll take a taxi home," I declared. And I stood up and started to walk out of Schwarzkopf's.

"The hell you will!" Gene said in his best John Wayne swagger as he got up, grabbed me and picked me up—yes, picked me up!—carried me to his Rolls, stuffed me in, and took me home.

I stewed for several days. I hate stewing—that low-level slow-cooking of your brain and emotions. It sets your jaw tight. It pinches your face ugly and makes you unrecognizable to you. It certainly does not allow you to be comfortable in your own skin. Worse, it was an insult to the memory of my father.

My father, that paragon of the easy-going man, that poster boy for unruffled feathers, that calm in any storm, that easy-smile, those twinkling-eyes, that man beloved by all because he never rubbed anyone the wrong way.

Wait a minute.

Was all that positive stuff? Or was there a dark lining of negativity to it?

Damn that Gene! I was mad enough at him to cause me to question my father. But wait another minute—it was my father that Gene was jealous about when he scraped my face against a stucco wall like scraping dog shit from his boots.

I hated stewing, hated it, and now I was stewing about stewing!

Hold on! Hold on! I had to adjust my skin, meaning my mental attitude, and recover the comfort, the calm—breathe deep, Adolphus breathe deep. And smile, damn you, smile!

I knew I had to call Gene, or rather, Eugene, yes, Eugene, I needed to put in a call to Eugene.

He was still in town, and his secretary and/or executive assistant (I think society was still in the middle of a change on this) put me right through to him.

"Look," I said immediately, "it's my turn to apologize. This higher education foundation of yours is fantastic. And Lori Needham—(that was the brightest student I had told him about)—well, it will absolutely alter her life. It couldn't go to a more deserving person. But as for me—"

"Say no more, Adolphus. I got the message. I've already found another candidate for the Ph.D. grant."

"Oh." Why did I have a sudden stab of disappointment? Goddammit! "Great! Good! I'm very pleased."

"I think Margaret will be very appreciative."

"Margaret?"

"Yes."

"Margaret who?"

"*Our* Margaret."

"Our Margaret? You mean, Peggy?"

"Yes, of course, Peggy."

"No one ever calls her Margaret."

"Oh, I'm sorry, I was just filling out the order for the grant and, of course, I was, you know, writing in her full name, Margaret Kathleen Bradford."

"You're giving *her* the Ph.D. grant?"

"Sure."

"She's not going for her Ph.D."

"She is now."

"But—but..."

"You sound surprised. Even unaware."

"But—but in what?"

"Um, let me see here—neuroscience. She wants to get her doctorate in neuroscience."

Of course, that made sense. If Eugene had said in education or educational counseling, I would have known he was putting me on. He wouldn't have known about her passionate interest in neuroscience. It's not something she would have talked to him about. But then, what the hell did I know about what she spoke to him about?

"You didn't know she wanted to do this for a long time?"

"No, we—well, we never—"

"You've never talked to her about it, have you?"

"Well, she never brought it up."

"Did you ever think to—"

"Ah, well, okay, this is, uh, great, um, wonderful. So I suppose she's going to go to—what?—UCLA or USC maybe? Somewhere local, of course, because, you know, she loves her house in Pasadena."

"No, no, it's a private university in Delaware, uh, here it is, Biden University. She says it sits right on the banks of the Brandywine River."

I went from stewing to a deep, strange, embarrassing sadness. But all that would have been mitigated if only I had known what it was really about, what was really going on in Eugene Carson's reptilian *Gene Pytka* mind.

―――――

I was genuinely happy for Peggy. At least I had convinced myself I was. I just had one question. "Why, Delaware? I mean, you know, Southern California, here, locally, we are not bereft of fine institutions of higher learning."

Peggy and I were taking a walk in my neighborhood, up to the city library and the lovely little park surrounding it, and to the coffee bar catty-corner to the library and the beautiful small park surrounding it. They had the best big fat moist orange-cranberry muffins. We loved those muffins more than any other person or persons could. We were, in fact, of the unstated joint opinion that the muffins existed only for us.

"Well," Peggy said, "Biden University has one of the top schools of Neuroscience in the country. As you know."

"Yes, as I know," I said, already feeling the sting of defeat.

"They do leading-edge research."

"Really?"

"Yes, of course. I mean, Biden has got some of the best brains on brains in the world."

"Oh, in the world. Not just America."

"They have a huge international reputation."

"And yet, such a small, such a little university."

"Intellectually intimate, I would call it."

"And it sits right there on the Brandywine River."

"Oh yeah, that's a plus."

"But is this really what you want to do? See, I'm having a hard time with that because you've always been so dedicated to others, you know the students, helping them further their education, especially young women."

The young woman behind the coffee bar counter with a ring in her nose, a metal piercing through her eyebrow that ended in what looked like a ball bearing, and fantastic butterflies with teeth tattooed up her arm, pointed out to us that we were next and now able to order. We did, ordering our muffins (warmed up) and coffee. During this short commercial transaction, we said nothing to each other. Once it was concluded, we gathered our consumables, grabbed flatware and napkins, and headed outside, finding a table on the sidewalk with a nice view of the park and library across the street.

A parrot screamed. There was a flock of colorful parrots in the branches of the trees in the park. Another parrot screamed, then several, serenading us as we blew on our coffees to cool them and cut our muffins into neat bite-size bits.

Peggy picked up our conversation as if she was a TV show coming back from a commercial. "I've done that. For years now, Adolphus. I've helped a lot of kids. I feel good about that. But I think I have a right to be selfish for a while."

"But, you know, all that dedication…"

"And now I'll be dedicated to unlocking the mysteries of the mind. I mean, Adolphus, think about it! Isn't understanding human consciousness the last frontier?"

I could not dissuade her, for I could not deny it. "You're really excited about this, aren't you?"

"Hey!—if it was sex, it would be a never ending climax."

"Well—pointedly, if crudely, put."

So there was nothing I could do about it. Not that I really thought that I was supposed to do something about it. I just figured it was a shame that UCLA or USC would be deprived of such an excellent, brilliant doctoral candidate.

It was a good ten months (or a bad ten months, depending on how you looked at it) before she would be off to Delaware. She had to finish out her contract with PCC first and put her Pasadena life into some sort of hold or something. She fretted a lot over whether to sell her house or to keep it and rent it. I urged her to keep it. As her last day at PCC approached, I took some small, unadmitted, pleasure-in-hope that she seemed to be growing sad. But I was mistaken. It really wasn't sadness, just pre-nostalgia for her times at PCC. Her database of the students she had helped would go with her, and she promised all of them that she would maintain communication with them. They, of course, were universally happy for her. But what the hell did they know?

The summer before she got started, she made some trips back to Delaware to arrange for housing and other things she needed to ease into her new life. Gene paid for it, flying her first class. She said she felt like royalty. And yet, got upset at me when I would call her "Princess Peggy."

Then the day came when she was going to go—and not come back. At least for a couple of years. Although I had a sinking feeling that it might be a permanent move. I pretty much had gotten myself used to the idea—steeled my nerves; girded my loins—when Peggy told me that Gene was going to take her back—himself—on his private jet!—and see that she was adequately installed into her new life.

"You mean, it's like your—like your *daddy* driving you to your first year of college."

"Well, sure, why not? Eugene is surprisingly paternal."

"The man is our age, for Christ's sake!"

"Oh, he's a little older than me. As are you, Ass."

"No, I mean, this is the problem. I mean, there is something sick about this, don't you think? The man loses his wife, the man really wanted children with his wife, the man refuses to even think about another wife, so he's got to get his 'children' from somewhere. First, he picks me, but I don't turn out to be a model son, so now he's picking you."

"That's absurd. Eugene doesn't love me like he loves you."

"He doesn't love me! It's—it's a weird sickness."

"Could be. And we've taken much advantage of it. And I, for one, am grateful. We are going to fly out of Burbank airport. Are you going to come and see me off?"

"Uh…"

"Adolphus?"

"Yeah, okay, sure. I mean, really, sure, of course, I'd be happy to."

And I did. Feeling a bit miffed because Peggy and Eugene were leaving about a week earlier than Peggy needed to. They had decided to spend a week in New York. "Some fun before her hard work," Gene said. They were going to see some Broadway shows (as long as they weren't Shakespeare), and Peggy wanted to take Gene to some museums. I'm not sure I was miffed because Peggy was leaving earlier than I had expected or because I was going to miss the fun.

At the airport, Eugene stood off to the side as Peggy and I said our goodbyes. We were standing on the tarmac with Gene's jet sitting off in the not-too-far distance. It was like that scene out of *Casablanca*. Or, worse, *Play it Again, Sam*. I dreaded that one of us might say, "We'll always have Pasadena."

"When I'm done, you know," she said, "I'm going to expect you to call me Dr. Bradford."

"I'll be happy to. And I'll be able to do it daily when you find a good position back here."

She looked at me and smiled sweetly with a tinge of pity on the side. "If I get through this and get a chance to do some significant research, I'll go to wherever that research takes me."

I felt like King George reading the Declaration of Independence. "Even though I'm here?"

"Well, hell, Ass, it's not like we're married or anything. Look, we've had some near-perfect times together, some, you know, great sex, which I don't expect to ever find again, but I'm going to be concentrating on the cerebral, not the physical in any case."

"Okay. If you can live with that. But, somehow, I doubt it."

"And how about you?"

"What do you mean?"

"Well, you know, when we first got together, we were, you know, we saw other people, right?"

"As I remember."

"But I don't think we have for quite a while. I know I haven't. How about you?"

"Are you expecting me to kiss and tell?"

"I'm expecting you to tell me if you've kissed."

"Only you of late. I mean, you've always been so handy."

"So I've just been a convenience for you?"

"No, I mean you give great hand jobs."

She laughed. She shouldn't have. It was an idiotic thing to say, but indicative of our relationship.

"Well, maybe you'll find someone else just as handy."

"Okay, yeah, I might just do that."

"No students, though."

"Peggy!" I admonished.

"You know, Sheila in Phys-ed, I think she's always had an eye for you."

"She's the women's basketball coach," I said aghast, if I may be allowed.

"You like basketball."

"She's ever so much taller than me."

"Mountains to conquer, Adolphus, mountains to conquer."

"Peggy," Gene called. "The captain says we better get going."

"Okay," she said back. Then she said, Goodbye. And I said, Goodbye. And then we gave each other the only awkward kiss we had ever exchanged.

She walked over to Gene, turning back to wave, then they entered his slick jet to most likely sit comfortably and drink copiously and share some laughs, possibly at my expense, as they winged their way to Peggy's—or, rather the pre-Dr. Bradford's—new life.

I went home and picked up the latest mystery novel that Peggy had recommended that I was only a third of the way through. I took it outside to my beautiful backyard (courtesy of Eugene Carson), to my reading Gazebo (courtesy of Eugene Carson), and began to read.

Damn, if I didn't figure out who-done-it before the denouement.

Ha! Take that, Margaret Kathleen Bradford!

25

Three days later, I was sitting in Dr. Eggers's office, and we were laughing about something. I don't remember what it was, but as we didn't have too many shared interests, it must have been something about the college. Maybe a student we found humorous, or one of the staff members. Or maybe Dr. Eggers told a joke. He told awful jokes. But being essentially the kind person that I am, I always laughed uproariously at them. In the middle of this laughter, his intercom buzzed, and he was told that there was a call for me and that it was Eugene Carson. Dr. Eggers picked up the phone, poked a button on his unit, and handed me the handset.

"Hello, Gene, what's up?" I said in a jaunty manner, wanting him to know that I was in a perfectly happy state of existence.

"Adolphus," his voice came over agitated and strange, "you've got to come to New York right now."

"What? Why?"

"It's Peggy."

"Huh?"

"She's been hurt. In a car accident."

I sat up straight—I had been slouching a bit in the chair—coming to attention. "What? What car accident? How is she?" I said rapidly, the urgency to do something, I didn't know what, but something compelled me to demand speed from the universe.

"Bad. She's very bad. She went off by herself in a taxi. I had—I had the car because I had a meeting downtown, and—and, you know, it was one of those—one of those intersection things, someone ran a red light, slammed right into the taxi, it flipped—flipped several times, they said—oh my god, Adolphus, it's like, I mean like, I feel like..."

"Gene." I heard the control slipping from Eugene, and I couldn't let that happen. "Gene, calm down." There had to be some sense in this, and only he could provide it.

"It's like Lavinia—it's like Lavinia again—all over again. Oh, Adolphus, you've got to come, you've got to come. She's hurt really bad."

"How bad, Gene?" He was so hysterical; I was thinking he was blowing it all out of proportion. Because of Lavinia, because Lavinia had died. But this was Peggy, not Lavinia, Peggy, sensual, funny, take-no-guff-from-me, very, very alive Peggy.

"They—they don't think she's going to make it, Adolphus. They don't think she has long. But...but she called out your name, and you have to be here, don't you? You have to be here."

But this is Peggy! I wanted to tell him, but I didn't. I found myself saying, "Yes, okay, Gene, yes."

He was starting to cry, blubber, actually. "Oh my god, Adolphus, it's like Lavinia, it's like I'm going through Lavinia again."

Indeed, he must have been. For the crying, the blubbering, it brought back clearly the day he walked into that South Pasadena high school classroom and announced Lavinia's death. So I could see him, as I saw him then, I could see the awful pain on his face, a sight I couldn't close my eyes to, the same eyes now suddenly filling with tears. "Okay, Gene, I'll get to the airport right—"

"No, no, I've got a car coming for you. Where are you?"

I started wiping tears with the fleshy part of the palm of my hand, noticing Dr. Eggers noticing that and becoming concerned and perplexed. He grabbed a box of tissues and placed them before me. "I'm at the college."

"That's what I thought. He's heading your way now." Eugene was calming down. Being in charge calmed him down. "He'll pick you up at the front, on Colorado. Get down there now; he'll get you right to the airport."

"But, Gene, I have to go home and pack,"

"No, no, don't worry about all that, I'll take care of everything."

"But—"

"No, you've got to come without delay—please—please." Each "please" was broken at the beginning into staccato Ps caused by short breaths leftover from his crying.

"Okay, Gene, I'll wait out front. I'll be there."

"He'll be there soon. I'll have another car pick you up at JFK. It'll take you right to the hospital. I'll meet you there."

"Okay—okay…"

"Please, Adolphus!"

"I'm coming—Eugene—I'm coming. Don't worry, I'll be there."

I hung up the phone, feeling as out of breath as if I had been underwater for longer than I should have been.

"What is it, what's happened?" Dr. Eggers asked.

"It's Peggy—car accident."

"Oh, shit!"

"They—they don't think she's going to make it. They think she's going to die."

"Oh my God—oh fuck! Well—well, what are you doing?"

"Eugene's sending a car. He wants me to go straight to the airport and come to New York."

"Of course, you must."

"Classes—I have classes."

"Don't worry about that, I'll take care of everything."

"I've got to go. I've got to wait out front for the car."

"Of course, of course. I'll come with you."

As we walked out of his office, he told his secretary, Sue, to take messages, there's an emergency, he'll be right outside, but he's not to be disturbed. Walking to my left and holding my arm, Dr. Eggers—George—took me out of the building. He later told me that I had started to hyperventilate, breathing in such short breaths that he kept telling me to breathe deeply, breathe deeply. He walked me down the front steps and guided me to the sidewalk facing Colorado Boulevard, walking past the long mirror pool—the mirror pool where the great Eugene/Adolphus chase had taken place. I remember asking him, "Why are you holding my arm?" just as my knees buckled and I gave way to gravity. But he caught me and held me up. "That's why," he said.

The Town Car pulled up just as we got to the sidewalk. The driver got out to help, but Dr. Eggers told him that he would take care of me. He opened the back door and deposited me on the back seat. "Let's get your seatbelt on," he said as I watched him doing it, wondering why I wasn't doing it.

"Thank you."

"Do you want me to come to the airport with you?"

"No—that's okay—I'll, um, you know, be okay."

"Right. I'm sure you will. As soon as you can, call me, even at home. Don't worry about everything here. I'll take care of everything."

"Okay. Thanks, George, I appreciate it."

"Don't mention it," George said, and I thought of my father as my father always said that, and in thinking of my father, I thought I was going to cry. But the driver started talking.

"We couldn't get a flight out of Burbank, so I've got to take you to LAX, sir."

"Okay."

"Mr. Carson said to stay with you all the way up to the gate. Your ticket is waiting for you. Anything you need, just ask. You'll find some bottled water back there if you need it."

"Okay. But why aren't we going?"

"It'll be just a moment or two, sir. Waiting for—ah, here they are."

Two California Highway Patrol motorcycle cops pulled up. The CHiPs, as they were famously known because of TV, gave the driver thumbs up, and he gave them the same, and they turned on their sirens, took the lead, and began to escort us down Colorado, then turned left and took us on up to the freeway.

"Holy shit!" I thought stupidly. "The power of a billionaire."

Once we got on the freeway, the CHiPs clearing the way, we must have traveled most of the time at close to a hundred miles an hour, or so it seemed. They escorted us all the way to LAX, to a white loading and unloading zone where we parked. The driver got me out of the car and took charge of me. The cops got off their motorcycles and stood there by the Town Car, guarding it, I assumed.

The driver rushed me to a gate for a Virgin Atlantic flight to New York, to JFK. Virgin—I suddenly thought for a moment that that was funny as hell, but I kept it to myself as the driver handled everything at the gate, getting my first-class ticket. He walked me on board and got me settled into my seat. He whispered to the flight attendant, a friendly, motherly type, that I was a special needs case, and told her the circumstances. And then he said goodbye to me and left. I think I thanked him. I hope I thanked him.

I was used to first-class travel with Gene, so nothing was new and strange and shiny. The luxury of this way of flying gave me no particular pleasure that day. I just sat there, letting the flight attendant take care of me, even putting my seatbelt on for me. The second time I needed this done that day. Like a child. Which I would have dearly loved to have been. I just felt numb. It's true; such a shock of information causes you to go numb. I suppose because you are trying not to feel what you're feeling. If it wasn't numbness, what would it be? Panic? Fear? Sorrow—deep, deep, gut-ripping-out sorrow? None of which, I'm sure, my body thought I could take at that moment.

Once in the air and once the captain told us we could undo our seatbelts—which I didn't—the flight attendant came by with a little pot of herbal tea. She said, "Mr. Carson thought this would be helpful."

"Really? I—I don't know if I want—"

"Mr. Cason really thinks you should drink it."

"Okay."

She pulled down the tray for me and put the pot down and a cup, and poured it for me, saying, "Afterwards, I would suggest reclining the seat and resting as much as possible. I've got a pack here with a blanket and a sleep mask, as well as a pillow."

"Thank you," I said. "And you are?"

She told me her name, but I can no longer remember it. But I thanked her, I did, I remember clearly that I thanked her.

I looked at the cup of herbal tea for a moment, looking at the liquid, captured by the cup, not dark, a bit translucent, a little bit of steam rising from its surface, the intersection between it and the rest of reality. I picked up the cup and brought it to my lips and sipped the hot liquid. It may have been chamomile tea or a chamomile blend, I really can't remember, and it really doesn't matter. I brought the cup down, setting it back onto the tray while not letting go of it. Then I raised it again to my lips and sipped again, then lowered it, then repeated several times this mechanical movement punctuated by a decreasingly warm but always wet sensation. I had not one thought during all this. Not about anything. Just a perception of moving the cup up, sipping, feeling liquid, the movement down. Then a thought came to me as I drained the last in the cup: Clever Japanese. I jiggled the small pot. There was more tea. I poured it all into the cup and took some pride in being able to replicate with precision my previously fine drinking of the tea.

When I was finished, the motherly flight attendant was right there to gather up the pot and the cup and store away my tray. She gave me the sweetest of small smiles, then quietly moved away.

I took her advice and reclined my seat and opened the pack she had given me. I pulled out the pillow, putting it behind my head, and the blanket, covering myself with it, and the sleep mask, something I had never used before. I secured it around my head to hold it in its proper place.

There is an odd beauty about darkness when you accept it—positive security in the negative. I liked, at that moment, being there, alone, unavailable to anyone else. I'm not sure I could have stood communicating with anyone else. And yet, the dark did not cut off, indeed it intensified, my surroundings. They just became a cocooning suite of sounds, muted sounds it seemed, off in some background, but prominently there nevertheless. Overall there was the white noise of the jet engines and the circulating air in the cabin. Chit-chat from the other first-class passengers and the cabin crew punctuated the background with words I could recognize, but not one coherent sentence. There were the click and clack of china plates and silverware (this was, after all, first-class), and the sound of a rolling service cart that had delivered the china and utensils and the food and liquid that gave them purpose. And there was the swish of cloth, clothing most likely, which reminded me of the swish of the entrance I heard a moment before I first laid eyes on Lavinia.

Lavinia. Such a vibrant presence. Radiant with life. Now dead.

Peggy. Not radiant. But always beautiful under illumination, accepting with pleasure the light. Soon to be dead?

I was hoping not to think of her, fearing to think of her. But there she was, laughing, kidding, looking at me askance. Sitting with her legs tucked under her on a couch, her nose in a book, her eyes scanning rapidly. She was a fast reader, faster than me. I had often cursed her for it. Eating with pleasure, drinking with satisfaction, fucking with abandon and a sense of play—

I put a stop to that thought, deflating the rising erection that seemed wholly inappropriate.

But then I thought of her on a bed because I knew she was at that moment on a bed—a hospital bed. Or maybe on an operating table. Were they operating? Gene said nothing about them operating, Just that—just that... So, no operating. Just bandages, she must be covered in bandages, head to toe, that's all I could see now. Tears. But I didn't want to cry, make a sound, intrude on the muffled, not sad sounds of the cabin that was my current reality. I just brought my hand up to my eyes and wiped away tears from under the sleep mask several times.

I must have fallen asleep, for the next thing I was aware of was the motherly flight attendant gently shaking me, saying, "Mr. Seruya? We've landed at JFK."

I got off the plane and came out of the gate and saw a man in a dark suit holding a handwritten sign: MR. SERUYA. He was also keeping in the crook of his right arm an overcoat and a long scarf.

I approached him and said, "I'm Mr. Seruya."

"Welcome to New York, sir." He was Puerto Rican. How did I

know that? Why did it even matter? "Mr. Carson thought you might need these." He dropped the sign and held out the coat for me. I put it on, and then he handed me the scarf. "One moment, sir. Mr. Carson wanted me to call him as soon as you arrived." He took out a gray Motorola flip phone and dialed a number. "Mr. Carson, I have Mr. Seruya here." He handed me the phone.

"Gene," I said.

"She's gone, Adolphus."

A quick breath taken in through the mouth, coming back out as, "Oh, no."

"She died about two hours ago."

"Oh, God."

"I know, Adolphus, I know." It sounded like he was beginning to cry, which I didn't want him to because where would that leave me? I heard him take a deep, recovering breath. "Look, there's no use going to the hospital. The driver will bring you to my hotel. I'm at the Plaza."

The Plaza. Eloise's Plaza. In the books. The kids' books by Kay Thompson. Kay Thompson was in *Funny Face*. Peggy loved that movie. Peggy loved those books.

"Okay, Adolphus? Do you understand? Just follow the driver, he'll take you to the car and bring you to me. Okay?"

"Okay," I said, and did, like a robot following the instructions of my creator.

I don't really remember the drive into Manhattan. I'm not sure I ever looked out of the windows of the car. I may have closed my eyes; I may not have. The numbness returned, and I was happy—although that's not really the word—that it had.

The driver delivered me to the Plaza, then up to Eugene's suite. He rang the doorbell. Eugene answered the door. "Thank you, Jesus," he said.

"You're welcome, sir," the driver said.

Eugene handed Jesus a hundred dollar bill, then said to me, "Come in."

I stepped into the suite—very luxurious. I could see a staircase. High ceilings *and* two stories! Well, Eugene was a big man, such a big man. Out of the windows, Central Park was bathed in twilight. The green was welcomed. Green is always welcomed.

"Adolphus—I can't—I can't tell you how sorry I am," he said, opening his arms just a little to punctuate the sentiment. But something in my brain, possibly something very primitive, saw it as an opening. I moved to him and between his open arms and encircled his torso with my arms, almost falling into him, my head landing on his chest, a new burst of tears wetting his shirt. And I squeezed, I squeezed tight. "Go ahead, go ahead," he said, "as tight as you want. You can't break my ribs."

My crying was loud, the tears were flowing, but it didn't last long. It was a burst, a quick one, that when done, was done. I broke away from Eugene, and he pulled a handkerchief from a pocket and handed it to me. I wiped, I blew, I soiled it rather well.

"Come over here. Sit down." He guided me to a gray couch, two chairs, a glass top table for all of them. I sat. I took a deep, broken-into-gasps breath. "Would you like something to drink?" Gene asked.

"Water, I guess."

"Nothing stronger?"

"No. Water will be fine."

He got it and brought it to me, and sat.

"The—the car that hit—the driver?"

"He's okay. He had airbags. No airbags in a New York cab."

"Arrested?"

"Oh, yeah."

"Fuck, Gene. Fuck!"

"I know. You guys were so close. The two closest people I've ever known outside of Lavinia and me. But we had so little time together. Whereas you guys…"

"Yeah. More than a few years now, I guess. When? Eighty-eight, I think. She started at PCC in eighty-eight. Liked each other right away, I think. Just always easy with each other. Eighty-eight. Not really that many years, but—"

The door to the suite opened, and in walked Peggy, ladened with packages. "Hey, Eugene, I'm back."

Eugene stood and approached her. "Good. Did you find what you wanted?"

What the hell was this? A wish-fulfillment hallucination? If I had been a heavy drug user in my youth, or even now, that would have made sense. But what was inducing this? Grief? Intense grief like I had never felt before. Not even at the death of my parents.

"Adolphus! What the hell are you doing here?"

It was no hallucination. Hallucinations surprise, but are never surprised, and Peggy's mouth was open in pleasant, if confused, surprise.

Gene's mouth was locked into an insane grin.

"He—Gene—told me you were dead," I told Peggy, speaking as one might to a specter.

"What?"

"That you were in a car accident—hurt badly—was going to die. He said I had to come."

Peggy dropped her packages onto the floor and turned to Gene. "You son-of-a-bitch! You did what?" She turned back to me. My face must have looked horrible. Puffy from crying, distraught, confused. "Look at him! What have you done? He's in pain, for Christ's sake." Peggy walked up to Gene and punched him in his belly to no discernible effect. "He always said you were a bully, a mean bully. But I wouldn't listen to him, I defended you, I said you were different now, but he said people don't change, I said that was ridiculous, but, boy, was he right. What a mean, rotten, lousy thing to do!" She said as she started to pound her fists on Gene's ample chest.

Gene didn't seem to mind. He just stood there—smiling. With a calm, not at all smug or self-satisfied, look on his face. In fact, it was beatific.

And that's when I started to laugh. Laugh uproariously. A full-throated, big belly laugh. An uncontrollable laugh. A screaming laugh.

"Now, look, damn it, he's hysterical!" Peggy ran over to me, sat beside me on the couch, and held me. I held her back but kept laughing and laughing. "Shhh, shhh, it's okay," she tried to comfort me as Gene came up, took my glass away, filled it again with water, and brought it back.

"Here," he said, handing me the glass.

"Thank you," I said gratefully, my laughs having diminished. I drank the whole of the glass down. "Ah, that's good, that's really good."

"Plaza water," Gene said, denoting the obvious.

"Wait a minute," Peggy stood up quickly. "Were you in on this?" she asked me.

"No!" Eugene and I said simultaneously with some panic.

"Well, what the hell!?"

I stood, standing Peggy up with me, keeping a hold of her hands, moving close to her. "Peggy, will you marry me?"

"What?"

"Don't you want to marry me?"

"Of course, I want to marry you. I've wanted to marry you for years."

"You never told me."

"You never asked."

"Hey, you're the feminist; why didn't you ask?"

"Because I didn't want to be rejected."

"Ah, yes. I probably would have."

"Yes, you probably would have."

"So?"

"Oh, yeah, sure, yeah, I mean yes, sure, let's get married. But Eugene is still a son-of-a-bitch."

"Yes," I said to Gene, "you are, you are still a fucking bully, you know that?"

"I disagree. I'm just a good businessman."

"A businessman? What business was this of yours?" I asked.

"Do we have to have that discussion again?"

"You love Adolphus," Peggy stated as if it was a first-time thought, as if the idea had not been presented to her before.

"Yes, I love Adolphus. I wanted what's best for him. I was determined to get it."

"But you were never pushing me to marry Peggy."

"No, just to get your Ph.D. Which Peggy wanted."

"What does one have to do with the other?"

"You guys are going to get married now, right?"

"Sure looks like it," Peggy said.

"So, Peggy, you're going to be in Delaware getting your Ph.D. And what are you going to do, Adolphus? Stay in California and teach your little classes?"

"Hey!"

"Of course not, you have to be in Delaware with your wife. So you might as well get your Ph.D. while you're there. What the hell else are you going to do? And Biden University has an outstanding history department—I checked. So you can both start together. Make it a competition. See who gets their Ph.D. first."

"Well, Gene, assuming I would even want to do this, I can't start right away. I would have to apply. I would have to be accepted."

"I've taken care of that. You're in. Ready to go."

"How?"

"On your own merits. I gave them all your academic records and history. And a small endowment."

"A small endowment? So you bullied them too. I don't know if you are a wonderful friend or a raging asshole."

"Look, Adolphus, I'm just a good businessman. You and I were in a negotiation about your future. Things weren't going my way. When things don't go my way in a negotiation, I don't give up; I change the conditions. So I changed the conditions of our negotiation."

"By making me believe that Peggy was dying, then dead?"

"It was radical, but you have only yourself to blame. You are so damn stubborn. It's hard to negotiate with a stubborn man."

"But you were so—so damn convincing. I mean the tears, the crying, the panic."

"Yeah, thanks. I took private acting lessons at the Pasadena Playhouse."

"You're kidding?"

"No. You want to hear my vocal exercises?"

"So, you've been planning this for a long time?" Peggy asked both appalled and impressed by the revelation she had received.

"Sure."

"You're one hell of a manipulative puppet master," Peggy, fresh off the revelation, conveyed to Eugene. "You do know that, don't you?"

"Sure. Like I said. A good businessman. Now would you guys like to get married here in New York—I could get the mayor to do it—or possibly in Delaware? Say, on the banks of that river Peggy keeps telling me about? That would be nice, wouldn't it?"

2 6

W e chose Delaware. Eugene, of course, arranged everything. He even sent his private jet back to Los Angeles to pick up Deb, Dr. Eggers, and several other PCC colleagues, a couple of my cousins I rarely see, and a few of Peggy's favorite students from then and the past who were still living in Los Angeles. Peggy, the only child of two orphans, both now deceased, had no other family. Gene had called Dr. Eggers right after he had put me in the limo and explained everything to him, including that he intended to buy me out of my contract. George was appalled, of course, but, being a good college administrator, he loved bread and always accepted whatever side a benefactor wanted to butter it. Gene gave him the task of gathering these few wedding guests and getting them to the airport at a date and time Gene would give him later.

We got married by a local judge on the banks of the Brandywine River. Gene, the bully, *insisted* on being my Best Man, and Eugene, the friend, gave us a fun reception in the hotel he was putting everybody up in. Deb was Peggy's Matron of Honor. Deb got really drunk at the reception and giggled a lot. But in a wholly charming way.

As we both had to start working on our doctorates immediately, there was no time for a honeymoon. That came later. A lot of love-making on Greek island beaches. Yes—lovemaking.

Then we went about having a brand new life, which I'm going to detail here as quickly as possible. The following is going to be a lot of telling and not showing, so you writing workshop wonks are welcome to leave the room if you want—shaking your heads all the way out the door, most likely. But I suggest you stick around.

We settled into the two-bedroom apartment Peggy had found and began our co-equal scholarship tasks leading to our doctorates. Although Eugene had tried to set it up as a competition between us, we never saw it that way. We shared a home office in the spare bedroom, supported each other when needed, and gave each other space when required. We shared various enthusiasms, frustrations, defeats, triumphs, and a whole hell of a lot of late-night pizzas. We were a bit older than most of the Ph.D. candidates at Biden, of course, but, having previous careers guiding students, we found ourselves not isolated or intimidated by the youths around us. We made friends among them but were also happy to be a solitary crew of two. I'm glad to admit that Peggy's was the tougher doctorate to achieve—cutting edge brain science being far more complicated than mere history. And she got crabby on occasion when she saw me sailing by smoothly waving a cheery "hello!" whenever she seemed to be stuck in a rowboat without oars. But we made it through. Our doctorates conferred upon us in the same hooding ceremony, which Eugene, beaming like a proud parent, attended.

We were soon to disappoint him. He had assumed that we would wind up with essential posts at significant universities and he had, in fact, started working diligently on our behalf toward this goal. It did seem the logical outcome for all the trouble we had gone through. And the money Eugene had spent. But Peggy had another idea.

"Eugene, you've spent a lot of money on me, and I'm deeply appreciative. And it's about time I start paying my own way, and a good position at a 'top-notch' university would be the way to do it. I could do fabulous research at such a place, even do some teaching, which would be fine. But I'd rather spend even more of your money. I mean, you've got so much, right?"

"Even more than I had before you started your Ph.D. Despite all the money I've spent on you."

"Well, there you are then. We've hardly scratched the surface. Look, here's the thing. There's a lot of politics in a big university, especially in the sciences when you're fighting for grants. Many of them come from the government or industry with different colored strings attached. Why should I get into all that when I've got my own grant-giving entity who only has love as his ulterior motive?"

"You mean me, of course."

"Of course. I know you and Adolphus have had your ups and downs, but you and I have always been pretty steady friends, right?"

"Sure."

"I mean, to some, you're a bit intimidating, overpowering, maybe even, at times, a bit of a bully. You know it's true, admit it."

"Admit it? I've cultivated it."

"But to me—well—to me, you've always been just a big, I don't know, what? A big teddy bear."

"A big teddy bear?"

"Stuffed with cash."

"I've always appreciated your honesty."

"Eugene, I want independence. I want to work in an atmosphere of pure science, with no bullshit pressure. I want to be beholden to no one."

"Except me."

"You I can handle."

Eugene smiled. "And I've never minded that."

"Good. Here's what we're going to do. I'm going to set up and run, and you're going to fund, The Consciousness Project."

"Which will be what?"

"An institute for research into human consciousness. I don't want to leave Delaware, so I think we can have a strategic alliance with Biden University without being controlled by them. I've found a plot of land right on the Brandywine, which would be a perfect place to build..."

I was privy to this conversation, my mouth wide open during much of it. One of Eugene's puppets had mastered the puppetmaster. Peggy got everything she wanted. I made a small contribution to it. I suggested it be called the *Eugene Pytka Carson Institute for Neuroscience —Home of The Consciousness Project.*

"Why add Pytka? I haven't used that name in years," Eugene asked.

"That's why. Oh, and the facing of this building should be any material but stucco."

"Christ, what a bully you are," Eugene said. "So, I suppose you'll have to get a job at Biden instead of Harvard or Yale?"

"Oh, maybe."

"What do you mean, maybe?"

"I'm playing something out, Gene. Let me see how it goes before I commit."

It was fun to toy with Eugene. I never thought I would be able to. And all because of an odd bit of fortune.

Going for your doctorate, to become a Doctor of Philosophy in your chosen field, to chase the recognition that being able to add Ph.D. to the end of your name gives is a monumental movement forward in one's life. It's a substantial commitment, setting the tone for and laying out the future of the rest of your life. It should not be taken lightly. Nevertheless—I did. I treated the whole damn thing as a joke, although a joke I kept to myself. I never would have admitted it to Biden University or Peggy and certainly not to Gene. Why should I have been so frivolous? Well, despite all of Gene's elaborate manipulations to get me to that point, I still didn't see the reason for it all. I just didn't care to get my doctorate; it was meaningless to me. The idea brought me no joy. But I now did care for (or finally knew that I cared for) Peggy. I happily accepted that our marriage—my becoming her husband, and her becoming my wife—brought me great joy. Believe me, no one was more surprised than me. So I would have done anything—even the standard climb any mountain, cross any ocean—to be with her, stay with her, until that horrid *'til death do us part* parted us. For death—or a very reasonable facsimile thereof—had already parted us before I knew what I now knew. But knowing what I knew, I wanted to keep knowing it uninterrupted until the real interruption of mortality, and either Peggy or I would not be suddenly walking through a door canceling grief.

If I had to go for my doctorate to maintain this new—and quite lovely—status quo, I would go for my doctorate. But that didn't mean I had to take it seriously. How does one not take a doctorate seriously? I gave that a lot of thought and decided that I would do it by making the subject of my dissertation something dull and unexciting and not in the current historical research zeitgeist, something plodding and ordinary and old fashioned. Maybe something that those who would read my dissertation and decide on my fate would find uninspired and say to me, sorry, no doctorate for you, little man. "Well, I tried," I could say, secretly happy that I had stuck it to Gene. Or, maybe that should be *stucco-ed* it to Gene?

I picked as my subject the life and times of the American Founding Father James Wilson. Ever hear of him? Probably not. Unless you are a fan of musical theater—as Peggy and I are—and especially the musical *1776*, a not historically accurate, although hardly ahistorical, rendering in song and dance of the deliberations of the Second Continental Congress. The musical's leading players were the querulous John Adams, the wise and witty Benjamin Franklin, and the laconic and horny, if finally eloquent, Thomas Jefferson. You know, the Stars, the ones with "It." But James Wilson is there as well, as he was in history, and the play maligns him horribly, turning him into a milquetoast sycophant shadow of John Dickinson. In reality, he was an intellectual, bright star whose writing was instrumental in giving a rationale for declaring independence. And Wilson was second only to James Madison in the drafting of the Constitution, thus in the structure, the very being, of our government. He was also a businessman who made a fortune in real estate and investments and one of our first

Supreme Court justices, although not our first Chief Justice, as he had hoped to be. Then, sadly, he died in bankruptcy. But all in all, James Wilson was a significant Founding Father. And yet, you've probably never heard of him because he just didn't have "It." What little legacy he had was being unflatteringly cemented by a Broadway musical. A very good one, but still…

Perfect, I thought, how more "un-sexy" a subject could I have picked? I entered into research on Wilson with a light heart, an unpressured mind, and a "fuck-all" attitude. And wrote a Pulitzer Prize winner.

What I knew and didn't reveal to Gene at our doctoral hooding was that my dissertation on James Wilson had gotten into the hands of a literary agent by a route I will not detail here. And that, at that moment, he was fielding two unusually generous offers from two major publishers. It seems I had written a "…fascinating, compelling, even witty account of the life and times of James Wilson, recovering him for all time as one of the most important of our Founding Fathers." Or so the *New York Times* said in their cover review. That damn book, *James Wilson: From Out of the Shadows,* became a bestseller, won, as I said, the Pulitzer Prize, and got me a lucrative five-book deal.

Ah, the sweet ironies of life.

The postdoctoral life of Adolphus Seruya and Margaret Kathleen Bradford (that's right, she didn't take my name. Are you surprised?) was quite sweet. The Consciousness Project she founded with Eugene's money became an important center for more-than-important scientific explorations of the brain, the mind, that wonderful sense of self so foolishly called a soul. I settled into a life of independent research and writing about whatever the hell I wanted to as an exercise in pure joy. We purchased an excellent three-story condo with an elevator that sat right on the bank of the Brandywine River, which flowed crystal clear and unimpeded, and we happily took that as a metaphor for our lives.

Gene Pytka, who had been the bane of my existence, turned into Eugene Carson, the boon of my existence. It is, I understand, a weird story. But as I was hardly the author of it, only a character, I finally settled into acceptance and appreciation and was happy to let it continue towards—what else?—a happy ending.

Eugene remained a part of our lives, but we saw less of him than we had before. We were busy. He was always very, very busy. He eventually sold Ramone International Aggregates, Inc. and became a venture capitalist entirely. His instinct for this was fabulous, and he grew even more affluent, which is a subtle way of saying, outrageously rich. We did meet up in New York for dinner and a show now and then, we ran into each other in Geneva once, he bought a basketball team and gave me a share of it just for the hell of it, and we managed to go to some of the games together. But, in truth, we now led separate lives. However, on the tenth anniversary of his hanging of the original Lavinia portrait in his great room, he insisted that Peggy and I come to the hanging of Lavinia painted ten years older. It was just the three of us and Maria, who now ran Eugene's domestic life with great dedication. The three of us and Maria with Lavinia, who was the beginning of this story. The evening we shared was a fine one. And remains a cherished memory.

Ten more years passed, and the twentieth anniversary of the hanging of the original portrait was approaching. I wondered if Eugene would call us to San Marino to witness the hanging of the twenty-year-on portrait of Lavinia that I knew was in that climate-controlled basement room. I decided not to wait. I decided to call Eugene.

And then the Earth shifted slightly in its orbit.

M aria answered the phone, as she always did, but instead of "Carson Residence," her official and standard greeting, she said, "He—hello?"

"Uh… Maria, hi, it's Adolphus. Is Eugene there?"

"Oh, Mr. Adolphus," Maria cried. "Mr. Eugene, he's dead."

"What? Huh?" It crossed my mind that it could be another bit of Gene manipulation, but Maria would never have gone along with such a thing, nor could she ever pretend to be as distraught as she now sounded, and for what purpose would he—

"He died this morning. I came in and woke him up, and he sat up on the side of the bed, then—" Maria sobbed deeply, painfully.

"Okay, Maria, you don't have to talk—"

"Then he just collapsed back on the bed and was gone. I tried the CPR he made me learn, but it was no good. I called 911, and the ambulance came, and they tried to—to revive him, but no good either."

"Where—where is he now?" I was afraid he was still on the bed, dead, freaking her out.

"They took him away. I—I don't know what to do now."

What could she do? Eugene had no family. Wait a minute—I'm

wrong. Peggy, me, even Maria, I guess we were his family. "Maria, Peggy and I will come out there. We'll get there as soon as we can. Would you want us to do that?"

"Oh, yes, please, Mr. Adolphus."

I was desperate to feel something. Eugene had been a part of my life —unwelcome, tolerated, accepted—since childhood. Gene's death was a shock, of course, but much like the death of a celebrity you've known about since childhood is a shock. It quickly became just information. As important as he had been in my life, it became clear that he had been important mainly as a catalyst. So maybe it's better to say not "in my life" but "to my life." I guess I never really liked Gene. He professed to "love" me and did much to benefit me, albeit in an almost bruising manner, so you would think I could at least have liked the guy and felt something at his death. But, let's all be honest here, he and I were not the types to ever really be friends. And yet—and yet we had this strange history together. Maybe that was my problem. I'm a historian, a "traveler" of the past. Gene was now dead, a "resident" of the past. Was it all just facts and data to me? Did it matter? Whether I was feeling something or not, our mutual history together, *The Adolphus and Eugene Story*, imposed upon me certain obligations that I was determined to fulfill.

I called Peggy at the institute and told her. She was struck sad immediately; I could hear it in her voice. But she also knew what to do. She knew Melinda Daniels, Eugene's lawyer, had worked with her often on matters to do with the institute. She called her and broke the news. Melinda said she would find out what she could, have a car pick us up at the airport, and meet us at Eugene's house.

Eugene had never moved from his mansion in San Marino. Nor did he buy any other properties, like so many other billionaires. Eugene seemed happy there—although I had never thought of Gene being happy—with only Maria to keep him company. But then he traveled the world dealing with his investments, living mostly in and out of hotels. On the flight out to Los Angeles, I thought about this: Did Eugene have any satisfaction in his life? Did he enjoy, I mean genuinely enjoy, anything? What a time to ask such a question—after his death. It might have been what we call "human" to have asked it during his life. But, well, okay, I guess it really wasn't *The Adolphus and Eugene Story*. Like almost every other person on earth, maybe it was only my story, and Eugene—Gene, boy, bully, man—was just a character in my story. Did that hold true for Peggy as well? God, I hope not. Maybe before—before Eugene opened my eyes by forcing tears out of them. But then, that would mean that Eugene was more than just a character in my life. And why did I never once understand that? Could I appreciate that now? I mean, he always said he did what he did out of a need to love someone after his great love, Lavinia, was gone. Why did I reject that as crazy? Did I ever accept it? I certainly got used to benefiting from it, although not taking undue advantage of it. At least, I felt I never did.

Peggy was asleep in the seat next to me. Even asleep, I think she was still feeling sad. Whereas I was feeling—nothing. I mean, I was beginning to perceive that a hole in my life had suddenly appeared, like a hole suddenly appearing in your sock. But the nature of a hole is to be a whole lot of nothing. So I was feeling nothing, which was understandable, given the hole.

Nothing in Eugene's mansion had changed. The furniture and its layout were as they were that night twenty years before, the night Gene first showed us Lavinia's portrait. The first one. That had changed, of course; it was the second one that hung over the fireplace now—Lavinia as she might have been ten years after her death.

Maria had greeted us at the door with a tear-stained, grief-strained face. Peggy immediately took her into her arms, and I felt compelled by convention to gently pat her back. We went into the kitchen where she had been preparing food, assuming we would be hungry. We were. We ate.

Melinda Daniels, Eugene's attorney, arrived shortly after that, and we all gathered in the great room to hear what she had to say.

"Eugene's death, as of the moment, is a bit mysterious. He was very healthy, with no apparent medical issues. So they are doing a full autopsy. They'll call me when they have an answer.

"Eugene had a will, of course, which I drew up for him some years back. I have it with me, but let me summarize it.

"His estate is to be broken up into several trusts, all to be overseen by my office and his long-time accounting firm. To be called the Maria Trust, the first trust is to be set up for Maria's benefit here and provide her with an income for life and covers all her medical expenses. There will also be a travel fund if she wishes to travel and finally take that vacation Eugene has been trying to get her to go on for years. This trust will also own this house, and Maria can live here, rent-free for as long as she wants. Upon Maria's death or leaving the house, it and all its contents are to be sold, the proceeds of which are to be split among no less than five charities chosen by Maria. The only proviso to that is that Lavinia's portraits are to be burnt now, and the ashes thereof gathered into an urn. Said urn is to rest on the mantle next to his own ashes. Maria is to make sure they are dusted each day. Upon the selling of the house, both urns become the property of Adolphus and Peggy. He instructs you to do what you want with the urns, but it would not displease him if you kept them and put them someplace prominent in your home.

"The second trust, to be called the Lavinia Trust, will be to the benefit of the Lavinia Public Library in Anders, Pennsylvania, and to Lavinia's surviving relatives—two brothers, I think.

"The third trust, to be called The Consciousness Project Trust, will continue to fund the institute.

"The fourth trust, to be called, rather weirdly, I think, the *Adoofus* Trust, is to be set up to provide grants of half a million dollars to scholars of exceptional merit in history. It is to be overseen by Adolphus and—Oh, wait a minute, maybe this is a typo and—"

"No," I said, "it's not a typo. The *Adoofus* Trust it is."

A small private joke from beyond the urn? I didn't think Eugene had it in him.

"And the last trust is to be a general charitable trust providing funds to a list of nonprofits he picked out. Well, that's about it as far as anything that concerns the gathered here," Melinda said. "Except he wanted the following to be read out, which he dictated in my office at the time he signed the will:

"'Well, I must be dead, or you wouldn't be hearing this. Whoever you are. Hopefully, Peggy and Adolphus are there because that means you outlived me, and that's good. Why? Hell if I know. If Maria is there I'm sorry to have left you such a big house, but you've lived there for years, and you've always said you wouldn't know where else you would want to live. So just stay, continue bringing in the cleaning crew, invite friends to stay with you, and be the queen I've come to think of you as. If none of you are there and I've outlived you all, well, isn't that just like me. Look, not that I believe in such crap, but if I had a spirit animal, it's the bull. Bulls are big and strong and hard to kill. They like to move forward, pushing anything in their way, out of their way. They don't like to stop. But that also means that they are dangerous in delicate situations—like in china shops. But I never gave a damn about china shops. That is until I met and fell in love with Lavinia. Lavinia, who, believe me, was not made out of china herself, taught me that much of the world and its people are china—beautiful if fragile things. She knew I couldn't be anything but a bull, but she showed me how to walk through a china shop and not break anything. And then she broke. At first, mad at whatever and whoever, I wanted to break all the china in the world. Hell, if I had had access to nuclear weapons, the world would be barren today. But I only broke Adolphus, or at least his ribs and arm and spleen. And he was only trying to comfort me. And I heard Lavinia chastise me, caution me that bulls have to be extra careful not to break the china. In fact, I think she told me that I had to be more than careful with china. I had to treat china as if it was my own. I didn't quite realize what that meant until I figured out that she wanted me to find the most fragile piece of china I could find and love it as I had loved her. Well, that, of course, turned out to be Adolphus, the most fragile person I had ever met. I mean, he is a man totally without aggression, ambition, adventure, a man just willing to sail along in life with no navigation, no destination, afraid of, or unwilling to experience pain. No bull him.

What's his spirit animal? The sloth? No, he always worked hard at what he did. Maybe the lovable panda, happy with his bamboo shoots. But why, Lavinia was teaching me, should everybody be a bull? Bulls may make things happen—but pandas are considered precious. Maybe the world needs both. Is this making any sense? Probably not. But if I had not loved Adolphus all these years, my life would have been a total waste. I've made billions. What's that? An accomplishment, sure, but once the billions are spent...? But I protected and cared for and loved someone who needed my love. And I opened him —a stubborn son-of-bitch panda comfortable in his bamboo tree—up to love. That's really my greatest accomplishment. Always love Peggy as I would have loved Lavinia, Adolphus. Or else I'll come back and rub your face against a stucco wall!'

"It ends there."

We were all silent, no one quite knowing what to say.

"Well, as you can tell," Melinda broke the silence, "he wants to be cremated. He says he doesn't want a funeral, but if you want to do something in his memory, that's up to you. If I may add a personal note. Eugene Carson was one of the strangest men I ever met. He was a bull, that's for sure—strong, tough, unrelenting. However, unlike others I deal with, Eugene never did anything, what I would call, mean in business. He was scrupulous about that. And yet, I never saw any warmth in the man. Still, I think I liked him. I certainly appreciated the trust he placed in me. I'll miss him."

Maria started to cry again. Melinda apologized for upsetting her. Peggy said it was okay; she didn't mean to. I said nothing. I was contemplating a hole.

After Melinda Daniels left, Peggy said to me, "Are you alright?"

"Sure. Why?"

"You look—I don't know—disturbed about something."

"Really?"

"Yeah."

"Well, guess I was just wondering how a man who for years had professed his love for me could say, um, well, rather unflattering things about me. I mean—a panda?"

"Pandas are cute."

"Yes, well, it was all that underlying stuff."

"Oh. Well, are you aggressive?"

"No, I guess not. But then, I never wanted to be."

"I think that was his point. And ambition, you've never really had any. I mean, not the world-beating type of ambition that Eugene would have understood."

"True. Again—wasn't my thing, was it? But still, to know this about oneself is different than to be *accused* of it. And I think I, in my way, like an adventure."

"Maybe he just got caught up in the alliteration of it all."

"Well, in all his alliteration, he forgot 'accomplished.' I'm certainly accomplished."

"That you are. Thanks to Eugene. As we—you and me—we are thanks to Eugene."

"Only by default. He didn't want me to be a best-selling author; he wanted me to be some revered Ivy League professor. I became an author completely on my own, and he never gave a damn about it."

"You don't think he provided you the conditions for that? Inadvertently, okay, but—"

"Yes, inadvertently, you're right about that. It wasn't what Gene was trying to manipulate, to bully me into. I won that round!"

"And us? Are we a married couple by default?"

"No, of course not. You don't think we would have eventually—"

"No, I do not. And neither do you."

"Okay, right, we'll always owe him for that. Big time. But a panda? I mean, I'll admit, I'm easy going, sure, always have been. Like my dad was an easy-going guy and very well-liked. So I'm easy going. Not as well-liked maybe, but, I think, liked well enough."

"Well, if so, maybe it's because you are at times a 'stubborn son-of-a-bitch panda,' to quote Eugene."

"See, that's the thing—if he loved me, why would he say such a thing to me? I mean, he intended me to hear it. He didn't love me; he was just a manipulative, weird bully who found a—a weird way to bully."

"You sound disappointed."

"Really? No. What I'm feeling is—don't laugh—hurt."

Maria had been sitting there, listening to this conversation. I had no idea if she understood or cared what I was going on about until she stopped the conversation.

"Mr. Adolphus, I want you to see something."

She took Peggy and me up to the only room in the mansion we had never been in. Eugene's bedroom. It was large, of course, decorated tastefully—the hand and eye of Lavinia here? I was worried Maria was taking us to see the bed he had died on so I would show more respect for the dead or something like that. But upon entering, she walked us over to a cabinet with glass doors, which she opened. There, displayed on two shelves, sat all of my books. There was my first book on James Wilson and my history of the building of the Erie Canal. My story of the Parthenon's construction and the years leading up to it, and the years after. And there was my history of early America, *Growing Pains: America from Revolution to Civil War*, my biggest bestseller. I had actually wanted to call it *Afterbirth*, but my publisher nixed the idea. I took *Growing Pains* out of the cabinet and opened it up to the title page where I had written in a bold hand, *For Eugene, Best Wishes, Adolphus Seruya.*

"These are the copies I sent him. I actually figured he'd just probably, I don't know, dump them somewhere."

"He had this cabinet built for them," Maria said. "He loved them. He was very proud of you."

"Proud of me? I always thought it fairly arrogant for anyone to be proud of another person. I mean, what right do they have to be proud?"

"Oh, stop being an ass, Ass," Peggy said with some disgust and other emotions. "Look how he kept them—like trophies. And not one of them did you dedicate to him, did you?"

"Well, I mean, it's not like he *really* loved them. I mean, I'm sure he never even cracked them open, never read them. They were just objects to him."

"Come here!" Maria commanded.

She took us into a large walk-in closet filled with big clothes for a big man. And one open bookcase in a corner in which other copies of my books were stored.

"Open up one of those," Maria said. "Open one up anywhere."

I did. The book was almost loose with use, and the pages that faced me, 189 and 190, were heavily underlined.

"He said you were his only real education. He read each book several times. Don't doubt he loved you, Mr. Adolphus, or that he didn't have the right to be proud of you. Now come here."

She marched us out of the closet and to a bedside table. There rested my latest book, my first work of fiction. Historical fiction, of course, a novel about Herodotus, the Father of History. I picked up the book. There was a bookstore receipt sticking out about mid-way. A bookmark, I assumed.

"I heard him laughing once while reading it," Maria said.

"I tried to bring some wit to it."

I opened it and turned some pages, looking at the print on paper, the gathering of alphabetic symbols into coherent words flowing out a story. As beautiful as any landscape to me. I was awed by the fact that Eugene's eyes had also scanned and read these words, entering them into his brain, his mind, his thinking. I teared up quite prominently.

"Oh, Honey," Peggy said. "What?"

"I'm just so suddenly, incredibly sad that he's never going to get to finish it."

M aria wanted us to stay the night at the mansion, and we did. We all agreed to honor Eugene's request and planned no funeral. With much to get back to, Peggy and I flew home the next day.

Two days later, Melinda Daniels called.

"We've got the results of the autopsy."

"Heart attack? Stoke, maybe?"

"Yes, a massive stroke caused by a brain tumor."

"A brain tumor? When did he get a brain tumor? He never said anything."

"Probably didn't know it. They said it had been there for years."

"Years? But—"

"It wasn't cancerous. It was benign. They told me it can be in a brain for years undetected."

"Years. Do they have any idea how many years?"

"Well, they were only guessing, but maybe twenty or so."

Peggy was at the institute when Melinda called. I didn't call her to give her the news. I had been working on my latest, another novel, having thoroughly gotten the fiction bug. But I stopped working. Socrates and Plato were just going to have to wait to take that utterly fictitious road trip I was plotting to send them on. It was late in the day, and I decided to make myself a cup of tea and sit out on our balcony overlooking the Brandywine and wait for Peggy to tell her then. And to talk to her about it. Anything important, the only person I want to talk to about it was Peggy. The true definition of a good marriage? But in this case, Peggy was even more pertinent than usual, being a brain person and all.

The tumor bothered the hell out of me. I didn't know why. Maybe because it was in the brain, and I am—now that I thought about it—a brain worker. I read, think, and write. That's brain work. Don't need to be aggressive about it, at least not in Eugene's way. Ambition doesn't really mean anything in such work. Desire, goals, plans, yes, but not really ambition—again, as Eugene would see it. And I'll fight with anyone—sorry, I'll debate with anyone—if they try to tell me that there is no adventure in brain work. Gene was all wrong about that. I have a natural bias in favor of the brain over other parts of the body. Maybe I was just sensitive over the idea of some alien growth lodging, uninvited, in one's mind. It made me shudder, like the idea of getting kicked in the balls makes most other men shudder. That's not to say the idea of getting kicked in the balls didn't make me shudder; it's just that a brain tumor was for me a more existential shudder. And the idea that Eugene's brain, a brain I kind of knew, suffered the indignity of tumor invasion brought it all home and made me deeply contemplative on the balcony—as one used to working his brain would be.

Peggy came home. I made us drinks. I told her the news. She did not react the same way I did.

"Oh. Really? Well, maybe that explains it."

"Explains what?"

"Well, you know—Eugene."

"You mean Eugene's death?"

"No, I mean Eugene, himself. You know, the Bull. And how the bull stopped breaking china—and," she smiled, "how a bull fell in love with a panda."

"What the hell are you talking about?"

"A tumor in the brain, depending on where it is—Melinda didn't tell you where in the brain it was?"

"No. Didn't think to ask."

"Well, depending on where it is, a tumor can affect a person's personality, sometimes radically, sometimes subtly, but causing a noticeable and often surprising change. You say Melinda said it might have been in there twenty years or so."

"That's what she said."

"Well?"

"Well, what?" I was slow to get it despite being a brain worker.

"When you knew Eugene as a kid, he was a mean bully who did you some physical harm?"

"Some?"

"And when you met him as an adult, some twenty years ago, he was a different person, right?"

"Aren't we all different as adults?"

"Are we? I'm not so sure."

"But he had, you know, fallen in love. Some people would say that can change you."

"Well, maybe. But aren't you the one who says people don't change? Aren't you the one who thought Eugene's behavior, his declared love for you, his need to love you was weird and strange and surreal?"

"Yeah, but what about Lavinia? Nothing weird about that."

"There wasn't? He told us that he'd only had prostitutes up till then. Not even any crushes, high school girlfriends, bar-hopping one-night stands. Obviously emotionally stunted there."

"Well, yeah, but Lavinia was—"

"Special, radiant, yeah, you both told me that. But how do we really know? Maybe he fell in love with her when the tumor first appeared. Maybe that's what caused him to suddenly open up to love."

"And what about me? Do I have a brain tumor?"

"No, I hope not. But you've always been impressed by well put together women, and from what you tell me..."

"Oh, Christ, I don't think—"

"It makes some sense. Look, I liked Eugene. I always did. Possibly because I thought someone should. Plus, he was a refreshing change from some of our other friends. But you've always been right; he was weird in his 'love' for you."

"Are you 'weird' in your love for me?"

"That's completely different, and you know it. Our love is completely normal."

"Oh, really? You find nothing special about our love at all?"

"Well, yes, to us, of course. But you know what I mean. Maybe 'normal' is not the word. Better said, our love is not abnormal."

"You used to be the big defender of his love for me."

"Well—it was advantageous, wasn't it? But with this information... Well, I am a scientist; I do know something of how the brain works."

It was the first time in years of marriage that Peggy had ever said or did anything to depress me. She didn't mean to, of course. But scientists are even more sensitive to the 'truth' than historians. Scientists always want an absolute reality, given the data at hand, while still open to a new reality if the data changes. Historians are happy to interpret reality, and sometimes even new data won't change their interpretations because historical data is never complete.

So what was Eugene Pytka Carson's history? And why was I changing my interpretation of it? Was he a man who had been altered by love? Was he a man whose soul, for lack of a better word, was so infused with love for one individual that—that individual having been taken away—he had to give that love to someone else—no matter how weirdly? Or was he a man with a brain tumor that caused him to go off his innate rails of bullyhood?

I'm pretty sure love is not a universal force, as the over-emotional would like us to believe. But I can pretty much accept that love is a personal force that is necessary and vital. But can it change a person? Can it make a complacent, happy-in-his-bamboo tree panda decide that, yeah, I'd like to share my bamboo tree with another? Can it make an aggressive, ambitious bull not necessarily leave the china shop, but to, more importantly, tread carefully within?

Or maybe it wasn't love that changed Gene. Perhaps it was hate. I can close my eyes right now and still see Gene's face before and after he scraped my face raw against that stucco wall. I have never doubted that I was looking into the personification of hate, hate as pure as possible. I could feel it batter against me, as the object of it. But Gene—Gene must have felt being it, having it within, like internal bleeding. That must have been a hundred times worse. Mr. Carson, who became Gene's stepfather, told my parents and me that Gene had come home very upset and immediately confessed. He wasn't reveling in what he had done, as he had reveled in whiplashing my butt with a wet towel. This scared him. And scarred him as much as it had scarred me. Bad enough that they had to hypnotize the memory out of him. But it was still there, of course. Did the experience dampen his emotions, the good and the bad? Did Lavinia—who was, I will always maintain, unique, and radiant if a lousy driver—reawaken those emotions and give him the strength to control them? And when he lost Lavinia, her love being violently yanked from him, isn't it—now that I think about it—utterly logical that he would pick me to receive his love, someone who he knew had become of some brief importance to Lavinia?

Or was all this the result of an undetected tumor in his brain?

We talk about the heart when we talk about human love.

We talk about the brain when we talk about human life.

When your heart stops, you don't die because the heart stopped.

You die because your brain is no longer being nourished with blood. Your heart doesn't die. Your brain, your mind, that is, *you* die.

A heart is nothing but a machine, an automated pump. Nothing goes on there but the flow of blood.

A brain is also a machine, but so much more than just the flow of blood goes on there—a whole universe of thoughts and feelings, pains and pleasures reside there. If love exists, it exists in the brain.

And yet, no one ever sent a brain-shaped valentine.

The heart is a metaphor—a cozy thought and intoxicating feeling.

The brain is a literal, physical repository of thoughts and feelings. Or do I mean the generator of thoughts and feelings?

Gene Pytka becoming Eugene Carson, was that the work of the heart or of the brain? The result of a life-changing experience of either hate or love or both? Or possibly the result of an unwanted mass of tissue, solid or fluid-filled?

I'm no ignorant fool, and I have a deep respect for the brain in the woman I love. I know what the most likely answer is.

But regarding *The Adolphus and Eugene Story*—and I wouldn't recommend this to you, in fact, I would cynically scoff at you if *you* made this choice, but, then, this isn't your story—regarding *The Adolphus and Eugene Story*, I think I'll go with the metaphor.

"Honey!"

Excuse me, Peggy's calling me.

"Yes!"

"The pizza guy was just here. I've got dinner laid out!"

"Great!"

"I got your cuttlefish!"

"Wonderful! I'll be right there!"

End

ABOUT THE AUTHOR

Bully 4 Love is Steven Paul Leiva's tenth work of fiction since 2003. Previous to that he was seen cavorting in the silly fields of Hollywood with such luminaries as Bugs Bunny and Betty Boop (although the latter was but a brief affair). His fiction has been praised by literary great Ray Bradbury, Oscar-winning film producer Richard Zanuck, NY Times bestselling author Diane Ackerman, and *Star Trek* actor John Billingsley, a voracious bookworm if there ever was one. He has received the Scribe Award from the International Association of Media Tie-in Writers. A traveler among several genres, his books include his witty Hollywood thrillers, BLOOD IS PRETTY and HOLLYWOOD IS AN ALL-VOLUNTEER ARMY; his Scribe Award-winning novelization of the indie family film, THE 12 DOGS OF CHRISTMAS; his Sci-Fi satire of first-contact told from the point-of-view of the aliens, TRAVELING IN SPACE; his comic look at happy-

ever-afters, BY THE SEA; his surreal political fantasia, IMP; his bizarre, possibly audacious, somewhat Sci-Fi novella, MADE ON THE MOON; his a contemporary "scientific romance" written in the tradition of H.G. Wells and Jules Vern, JOURNEY TO WHERE; and CREATURE FEATURE: A HORRID COMEDY, which combined a spoof of old monster movies with political satire because, well, why not?

You can find Steven on Facebook, Twitter @StevenPaulLeiva, and he muses and on occasion amuses at http://emotionalrationalist. blogspot.com/.

www.ingramcontent.com/pod-product-compliance
Lightning Source LLC
Chambersburg PA
CBHW060854250626
47159CB00008B/2727